Nightwatchers

Nightwatchers

a novel by
Vincent Wyckoff

North Star Press of St. Cloud Inc.
www.northstarpress.com

North Star Press of St. Cloud Inc.
www.northstarpress.com

Cover Design and Layout by Elizabeth Dwyer.

Text body set in LTC Caslon Pro Regular, with P22 Franklin Caslon Italic headings, and Tenez section heads.

Frist Edition, September 2020.

For Samuel, Autumn, and Trevor
with love.

Nightwatchers
The night is tranquil,
The stars hang low.
The inland sea turns silver
In the moon's eerie glow.
Creatures of Earth turn homeward
As eventide falls;
Silence hangs in the mist,
And the Nightwatchers call.

-Dorothy Wyckoff, 1919-2010

Prologue

*I*n *the gray light of dawn, above the narrow gorge over the Black Otter* River, a large shadow slides away from a stand of small balsams. Flickering silently through the woods, it vanishes in the fog off the river and reappears moments later, mingling with the darker recesses under the canopy of trees. This shadow isn't rooted to any one spot, but blends effortlessly into its surroundings, becoming a part of the scenery wherever it happens to be. Indeed, to an observer it would be easier to follow the movement of the shadow rather than the dim form that casts it.

Gliding forward through the underbrush with a slightly hunched posture, arms held tight and motionless along its side, the head bobs and weaves like a boxer to prevent disturbing the brush it passes. The agile body cants from side to side with the head to slip undetected through the foliage. Years of hunting and trapping experience lead the moccasin-clad feet unerringly over hidden roots and rocks, past sticks and branches that could snap underfoot.

This shadow doesn't need a trail or path to move quickly through the forest. It's more comfortable closely surrounded by the cover of heavy undergrowth. It flits and darts like a veiled light passing through the woods. Heavy eyebrows shade keen gray eyes that take in everything, looking at nothing in particular but seeing everything at once. They note every blade of grass that moves, every leaf that twirls overhead. A thick mass of dark-brown beard covers the narrow face, the growth long enough to allow for a tight, narrow strand of braiding below the lips and over the chin. The lighter blond hair is also braided, a loose plait interwoven with beaded leather bands, feathers, and a thin silver chain. The mouth remains closed, breath passing through the long nose as it identifies and files away the pungent woodland aromas it encounters.

Taken individually, the shadow's features are striking, in some ways even handsome, but in combination they form an almost ghostly apparition in the dim light of dawn. And the way it glides through the forest could be considered natural and elegant, but the shadows it casts reek of a bitter disappointment. Smaller forms flitter beside the larger, like quaking leaves attached to a tree; four-legged shadows bounding off in all directions through the underbrush. The woods become silent when the crepuscular shadows pass, as if creatures great and small realize a restless soul moves among them.

The hunter has been on the move for days—weeks, actually; for most of the past summer months. From a small native village in the hinterlands of Canada, up north beyond hundreds of unnamed lakes and streams and mosquito-infested bogs, he's traveled south, leaving behind a desolate setting of poverty and despair. That place and the wretched life he'd been exiled to as a child had never really been home for him. It seemed that loneliness had been inflicted upon him, until he'd finally been able to walk away from it, to seek a place of comfort and well-being.

An opportunity to search for a place to call home.

The shadow pauses to take a deep breath. He can still hear the roar of the river as it crashes over boulders on its way to the sea. Lake Superior. An unfamiliar emotion arises in his chest. The forest is beautiful at this quiet time of day. He stands still under a canopy of red and yellow leaves as the accompanying shadows drift away, their panting yelps fading to nothing. Yesterday he'd stumbled upon a small cottage in the woods not far from here, and was offered a job by the man contracted to roof the place. Earlier, he'd found a shallow cave near the headwaters of the river. It opened to the south, as if offering light and warmth to anyone wishing to abide there.

An open doorway to shelter and rest.

The hunter turns to follow a hiking trail paralleling the river. He wonders if this is the same trail he's been crisscrossing for weeks now on the walk south. The Superior Hiking Trail. A solemn grin spreads across his face with the notion that perhaps better times are ahead. This is a good place, he thinks, and maybe far enough away from his past to become a home. A grouse flushes on the trail ahead, causing his thin-lipped grin to open in a broad smile of delight. His stride lengthens to an easy jog, sure-footed and calm, remembering a wolf attack he'd witnessed a couple years ago in Canada. The lead wolf, his good fortune in tracking down a small deer making him overzealous, leaped so high and hard he'd flown harmlessly over the back of the frightened animal while his teeth barely grazed the neck of his prey. The hunter had laughed out loud at the episode, but admired the strength and primal instincts at play. He'd followed the pack through the seasons, often gone for days at a time, ranging far afield. At some point they'd accepted his presence, apparently understanding that with him nearby they avoided the bullets and traps set out for them. And now, as he travels through these new lands, he appreciates their cunning senses guarding his constantly moving perimeter.

A hundred yards up the trail the man's long, straight nose picks up the faint scent of sweat and deodorant. The smile disappears and he changes course, slicing along an animal path at an angle quartering away from the hiking trail. Until yesterday he hadn't seen anyone in weeks, and he was comfortable with that, certainly much more comfortable than an unexpected early morning meeting with strangers. It seemed an unlikely hour for trail hikers, but there was a town nearby, so who could say. Leaving the trail is second nature for the hunter, and he takes comfort in blending back into the forested shadows. Soon, he turns and runs hard for the dense cover along the riverbank, leaving the sour, pervasive human odors behind. Moving fast through the woods always exhilarates him, and the smile returns moments later as he slips through invisible leafy passageways, setting a course to follow the river to the headwaters.

A place that just might become home.

Part I

Chapter 1

*A*bby *Simon leaped down the steps, leaving the screen door to* slam behind her as she jogged across the front lawn. Slinging her backpack over her shoulders, she set a brisk pace down the hill into town. It was still dark, but in the distance a brilliant pink glow hovered over the eastern horizon of Lake Superior. Abby's breath billowed around her as a steamy vapor in the near-freezing pre-dawn. While maintaining a stiff-legged, energetic pace, she thought about her younger brother, Ben. It would be a couple hours yet before he came out to meet the school bus. Because of the family's near-tragic adventures of early summer, when Ben had been kidnapped for several weeks, her father still waited outside with his youngest until the bus arrived. She couldn't blame him for worrying, but Abby had to admit that waiting for the bus with his eight-year-old son was better than last month, when the new school year started and Matthew insisted on driving Ben the half-dozen miles to school up the shore.

Rooftops over Black Otter Bay cast dark-angled edges into the early dawn as Abby strode onto Main Street. Main Street was simply a narrowing of old Highway 61 as it passed through town and across the steel-girder bridge spanning the Black Otter River. Small gift shops rose up stark and deserted, some already closed for the season, but lights glowed from the dock area behind the post office. Up the hill overlooking Main Street, Abby spotted the all-night streetlamp in front of the stone, timber, and concrete-block sheriff's office. It cast a soft illumination over the fall foliage lining the ridge behind town. And just beyond the stingy range of the sheriff's streetlamp, the town cemetery sprawled out beneath a shelter of pines, the stories and memories of indigenous and immigrant settlers resting together quietly.

A car door slammed, and Abby broke into a jog again. Lights inside the Black Otter Bay Café lit up like directional beacons for the daily rush of local morning regulars.

Abby hustled up the steps and opened the door to the welcoming smells and sounds of the small-town café.

"Hey, girl," Marcy called from the swinging doors to the kitchen.

Abby peeled the backpack off and stashed it on a shelf below the counter. She straightened her Minnesota Twins baseball cap, tightened her thick black braid protruding from the back of the cap, and looked up to see Red Tollefson eyeing her from across the counter.

"Well, Abby, those Twins broke our hearts again, didn't they?" he said.

She started to respond, but a smear of powdered sugar surrounding his lips distracted her, so while reaching to hand him a napkin, she pantomimed wiping his face. Marcy returned from the kitchen, placed a platter of pancakes in front of Owen Porter, and then reached a hand around Abby's neck and kissed her on the cheek. "Morning," she said.

Abby smiled as she slid the maple syrup pitcher across the counter. She took comfort in this early morning routine. Like the maple syrup to Owen's pancakes, these people, this place, the aromas, and the inane conversations fulfilled her. She couldn't imagine any other place to call home.

With an arm still draped around Abby, Marcy nodded back toward the door. "Spread that bundle of newspapers along the counter, and then we need to get more silverware and napkins."

Abby retrieved the newspapers, and as Marcy dashed off to refill coffee cups, she grabbed a utility knife from under the counter and slit open the bundle. The two of them had become very close after Marcy helped Abby last summer with her run-in with the Chicago mafia. Not to mention the fact that Marcy was now dating Abby's father.

Owen Porter asked, "How's Matt doing these days?"

"Dad is fine," she said, sidling along the counter with the papers. "He's still a little freaked out about what happened, but I think he's doing pretty good." The truth was she hadn't seen her father this happy in a long time. After getting through those frightening weeks of early summer, his family was together and safe, and the new school year had gotten underway with no major problems. Abby knew that as a single father he constantly fretted over and doubted his parenting skills, but she also knew he cared more about his children than anyone could know. And now that Marcy was in the picture, he had someone to confide in. As far as Abby was concerned, even if Marcy should one day become her stepmother, she'd always be like a big sister to her.

Marcy had been the one to suggest that Abby could help out in the café. While she wasn't exactly an employee—at fourteen, she was too young for that—Marcy still expected her to show up every day, and Abby was only too happy to oblige. Marcy often passed along a couple dollars in tips to the girl before taking a short break each day to drive her up to school.

Red Tollefson clinked his coffee cup in its saucer by way of asking for a refill, and then squinted up at Abby behind the counter. He licked his lips, glanced over his shoulder, and finally blurted, "What about your mom? What do you hear from Jackie?"

Abby retrieved a plastic bin of recently washed silverware and looked at Red. He'd spent a career in charge of a state highway maintenance crew, running heavy equipment in all extremes of weather while managing personalities nearly as big as his own. He'd always made the decisions, gave the orders, and in retirement he still had viewpoints and opinions he was sure people wanted to hear.

Marcy slipped up behind Red and reached the coffeepot around his shoulders. Splashing coffee in the cup, over the saucer, and all around his place setting, she spoke directly into his ear from six inches away. "Back off, Red. Leave her alone."

Abby stepped back, covering a grin, not sure if it was because of the way Marcy jumped in to protect her or the ridiculously childish expression of dismay on Red's face.

"What did I say?" he asked, incredulous.

"It's okay," Abby interjected.

"Jackie is just fine," Marcy stated. "Abby talks to her every week."

From the sink behind her, Abby snatched a dishcloth to wipe up spilled coffee. When Marcy left to return the coffeepot behind the counter, Abby collected the bin of silverware and set it in front of Red. She grabbed a handful of forks, and using a dry dishtowel, began wiping off handles and tines. "Mom is working off the judge's sentence," she said, aware that Marcy had paused behind her to listen. "She's got like a year's worth of hours to volunteer, mostly at one of the homeless shelters in Duluth."

Owen asked, "She still living at Randall's place?"

"For now," Marcy cut in. "He won't be back for a long time."

"With all the court-ordered hours, Mom can only work a part-time job, so it's going to be hard for her to get a place of her own."

"Maybe she'll end up in the homeless place herself," Red exclaimed.

Marcy lunged back to the counter, but Abby cut her off. "You know, I think Mom actually likes working there," she said. "She feels needed." Abby picked up another handful of silverware and continued. "But she really knows a lot about art and stuff, so I'm sure one day she'll find a better job."

"Another thing the court stipulated," Marcy added, "is that Jackie can't go to the casinos anymore."

"Well, I'm sure she can't afford it anyway," Owen said.

"Never bothered her before," Red declared, prompting another bluff charge and glare from Marcy.

"I think the hardest thing," Abby began quietly so just the four of them could hear, "is that she can't see us right now." She pursed her lips in thought, and then looked at Red. "She said she never knew what Randall was up to, and I believe her. He told her that Ben was safe, and she went along with it. That was her crime." Abby looked down at the silverware in her hand and gave a powerless shrug of her shoulders. "Even Dad feels bad about that. But the judge can throw out the restraining order when she finishes her community service."

The door opened and Sheriff Marlon Fastwater and the postmistress, Mrs. Virginia Bean, stepped in. The sheriff acknowledged greetings with the briefest of nods. He was a big man without being overweight, and carried his large frame with a fluid grace. He stopped next to Red and scanned the roomful of morning regulars. Mrs. Bean reached across the counter to squeeze Abby's forearm.

"Good morning, Mrs. Bean," Abby said. "Can I get you coffee?" Abby was already stacking a coffee cup on a saucer in front of the sheriff. Mrs. Bean didn't often come in this early, preferring to wait until later in the morning for a coffee break.

"No, dear, but thank you," she said. Placing a hand on the sheriff's shoulder, she added, "I think I'll just head over to the post office and get a fire going. It takes a while to warm up that old building."

"I'll help you," the sheriff said, turning back toward the door.

"I know how to light a fire, Marlon," Mrs. Bean said. "Drink your coffee."

Marcy scooted over with the coffeepot, and before the sheriff even settled on a stool, she'd slid a steaming cup of coffee in front of him.

"Did you hear those wolves last night?" Red asked the sheriff, but in a voice loud enough for the whole room to hear.

Fastwater ignored him as he awkwardly attempted to jam a huge index finger through the coffee cup handle.

From the door, Mrs. Bean turned back to ask, "What wolves? I didn't hear any wolves last night." She said it with a tone of voice that implied that if she hadn't heard them, they hadn't been there.

Fastwater gave up trying to poke his finger through the cup handle and finally wrapped a large fist around the mug. Lifting it to his lips, he slowly turned to stare at Red. Between Mrs. Bean's derisive scowl and the sheriff's intimidating gaze, the retired foreman leaned back and looked away. To Marcy now, he declared, "Lots of wolves. All night. Well, maybe not all night, because I was sleeping." He dared a quick glance at the sheriff. "But this morning, before dawn. Yipping and yapping like they were on the run. Hunting. But howling, too."

Mrs. Bean pulled the door open and said, "You need to get your medications checked, Red."

That brought smiles and chuckles all around, but Red sat up to defend himself. "Up over the ridge, Sheriff. I had to get up to, you know, get up to use the little boys' room." He paused to peer sheepishly over at Marcy. "Wolves were out there, Sheriff. I heard them plain."

Mrs. Bean smirked and walked out. Fastwater used two hands to gently set his cup back on the saucer. Looking at Abby still polishing silverware, he winked and asked, "Did you hear wolves last night, Abby?"

She shook her head. "I've heard them before, though. But not last night." She looked at Red, and added, "And never right up behind town."

"Well, I heard them," Red declared. "Plain as day, only it was night."

"You sure, Red?" Owen chimed in. "I've never heard wolves that close to town."

The door swung open again, and in the sudden quiet with everyone turning to look, Red blurted, "Of course I'm sure! I've heard wolves a million times. And it was a bunch of them."

Nichole Nielsen slid up to the end of the counter, an uneasy grin playing over her face. She studied Red as if waiting for another outburst, and then raised a questioning eyebrow at Marcy as she placed a water bottle on the counter. "Any chance you could fill this up for me?" she asked. "It seems I forgot in my rush to get out the door."

"Of course, " Marcy said, passing the bottle to Abby.

A real estate agent originally from Duluth, Niki had moved up here two years earlier when she'd seen the spike in lakeshore property values coming. Of course, to the locals she was still an outsider, and probably would be for a couple more decades, but they'd grudgingly accepted her after she survived the first winter here among them. In her mid-thirties, single, and attractive, she'd made several friends in town besides Marcy. She drove a Volvo, however, which didn't help endear her to the predominately Ford- and Chevy-driving townsfolk, but she claimed it was useful when showing expensive lakeshore properties to rich folks from Chicago and the Twin Cities.

Niki glanced at Red again, but he'd resumed his discussion with the regulars at the counter. The sheriff sat head and shoulders above them, all except Owen Porter, who was just as tall but carried half the bulk of the sheriff. She didn't know much about the big lawman except for what people said: he was tough but fair, and his family lineage went back to before the white settlement on the shore. His weathered, dark complexion glowed with vitality.

To Marcy, Niki asked, "What's all this about wolves?"

Marcy snorted. "Red's nightmares. Claims he heard wolves howling last night."

"It wasn't a nightmare," Red stated. He looked at Niki as if expecting her to agree, but she simply shrugged and looked away.

Abby returned the filled water bottle to the counter. "Going for a run?" she asked.

"Yup. I have a meeting later this morning, but plenty of time to run the loop up along the river."

"It's supposed to be sunny today," Abby offered. "The woods will be beautiful up there when the sun gets up."

"As long as it isn't snowing, I'm happy," Niki said. To both women, she asked, "Are you going to decorate the place for Halloween?"

Marcy was known for her wild get-ups, like green hair for St. Patrick's Day, a Santa hat and beard for Christmas, or an Uncle Sam outfit for the Fourth of July with a small fireworks display out in the parking lot after dark.

Marcy looked at Abby and winked. "Oh, I think we'll come up with something."

Abby smiled, unaware of any Halloween plans, but sure her friend would come up with something when the time came.

Marcy suddenly reached over the counter and grabbed Niki's arm. "Oh, remember last year? Remember your Little Red Riding Hood costume?"

Niki burst out laughing, a blush rising on her cheeks. "I've had that costume for years."

"Well, it works for you, girl. You were hot!"

Still grinning, Niki said, "That's another reason I'm running; I'd never fit into that thing looking like this."

Because everyone within earshot remembered the sensation Niki's costume had caused last year, the string of men at the counter followed this new line of conversation with rapt attention. Owen Porter leaned forward to speak around Red and the sheriff. "There's going to be a masquerade dance down at the bar again this year. Everybody in town will be there. Are you going to be around?"

Owen was almost abnormally tall, and skinny as a stick. He perched on the counter stool like a prehistoric insect, all arms and legs. He worked the day shift down at the taconite processing plant, and was known for telling tall tales about his alleged dating life in Duluth. So far, however, no one had ever met one of these women, just as no one had ever heard him utter these many words to a female before. So, while it wasn't exactly a request for a date, everyone still looked at him with mild surprise.

It was Marlon Fastwater who finally broke the awkward silence. "Mrs. Bean says she wants to go as the Queen of England."

Everybody looked at him, stunned, until Marcy burst out laughing. "You're kidding, right? So what does that make you, the king?"

Then everyone tried speaking at once. The sheriff looked down the counter, surprised to see everyone laughing, apparently at his expense.

"He'll be the Sheriff of Nottingham," Red snorted, slapping Owen on the back.

While the jibes continued, Marcy and Abby leaned over the counter toward Niki. Abby said, "Marcy and my dad are going as Raggedy Ann and Andy. I helped Dad dye a mophead bright orange last night for his wig."

Marcy rolled her eyes. "He's all worried about his beard. Like Raggedy Andy couldn't have a beard."

Niki gazed at Abby. "What about you? You're too old for trick-or-treating, and too young to go to the dance at the bar."

Abby shrugged her shoulders. "I'll take Ben out trick-or-treating, then we'll probably just stay home and watch a scary movie or something." She cast a bashful glance Niki's way. "So, are you going as Little Red Riding Hood again?"

At the mention of Niki's costume, conversation along the counter fizzled out. "You bet I am," she replied. Picking up the water bottle, she added, "If it still fits."

"You're not going running up over the ridge, are you?" Red asked.

"That's the plan," Niki replied.

"But I heard all them wolves up there last night."

"Oh, Red," Marcy scoffed. "Just stop it. Even if there was a wolf up there last night, it's long gone by now."

"Wolves, Marcy. Plural. I heard a whole pack of them."

Niki looked from Red to Marcy, a wary, pensive expression wrinkling her brow.

Owen got to his feet and took a few tentative steps toward Niki. "The wolves won't bother you," he stated, rather formally, trying to reassure while not making eye contact. "There's never been a confirmed wolf attack on people before." He lost his nerve when Niki looked at him. "At least not on grown-up people," he added as he stopped behind Red, keeping the sheriff's bulk as a protective wall between them.

Silence lingered until Marcy finally rolled her eyes and turned her attention back to Niki. "Are you going to the dance with someone special this year?"

Niki's expression darkened even more, causing Marcy to wonder what she'd said wrong. Sneaking a glance at Abby, she noted the young girl's confused stare.

Niki backed up a step before turning to leave. "I better get a move on," she said over her shoulder.

"You're welcome to go with Matt and me," Marcy offered.

Niki was at the door. "I really need to get this run in," she said. "Thanks for the water, Abby."

Everyone watched her slip out the door, until Red called, "Watch out for them wolves, young lady."

Marcy slapped the counter in front of Red. "That's enough about wolves," she said, but everyone's attention was still focused on the door where Niki's surly, dour expression seemed to linger.

"What was that all about?" Abby asked, but no one had an answer.

"I probably shouldn't have told her about the wolves," Red said. "But really, she needs to be careful up there all alone."

"I don't think it's about wolves," Marcy said.

It took a few minutes for the uneasy feeling to pass, but by the time the sheriff stood up to leave, it felt as though a darkening cloud cover had finally drifted out and away from the room. Aware of Marcy's tip-sharing ploy with Abby, Fastwater dropped a few extra dollar bills on the counter for his coffee and smiled at Abby. "You need a ride up to school?"

Marcy said, "I'll take her, Marlon. But thanks." She looked a little pale under the garish lights of the café, as if still reacting to Niki's mysterious behavior.

"Well, good enough, then," he said. "I think I'll go see if Mrs. Bean got that fire started."

•   •   •   •

The sun was up, and after sitting under the old fluorescent lighting in the café, the world outside sparkled in the bright fall sunshine. Sheriff Marlon Fastwater stood beside his squad car, squinting against the light at the lone figure dropping into deep knee bends on the steel-girder bridge's walkway over the Black Otter River. He watched as Niki stood, stretched her arms high over her head, and then jumped into an easy lope across the bridge. At the far end she angled through a wide mowed ditch to the narrow spur trail following the cascading course of the river. From where he stood, he couldn't see the water in the depths of the gorge beneath the bridge, but he heard the waterfalls and rapids crashing over boulders on its final descent to the sea.

When Niki disappeared into the fall foliage lining the river gorge, a brief shudder tickled across his shoulders. He took a deep breath, sucking in the earthy aromas of damp rock, driftwood, and cedar trees. From his maternal grandmother he'd inherited the capacity to sense things not generally apparent to others. However, unlike the tales he'd heard of Floating Bird's insights, he had no control over this ability, nor did he usually understand its meaning. He closed his eyes and breathed deeply, remembering Niki's Little Red Riding Hood costume from last year, as well as the cleavage-revealing nature of the outfit. Another shiver prickled up his spine when he recollected bits of the frightening children's folktale, a story that was eerily similar to one in his own culture. Then he opened his eyes to the wide expanse of waves rolling across Lake Superior and contemplated the sinister appearance of the Big Bad Wolf in those tales. Turning his gaze back upriver, he exhaled a long sigh of misgiving when he spotted the empty trailhead where Niki had vanished into the forest.

Chapter 2

*C*harles, *come help Mommy put these pumpkins in the wagon."*
Anna Eskild bent to the task and soon four-year-old Charlie ran
up beside her. "Punkins!" Charlie exclaimed, wrapping his short
arms around one of the orange gourds his mother had cut loose from the
vine. He strained under the weight, exaggerating a groan as he tried to
straighten up.

"Don't drop it, honey. Put it in the wagon with the others."

Little Charles Eskild-Hagen stumbled from side to side as he made
his way through the tangled mass of branches and vines to the wagon. His
mother followed with two more pumpkins, and together they placed their
loads in Charlie's bright red wagon.

"Jack-o' . . . jack-o' . . ."

"Jack-o'-lantern," his mother finished for him. "We'll keep the best
pumpkin to make our own jack-o'-lantern, but the others we have to sell
in town."

"Jack-o'-lantern," Charles repeated, jumping up and down with
delight.

Michael Hagen, her husband, had dropped the two of them off at the
end of the driveway on his way to work. He drove an old Chevy pickup,
and little Charlie loved these early morning rides in the bed of the truck

down the half-mile-long driveway. From there, mother and son usually walked back to the house for breakfast, surveying the garden beds along the way, checking the weather, and plotting the daily workload. When Anna had seen the ripe pumpkins, however, she decided to harvest them immediately. They'd quickly sell in town if she could save them from marauding red squirrels and chipmunks.

Anna noted the potatoes and carrots ready for picking, and several bell peppers and cucumbers that had finally ripened. She looked at the few puny tomato plants and wondered how any of them had survived the recent cold nights.

While Charles picked up stones from the road to hurl at make-believe targets in the forest, Anna stuck her hands in her jacket pockets and studied the tiny gardening enterprise hewn out of the edge of the woods. They'd chosen this spot along their gravel driveway for the vegetable garden because the land rose gently away from the road, the angled slope facing south, giving the plants as much sunlight as possible in this region of short growing seasons. Each year they cleared out a little more area, edging the plots with rocks dug out of the ground and timbers cut in the clearing process. But the soil was poor—acidic and rocky—so each fall she turned over the dead plants and worked them into the earth where they'd build up nutrients for the next year's crop.

The driveway was a discarded gravel logging road, in most places just a two-rut passageway connecting their house with the county trunk highway leading inland from Lake Superior. The highway out here wasn't used much, mostly local folks avoiding tourist traffic down on the shore, or as access to the parking lot for a spur trail leading into the Superior Hiking Trail, which ran nearby. The parking lot was just across the road from the entrance to their driveway. She'd noticed a car parked there when she'd scooped Charlie out of the back of the truck, but during camping season there usually were cars parked there, so she hadn't paid it much mind. They were nearly five miles inland from Black Otter Bay, and while the huge, cold lake moderated temperatures down along the shore, the big body of water couldn't influence the whims of Mother Nature out here. It never got really hot; ninety degrees Fahrenheit was unheard of, but forty below zero wasn't uncommon on a clear winter night.

Anna sighed to herself as she thought of all the work they had to do before snowdrifts buried her gardens. It was mid-October, meaning winter was still a solid three or four weeks off. The first killing frost was a couple weeks overdue, however, and would arrive any day now. For the next month she'd be busy picking and canning whatever vegetables could be saved, digging up and composting the garden beds, as well as finding time to sell a part of the harvest in town.

Grabbing the handle of the wagon, she began the slow trudge up the road to their house. It was beautiful here, quiet and peaceful, and the woods resounded with the busy calls of birds and scampering critters putting away their own stockpiles for winter. Deer and moose tracks littered the road, and she'd had to string chicken wire in spots to deter animals from eating all their produce.

"Come on, Charles," she urged. "Let's get this load put away and make some breakfast."

Charles ran ahead, his coat flying open around him while he jumped and threw rocks at targets on both sides of the road. She smiled at his energy and antics and thought how wonderful it was to raise a son in this rural countryside. Anna had grown up in Black Otter Bay and couldn't imagine living anywhere else. A full year older than her husband, she'd just turned thirty-three the previous summer. The hardworking lifestyle they'd chosen for themselves became evident toward the end of the day in a slight slumping of her shoulders. But Anna was strong and self-confident, and the outdoor work added a healthy luster to her complexion. A splash of freckles across the top of her cheekbones and nose highlighted her sparkling Nordic blue eyes. Thick strawberry-blond hair, held away from her face with tortoiseshell barrettes, fell in loose waves over her shoulders.

Her husband, Michael, was originally from Minneapolis. The first time he'd traveled up the North Shore, almost ten years ago now, he'd fallen in love with the quaint lifestyle and natural beauty of the area. He had his own construction and remodeling business, and he'd spent his first summer here working for room and board until he'd lined up enough jobs to make the move permanent. His construction business had never become really successful, however, and most of the long winter he was idle. But he'd never lost his initial infatuation with the north woods. Building their home and life out here was a full-time job in itself, and both of them toiled from before sunup to well after sundown to make it work.

Anna used a hand to shade her eyes as she looked up the road in the direction of their house. After winding past the vegetable plots, the gravel driveway dipped through a low, marshy area. It wasn't a place they'd ever be able to garden, but it was one of her favorite spots, nevertheless. The wet ground, containing half a dozen seeping springs, fed a small, unnamed creek that eventually found its way to the Black Otter River. Each spring, as the sun got a little higher and warmer, Anna eagerly watched for the marsh marigolds to poke up their yellow heads, the first true sign that spring was finally on its way. Hundreds, probably thousands of the big blossoms would open, often pushing their way through the last vestiges of snow still clinging to the shady, wooded landscape.

Michael had built a small tool shed here, a place they could store gardening equipment without having to haul it back and forth to the house. They only had one vehicle, the old Chevy three-quarter-ton pickup that Michael used for work. The big red truck had a detachable plow, and with the back end loaded with extra firewood for traction, they managed to keep the road open all winter. Anna used the truck for errands and to haul her vegetables to town, but when Michael was off on a job she worked the gardens with a wheelbarrow and Charlie's little red wagon.

She left her small hand tools in the shed and pulled the wagon up the short hill leading away from the marsh. Here the road leveled out and grew narrower as it snaked through birch and conifer forests. About a hundred yards from the house it finally opened up again, and this was where the flowerbeds began. These were her pride and joy and the focal point of her small business, Anna's Gardens and Toolshed. Tiered plots of annuals and perennials on both sides of the road were neatly marked with hand-painted signs, and woodchip-lined walkways wound between them. This was where their gardening efforts had begun, and after seven years of expanding and adding more plants each year, they now had more than an acre under their diligent care.

Folks from town bought all their gardening supplies here, and over the years many tourists had discovered the little backwoods nursery, too, buying hearty yarrow plants or tall spikes of lupine to bring back to their own gardens in Duluth or the Twin Cities.

A much larger garden shed stood here, full of bags of potting soil and fertilizers and gardening tools for sale. Anna loved to work out here, making up hanging pots and drying flowers to sell in the tourist shops in town. A makeshift greenhouse was attached to one side, the walls and roof made of heavy-gauge polyvinyl. A dozen windows Michael had salvaged from a job down on the shore were stacked against one wall of the shed—they'd saved them to begin construction next spring of a permanent greenhouse.

"Let's put these pumpkins in the shed, honey," Anna said to Charles when they arrived at the shed. There were no doors or windowpanes in the building—air and sunlight were allowed to flow freely through the building to prevent the growth of mildew and decay. She selected a couple wooden crates from a stack outside, brought them in and set them on the floor, then went out to retrieve the load from the wagon. She paused in the doorway and looked across the road into the woods. A movement had caught her eye, and she scanned the trees beyond the farthest garden plots.

Anna had been born and raised in this north country, so the woods were a familiar place to her. As an only child, she'd accompanied her father every fall on his deer- and grouse-hunting excursions. She'd been the son he never had, and as she grew up she'd learned there was nothing to be afraid of in the woods—that is, nothing to fear if you kept alert and used a little common sense. Those early years spent with her father had taught her a respect bordering on reverence for the life that lived and survived in this harsh environment.

Now she saw it again, at the far left of her range of vision. Just a flicker of movement, nothing she could focus on. Leaning against the empty doorframe, nibbling on a piece of mint, she studied the brushy area beyond the small herb garden beds. After concentrating her attention for several moments, however, she could see nothing that didn't belong out there. Anna knew if she stood still long enough whatever it was would reveal itself, but she had work to do, and coffee and breakfast were waiting.

Charles played toy soldier, marching with swinging arms toward the house. Anna grabbed the largest of the pumpkins and placed it on the floor in the shed. A minute later she returned for a second load but stopped short in the doorway, caught her breath, and scanned the trees across the road. The woods stood silent before her, but she knew something was there. She couldn't see any movement but rather felt a presence lurking just out of sight, watching her. She heard Charles's scraping steps on the gravel and looked at her son, his little body rocking side to side as he counted his steps. One-two, one-two.

It was probably a deer—or more likely several deer—coming to raid the herb garden now that it was maturing. But she couldn't shake the uneasy feeling creeping over her. She'd learned to trust her instincts about these things, and she'd never heard the woods go so quiet just because a deer passed by.

A bear? Maybe, but they generally didn't come around in the daytime. Whatever it was knew she was there. She could feel it watching her, and suddenly she felt very vulnerable. Her son was twenty yards away up the road, and the safety of the house was another eighty yards beyond him.

The notion that something was watching her became very real, as real as if she'd actually seen it. She couldn't explain her fear, but the clenching spasms in her stomach were proof enough that a malevolent creature stalked her, watching from the covering growth behind the seemingly tranquil gardens.

"Charles? Charles!" she called impatiently as she stepped out of the doorway. "Let's play a game, sweetheart." Out in the open now, walking in the middle of the road, her fear intensified. It threatened to engulf her like an invisible riptide overwhelming a swimmer. She couldn't make herself turn her back to the trees across the road, so she sidestepped toward Charles, all her senses tuned to the mysterious dark silence watching her.

She squatted down as her son ran up to her. "Remember Mommy's special watch, Charlie?" Anna had to concentrate to keep her voice calm. "Remember the stopwatch we use to time things?" She pulled her jacket sleeve back so he could see her Swiss Army watch. She looked into the woods again, where the menacing presence seemed to darken the cheery morning sunlight.

"Let's see how fast you can run to the house, okay? I'll time you."

Charles stuck his finger on the glass face of the watch, leaving a muddy smudge. "You count me, Mommy. One-two-three," he shouted with delight.

"That's right, honey, I'll time you. Now hurry—run up to the house and go inside. And show Mommy how you lock the door, okay?" She made him look her in the eye and she repeated, "Lock the door when you get inside. Understand?"

Charles nodded and bounced his impatience.

"Okay, sweetheart, run as fast as you can." Anna turned him around and faced him up the road toward the house. "One, two, three, go!"

After Charles took off running, she glanced over her shoulder at the stoic stand of birch and maples across the road. Nothing moved. Not a sound could be heard but the beating of her heart and the nervous intake of her breath.

Still squatting in the middle of the road, one hand skimmed over the gravel beside her until it found a fist-sized stone. She took a moment to glance back at Charles and his short legs chugging him home. Then she slowly stood while working the keys of her key ring between her fingers so they stuck out of her fist like claws. With the rock clasped firmly in her other hand and both fists concealed inside her jacket, she took a deep breath and set out at a brisk walk up the road behind her son.

Vincent Wyckoff

When she turned her back on the forest she almost choked on her fear. She walked faster, started jogging, hoping to leave the dark presence behind. The absolute silence around her resounded in her ears. Soon the gardens ended again and the woods closed in tighter against the road. Charles was almost to the house, and she was halfway, but the grip of fear wouldn't let go.

Then she saw movement again, something paralleling her in the woods on the left side of the road. It was closer, angling toward her to intersect her path to the house. She ran harder, let go of the rock and keys in her pockets and began pumping her arms to run faster. Panic was overcoming her, and she yelled up ahead to her son, "Run, Charlie, run! Get in the house!"

He looked back at her, saw her running and thought it was now a race between them. He started giggling as he churned up the last few yards of the driveway. Anna knew exactly where the unseen presence was. The whole woods, with its brooding silence, betrayed the location.

She saw Charles laugh as he pushed his way into the house and slammed the door behind him. She sensed her pursuer moving toward the road, closing in on her faster than she would have thought possible. She didn't dare break her pace by turning to look, keeping her focus on the door of the house. She willed herself to get there; nothing was going to stop her.

Nearing the end of the driveway, she heard a clatter on the gravel behind her. The sound roared through her ears and in her panic she ran full speed up to the door and crashed against it, gasping in relief and yelling to her son, "Open the door, Charles!"

She grabbed the handle and felt its rigid resistance, heard Charles laughing inside. She pounded on the door once, twice, yelled again in desperation, then fumbled in her pocket for the keys. The crunching of gravel drew close behind her and she pressed herself flat against the door.

The balled-up wad of keys finally popped out of her pocket, but in her haste they flew out of her hand and landed in the dirt beside the door. She fell to her knees, totally consumed by the approaching presence on the road.

Shaking and nearly hysterical, unable to grasp the keys, she clenched her fists and spun herself into a desperate lunge while emitting a shout of defiance.

The big red pickup truck slid to a stop behind her and Michael jumped out of the cab. He ran to her, calling, "Anna, Anna, honey, what's wrong?" He grabbed her shoulders as she slumped to a sitting position against the door. Her face was pale and she shook uncontrollably while trying to see around him. The woods remained silent, revealing nothing of the menacing presence she knew had been out there.

Michael pulled her to her feet as tears trickled down her face. He embraced her and held her tight, but Anna couldn't take her eyes off the woods beside the road. He whispered soothing words in her ear, then asked, "Where's little Charlie? Is he inside?"

She nodded against his shoulder.

"Sorry if I frightened you," Michael said. "I came back home because I forgot my scheduling books and estimates. I saw the wagon of discarded pumpkins, and when I saw you running I got so scared. I'm sorry."

Chickadees were calling from the edge of the forest, then she saw a half dozen of the little black-and-white birds winging through the trees. It seemed as though the sinister veil had suddenly lifted, and life had returned to normal in the woods.

"Something bad, Michael," she choked out. Anna cleared her throat and started again. "There was something chasing me—something evil."

He looked over his shoulder down the road, and when he turned back to her she tried to force him to believe her with the intensity of the stare she leveled at him. Then an involuntary shudder racked her body and she buried her face in his chest.

She heard the deadbolt unlatch and Charles twisting the door handle. "Daddy's home!" he exclaimed when he finally managed to pull the door open. Anna stepped aside so Michael could scoop up his little boy.

She folded her arms across her body and continued her surveillance of the woods. Behind her, she could feel Michael watching her. Using the back of her hand, she wiped the tears from her cheeks, but when she turned to them and smiled, she saw his worried expression. She grabbed his free hand and kissed it, mussed up Charles's hair with her other hand, and said, "We sure have a fast runner here, honey. Do you know he beat me in a race up the road?"

Michael laughed and carried Charles into the house while Anna lingered for a moment in the doorway. This time of year the sun never got very high, but even with the long shadows the forest seemed peaceful again. She wanted to believe the whole thing had been a trick of her imagination; a breeze twirling some leaves, maybe a wolf stumbling into them by accident. But the sense of dread was slow to leave, so with a final glance at the awakening woods, she shook away the memories and followed her family into the house, sliding the heavy deadbolt home behind her.

Chapter 3

When the call came in, *County Sheriff Marlon Fastwater* was down at the Black Otter Bay Post Office debating the merits of computer technology with the postmistress, Mrs. Virginia Bean. It was an argument they'd had before, and no matter how many times they went around on it, they never moved so much as an inch closer to agreement.

"So, the Postal Service sets you up with a computer and all the programs to run the office here," Marlon stated once again, waving an open hand around the back room. "Now they expect daily, probably even hourly reports. And what do they want to know? How many pieces of mail you have to sort, or how many missent items come through here. How many pieces of parcel post." He snorted. "Who cares? All you need is a truck to drop off the incoming mail in the morning, and another to pick up the outgoing mail in the afternoon. End of story."

Mrs. Virginia Bean smiled. The sheriff was a big man, handsome and masculine in a rugged, northwoods sort of way, but he really had no clue about the workings of the modern world. His massive, malamute-husky lay sprawled at his feet.

"It's all about efficiency, Marlon," she said, cinching closed a small sack of outgoing mail. She reached for the identifying zip code label to attach to the bag. Her long, slender fingers, encrusted in rings, twinkled in the fluorescent lighting as she worked the leather straps on the satchels. Years of handling the mail had given her movements a proficient purpose.

"The main office in Duluth needs to know that we're a viable office up here," she explained, handing the bag to the sheriff.

"A viable office?" he retorted, dropping the bag in a gurney for her. "You work all day getting folks their mail. You're more than viable. You're an absolute necessity."

She loved the way his black eyes glittered when he got upset. Sometimes she'd start these conversations just to see those eyes sparkle, and to hold him here keeping her company as long as possible.

"It's a big waste of time," he continued. "A bunch of paperwork to validate their jobs, because they don't have anything else to do. It just makes more work for you."

Fastwater's whole existence revolved around his clearly defined common sense. A direct approach, with no shaded areas of "what ifs" or "maybes," guided his outlook.

"Think about your job, Marlon," she said. "The computer has completely changed law enforcement. All the information you need is right at your fingertips."

Marlon scoffed. But he admitted to enjoying those evenings when Mrs. Bean came up to the station to give him lessons on the computer. How did she know all that stuff? He still couldn't tell a file from a folder, or when to quit a program or simply close a document.

Technically, Mrs. Bean wasn't a missus anymore. She'd lost her husband thirty years ago in a late-night, one-car, alcohol-induced crash on an old stretch of Highway 61 leading up from Duluth. They'd had no children, and instead of returning to her childhood home on the east coast, the young widow stayed on with her job in the post office, collecting a steady paycheck and benefits. She'd never remarried, and townsfolk knew her simply by the name etched in the postal nameplate on the window counter: "Mrs. Virginia Bean."

But for a long time now there'd been rumors about the nature of the friendship between the postmistress and the sheriff. Of course, speculation about such a relationship wasn't the sort of thing people in Black Otter Bay would discuss in public. Even though the sheriff and the postmistress were about the same age, Mrs. Bean looked older. She was at that indeterminate middle age, somewhere around fifty years old, and even though she often wore "old-ladylike" floral print dresses, topped with a bulky postal sweater, today her thick graying hair hung in gentle waves down her back in the style of a much younger woman. Her lively violet eyes were her greatest asset, however, whether sparkling with laughter or flaming up in anger.

As for the sheriff, he stood three or four inches over six feet with the thick, rounded shoulders of a powerful man. His torso was long and lean, with big hands at the end of heavy, muscular arms. But it hadn't always been that way.

Scrawny and shy as a youngster, a loner by nature, and the only Native boy in the local public school, Marlon learned early on about bullies and racism. His older sister, Arlene, had been the exact opposite. Loud and large, Arlene crashed through their childhood with aplomb and self-confidence, employing her own style of brassy intimidation.

Marlon's mother rarely left their rural homestead, and his father, a part-time cop in Black Otter Bay, missed the early signs of his son's struggle in school. It wasn't until Marlon began skipping classes in bunches that his parents became aware of the problem. He spent much of the fall of his first year in junior high out in the woods. As winter approached, he mapped out a trapline and turned all his energy into understanding the rhythms and cycles of the wilderness.

With his father lecturing and threatening punishment, Marlon retreated further into himself. It turned out that the only venue for communication known to either of them existed in the woods. So, at his father's request, Marlon showed him his snares and well-hidden trapline. When the first snowfalls began filtering down out of Canada, they spent whole days together in the woods, talking and telling stories. By the time the rivers and lakes froze over, Marlon's father had a good hunch as to what troubled his son, and furthermore, an idea as to how to fix it.

Ice skating is a popular winter pastime in Black Otter Bay, but hockey is the king of outdoor winter sports. With frozen lakes and rivers everywhere, finding a place to ice skate involves no more than a hike into the woods and the time it takes to shovel snow off a patch of ice. But outdoor skating is often hampered by rough and uneven ice, in some cases even open stretches of water. To play hockey, snow is shoveled off the ice into a berm around the rink, and while that helps keep the puck in play, it doesn't work nearly as well as the wooden boards found in real hockey arenas. Year after year the local high school players found that out when they competed against teams from larger cities.

Early in the winter of Marlon's eighth-grade year, his father came home with a truckload of plywood sheeting. Every evening for a couple of weeks they worked building a homemade hockey rink on the flat, open acre in front of their house. Then for an hour every morning before school and work they flooded the rink with garden hoses, gradually building up a solid, smooth surface. Finally, just before Christmas, Marlon's father put the word out around town. Carloads of parents and kids began showing up. A sunflower heater turned the garage into a warming house, and before long the Fastwaters' house was considered hockey central in the area. Neighbors contributed floodlights, attaching them to spruce poles placed around the rink. A generator, donated by the local general store, kept the lights on all winter.

With the completion of the hockey rink, Marlon's social status quickly changed. Every weekend brought sleepovers at the Fastwater house, and kids clambered to hang out with him in school. And along the way the motley bunch of local kids became pretty good hockey players. Within a couple years, Marlon experienced his teenage growth spurt, and with his newfound self-confidence, allowed his thick black hair to grow long. When his high school hockey team finally boarded a bus to confront their Iron Range rivals, the big Indian kid led his teammates onto the ice, his flowing hair and graceful, large frame giving pause and creating doubt along the opponent's bench.

He wore his glistening black hair short now, military style, usually covering it with a tattered old ball cap. From her position at the far side of the gurney of outgoing mail, Mrs. Bean thought he looked like an awkward, overgrown child again, unsure of himself in this conversation and uncomfortable with his presence in the back room of the post office.

The sheriff noticed her staring at his trousers. Looking down, he asked, "What?" Then he felt the droning vibration of the cell phone in his pocket. Grabbing for the phone, he ignored her grinning smirk. Ringing telephones grated on him, so he kept the cell on vibrate; that is, when he had it with him at all.

The caller ID revealed it was his nephew calling from the police station. Fumbling the phone with awkward, thick fingers, the sheriff finally answered, "Yeah, Leonard?" while pushing the gurney of mail through the back-room clutter toward the dock door.

"Marlon, we just got a call through the 9-1-1 service."

The sheriff stopped and lowered his voice. The cell phone disappeared into the mitt of his big hand. "What happened?"

"A couple backpackers found a body up the Black Otter Trail. I already notified the rescue squad."

Marlon opened the back door of the post office and stepped outside. The big husky joined him on the landing next to the dock. As he closed the door, he glimpsed Mrs. Virginia Bean shuffling papers on her desk, all the while watching him and trying to overhear his conversation.

With the door shut, he turned his attention to the problem at his fingertips.

"What do we know, Leonard? Where did the call come from?"

"A couple young guys, up over the top of the ridge. They were just hiking through when they spotted her a few yards off the trail."

"Her?"

"Yeah, I guess so."

"They still on the line?"

"No. They're pretty upset, Marlon. They wanted to come into town, but I told them to wait until we get there. You know, to keep anyone from disturbing the scene."

"That's good, Leonard. And Eckman and his crew are on the way?"

"Yeah."

"All right. Let's keep this quiet until we get a handle on what's going on. I'm on my way." He opened the door and strode back through the post office. "Have Eckman and the rescue squad meet us at the station. We'll go up together."

"Marlon?" Leonard said before hanging up. "These kids are pretty spooked."

"I suppose they are," Fastwater answered, trying to sound nonchalant as he looked at Mrs. Bean, who studied his expression in return. To her perpetual frustration, he was a master at revealing nothing.

"They said it's a woman's body. They think she had a small ponytail. But the face is in rough shape, Marlon. They said her nose was broken, so there was a lot of blood."

Fastwater didn't blink an eye. Turning slightly to face away from the inquisitive postmistress, he mumbled into the phone, "Did they have an idea how long she's been out there?"

"It's fresh, Marlon. The blood hasn't even dried."

"All right, then," the sheriff responded, once again looking at Mrs. Bean. "I'll be right there."

Returning the phone to his pocket, he gave the postmistress his usual blank stare. "Gotta go," he said. "Leonard needs me up at the station." His dog was already at the door, looking back in anticipation.

"What's going on?" she asked.

Mrs. Bean had many strong character traits that Fastwater found appealing, but her reputation as the premier town gossip was not one of them. If he told her what Leonard had said, the whole town would know a body had been found before he even got up there to see it himself.

"I'll get back to you later," he said, slipping around the counter and heading for the front door. He was already processing information and formulating questions to ask the young hikers. He knew there were many ways for a person to get into trouble in the woods, any number of ways to get seriously hurt: camp hatchets, knives, hypothermia. Slips and falls. But to actually get your face knocked in, now that took some real effort.

Acknowledging the postmistress's expression of concern, he pulled the door open and added, "It's all right. We'll talk later."

A cold gust of wind blowing in off Lake Superior met him at the corner of the building. A chill infiltrated his jacket collar, sliding down his back, while the dog's thick fur ruffled up with the breeze. Absentmindedly scratching the dog's ears, he considered what it would take for a person to stumble over a tree root and crash face-first into a rock. Or to lose control from a stroke or heart attack and tumble into the ground. He paused at the squad car door while the big dog jumped in, thoughts of bad luck and accidents fading as a premonition blossomed, the second such experience of the morning. Squinting past the mini mall and café toward the steel-girder bridge over the Black Otter River, he understood all too well just how vague the line could be between bad luck and murder.

Chapter 4

C *harles* *sat on the living room floor next to his father, listening and* laughing as Michael read to him from the comic section of the Duluth newspaper. A daily ritual, Michael brought the paper home after work each day and together they followed the adventures of the Peanuts gang and Mark Trail and Dennis the Menace. Anna set her wooden stirring spoon next to the stove and listened to their familiar chatter. Hearing Michael's voice and Charlie's delighted laughter went a long way toward calming her nerves, but the episode from early that morning hadn't completely left her.

They'd taken a walk together around the garden plots, discussing the condition of the flowers and herbs and the work to be done to put the beds to rest for the winter. Their talk was lighthearted for Charles's sake, not unlike anything they'd done almost every day this summer. But around the heavily wooded exterior of the gardens, both she and Michael had looked for signs of an intruder—tracks in the dirt or a broken branch, something to indicate her fears had not been imagined. They'd found nothing, however, and despite Michael's reassurances, Anna hadn't been able to shake the chill from the certain knowledge that something had been out there.

In a way, Michael had been unnerved by Anna's story, too. Not so much her description of what she perceived to have happened as her reaction to it. The look of terror on her face when he unexpectantly came home this morning was something he'd never seen before. Something he wouldn't have imagined possible from her. It was easy to assume that Mother Nature had been playing with Anna's imagination. After all, the angle of the sun at this time of year often blended shadows and crisp lighting into strange configurations, and sounds traveled farther in the cool, dry air while being distorted and exaggerated. But Anna knew all that. He respected her knowledge of the woods and her quiet Scandinavian self-confidence. He considered her too solid and aware of her surroundings to fall for a simple trick of nature.

On the other hand, on his way to work for the second time this morning, he'd spotted the rescue squad and the sheriff's squad car in the parking lot access to the Superior Hiking Trail across from their driveway. He'd stopped to inquire, but no one was around, and he found the absence of people and noise a little unnerving considering the uncommon presence of official vehicles so far into the woods.

Walking over to the wide entryway to the living room, Anna crossed her arms and leaned against the doorframe, her heart warming at the sight of her husband and son sitting together on the floor studying the newspaper. Michael looked up at her and smiled, then asked, "What's cooking? Sure smells good."

"Leftovers," she replied. "That venison stew we had last night. But I have a stalk of broccoli and some greens for a salad, too."

"Don't tell me one of your tomatoes finally ripened?"

Anna dropped her arms and wandered into the living room. "No," she snorted. "But there are green peppers and cucumbers and baby carrots."

"Ick!" Charles exclaimed, wrinkling up his nose and sticking out his tongue. "Carrots!"

They both laughed, and then Michael said, "Oh, I almost forgot. I invited that new guy in town over for dinner."

"What new guy?"

"Some fellow down from Canada, a French-Canadian named Luc. I hired him to help with the tear-off on Selstad's roof. You know, up the Moose Lake Road?"

Anna stood in front of the fireplace and slid her hand along the mantel. "I haven't heard of anyone new in town," she said. "Where's he staying?"

"Right now he's camped out up at the headwaters of the Black Otter, by the old beaver dam. He grew up with the Cree Indians—knows a lot about the woods. I don't know where he'll be living come winter. I suppose he'll head back up north." Michael looked past Anna into the kitchen. "Is there enough of that stew to go around?"

Anna smiled. It was just like Michael to invite someone over on the spur of the moment. But that was one of the things she liked about him— his generosity. Life could get tedious and hard out here in the woods. A little spontaneity lightened things up, and company was always welcome. "There's enough stew to feed an army for a week," she said. Then, cocking her head to the side, she asked, "How did you meet him? I mean, you said he lives in the woods."

Michael shrugged. "I saw him yesterday trotting along the snowmobile trail beside the road. I stopped to offer him a ride, and before long we were talking and he rode up to the Selstad place with me. He helped me get things ready for tomorrow, and I offered him a job."

Anna went to stand over Charles where he sat on the floor. Absently stroking her son's hair, she said, "Well, maybe he'll take some leftovers home with him."

"He doesn't have a car, honey. He doesn't drive, so more than likely he won't even show up." After pausing for a moment, Michael continued. "To be honest with you, the guy is a little different. He has a long beard, and makes most of his own clothes. But if today is any indication, I can tell you one thing for sure: he's strong and he isn't afraid of work. He unloaded two bundles of shingles at a time from my truck. If he sticks around, he'll be the best help I've ever had."

Anna stepped to one side of the fireplace and looked at a grainy, overexposed photograph on the wall next to the stone chimney. The couple in the picture was her great-great-grandparents, Gilbert and Ingebord Eskild. They'd arrived in Black Otter Bay in 1899 to homestead land, and Anna's living room, with its twelve-inch-thick, square-hewn logs, was the original home they'd built. She didn't know much about the figures in the photograph, but, because she'd grown up in this wild country, Anna had always wished she could have talked to them, especially her great-great-grandfather, Gilbert. She recalled what little she knew of them. He was a farmer, recently arrived from Finland, and Ingebord's family had emigrated from Norway. When the two met, Inga was fifteen years old and working in her father's dry-goods store near Sandusky, Ohio. In the story handed down to Anna, Gilbert hadn't been approved of as a suitor. The Finns, in Ingebord's parents' opinion, were slovenly and not a suitable match for their daughter, so the young couple eloped. It must have been a frightening and exciting adventure, Anna thought, as they boarded the first steamer packet available. Gilbert had dreams of homesteading a farm in Minnesota, but as chance would have it the little steamboat docked them at Black Otter Bay, which at that time was a tiny fishing village clinging to the shores of Lake Superior and populated predominately by Finnish and Norwegian immigrants.

While studying the photograph of her ancestors, Anna slid her palm along one of the flat, smooth logs comprising the wall of her living room. She could picture her great-great-grandfather carefully working the log to fit it in place. Then the years Ingebord had spent scrubbing the walls, removing fireplace soot and grime until the grain in the cedar glowed. She felt close to them then, her eyes studying their faces while her fingers felt their handiwork.

Anna leaned in closer, as she had done hundreds of times before, to scrutinize the faces of the couple photographed outside their cabin, now Anna's living room. As a young girl studying the photograph, Anna had made an interesting discovery: Gilbert's eyes appeared very light compared to the black dots glistening below Ingebord's eyebrows. The stark black-and-white photograph was more than a hundred years old, but from it

Anna had been able to surmise that Gilbert's eyes had been blue. In a family with generations of dark brown Scandinavian eyes, Anna's eyes also happened to be blue. Because of this she'd grown up with an affinity for her great-great-grandfather, a familial bond that spanned generations.

Gilbert's face exuded character, and Anna was sure it was the humorous, twinkling glow of his expression that had attracted Ingebord. His smirk was one of self-mockery, highlighted by radiating wrinkles at the corners of his eyes and mouth, like rays of sunlight emanating from his face. A tall, lean man, his arms hung loose at his sides, ending in the huge hands and thick fingers of a workingman.

Ingebord's expression was more withdrawn, as if she'd found her new life in northern Minnesota to be harder and more isolated than she'd expected. In the family history passed down to Anna, it was said that no one had ever found Gilbert and Ingebord's marriage certificate. Anna had often wondered about that. Had they run away so quickly that they hadn't dared to stop long enough to get married in Ohio? Several years ago, she'd looked through the early population census of Black Otter Bay and discovered that there hadn't been a priest or minister in the region until 1905. By that time, Anna's great-grandfather had been born, as well as a great-aunt. She could imagine the difficulty in coming forward to get married in the village after already having two children.

Gilbert had tried to tame the land; in fact, some of Anna's gardens were planted in areas he had originally cleared. But a plow was no good here. A limitless supply of rocks and roots dulled the blades, or simply cast them aside. Fortunately, the lumber industry moved into northern Minnesota by the turn of the last century, and Gilbert had found work as a lumberjack, his dream of starting a farm disappearing as quickly as the towering pine forests around him.

Anna grabbed the cast-iron knob for the fireplace damper and turned it to open the flue, then looked back at Michael and Charles, listening for a moment to her husband's description of one of the cartoons. "Think it's cool enough for a fire tonight?" she asked, and when they looked up at her, she said, "How about you guys get one going when you're done there?"

They immediately dropped the paper and scrambled across the floor to the fireplace. "Let me light it, Daddy," Charles called as Michael opened the fire chamber. "I want to light it!"

"Okay, okay," Michael said. "But first we have to get the kindling and more wood. You can help me get it ready."

Anna smiled as she watched them digging in the wood box, but when she turned to go back to the kitchen, a movement in her peripheral vision caught her attention. In an instant the immobilizing sense of dread from earlier in the day returned. Looking at the window over the kitchen sink, she choked out a scream at the sight of a man's face framed in the glass, passively looking back at her.

All of her irrational fears came rushing back, gagging her in their intensity. Her hands flew to her face as she staggered backward under the weight of the fear. Michael jumped to her side, grabbing her shoulders to steady her retreat. "What is it, honey?" When she didn't reply, he gently shook her. "Anna! What's wrong?"

She couldn't make herself look up again, but she pointed toward the kitchen sink and stammered, "The window." Her hand trembled as she pointed, then she blurted, "Someone was looking in the window at me."

Michael released his grip on her and ran to the window. After a quick look outside, he said, "There's nobody there, Anna. Not now, anyway. I don't see anything." But as he craned his neck for a better view, a sudden loud knock at the kitchen door made them both jump. Anna resumed her stumbling retreat into the living room, where she grabbed Charles and took a seat on the far end of the couch. Michael watched her sit down, gave her a smile of encouragement, then turned and took three long strides to the kitchen door.

Even Michael sighed in relief to see his new friend Luc at the door. From the living room, Anna heard the man admit to looking in the window. Now, while she composed herself, the two men stood in the kitchen laughing over the scare he'd inadvertently thrust on them. Using her hands to straighten her hair, she sniffled and cleared her throat as her eyes darted from object to object around the room: the photograph, the mantel, the newspaper spread out on the floor. A moment earlier she'd been scared to death, and now Michael stood at ease in her kitchen with a stranger. Charles crawled back to the wood box, dragging out sticks to make a fire, littering them across the hearth.

"Anna, honey," Michael called as he led his friend in from the kitchen. "I want you to meet Luc Trembley. He's the fellow I hired to work some jobs for me this fall. Luc, this is my wife, Anna, and over there is our son, Charles."

Anna sucked in her breath to steady her voice, and then stepped forward to greet their guest. Her first impression of the stranger was that he was a big man, but then she realized he wasn't large in a bulky sort of way. Rather, his overall presence seemed to take up more space than his physical body could account for. His shoulders were wide under a green-and-black buffalo-plaid flannel shirt, but his waist was narrow where the shirt tucked into belt-less denim jeans. Shaking his hand, Anna felt raw power emanating from the man, but as he stood before her, calmly balanced in his moccasins, she sensed a spiritual quality about him, as if all that power and bulk were merely a façade to conceal an even greater inner strength.

"How do you do, Mr. Trembley," Anna offered. She noticed his skin was deeply tanned, and its texture was like that of leather, not unlike the heavy moccasins covering his feet. His long, dark beard was brushed out and looked soft, while his sun-lightened hair was pulled back into a tight braid. She saw that interwoven in his hair was a thin silver chain with a tiny locket attached to the delicate, tarnished links. Looking into his eyes she felt another jab of anxiety, and for the first time noticed the acrid taste of fear lodged in her throat. Other than his cold, gray-blue eyes, she admitted that his countenance seemed passive. However, the gut-wrenching sense of dread wouldn't let her go.

"I'm so very sorry for upsetting you, Mrs. Hagen. Believe me, that was not my intention." His words were heavily accented in French, and the tenor range of his voice surprised her—with his size and strength she would have expected a deeper voice. She thought his speech seemed formal, studious, then she realized English was probably a second language to him. He dipped his head to her with his greeting—perhaps a nod of respect, she wondered. "I was just looking in the window to be sure I had the correct house."

"Well, it's not like there are a million houses around here," she said too quickly, then immediately regretted her lack of courtesy.

"You must have seen my truck out front," Michael interjected. "Didn't you recognize my old Chevy?"

The man's gaze finally left Anna's face as he slowly turned to look at Michael. "I didn't come that way," he said softly.

"Well, how did you get here, then?" Michael asked, a tinge of sarcasm coating his words. "Through the woods?"

"Mais oui. The shortest distance—"

"Michael," Anna interrupted, her voice at last under control. "Where are our manners? Your friend has walked all this way . . ." Turning to Luc, she said, "Please come in and sit down, Mr. Trembley." She stepped aside to allow him to enter the living room, ushering him toward the couch. "Can I get you something to drink?"

"Please call me Luc," he said in his strangely soft voice. "And I'll just wait. A glass of water with dinner will be fine."

"Anna had a terrible scare this morning," Michael explained as he and Luc sat down. "She imagined something stalking her in the woods, and she's been kind of jittery ever since."

That doesn't even begin to describe it, Anna thought as she went back to the kitchen to check on the stew. Uncovering the kettle, she grabbed the ladle and gruffly swished the contents around. And I didn't imagine anything! She felt a tremble in her hands, and her legs still shook.

Returning to the living room, she saw Michael helping Charles stack kindling in the fireplace. From his seat on the couch, Luc looked up at her and asked, "What sort of creature do you think was watching you? Did you get a look at it?"

"I never actually saw anything," she replied. "It was just a feeling I had." She turned to watch Charles carefully stacking twigs and sticks in a neat pile in the fireplace. Her next comment was directed at Michael's back. "But I wasn't imagining anything."

"I'm sure you weren't," Luc said, and when she looked at him, he continued, "I saw wolf tracks on my way in. Not coyotes or brush wolves, either. These were the real thing—timber wolf tracks."

Michael stopped what he was doing and looked over his shoulder at them. "I didn't see any tracks out there. Are you sure?"

"Oui. I can show you." His face softened when he spoke to Anna again. "Canis lupus has much power, madame. He is an animal of great spirit. You can feel when he is nearby because his life force is so strong. You need not see him to know he is there."

Anna watched his arm and hand gestures as he spoke. At times it appeared he used them as walking sticks to balance his way through the English words, while at other times he looked like a maestro conducting language rather than music. But most of all he seemed to be using the gestures to help his listener understand the essence of his speech.

Michael stood up. "Well, I think it's still light enough to see outside. What do you say we go have a look at those tracks of yours?"

Luc led the way outside, followed closely by Michael, and Anna took Charlie's hand after promising he could light the fire when they returned. The long gravel road leading up from the highway ended in a cleared-out parking area by the kitchen door. Michael's truck was parked there, beside a covered stack of firewood and assorted tools he used in his business. Instead of walking down the road to the garden plots, however, Luc turned and followed the kitchen wall to the side of the house, then turned again and walked along the length of the building, past the log-walled living room and the addition Michael had built on the rear of their house. The addition was used primarily as a utility room and storage area, but he'd also built a loft above it for Charles's bedroom. With a wooden ladder for access, the loft was like a tree house to Charles, and when he went to bed at night, he fell asleep to the sights and sounds of his parents below him.

Luc headed into the woods, and Anna marveled at the way he moved. He glided soundlessly into the underbrush, and his agility became even more apparent when Michael entered the woods. Her husband's heavy boots crunched the forest debris underfoot, and his arms and shoulders roughly pushed branches aside in his effort to keep up. They quickly disappeared, but Anna and Charles managed to follow by listening to Michael's movements through the trees.

When she caught up to them, they were kneeling over a soft spot in the dirt. Luc was carefully picking away fallen leaves from the ground. "Here, you see?" He pointed a long index finger at a faint sign in the mud. "See the rounded toe mark? And here, the point where a claw poked the ground?"

"Are you sure about that?" Michael asked. "I can't see where you get a wolf print out of that—it's just a smudge in the dirt."

After Anna had squatted down to look for herself, she wouldn't deny that it could be a wolf print, but she had to agree with Michael—it didn't look like proof of a track, either.

"You must learn to see the whole picture," Luc explained. From his position on all fours, he brushed his hand along the leafy understory beside him and said, "See the wolf move here. He trots along, keeping his body low to the ground." Now Luc's hand swung out in front of him toward Anna. "He knows the house is nearby. He can smell you, and he hears the strange human sounds." Luc dipped his head toward a small opening in the prickly bushes next to Anna and directed his outstretched arm into the passageway. "He turns sharply here to move through this opening, and when he does, one of his claws digs into the dirt to help him turn." Now he looked up at Anna again. "So, my friend, he leaves us this print as proof of his passing."

Everyone huddled around him as he stood up, and Anna was thinking that he still hadn't proved anything to her, although he certainly told a good story.

"Jeez, Luc, I don't know . . ." Michael began, but Luc leaned forward and reached into the briars. When he extracted his fist, he opened it to reveal a small clump of gray and white hairs in his hand.

"What the?" Michael said under his breath. "Is that wolf fur?"

"Certainement, monsieur."

Charles began pulling on Anna's hand. "Mommy, I don't want to see a wolf!"

Anna scanned the forest around them. Darkness was descending quickly, and what little breeze there'd been during the day was gone. The woods were silent and still, and it wasn't hard to imagine furtive eyes watching them from the cover of brush and shadow. She looked into Luc's eyes and trembled as a shiver rattled up her spine.

Charles kept tugging, more earnestly now. "Mommy, come on!"

"Okay, honey. Let's go back to the house." She let him lead her through the bushes, the glow from the kitchen window promising warmth and safety. But a chill in her bones betrayed her inner doubts, and then she wondered, how had Luc spotted that track in this dim light on the leaf-covered forest floor?

• • • •

Dinner that evening was quieter than usual. Despite Charlie's voracious appetite, Anna could see he was worn out from spending the whole day outdoors with her. And he was probably just a little shy because of the long-haired stranger sitting at the table with them. Michael usually spent this time talking about the job he was currently working on, or catching them up on village gossip. But he seemed a little pensive, too, ever since their excursion into the woods before dinner. Anna knew him well enough to know that he was probably worrying about the possibility of wolves ranging so close to the house. It was a scary thought, she admitted, especially with Charles playing outside so much. She wondered what they could expect this winter when the wolves' food sources became scarce.

For herself, Anna couldn't shake her feelings of misgiving, and to make it worse, she couldn't get a handle on the exact source of her dilemma. She was convinced that somehow the strange events of the day were related. In all the years spent with her father in the woods hunting, camping, and backpacking, she'd never felt the sinister terror she'd experienced that afternoon. It had so unnerved her that when she'd spotted Luc looking in the window, she'd completely lost her composure. And there was something else about this stranger Michael had invited into their house. When she looked into his eyes, she shivered at an untamed element glistening there, an animal-like wildness that recognized neither master nor compassion.

But Luc Trembley was a perfect gentleman at the supper table, and twice he complimented her stew. "May I ask what seasonings you use, Mrs. Hagen?" he asked. "They add so much flavor without covering the taste of the venison."

To Anna, it seemed like such an odd question to be coming from a man who was basically homeless, a man who made his living from hunting and trapping, and probably did his own cooking over an open fire.

"Earlier in the year," she replied, "I always use Vidalia onions. They're my favorite. Vidalias and whatever else are available. Of course, the broth is a lot thinner than this. But this time of year I throw in vegetables from the garden, and fresh herbs like Shepherd's basil, thyme, and a little sorrel. I get mushrooms down the road by the seeping springs. I try to use the stuff while it's fresh, then I dry or pickle or can whatever's left over." She smiled at his nod and grin of admiration. "I'm glad you like it," she concluded.

From her place at the table, Anna studied their guest. He was an enigma to her, wild and independent, yet polite and well-spoken. She wondered what sort of questions she could ask him without sounding pushy or rude. "Michael tells me you're from Canada, Mr. Trembley; whereabouts?"

"Actually, I'm originally from France. La Tremblade, a town on the Bay of Biscay, near Rochefort and La Rochelle. But please, Mrs. Hagen, my name is Luc."

"France?" Both Michael and Anna looked at him in surprise. "My gosh," she said. "Excuse me, it just seems so odd. How did you wind up living with Indians in Canada?"

"My uncle lives there. I was sent to live with him when I was seven years old."

The conversation seemed to hit a dead end while Luc continued spooning his bowl of stew. Anna worried that he wasn't going to tell them more, but after an almost awkward time of watching him eat, he finally looked up and said, "My father is a sailor. He captains his own fishing boat out of Royan, on the mouth of the Gironde River. It was hard for him to care for a small boy when he was gone to sea so much, so he wrote to his brother in Canada and asked him to take me."

He said this so matter-of-factly, Anna thought, and without any feeling. And yet, he'd been just a little boy . . . "What about your mother?" she asked, without considering the rudeness of the question.

"He had the biggest trawler in the fleet," Luc said with obvious pride. "When I was very young, he took me on the boat sometimes."

Anna arched an eyebrow and looked at Michael to see if he'd noticed how Luc had ignored her question. He must have, because he asked, "Did something happen to your mother, Luc? Where was she?"

Luc deliberately finished chewing and swallowed his food, then reached for his glass of water. Anna watched the glass reach his lips, tip as he drank, and when she looked at his eyes beyond the rim of the glass her heart froze. She'd seen eyes like that before! Years ago, on a cold November day while deer hunting with her father, she'd shot a young buck, but only wounded it. Her father had led the way as they trailed the injured animal for hours through the woods. Toward evening they'd finally spotted it, on the far side of a small stream, but a pack of wolves had found it first. Hidden at a short distance, they'd watched the bloody carcass being ripped apart and devoured, until one member of the pack broke away and came toward them to the stream to drink. He'd lowered his mouth into the water and silently sucked, not lapping at it like a dog. And all the while his eyes darted around, constantly searching for danger. Somehow the wolf had spotted them, and she'd watched as his nose wrinkled up in a snarl. In the next instant the whole pack disappeared over a ridge. She'd never forgotten those eyes, cold, ruthless, and completely wild. Now she looked at them again over the rim of the glass.

"I never knew my mother," Luc said, straining to keep his voice steady. "She was a drug addict and prostituee. Une putain crasseuse."

Wondering if they'd understood his French correctly, Michael and Anna stopped eating and looked at Luc. A moment later he simply said, "My mother was a whore."

Anna realized the conversation had definitely hit a dead end, and even though she had more questions now than before, she decided to keep quiet. Getting up, she retrieved the cast-iron kettle of stew from the stove and passed it around the silent table. She exchanged some questioning looks with Michael, but Luc asked him about the roofing job they'd start tomorrow, and in the end, nothing more was said about his parents.

• • • •

After dinner, everyone helped clean up, then Charles finally got to light the fire in the fireplace. He quickly fell asleep in his father's lap, the boring conversation about roofing a house acting like a sedative. It was having the same effect on Anna, so when the men began calculating how long the tear-off would take on the Selstad roof, she volunteered to haul Charles up to bed.

When she was upstairs, she heard Michael take out the wine glasses, and soon she heard the pop of a cork from one of her father's bottles of homemade wine. Michael explained to Luc, "Anna's father makes his wine from berries he picks out here each summer. Chokecherry, blackberry . . ." He held up the bottle to look at the handwritten label. "This one's raspberry, from last July. Hmm, three months old," he said with a laugh. "Should be a very good vintage."

From upstairs, Anna heard the wine being poured, then looked over the edge of the loft to see the fireplace aroar and Michael taking a seat on the couch. "This used to be her father's house," he said to Luc. "In fact, Frank built the back bedrooms and bathroom when Anna was just a kid. He moved into town when Edith died—that was his wife, Anna's mom. Frank's a really cool guy," he continued. "He gave this place to us when he moved. This living room was his great-grandfather's original house."

Anna sat on Charles's bed, stroking her sleeping son's forehead and brushing the hair back from his face. She couldn't see the men sitting below, but she watched the same fiery shadows that they saw flickering around the room, and she could hear their quiet words of conversation.

"What do you think I should do about the wolves, Luc?" Michael asked. "I don't like them coming so close with little Charlie running around."

"You live in the woods," Luc replied with a shrug of his shoulders. "The wolves live in the woods. There is much room for both of you."

"Well, I just don't like it. Hell, I'd leave them alone, but I can't trust that they'll leave us alone. Especially with winter coming on."

"They are protected here, non?"

"Well, sure, but it's my job to protect my family, too." It was quiet for a minute while the men were thinking, and Anna began climbing down from the loft.

"I tell you what, Luc," Michael continued, "and I don't care who hears me say it. I'll shoot them if I have to, to protect my family."

"You're not going to be shooting any wolves, Michael," Anna said with irritation when she got to the bottom of the ladder. "They're not hurting us—shooting them is just absurd. There must be some other way of dealing with them. Maybe we'll get a dog. Charlie's been wanting one."

Her brusque words hung in the air as she joined them, sitting on the couch next to Michael and taking the glass of wine he offered. Detecting a smirk on Luc's face, she blushed both from anger and embarrassment. Sitting in an overstuffed chair beside them, Luc's attention was directed at the fireplace, so he missed her glare of rebuke. With just the little light from the kitchen sneaking into the room, the roaring blaze cast wavering shadows around them. Her great-great-grandfather's hand-worked logs reflected a burnished gold warmth throughout the room. Anna's first taste of wine began easing the tension she'd carried all evening.

"Have you ever tried trapping wolves in Canada?" Michael asked Luc.

"Oui, many times."

"I've tried trapping fox and brush wolves around here, but I've never had any luck. Remember last winter, Annie? I spent a whole day on that one set to make it perfect. I tell you what, Luc, there wasn't a flake of snow out of place. Later, I found fox tracks circling the set, but they wouldn't come in. How do they know?"

Luc shrugged his shoulders. "Maybe your work was too good. Nothing in the woods is perfect, non? It is a place ruled by chaos. To make your work natural to the animals, it must be just a little messy, too."

"Well, if those wolves become a problem this winter, maybe you could help me set a trap. If we take out one or two of them, the others might leave the area."

Luc ignored the remark and looked aside at the wine glass in his hand. "My uncle's trapline in Canada covered forty miles," he said. "It took us three days on snowshoes to cover the whole route. When we'd get back, we'd spend a day or two skinning hides and repairing equipment, then we'd head out to do it all over again. Each family in the village had their own parcel to trap—they were handed down from generation to generation. My uncle paid a family every year for the right to trap their area, and now, after many years, they have given it to him. But trapping does not make a very good business, non? It is not like it used to be."

Michael and Luc continued talking about the woods and hunting, a subject Anna was usually interested in discussing, but her exhaustion, and the potent homebrew wine, soon set her mind to wandering. She wished she could put a name to the fear she'd experienced that afternoon or find some proof as to what had been watching her. She was convinced she would have spotted a stray backpacker or hiker. If someone were lost, say wandering off the Superior Hiking Trail, why would they hide in the woods and not ask her for directions? For a while, she'd thought it could have been a bull moose—after all, it was the rutting season, and they were wandering far and wide in their search for a mate. But an aggressive bull moose wouldn't have been so shy; he certainly wouldn't just stand out there watching her. Besides, they'd never found any tracks, and a bull moose in rut cuts a wide swath in his passing.

From her dark corner on the couch, Anna felt the evening chill, even with the blaze across the room in the fireplace. She looked at the shadows silently playing around the smooth cedar-log walls like exotic dancers, or pagan worshipers. The conversation around her continued in quiet tones so as not to disturb Charlie's sleep. At times like these, she mused, we're not so far removed from the woodland tribes who lived here two hundred years ago. And it was comforting to think that her great-great-grandfather had sat in this same spot, watching the flames of a long-ago fire cast shadows over these same walls.

A loud pop in the fireplace shook her out of her reverie. Michael jumped, too, and then laughed when he realized it was just a chunk of pitch exploding in a pine log. Anna looked at Luc's profile in the light from the fire. He was slouched comfortably in the big chair, staring into the flames. She asked him, "How do you know that the wolf that made those tracks you showed us is the same one who scared me earlier today? I mean, that track was out behind the house, but I was way down the road when I felt something watching me."

Luc took his time responding, slowly sitting up straighter and breaking his attention away from the fire. He set his empty wine glass on the end table, and then turned to look at her. "The wolf is always moving, madame. He leaves you his track here, he watches you there, tomorrow he is gone."

"I don't know," Anna said. "I'm sure I would have seen it . . ."

"Where there is one wolf, there are probably more."

"But I've seen wolves before, Luc. Why did I get so scared this time? It was like something evil was watching me." The fire's glow against Luc's face was creepy, she thought, like the lighting in an old movie highlighting the face of a bad guy.

"Maybe it was Manitou," he said softly.

"What?" Michael asked.

"Manitou?" Anna repeated, sitting up straight. "You mean, like an Indian god?"

"Not a god," Luc explained. "More like a spirit. They roam the woods, mostly avoiding people, but sometimes when they encounter a person, they take the shape of an animal."

"Oh, come on, Luc," Michael scoffed. "Now you're telling ghost stories."

Anna held up her hand to stop her husband from saying more. "Could Manitou take on the shape of a wolf?" she asked.

"Certainement. Or a bear, or any other animal. It depends on which life force it takes its power from. Matche-Manitou, a very evil mystery, has the snake magic—"

"Snake magic?" Michael interrupted. "I don't think there's any snake magic around here," he added with a tone of sarcasm.

Anna playfully slapped his shoulder to shush him. To Luc, she said, "That would explain the bad feeling I had." She wanted to ask more, but then they all heard the faint howl of a wolf somewhere out in the night. It was a long, lonesome wail that faded away slowly. Anna looked to the window, half expecting to see another creature watching her. But all she saw was darkness. They sat in silence, the glowing shadows from the fireplace gyrating around them, and soon another wolf could be heard answering from farther away. Anna found herself settling closer against Michael's warmth.

Luc stood up and said, "And so it is time for me to go. Thank you so much for dinner and your hospitality. It was a pleasure to meet you and your son, Mrs. Hagen."

Anna looked up at him in disbelief. "But you can't go out there now," she said. "It's dark—can't you hear the wolves?"

"Let me give you a ride," Michael suggested.

"That won't be necessary," Luc responded. "I walk everywhere, and there's a moon tonight to light my way. Besides, you can't drive to where I live."

"I know, but then at least stay here tonight. We can ride together to work tomorrow."

"Thank you, but I must go." To Anna, he bowed and said, "Madame, it was a pleasure to share time and dinner with your family. The food—I would like to know more about how you prepare it."

"Of course," she replied, at a loss for words due to his sudden decision to leave. She shuddered at the thought of him walking off alone into the darkened forest.

They followed him to the kitchen door, where her mood suddenly lightened. For all his table manners and pleasant conversation, her apprehensions hadn't left her all night, and now she could feel her misgivings preparing to walk away with him. It had been like having a wild animal loose in the house. When he opened the door, he turned to Anna and said, "You need not fear Manitou, Mrs. Hagen. Sometimes he just watches. He is very curious." And then he turned and disappeared into the darkness beyond the meager realm of their yard light.

Chapter 5

The next morning found Sheriff Marlon Fastwater sitting in his office entering details of the investigation into his computer. The day had started early and no doubt would run late. He paused as a huge yawn overtook him, then rubbed his eyes and looked at the clutter on his desk. Yesterday had been a nightmare, reminiscent of the chaos the little village had endured last spring with the death of Rose Bengston. And just like that event, there was no reason to think this would be over any time soon. Once again, he scanned the summary of reports sent up early this morning from Duluth. Apart from the fact that the real estate agent was dead, the worst thing he read in the communication was that a rookie detective was on his way up to see him. "To confer and lend assistance," the report said, but Fastwater figured the visitor would more than likely just get in his way and piss him off.

The sheriff had accompanied the rescue squad to Duluth yesterday, where Nichole Nielsen's body had been formally identified. Talking to some of her friends and family, he'd learned that they were used to her independent lifestyle, her coming and going whenever she wanted. No one was aware of a disgruntled boyfriend, just as no one could imagine anyone wishing her harm.

Putting the computer to sleep for a while, he leaned back to look at the wide-angle view of Lake Superior outside his office window. He thought that sitting here waiting for the detective to arrive was like hanging around waiting for the onset of a migraine. Clasping his fingers behind his head, he stretched his legs out on the desktop. The distant motion of whitecaps breaking over themselves always had a calming effect on him. Walking along the rocky shoreline was even better. He found the sound of the surf and the fresh air to be a perfect antidote to the pressures of his job. He'd be willing to bet that after the upcoming meeting with the detective he'd be in need of a long walk.

The police station, or "headquarters" as Sheriff Fastwater usually called it, was tucked into the side of the hill behind Black Otter Bay. When the leaves were down, as most of them were now, he could see many of the rooftops in town, part of the highway, and the steel-girder bridge spanning the Black Otter River. The office itself was small and spartan, the only picture on the walls an old black-and-white aerial photograph of the shoreline. Taken from out over the water, the photo was from the 1940s and showed the fleet of local fishing boats in the harbor. In the background, the tiny cluster of clapboard buildings comprising Black Otter Bay looked raw and precarious, virtually obscured by the vast coniferous forest surrounding it. Even today, Fastwater thought, the photograph was an accurate depiction. Not much had changed, at least as far as the number of buildings in town. If anything, the forest was even taller, darker, and more imposing as it crowded in around them.

The sheriff liked this perch up on the hillside; in a way, he felt it kept him and the law away from the general public. To his way of thinking, law and order was a goal worth striving for, and locating the sheriff's office apart from and above everyone else seemed appropriate. The little building was only two rooms: his office and a tiny bathroom with a toilet and sink. It didn't even have a jail cell. The few times he'd needed to lock someone up he'd simply left the offender in the office and padlocked the door on his way out. No one from town, whether sleeping off a drunk or in some sort of trouble, would ever consider breaking one of his windows to escape. He knew the townsfolk didn't think that way. Besides, Fastwater's dog, Gitch, spent his nights in the police station. The sheriff figured the dog, from his sleeping spot on the braided rug in front of the door, was more reliable than any lock or security system he could have installed.

Fastwater's gaze wandered over to the dog sprawled out by the door. Gitchi-Gami was his constant companion, named after the Ojibwe name for Lake Superior, meaning "big water." He was mostly malamute and Alaskan husky, with enough German shepherd in him to give him that "police dog" look. From his sled dog ancestry, Gitch had inherited one brilliant blue eye. The opaque blue of that eye reminded Fastwater of the colors reflected in the ice floes heaved up on the shore of the big lake each spring. For the most part, the slabs of ice were clear and clean, but when the sun hit them just right and picked up the blue colors of the lake, the result was a glistening pile of ice shards that looked like an overflowing treasure chest of gems and jewels. Gitch's one blue eye looked as if it could have been plucked right out of that mass of glittering, brilliant blue ice.

Gitch lay at an angle across his rug by the door, facing inward just enough to be able to keep watch over his master. As if sensing the sheriff looking at him, he raised an eyelid and studied Fastwater. After deciding there weren't any imminent plans to get up, however, Gitch adjusted the position of his chin across his front paws, let out a sigh, and drifted back to sleep.

Fastwater thought back to the day Gitch came to live with him. What a bizarre night, he thought with a wry grin. It had been four years ago now, on Halloween. Every year the town's municipal bar hosted the annual Halloween dance and masquerade party. Just before midnight, the sheriff had taken a walk through town, jiggling and testing store locks while greeting the various ghouls and costumed revelers he met on the sidewalk.

He'd stopped in at the bar to check out the proceedings, ordering a cup of coffee to go. Toby, the full-time manager, and two of his employees ranged back and forth behind the polished wood-plank bar, serving out tap beers and mixed drinks while refilling bowls of nuts and grabbing empty beer bottles in a frantic rush of non-stop movement. Toby's white shirt, sleeves rolled up beyond the elbows, hung out haphazardly at the waist. His thick hands and forearms worked with a fluid grace acquired from years of tending bar. He splashed a cup of coffee across the bar to Fastwater, waved off the sheriff's tendered payment, and then continued his maneuvers along the line.

It was clammy and hot inside, a humid heat radiating from the sweating dancers and pool players crushed together shoulder to shoulder. The interior of the bar was paneled with rough-sawn cedar slabs, the floor a scuffed and dulled tongue-and-groove fir. Crammed into a corner on a raised platform, a local country and western band belted out high-energy music. The dance floor was full and the lively, gyrating partiers had sprawled out around the dozen or so tables scattered about the room. Fastwater thought he'd never seen so many happy people together in one place before. Everyone wore big, drunken smiles, and bursts of laughter erupted from every sector of the room.

About the time the sheriff had decided he'd seen and heard all he could stand, the tall and rangy Owen Porter lunged through the door. Owen had a reputation for telling stories that were just a little hard to believe. Despite the tall tales, Owen wasn't much of a drinker, so the wild look in his eyes caught Fastwater's attention and drew him to the newcomer.

"Sheriff!" Owen exclaimed upon seeing the lawman.

Fastwater put his hand on Porter's shoulder and coaxed him to turn around and go back outside. Before the screen door slammed shut, Owen was waving his arms and stammering, "I'm sure glad I found you, Sheriff! There's a crazy kid up the road there, and blood everywhere. I can't make any sense out of what he's saying, and—"

"Hold on a minute," Fastwater interrupted. "Just slow down, Owen, and tell me what's going on."

"He said he killed someone, Sheriff! A girl. His girlfriend. He said he killed her!"

Fastwater stopped walking and turned to face the excited young man. Owen Porter was one of the few people in town as tall as the sheriff. Fastwater moved in closer, pinning Porter to the spot by staring him straight in the eye. He sniffed for alcohol, but all he detected was the fetid odor of stale cigar breath.

He put out a hand and gently patted Porter on the chest. "Okay, let's go easy now," he said. "Start at the beginning. Where did you see this fellow?"

"A couple miles down the highway there," Porter explained, pointing south toward Duluth. "I was coming home from a date. Me and Joanelle, we went to a movie and stuff in the city."

"That's fine, Owen. Great. Now about this kid . . ."

"I saw him walking along the shoulder of the highway, so I stopped, you know, to see if he needed any help. Like a ride or something."

"Okay, so you stopped. Then what happened?"

"This kid, I couldn't believe it, man. He had blood all over his shirt and hands, even smeared on his face. He pointed at the woods and said, 'I killed her. She thought she could run around behind my back, but I found out. Now she's dead, and I buried her out there under a pile of rocks.' He kept saying that, about killing his girlfriend and burying her. I tell you, Sheriff, it scared the heck out of me."

Fastwater studied Porter's face, looking for a lie or another tall tale. All he saw were signs of shock and anxious fear.

"Where is this guy now?" he asked.

"He walked off into the woods, saying he'd show me the body. Hell, Sheriff, I don't want to see no dead body. So I jumped back in my truck and hightailed it into town. Looked for you up at your office, then came straight down here to get help."

"So it was only fifteen or twenty minutes ago that you saw this guy?"

Porter nodded. "Fifteen minutes tops. He's just a kid, Sheriff. Can't be more than sixteen or seventeen years old."

"Okay, Porter, here's what we'll do." He grabbed Owen's arm and led him into the parking lot. As they walked, he said, "Give me a ride up to my car. I'll call my deputy and we'll follow you out to where you last saw this kid."

"Sure, Sheriff, whatever you say."

Twenty minutes later, Fastwater's nephew Leonard had joined him. They tailgated Porter's pickup truck south out of town on old Highway 61. Leonard Fastwater hadn't been a full-fledged deputy at that time. He was going to school, though, and the sheriff had him tag along whenever possible, just for the experience. Leonard had spent several years on what he called his "spiritual quest," a solo journey that had taken him to Native American communities throughout the north country. He'd studied with tribal elders and shamans from the Dakotas to Hudson Bay.

Since his return to Black Otter Bay, he'd kept whatever wisdom, personal insights, or magic he'd learned to himself. He was a man of few words, so Fastwater was surprised to hear him say, "I always thought those mud flaps looked silly." Leonard nodded ahead at the twin chrome silhouettes of nude women reclining behind the rear wheels of Porter's pickup. In the dark front seat of the big county cruiser, Leonard's voice sounded far away and only half awake.

Fastwater had just enough time to glance at the mud flaps when the truck ahead of him suddenly veered to the right and slowed down on the shoulder of the road. In the middle of the opposite lane, a lone figure could be seen in the peripheral glare of the headlights. The sheriff let out a "humph" of surprise. Until now, he'd still thought that somehow this was just another of Porter's crazy stories.

They got out of the car and walked across the highway, the sheriff unsnapping the holster of his handgun. Approaching the muddy, bedraggled teenager, Fastwater saw he carried a bulky bundle under one arm. Leonard produced a flashlight, and in a move to disorient the kid, shined the beam of light straight into his eyes. Fastwater was taken aback at the sight of blood smeared across the lightly bearded face.

"What's going on here, young man?" was all he could think to say.

The kid muttered to himself, like he wasn't even aware of their presence. With the light in his face he'd stopped walking, but he continued his vehement conversation with himself.

"Hey!" Fastwater shouted to get the kid's attention. "Look at me."

The kid leveled a dull stare of absolute hatred at the sheriff, a glare void of light, as if the person behind those eyes resided in another world.

"You having some sort of trouble or something?" Fastwater asked.

"I didn't even bother to bury her deep," the kid said. "Just piled rocks over her backstabbing body."

"Whose body?"

"She used to be my girlfriend," came the matter-of-fact reply.

A whimpering sound came from under the boy's arm, and Fastwater saw that he clutched a struggling puppy tightly to his side.

"What's that?" the sheriff asked.

"My wolf dog," the kid said, hauling the puppy up to hug him against his face. Smacking sounds of kissing came from the boy's lips. Blood was caked to his arms and hands and matted in the dog's fur. Strips of rawhide in various widths were knotted up in tangled masses around the boy's neck and wrists, with a wider one around the puppy's neck.

Fastwater looked at Leonard and found an expression of revulsion on his face.

The puppy increased his efforts to free himself, and the kid grabbed him tight with both arms.

"You suppose you could show me where you buried her body?" Fastwater asked.

"Sure I can," the boy said. "But I don't want to see her no more."

"Well, just show me where she is, then."

The kid promptly turned around and walked back along the ditch. Fastwater heard the incessant muttering start up again. "Follow him," he said to Leonard, and then he jogged back across the road to his car. On the police radio, he put in a call to the volunteer rescue squad, then switched on his flashing squad car lights. They'd work as a beacon for the rescue crew to home in on.

He extracted a flashlight from the glove box, looked at the shotgun mounted before the dash, decided against it, then jumped out of the car and slammed the door. At Porter's truck, he thanked the young man for his help and told him to head on back to town.

"Are you kidding?" Owen answered. "I found him; I want to see how this thing plays out."

"Well, suit yourself," Fastwater replied, impatient to catch up to his nephew. "Come on if you want. We're going out to look for the body."

At that, Porter hesitated, but when the sheriff turned to leave, he flung his door open and swung his long frame out. Grabbing a flashlight from a toolbox in the back of his truck, he switched it on, nodded with satisfaction to see it light up, then turned to follow the sheriff. "Hang on," he called. "Hang on, Sheriff. I'm coming."

Fastwater spotted Leonard's flashlight bobbing into the woods. The ditch here was deep and soggy and before he knew it his boots were full of water.

"Damn it," he cussed as he heard Porter splash and stumble through the icy water behind him. Following their bouncing flashlight beams as fast as they could over the rocky terrain, they quickly caught up to Leonard and the boy. It soon became apparent that the kid was wandering with no particular destination in mind. He'd meander one way for a while, stop and look around while muttering to himself, then march off into the dark in a totally different direction. Fastwater detected movements in the woods around them, but he wasn't fast enough with the flashlight to discover what was out there. Maybe deer, he thought, beginning to herd up for the winter, or possibly wolves, attracted to the scent of blood and the whimpers of the puppy.

Finally, the kid stopped and clearly said, "I think it's right around here somewhere." The three men pointed their flashlights into the woods, revealing the darkened voids and secret hiding places of the forest floor.

Huge boulders seemed to materialize out of nowhere when the light fell across them. Downed trees gave off shadows like animals lurking in the dark. And always in the background, the pounding surf of Lake Superior could be heard crashing against the shoreline a few hundred feet away.

"This is just too weird," Fastwater thought out loud. And on Halloween night with an October full moon, a blue moon at that—the second one this month. Looking up, he saw clouds scuttling across the face of the moon. A perfect picture of Halloween, he thought. The only thing missing is the witch on her broom. Next to him was the lanky form of Owen Porter, with his protruding Adam's apple and wavy mass of black hair resembling Sleepy Hollow's Ichabod Crane. Even a murky fog laid thick and eerie in the low spots in the forest. He half expected to see Boris Karloff appear out of the gloom.

The search spread out. In the darkness and fog they called to each other to prevent getting separated. They followed their flashlights around in vain until they heard the rescue squad's siren up on the highway. Needing no encouragement to leave, they followed the sound out of the woods. Parked behind the sheriff's car were three members of the rescue squad gathered around their ambulance.

"What's all the fuss?" Dave Eckman called when he saw the sheriff clambering out of the ditch, a surly-looking kid in tow. Turning around in a circle, the ambulance driver swung his arms up in a gesture of confusion, saying, "With all this fog we expected to see a car off the road or something." He looked at the young man standing behind Fastwater, then across the road into the woods, as if there must be something more to see. Incredulous, he asked, "You called us out for this?" Eckman had his hair slicked back and wore white face paint and the fangs of Dracula.

Fastwater groaned. They must've been at the Halloween dance in town. He'd just wrecked their evening, and probably for nothing. He sent Leonard, Ichabod Crane, Dracula, and the mummy, who'd removed the wrappings from around his head, back into the woods to finish off the search.

He loaded the kid into his squad car and spun the rear wheels in the shoulder's gravel turning the big car around. In an attempt to add some credibility to the evening, he switched on the police siren and raced full speed back to headquarters. The kid continued his running monologue, a series of phrases and words that made no sense to Fastwater. With the kid gesticulating wildly and rocking a rapid rhythm across the front seat from the sheriff, the puppy finally made his escape. He slunk across the seat and tentatively crawled into the sheriff's lap. With a big, warm hand, Fastwater stroked the muddy head of fur draped across his leg. The puppy twitched and whined, let out an exhausted sigh, and before they reached the outskirts of town, he'd fallen into a whimpering sleep.

In the end, they never did find a body. The kid had walked away from a juvenile psychiatric ward in Duluth two days earlier. The blood was his own, from self-inflicted wounds on his arms and wrists. Authorities from Duluth who came to retrieve him had no knowledge of a girlfriend. They also had no idea where the dog came from.

Fastwater had made a half-hearted attempt to find the owner, but he hadn't been disappointed when no one showed up to claim the puppy. Gitch had moved himself into the police station as if he'd finally come home, as if this was where he was supposed to be. And that had suited the sheriff just fine.

• • • •

As if he knew that Fastwater had been thinking about him, Gitch raised his head and looked at the sheriff lounging behind his desk. Slowly getting to his feet, the dog stretched, then walked over and laid his head against the sheriff's leg. Fastwater petted and scratched the furry ears, saying, "That was a crazy night, wasn't it, old fella." From a desk drawer he withdrew a dog biscuit and offered it to Gitch. Solemnly taking it between his front teeth, like a churchgoer receiving a communion wafer, the dog returned to his rug near the door and lay down again.

Sipping coffee from his thermos cup, Fastwater sat back to consider the few facts he knew about yesterday's early morning attack in the forest behind town. While he'd be the first to say there were many innocent yet tragic ways to die in the woods, he was convinced that Niki's death had been murder. The young lady had put up a fight. Even hours after the incident, the sheriff had sensed the fear and anger lingering in the earth beside the trail. He rubbed a hand over his clean-shaven jaw as he considered that there wasn't much to go on. His counterparts in Duluth were doing forensic tests, however, so maybe this hotshot big-city detective would shed some light on the specifics of Niki's death.

Accompanying him to headquarters this morning, Mrs. Bean had helped him retrieve the overnight communications from Duluth off his computer. But, like all the high-tech gizmos they'd thrown at him lately, he considered the reports and paperwork to be useless. The hardest part had been keeping Mrs. Bean from reading the dispatches as they printed them out.

Scanning the reports once again, he thought the only item of interest was that the lab would be running tests on the victim's clothes. From that information, forensics would determine not only the cause of death, but the nature of whatever weapon had been used. He wondered what the forensics people expected to find. He'd seen the outcome of many barroom brawls, and he could tell them straight out about the murder weapon. Find me some broken knuckles, he thought, and then we'll be getting somewhere.

What he did know was that the attack had taken place not long after sunrise, because he'd seen Niki that morning in the café and watched as she started her run into the woods. Later, at the scene, he hadn't spotted much sign of a struggle, or evidence pointing to a motive or killer, but he had found several sets of wolf tracks. Probably from before the attack, he admitted, but fresh, and more tracks than he'd seen together in a long time. They seemed to back up Red's story about wolves howling nearby the night before.

Vincent Wyckoff

He knew strange things tended to happen this time of year. Wildlife behavior could be unpredictable with mating seasons going on and everyone getting anxious about the upcoming snow season. Or maybe it was just Halloween, with another full-moon cycle approaching. The sheriff quietly lowered his feet to the floor and sat up. The full moon. Could that have anything to do with this case? he wondered. Then he laughed to himself as he conjured up the image of the costumed rescue squad searching the woods on a full-moon Halloween night four years ago. The night Gitch had come to live with him.

With a lopsided grin still dangling across his face, Fastwater watched a shiny new, dark blue Mustang pull up next to his squad car. Gitch bounded to the window at the sound of tires on the gravel outside. He put his front paws on the sill to prop himself up and eagerly studied the newcomer. Not many people drove up to the police station, and Gitch was familiar with the half dozen or so vehicles that regularly stopped by. Usually, after recognizing the car, his tail would start wagging and he'd whine with the anticipation of greeting a friend. But when the car wasn't familiar, as in this case, he'd emit a barely audible growl while his tail and body went rigid.

Looking like a man who's resigned himself to having a bad day, Fastwater watched the dust settle around the car outside. Without trim molding or official markings, with black sidewalls and tinted glass, the detective's vehicle looked like no squad car Fastwater had ever seen. Through the double-paned window he could hear and feel the throaty rumble of the idling engine. It was a little disconcerting to think that the detective's slick new squad could probably run circles around his bright burgundy sedan, with all its flashing lights and fancy gadgets. When the young detective finally eased himself out of the car, Fastwater watched him adjust his regulation aviator sunglasses before turning to scan the rooftops of town and the big lake beyond. Feeling his indigestion begin to burn, Fastwater let out a sigh and gave a last thoughtful look at the severed tail of a wolf he'd found near Niki's body. He'd brought it back in a plastic evidence bag, but after puzzling over its significance, he'd been unable to piece together how it could be involved in the young woman's death. There was no evidence to suggest she'd been attacked by wolves, and there was no blood on the tail. As the detective approached the office door, Fastwater slipped the plastic bag into the top center drawer of his desk. Technically, he'd admit that he could be accused of withholding evidence, "But he's here to help me," he said to himself, his anger already rising. "Let him find his own damn clues."

Sergeant Bryce Jepson was young, clean-cut, and far too "regulation" for the sheriff's liking. After introducing himself and shaking hands, the detective took off his sunglasses and stood in the sparsely decorated office's entryway, looking at the bare walls and sizing up his small-town counterpart. Fastwater knew what the man was thinking. Every time an outsider visited for the first time, they had the same expectations. They'd see this big Indian standing there and expect to find historical artifacts on display: arrowheads and beaded pouches, maybe even a tomahawk or war club. To them, the office should have knotty-pine paneling and warm wooden furniture. That's why he'd left the unpainted concrete-block walls bare and unadorned. It was not only easier to keep clean, but he took pleasure in disappointing his unwelcome, meddling visitors.

After the sheriff assured Gitch that everything was okay, the dog returned to his rug by the door, this time lying down at an angle that allowed him a full view of the stranger. Fastwater motioned to a plastic chair next to his desk and watched as the young detective sat down, first pulling up his pant legs to prevent stretching out the knees. What the hell kind of a name is Bryce, anyhow, the sheriff wondered to himself.

"Interesting place you have here, Sheriff," Jepson offered, looking around the room again. A tight-lipped smile ran across his face. "Quaint and sort of . . . I don't know . . . uncluttered."

Fastwater ignored the detective's sarcasm. Instead, he let his thoughts wander away as he turned his attention back to the window and the deep, rolling sea beyond.

Vincent Wyckoff

"But I suppose you don't need that much equipment," Jepson continued. "I mean, in such a small town, there probably isn't much need for high-tech law enforcement."

Fastwater's gaze slid back to the detective's face. He noticed how smooth and unblemished the young man's skin was. White and soft, too clean, not even a hint of shadow from shaving stubble. Then he locked eyes with the detective. What were they thinking when they decided to send this punk up here? he wondered. He could picture Captain Simanich, his old friend, and head of the Special Investigations Bureau in Duluth, having a good laugh at his expense.

Originally from Eveleth, over on the Iron Range, Phil Simanich and Fastwater went back together a long way. They'd played high school hockey against each other, and, after a few years of secondary education, they'd served together in the marines during the First Gulf War. Over the years they'd kept in touch, occasionally meeting for drinks at the VFW in Duluth. While developing their respective careers in law enforcement, they'd shared information as well as good-natured fun and teasing along the way. But, while Fastwater was content to police his own little neck of the woods, Phil Simanich was more ambitious. He was a tough cop, Fastwater knew, an intelligent, honest man with a good war record and the credentials to help him move quickly up the ranks at police headquarters in Duluth.

The sheriff's stare hardened as he thought about his old friend. Simanich might get a kick out of meddling in his local business, but Black Otter Bay was still Fastwater's jurisdiction. Jepson, thinking the sheriff's glare was directed at him, broke eye contact and turned to look around the room again. That strange dog with the intimidating blue eye was watching him.

Finally, swinging his gaze back to the desk and the large uniformed man sitting behind it, Jepson nodded at the papers in front of the sheriff, cleared his throat and muttered hoarsely, "You had a chance to look over the reports we sent up from Duluth?"

Carefully, like an uncertain student pulling out his wadded-up homework, Jepson retrieved his own folded copies of the report from an inside pocket of his sport coat. Fastwater got a glimpse of the butt of a department-issue .38 slung in the young man's shoulder holster. The sheriff smirked. Up here, folks would laugh if they knew their sheriff carried a toy like that. For himself, he packed a stainless steel .44-caliber Magnum in a tooled-leather holster on his hip, like the old western gunslingers. He also kept a twelve-gauge pump shotgun loaded with #4s in the squad car, and he'd never known Black Otter Bay to need any more firepower than that.

Shuffling the reports around on his desk, Fastwater kept quiet and watched the young detective. Another thing ignorant folk expected out of an Indian was silence, and he usually obliged them in circumstances such as this. Let them talk and show their hand, he figured, because this was his turf and his people, and he was in charge of their welfare. Besides, he hadn't invited this stranger up here, so if he didn't feel like talking, that was his prerogative.

Trying again to get the conversation going, Jepson commented, "I suppose you've had time to look over the crime scene. Anything else you want to add to these files?"

Looking at the reports on his desk, Fastwater said, "I don't see where they've classified it a crime yet. Until the coroner's report is final, we won't know how she died."

"Well, come on, Sheriff," the detective said with a know-it-all smirk. "It seems kind of obvious, doesn't it? A good-looking young lady alone in the woods."

Glaring at the detective, Fastwater knew his first impression had been right. This kid was going to piss him off. Leaning across the desk, he asked, "So, what are you implying, that she was asking to die?"

Jepson sat back, took a deep breath, and exhaled slowly. Fastwater could see more bulk to the young man than he'd previously noticed. He had a thick chest and shoulders with heavy upper arms, the type of body mass and muscle definition acquired through hours in the gym, not manual labor.

"Listen, Detective," he began with a heavy dose of warning in his voice. "Don't come around here telling me what's obvious and what's not.

Duluth saw fit to send you up here, so I'm assuming you've worked murder cases before." He paused before adding, "You have, haven't you? Worked murder cases before?"

The detective waited before responding. He held the sheriff's eyes for several seconds before barely tipping his head in a nod.

Fastwater thought he'd seen better bluffs during Saturday night poker games. But, in a disarmingly friendly voice, he said, "Good, good—that's good. Then I take it you've captured a killer before." The detective didn't respond, but Fastwater gave the kid credit for holding his gaze. "Ever shot a man?" he asked.

The detective rolled his eyes and looked down at his fingers drumming on the sheriff's desk. Fastwater saw his questions hitting the mark. The kid thought he'd come up here and push some stupid small-town cop around. Getting no more responses, the sheriff asked, "Tell me, Detective, have you ever shot a man, or sat down after a gunfight and inhaled the smell of burnt powder?"

Even Fastwater was startled when the young man lurched to his feet and slammed a fist on the desk. "What's the matter with you?" he blurted, his jaw clenching in anger. "What's with all these stupid questions?"

Fastwater regained his advantage by standing up and leaning his large frame toward the detective. "I just need to know what sort of experience you bring to the job." His voice sounded polite and subdued after the detective's outburst. Then he stuck his thick index finger into the detective's chest and leaned even closer. "And now I understand. You don't know shit." He stepped back, still holding the detective's glare. "Don't come up here presuming to tell me what's obvious. This is my town, and I still command jurisdiction in this county." He paused to let his words echo around the small office. Then, drawing a deep breath, he concluded, "Do you understand me on this? It's really important, Detective, because if you don't think you get it, you might as well pack up your reports and grab your ass and haul them on out of here right now."

He didn't bother waiting for a reply, but sat down and slowly took a sip of coffee. There really wasn't any way for the young man to save face, the sheriff knew, and he let him squirm for several more seconds before telling him to sit down.

With a little apprehension, the detective lowered himself back into the chair. Fastwater figured the rules for this meeting had finally been established. The two men discussed the few facts that were known. The discussion stayed professional, factual, and proceeded smoothly, with the sheriff doing most of the talking. He described the scene where Niki's body had been found, and the tangle of wolf prints around the area.

Eventually, Sergeant Jepson relaxed, and he offered enough astute observations for the sheriff to realize the kid was no dummy. At the mention of wolf tracks, the detective frowned. "Wolf prints? Are you thinking wolves killed her?"

Fastwater shook his head. "No, but they were there."

"I'd really like to inspect the scene myself," Jepson said, a timid question mark appearing in his voice.

The sheriff nodded. He took another sip of his now-tepid coffee and wished he could dump it out and replace it with a hot refill, but he'd have to offer the detective a cup, and the only mug he had was the dented thermos cover.

"What about relationships?" Jepson asked. "Did she have any boyfriends?"

"Not that I'm aware of. She had friends, and I know she went snowmobiling with some of the young men in the local club. But she spent a lot of time in Duluth."

Jepson nodded. "You have any hotshots around here?"

The sheriff raised a questioning eyebrow.

"You know, a tough guy, maybe one of those fellows in the snowmobile club. Someone she might have dated but rejected."

Fastwater grinned, but then shook his head. "We don't get too many accomplished, professional young ladies around here. None of those boys would have had the gumption to ask her out."

"What about the backpackers who found her? What's their story?"

"They went home to Minneapolis. They're not much more than teenagers. After what they saw, they'll probably never go camping again."

Jepson nodded and began stacking his reports. "Well, I'd really like to see where the body was found."

Fastwater pushed his coffee cup away and stood up. Tucking in his shirt and adjusting his holster and belt, he said, "I'd like to show you something first, Sergeant Jepson. And then we'll go see where they found her. Follow me, would you?"

The detective's expression lightened at the seeming warmth in Fastwater's voice. Feeling that the discussion of the case had progressed well, Jepson said, "Why don't you just call me Bryce, Sheriff? We're going to be working on this case together, and Sergeant Jepson sounds so formal."

Fastwater looked away to hide a snicker. "Just come with me, Sergeant," he said as he grabbed his coat off a hook by the door. Gitch was on his feet with wagging tail as the sheriff opened the door. "Come on, old buddy," Fastwater said to his dog. "Let's take the detective here for a walk."

They went outside, around the corner of the building, and took a short path through the woods. Gitch picked up a softball-sized rock and, like a kid grabbing a piece of candy, turned his bicolored eyes up to his master, as if asking permission. Fastwater patted him on the head and motioned for him to take the lead. Noticing that Jepson had watched this strange routine, Fastwater felt compelled to explain.

"Gitch has a habit of carrying a rock around with him when we're in the woods," he said. "Don't ask me why. Maybe he has some retriever blood in him."

"I don't suppose it can be too good for his teeth," the detective commented.

"Well, I guess everyone has a right to at least one bad habit."

Gitch trotted a short distance ahead, the rock in his mouth seeming to have little effect on his mobility. It was cold out, but the sun was shining and Fastwater anticipated the day warming up nicely if only the wind would stop blowing. He knew they'd been lucky on the weather so far. In another month, by deer hunting season, they could have six inches of snow on the ground.

Fifty yards down the path the woods opened up on a small cemetery enclosed by a low rock wall. Fastwater led the way toward the back, to the area with the oldest graves, and stopped before a row of tiny black headstones. He knelt down and reverently ran his hand over thinly etched letters. "These are my people," he said, as much to the headstone as to the detective. "My mother, father, grandparents." He nodded further down the row. "My uncles and aunts—they're all here."

He stood up and pointed at the row of headstones behind them. These were bigger, the printing more legible, with names like Moen, Fjeldmir, and Ingvarsson. "Buried right next to the white folks that settled here. We helped them, welcomed them, and became a part of their new community. You can look around here and see that what I'm telling you is true. My people lived and worked and died side by side with the whites, and even in death we continue to reside among them."

The detective stepped forward and bent down to look at the gravestone the sheriff had been touching. He could see the lettering wasn't really engraved. It looked as if someone had simply tried to scratch a name in it with another stone. "Float . . . Bird?" he asked out loud.

"Floating Bird, my grandmother," Fastwater said. "She had powers, or so my mother told me. She died before I was born."

"What kind of powers?"

The sheriff shrugged. "Medicine. I don't know, it's hard to explain. She felt things." He had no intention of telling the young man that some of those powers had been passed on to him; that he had occasional visions and insights, too.

The detective stood up and looked around the quiet little cemetery. He finally let his gaze wander back to the sheriff, and with a grin, he said, "So, what are you trying to tell me—that we're going to use her powers to solve this case?"

Fastwater didn't return the smile, but looked up at the leafless branches of trees reaching over the cobblestone wall. Shoving his hands into his pockets, he leaned back and smelled the cold, dry air, then sighed deeply and looked at the detective. "What I'm trying to tell you, or show you," he began, with a gesture toward the headstones, "is that I'm a lifelong member of this community. I've got roots here. I know every single person living around here—every man, woman, and child. I know everything about them: their names, what churches they go to, their whole family histories. I know who's divorced, who's having affairs, and who drinks too much. I know how folks around here think and act, what motivates them and what doesn't." He paused when he saw the detective's eyes glass over with boredom.

Abruptly, the sheriff turned and headed back to the office. Behind him, he heard the detective scramble out from the row of graves and jog up beside him. "Wait a minute, Sheriff," he pleaded, but Fastwater kept walking, all the way back to headquarters and the vehicles parked outside.

"Hold on now, Sheriff. I didn't mean any disrespect back there. We're supposed to be working on this thing together."

Fastwater stood at ease, a glowering giant looking down on the young man. "What I was trying to tell you back there was that I know in every fiber of who I am that nobody from around here committed that crime." He leveled such a withering look at the detective that about all the young man could do was settle backward against the sheriff's squad car and hope he wasn't going to launch into another tirade. But Fastwater was looking past the car, his jaw muscles clenching while he studied the rhythmic movements of waves on Lake Superior.

Gitch ambled over and with great ceremony dropped his rock next to the front wheel of the car. He looked up at the sheriff, his tongue busy licking residual dirt and grit from his lips. Getting no reaction from his master, however, he sauntered over to lay down by the door of the building, lying at such an angle that he could watch the two men finish their discussion.

The detective let his gaze follow Fastwater's down to the small harbor and the miles upon miles of open sea beyond. "You want to talk about powers, Sheriff, that lake has medicine to spare. Bad medicine, I imagine. The November gales should be blowing in any day now."

Fastwater didn't hear the detective. He was working a problem over in his mind and a plan was finally taking shape. He needed time alone to work this case, to get a feel for what he was up against. And he couldn't accomplish that while placating Duluth and babysitting this kid. He needed to keep the detective busy for a few days, keep him away from Black Otter Bay. To do that, he'd use Jepson to handle the tedious research and paperwork that needed to be done. And maybe that would keep Simanich off his back for a while, too.

With that in mind, he turned to the young man and said, "You sure you want to help me on this case, son? Because if you do, I can use the help." He hoped he wasn't laying it on too thick. "I need you to get back to Duluth and work that end. Dig up as much information as you can."

"Ah, come on, Sheriff . . ."

"Listen to me, Jepson. We could go from house to house, cabin to cabin, asking questions and interrogating people around here until we're blue in the face, but it won't shed any light on this case. To get anywhere at all, we'll need information, a break or a clue, and you're the man to find it for me."

Sergeant Jepson looked at the sheriff with disbelief. "What can I possibly find out down there that's going to help?"

"First of all, get after that medical examiner. There could be DNA to run. And find out exactly how Niki died. If he gives you some runaround about blunt instrument force, press him to be more specific. Ask him questions. Could a branch or rock swung by an attacker do that kind of damage? How about a moose hoof, or a deer hoof for that matter? Is it possible she could have tripped while running and hit a rock so hard she killed herself?"

The detective jotted notes on a small pad, scribbling down Fastwater's stream of ideas.

"We need to know anything the examiner can tell us about a sexual assault," he continued. "Once we have some parameters to work with, we can develop ideas about motives." He looked at Jepson again. "It's okay to be a nuisance. Just keep after him. If you ask enough questions, you just might hit the right one. There's no obvious sign of rape, but she was jogging, so what's the motive for robbery?" The sheriff paused, thinking, then shook his head. "It had to be some sort of sexual assault."

Fastwater paused in his monologue, thinking, trying to decide how to work this case from the outside in. He knew he wasn't going to solve it with what he had to go on around here. And he didn't think there was much chance the medical examiner would turn up anything useful, either. He looked at the detective slouched against the car, still taking notes. "Take some time to look through open case files, too. Check with the Twin Cities, and Chicago."

The sergeant nodded, kept writing, and Fastwater finished his thought. "I'm convinced we're not looking for a local on this one, so maybe you can find a similar case somewhere else to tie into it." He snapped his fingers and pointed at Jepson. "Oh, and we had a fellow up here four years ago. An escapee from a psychiatric ward. Claimed to have killed a woman, but we never found a body. I'll forward his name to you, along with the rest of my incident report. Find him, check out what he's been up to."

He waited while the sergeant finished writing, then said, "So, are we good?"

"I still don't know what I'm supposed to tell them . . ." the sergeant said, a hint of a question in his voice.

"Tell Simanich I'll make an arrest in a few days," Fastwater interrupted, impatience making his voice gruff. But then he paused to take a deep breath. "Listen, I don't care what you tell him. Make something up. Tell him I said to go to hell if you want to; he'll understand." It took a conscious effort for the sheriff to soften his expression. "I really need you on this, Jepson. I need you to dig around and find me something."

The sergeant displayed a grim nod of acknowledgement. "All right, Sheriff, I'll see what I can do. But I'd really like to get a look at the crime scene. And just so you know," he continued quietly, "they'll probably send me back up here later this week."

"That's fine, Detective. Just don't let them send the Feds up here. We'll never get anywhere with a bunch of tourii traipsing around the woods."

"Tourii?" the sergeant asked. "Is that French?"

"No. It's mine. Tourii, plural for tourist. We had a boatload of law enforcement up here this summer. My office was so full of sport coats and ties Gitch could hardly find a place to sit. Now, let's take a drive. I'll show you where we found Niki's body." He opened the back door of the squad car and whistled softly to Gitch.

Jepson stepped around to the other side, and as they climbed in Fastwater's thoughts jumped ahead to the parking lot off the trunk highway. Anna's Garden and Toolshed was right across the road, and he smiled at the thought of the fresh berry pies she'd be baking now, and all the produce she would have harvested in the last few weeks. Maybe he'd stop in to ask if she'd noticed anything odd yesterday, and while he was at it, buy a bag of her homegrown vegetables.

Chapter 6

*M*ichael *used his morning drive to the jobsite to organize his* day. Today, he had a half-hour drive—fifteen minutes to town, and then another fifteen minutes up the Moose Lake Road to the old Selstad property. He used the time behind the wheel to set goals and plan the daily workload. But this morning was different. He found himself distracted by thoughts of a conversation he'd had with Anna the night before. After Luc had left and he and Anna had gone to bed, he'd asked her what she thought of Luc.

"He makes me uncomfortable," she'd blurted, so quickly that Michael realized she'd been expecting the question. "There's something about him that gives me the creeps."

"How can you say that?" In the dark, Michael began counting off Luc's attributes. "He loved your stew, and I told you he's a great worker. He's polite. . ."

"It's none of that, Michael." Anna paused a moment to collect her thoughts, and while they lay side by side in bed, he listened to the fire popping in the next room. He'd loaded up the fireplace before they went to bed and closed the glass doors to build up the heat. Soon he heard the blower fan click on.

When Anna finally spoke again, he detected a trembling urgency in her voice. "I've lived out here all my life, Michael. Until today, I've never been afraid of anything in the woods. I know how everything works out here—it's predictable, reliable. But today, for the first time, I was overcome by a fear that I don't understand. Then I find a strange man looking in the window at me, and later he talks about spirits and ghosts and Manitou. It's just too bizarre."

"Ah, come on, Annie." Michael groped for some comforting words. Anna was usually so strong and confident; he wasn't accustomed to finding words to relieve her fears. "Listen, you had a bad scare. It's only natural to feel a little unsure when you've been shaken up like that."

"It's more than that, Michael. It's too much of a coincidence, all these strange things happening on the same day. There's something about that guy . . . what did he mean when he said I have nothing to fear from Manitou? How does he know? He said they're just curious. What is that supposed to mean?"

"I'm telling you, Annie, he's all right. I know it's weird that he lives in the woods, and it's tragic about his mother, but he's a steady guy. He knows everything about the forest, and he said he'd help me work out a trapline this winter when my construction jobs dry up."

"He never said anything about helping you trap. Didn't you notice how he decided to leave right when the wolves started howling? It's like they were calling him."

Michael shook his head in the dark. "Well, anyway, it would be nice to have him around this winter."

"So he's going to stay here all winter? Camping out in the woods?"

"I don't know. I doubt he'll live outdoors all winter, though."

"Well, before you get any ideas, I can tell you right now he isn't going to be living here." Her words sounded too harsh in the quiet darkness, almost hysterical, effectively ending the conversation and leaving Michael to wonder how she had known he was thinking of asking Luc to overwinter with them. After a while Anna turned and wrapped an arm around him, nestling her cheek into his chest. "I'm sorry, Michael. I know you like him, and maybe he really is okay. But you know I've always trusted my instincts, and right now they're sending up bright red flags."

"I know, honey." Michael kissed her forehead and stroked the back of her head and neck as they settled down to sleep.

This morning, from his perspective behind the wheel of the old pickup truck, he thought that whole conversation seemed absurd—except the part about Anna's intuition. He knew her insights were uncanny, and he couldn't simply disregard her feelings about Luc. Several years ago she'd explained her ability to sense things about people as a gift she'd learned from the woods. "Everything comes at you straight on," she'd told him. "There's no cheating in the forest. No quarter given or taken. Oh, sure, there's camouflage and the appearance of deception, but ultimately everything lives or dies by its own merit, so why waste time pretending to be something you're not? You survive by being stronger or smarter or faster, by using your own inherent skills. After struggling with situations at their face value, it becomes easier to see when things are not what they appear to be—and that's especially true with people."

Michael shook these nagging thoughts, and the suspicious implications of Anna's intuition, from his mind as the truck chugged up the last hill before topping out on a scenic overlook of Lake Superior. From here, the highway dropped off dramatically into the town of Black Otter Bay, another half mile down the road on the shore of Lake Superior.

The Sea Superieur, the French voyageurs had called it, and Michael repeated the name every time he drove over the crest to look out on the largest freshwater lake in the world. Gordon Lightfoot, in his ballad about the sinking of the Edmund Fitzgerald, said, "the lake never gives up its dead," and Michael had learned to what extent that was true. The lake is so deep, with depths up to 1,300 feet, that locating a body is nearly impossible, much less attempting to recover it. In other bodies of water, when a person drowns, bacteria in the body begin decomposing the flesh, and the carbon-dioxide gasses emitted during the process cause the body to bloat and eventually come to the surface. But Lake Superior, with an average water temperature of less than forty degrees Fahrenheit, is too cold for bacteria to survive. So when a body descends to the depths of the great lake, it generally stays there.

But this morning the lake looked peaceful and serene, a glittering, dazzling blue-white in the early sunlight. Looking to the southeast, Michael could see the Apostle Islands scattered off the north shore of Wisconsin, but when he looked straight ahead to the east or northeast, there was nothing but water. For 350 miles and more the ice-cold water rolled on, past Wisconsin in the south and up north beyond Isle Royale to Canada. The northern shore extended halfway across Ontario, all the way east to Sault Ste. Marie in Upper Michigan. From his vantage point on top of the hill, Michael knew the thirty or forty miles he could see out to the horizon comprised nothing more than one little corner of the lake, but still it contained more square miles of water than most freshwater lakes in the world.

In the distance he could see two iron-ore freighters, one of them a huge, square-sterned thousand-footer. Closer in was a foreign ship, probably headed for Duluth and a load of Midwestern grain. Anna had showed him how to identify the foreign ships by the configuration of structures on their decks. It always amazed him to think that oceangoing vessels could make it all the way to Duluth, in the center of the continent, literally thousands of miles from their saltwater shipping lanes.

It was this panoramic overlook, and many other scenic views like it, that had hooked Michael the first time he'd visited the North Shore. Lake Superior had beckoned to him with her beguiling siren call, lulling him with her crystal-clear ebb and flow. She could be a treacherous suitor, but that, too, had been part of the attraction. Michael never ventured out on the lake. She wasn't a place for amateurs, and mistakes on the big lake were not forgiven.

But he'd found the lake's raw beauty to be so stark and natural, so bold and invigorating, that he knew he wanted to live near it. He'd immediately begun planning for a permanent move. Thinking back on those days brought a smile to his face as he approached the turnoff to Highway 61. How simple life had been then! He hadn't had a care in the world—hadn't owed a penny to anyone. His old truck had been new then. He'd camped out in the back of it with his tools and a few other belongings while he'd hung around town looking for odd jobs to tide him over.

At the bottom of the hill he turned onto Scenic Highway 61 and, in second gear, idled along the main street of town. He knew the café had been open for a couple of hours already, and he could see smoke coming from the post office where Mrs. Virginia Bean had the woodstove heating up the little building. Other than for a few hours over the weekends, most of the tourist shops were closed for the season, but Michael knew the rest of the town got up and about their business early. The townsfolk generally lived and worked by the light of day. Michael often wondered if it was a throwback to the days when Black Otter Bay had been primarily a fishing village. Lake Superior was notorious for throwing frequent, unannounced temper tantrums, and the early commercial fishermen in their small boats were no match for the combination of high winds, high seas, and rocky shorelines. Therefore, by the time the sun set beyond the ragged hills behind town, all the boats were sure to be in and securely lashed to their moorings. And the whole town had adopted that schedule. The cafe was open by six o'clock every day, but didn't stay open to serve supper. Tourists driving along Highway 61 after dark often missed the little village because the townsfolk were not only home and off the streets after sundown, but usually in bed asleep with the lights out.

At the far end of town, Michael turned inland again after crossing the steel-girder bridge over the Black Otter River. The Moose Lake Road was a gravel forest trail that angled away from Lake Superior and wound through the hills north of town. There were several lakes along the way, and Michael liked to bring Anna and Charles up here on Sunday afternoons for picnics, swimming, and fishing from shore. This morning a heavy, wet fog had settled into the low areas of the road, and Michael had a hard time distinguishing the shorelines of the lakes he passed. Strangely enough, none of the lakes were named Moose Lake. Michael had been told that the narrow forest road had been named for the large numbers of moose that used it to travel from one boggy watering hole to the next. At the top of the hill he passed the overgrown turnoff to the deserted boat landing on Big Island Lake, where Rose Bengston's body had been found last spring.

The people who lived up here were a wild, independent bunch: loggers and lumbermen, fishing and hunting guides. The Selstad brothers lived out here, too, and it was their house that Michael had bid to reroof. Ingvald and Nels were in their upper seventies or early eighties, and Michael figured if they'd roofed their house ten years ago when it first needed it, they probably could've done it themselves. Lifelong bachelors, they'd never moved away from their parents' homestead, and Michael had heard the rumors claiming they'd never traveled even as far as Duluth in their lifetimes.

Turning onto their road, Michael chuckled out loud at the memory of his recent visit, when he'd stopped by to estimate the roofing job. The brothers were known to argue over everything, yelling at each other and swearing and throwing fits of anger, sometimes lapsing into Norwegian in their quest for the meanest turn of phrase.

"I'll park my trailer on the lawn out front," Michael had explained to them a week ago while sitting at their kitchen table. "It'll make it easier to load up the old roofing as I tear it off." Michael thought he was being generous by calling it a lawn. It was almost impossible to tell where the washed-out road ended and the weedy, stone-filled yard began.

"Park any danged place you want," Nels had said. Tobacco juice splattered down his chin and the front of his shirt. "But we ain't paying no dumping fees if you're hauling that old roof to the municipal dump."

Before Michael could respond, Ingvald had erupted, spinning around on his brother from his place at the stove. "Just who the hell do you think is going to pay for it? It's our gol-darned roof!" For emphasis he jabbed the dripping ladle at his brother. A horrible aroma filled the room, and Michael had no idea what the man could be cooking. It smelled like rancid fish parts and onions, or maybe something with cabbage. Michael had never seen Ingvald without several days' worth of white beard covering his face. When he started shouting, the veins in his neck and on his forehead bulged. Michael wondered how the eighty-year-old's heart kept up.

Nels waved off the thrusting ladle. "So what are we paying property taxes for, you old moron?"

"What the hell do property taxes have to do with our roof?" Ingvald wanted to know.

Michael would have laughed at their childish bickering, but the smell from Ingvald's cooking was suffocating him. "Listen, you guys," he began, but a sudden scolding rant in Norwegian brought him to his feet. He started to speak, but a gob of brown tobacco juice bubbling out of the corner of Nels's mouth caught his eye. It dribbled down his chin, and Michael watched as it hung in an ever-enlarging wad before finally dropping with a heavy splat on the front of his shirt.

Totally unaware of his brother's ongoing tirade, Nels turned his rheumy old eyes at Michael and said, "We ain't paying to have that old roof—"

Michael threw up his hands. "Wait a minute. Wait a minute!" he yelled. He looked from Nels to Ingvald and back to Nels again. The brothers were finally quiet, so he said, "I'll pay the dumping fees, okay?" He stepped toward the door and fresh air. "We've agreed on a price for roofing your house. Just let me park my trailer out there in the yard, and I'll take care of everything else." His eyes began watering from the cooking fumes as he pulled the door open.

"Park anywhere you want," he heard Nels say behind him. Michael gulped fresh air and wiped his eyes on the sleeve of his shirt. Closing the screen door, he looked back inside at the two brothers.

"I don't want nobody driving all over my lawn!" Ingvald shouted at his brother. The cooking ladle clattered to the floor, and the forehead veins began bulging again. "Ah, reis til helvete!" he exclaimed in disgust. Michael ducked his head, turned, and walked away, figuring the argument had nothing more to do with him.

Vincent Wyckoff

Driving up to the house this morning, he noticed their rusty old Allis-Chalmers tractor was gone. The brothers didn't own a car, and Michael had heard that neither even had a driver's license, so they drove the tractor whenever they needed to go somewhere. They could often be seen cruising the lakeshores and back-road culverts collecting aluminum cans to sell to the recycler when he made his monthly stop in town. Once or twice a month they'd drive the ugly orange tractor into town to pick up mail, supplies, and maybe a bottle or two from the municipal.

Michael had seen them driving the tractor many times. Ingvald, the older brother, usually drove, and he'd sit hunched over on the swaying tractor seat, his back curled in a loop as he slouched under a wide-brimmed felt hat. He seemed to know only one speed, and that was with the throttle lever wide open. They'd careen down the narrow forest roads at full speed, kicking up clouds of dust and stones around them. When they were working—as they termed their aluminum can retrieval service—they passed a pint bottle of peppermint schnapps between them.

While Ingvald drove, Nels sat up high on the steel fender, rocking back and forth as he hung on with both hands. Nels had fallen off the tractor many times, and though he'd never managed to get run over, he'd broken his arm, both wrists, and wore assorted bruises, lumps, and lacerations over the years from banging into the ground. And Ingvald, while somehow avoiding injury, was prone to tipping the tractor over in the roadside ditches, requiring assistance from the town wrecker. He'd knocked the headlights off years ago when he'd lost control and inadvertently blazed a trail through the brush. On another occasion, the exhaust stack on top of the manifold had been lost to a leaning deadfall, the height of which Ingvald had miscalculated. They now had burlap sacks wired onto the brackets where the headlights had once been, and here they stored the cans and other salvageable items they encountered.

But the beat-up old tractor was not in sight this morning, so Michael figured the Selstad brothers were already out on one of their lunatic errands. As he approached the house, he saw Luc on the roof, wielding a short-handled spade. Michael noticed how he'd maneuvered the trailer under an eave at the edge of a dormer, using the roof valley to channel loosened shingles toward the trailer. Yesterday they'd torn off the top few rows, covered the exposed roof boards with tar paper, and hauled a couple dozen bundles of shingles to the peak, where they'd stacked them out of the way.

Michael tapped his horn to acknowledge Luc's wave. He had almost half the front roof torn off already, and Michael grinned and shook his head in amazement. He must've gotten started before sun-up, he thought. With such an early jump on the tear-off, Michael calculated how far they could get with the shingling by the end of the day.

"Slow down, Luc," he called with a laugh. Grabbing a short-handled shingle fork out of the truck, he hustled up the ladder. There wasn't any hurry, he told himself, but Luc's steady, rhythmic pace was contagious.

Working up a sweat in just the first half hour, he stopped long enough to take off his flannel shirt. Luc wore thick moose-hide moccasins, and Michael noticed how sure-footed they made him. The tough leather soles clung like sandpaper to the slippery, angled surface. As Luc leaned against the spade to rest, Michael looked at his hard-working partner. "Those moccasins seem to work pretty good up here," he commented. "I should see about getting a pair for myself. And those leather chaps, where did you find them?"

Luc looked down, then carefully brushed shingle residue from his knees. "I made the moccasins myself," he said. "From a moose hide I got from an old man up north. It's the best material for moccasins—the thickest and toughest." He looked up at Michael. "It's all I wear, non? So I'll use the whole hide for moccasins." With a dismissive flick of his hand, he added, "I will give you a pair."

"Really?"

Luc gave an emphatic nod. "It is something I do when campfires burn low at the end of day. There is still more of the hide, so I will make you some."

Pausing a moment to think about Luc's words, Michael self-consciously looked down at his own scuffed and worn lace-up boots. "So you, ah, you're planning to hang around here this winter, then?" he asked.

Luc looked away, squinting up at the sun rising higher in the sky. "Je ne sais pas," he said.

"You don't know?" Michael's question sounded more like an accusation. "Well, you must have some sort of plan. You can't very well live outside all winter."

"Living outside is not the hard part," Luc responded. "Living in town is much worse."

Michael laughed and shook his head, but Anna's warning danced around the edges of his thoughts.

"Where you live is very nice," Luc continued. "You have shelter and warmth—all the modern comforts. And you don't have people digging in your business."

Michael didn't laugh this time. "Heck, Luc, there's always people nosing into a fellow's business, no matter where you live."

"Not where I live," Luc said with a tone of belligerence.

Ignoring Luc's remark, Michael said, "I think I had more privacy when I lived in Minneapolis. In a small town everyone knows everyone else's business." He thought about it for a moment, and then said, "It's nice to be part of a community, though. If I ever need help, I have people I can count on, and they know they can call on me, too."

"It's not good to rely on people," Luc stated with authority.

A reference to his parents? Michael wondered. He studied the longhaired, bearded man before him. Dressed in homemade moccasins and leather chaps, he conjured up in Michael's mind images of mountain men and French-Canadian voyageurs, from a time when men were answerable only to their own fears and shortcomings. But what sort of fears could this man have? What shortcomings made him shun society and the comforts of town? Michael frowned and took a hard look at his companion leaning easily against the roofing spade. He wanted to ask more questions in the hope of getting answers that would alleviate Anna's misgivings. Before he could go on, however, Luc straightened up, hoisted the heavy steel spade, and dug into another row of shingles.

Watching him work, Michael found it impossible to maintain the thought that Luc could have an evil side. The smile returned to Michael's face, and as he got back to work, he said, "Let's finish ripping this sucker off, Luc, and haul it to the dump. I might just spring for a cup of coffee while we're in town."

Luc didn't respond, didn't break his swinging, shoveling stride, but Michael thought he detected a slight tightening of his friend's facial features, as if the thought of a trip to town made him uncomfortable. Michael wedged his spade under a row of shingles and shrugged to himself. He knew it was none of his business, but maybe he could help Luc break out of his self-imposed exile. And if he could do that, he figured Anna just might warm up to him, too.

• • • •

For more than one hundred and thirty years the Black Otter Bay Café had been serving food to locals and tourists alike. Over the decades it experienced several reincarnations, from serving hungry logging crews home-cooked meals out the back door, to hiding gangsters during Prohibition, and more recently providing a comfortable rest stop for busloads of tourists and hungry families traveling along the shore. Marcy Soderstrom currently ran things, and would tell anyone who'd listen that the original owner, Agda Hjemdal, haunted the place. Marcy claimed that doors and windows randomly opened and closed by themselves. She'd witnessed items falling off counters and tables, as if someone had accidently dropped them. She even ran up to the sheriff's office one evening when, after closing up and locking the café, she'd looked back and seen every light in the place blazing away. Of course, in a provincial setting such as Black Otter Bay, talk of ghosts and spirits didn't go very far, but, like the café itself, Marcy held an honored place in the hearts of the townsfolk. She was one of their own, and the fact that she changed hair color on an almost daily basis, wore quirky outfits to work, and thrived on teasing the noble sheriff with off-color jokes only added to her reputation.

She opened the café every morning without fail, served out coffee and the Duluth newspaper to regulars, and listened to their small-town stories and complaints with good-humored candor. Last spring, it was Marcy who played a significant role in uncovering the money laundering taking place in an art gallery in Duluth. While she didn't get much of the news headlines, everyone in town knew that if it hadn't been for Marcy, young Abby and Ben Simon would have come to a bad end. Still single at the time, Marcy had always claimed that her Prince Charming would one day walk through the café's door, and technically that had actually happened. Matthew Simon, the divorced father of Abby and Ben, had been walking through that door his whole life, but Marcy had only recently taken note, and the café regulars now quietly cheered on their budding relationship.

Despite no-smoking laws, it was obvious that throughout the early years of the café's existence patrons had smoked in the main dining room. When Luc and Michael walked in, the smell of fried foods wrapped in old cigar and cigarette smoke and seasoned with the mustiness of antique furniture hit them head-on. It was an odor that couldn't be scrubbed out, sanded off, or painted over. Marcy could attest to that because she'd tried. Upon entering, even Luc stopped in his tracks, wrinkled up his nose, and surveyed the room full of regulars.

Behind the lunch counter, hanging on the wall over the cash register, was a gigantic mounted lake trout. For years the monster had hung over the doorway. The relic had been an ugly specimen, covered in years of grease, soot, and smoke. The past summer Marcy had taken it down, spent weeks degreasing and cleaning it, even touching up some of the paint, until it looked so good she decided it needed a new home. Michael had offered to hang it for her, and now it commanded center stage on the wall over all the action.

Michael nodded at some of the local townsfolk and greeted others as he passed, but in deference to Luc's wish for anonymity saved introductions for another time. They took a booth out of the way; the locals usually preferred to cluster around tables or the lunch counter, leaving the booths to the citified tourists. Michael put on an air of jocularity to lighten his friend's mood. "This is where I met Anna," he explained while looking over the menu. He wasn't really reading it, he knew it by heart, but he wanted to give Luc a chance to pick something out. "That was probably ten years ago now. She was a waitress—she'd only been out of high school a few years. Anyway, it was the middle of the afternoon and dead quiet. I don't think anybody else was in the place."

Marcy swung by their table, interrupting his story while snapping a wad of gum and inspecting Luc's rough-worn appearance. To give his friend another moment, Michael ordered a BLT with fries and coffee, but because that was his regular order, Marcy didn't bother writing it down. Instead, she continued her blatant surveillance of Luc until he finally looked up from the menu long enough to nod, shrug his shoulders, and say, "Moi aussi." He sat back uneasily when Marcy snatched the menu out of his hands.

Standing close to Luc, she placed silverware and napkins on the table, then looked over at Michael and said, "How's Annie? I suppose she's getting ready for winter?"

"Well, Marcy, you know how Anna is, " Michael said with an easy tone of familiarity. "Winter doesn't much bother her. But, yeah, she's getting ready to put the gardens to bed for the winter."

"She's some kind of woman," Marcy commented. "Living way out there—no TV, no car."

"Hey, that's the way she likes it. You'll never catch Anna living in town."

Luc jumped when Marcy's hand dropped to his shoulder. She asked, "Who's your friend, here, Michael?" Introductions were made, but Luc kept his eyes on the table until Marcy withdrew her hand. She nodded her head toward a table of three young women Michael had never seen before. "Those girls are hiking the Superior Hiking Trail," she said, lowering her voice. "They told me they're from Duluth. Played softball together at UMD. They've got one of those fancy dome tents, Gore-Tex rainsuits and boots, and goose-down sleeping bags. And, get this, they eat at restaurants so they don't have to carry their food and cook out. Can you believe it?" Marcy stuck her pen in her apron pocket, then leaned over the table and in a loud whisper said, "They live better than I do, and they're camping out!"

Michael laughed and looked across the booth at Luc, but his companion was studying the young women Marcy had pointed out.

"Camping in luxury," Michael said as Marcy turned to leave. "The only way to go."

"I'll bring your coffees right away," she said over her shoulder.

Michael aimed his smile back at Luc and resumed his story about meeting Anna. "So anyway, I'd gotten a fancy cowboy hat from a friend when I bought my new pickup truck. You know, that whole good-ol'-boy thing." Michael noticed that Luc was slow to swing his attention back to the story, but he grinned at the obvious interest his friend showed in the three backpackers. "I'd been watching her all afternoon," he continued, "and I knew she'd been eyeing me, too. You know how sparks seem to shoot between people sometimes?"

Michael paused for a moment and scanned the restaurant, then looked back at Luc and was glad to see him patiently waiting for more of the story. "So finally, she comes over to my table to pour another cup of coffee. This is like the hundredth time, and we'd been too shy to say anything before, but I could tell she was going to speak to me this time. So, she pours my coffee, then sets the pot right here on the table." Michael used an index finger to indicate the outside edge of the tabletop. "Then, before I could react, she reached out and swatted my hat right off my head! 'You're no cowboy,' she says to me. I couldn't believe it! What the heck was I supposed to do? I couldn't think of a thing to say. We just sat there looking at each other until both of us cracked up laughing."

A grin appeared on Luc's face, but he didn't offer a comment, so Michael concluded his story by saying, "Man, you got to like a woman with spunk like that!"

Marcy returned with the coffees, and then lingered for a moment at their table. "Can you imagine how long those three girls would last living out at your place like Annie?"

Michael sighed while making a face. "Come on, Marcy, they'd probably do just fine. It's not like we live out on the frontier or anything."

"Hah! I can just see the first time one of them breaks a fingernail." Marcy's expression changed as she put on her best Valley Girl impression, and in a loud, whiny voice said, "Oh my God! Like, I'm gonna die! I need a makeover, a manicure! Someone help me!"

This coaxed a befuddled expression out of Luc, but Michael and Marcy broke into fits of laughter. The harder they laughed, the funnier it became, until Marcy had to lean against the table to support herself. When Luc finally grinned at their hysterics, they laughed so loud and hard even the three objects of their ridicule turned to look at them.

"I better get back to work," Marcy said while wiping tears from her face. "Two BLTs coming right up."

Michael watched her walk away, and then glanced at the table of three backpackers. They were very young, he noted, probably just a year or two out of college. They all wore flannel shirts and khaki shorts with thick knee-high socks and hiking boots.

Interrupting Michael's surveillance, Luc asked, "What's the Superior Hiking Trail?"

Michael quickly turned to face his friend again. "It's a hiking trail, goes all the way from Duluth to the Canadian border. Two or three hundred miles altogether."

Luc nodded in understanding while fidgeting with his coffee cup. "Must be the path I walked this summer to get here," he said.

"I suppose. Coming up from Duluth it crosses the county highway out by my house, then ties into the Black Otter Trail out here." Michael swung a thumb over his shoulder to indicate the general direction where the trails met. "On the north end of town it heads inland again. Goes out near the Black Otter's headwaters and through the lakes region where we're working. You must have been on parts of it with all the hiking you do."

Luc grunted an acknowledgement, then Michael watched as his eyes shifted back to the three women. His face was expressionless until a chorus of ribald laughter erupted from the girls' table. Michael thought he saw an intensity bloom across Luc's face—a tightening of his jaw and a slight twitching in the focus of his eyes. But it was hard to tell; it could have been a change in the lighting, or perhaps just a shadow crossing the room.

Then the door opened and Sheriff Marlon Fastwater walked in, followed by his nephew and part-time deputy, Leonard. A third man trailed behind. Michael watched as they slowly made their way to the counter and the red, vinyl-covered stools. As soon as Marcy saw them she began pouring coffee, sliding the cups across the counter almost before the men sat down.

Michael had never seen the newcomer before. Even wearing a sport coat, he could see that the young man had a robust physique, thick across the chest and shoulders, but the fancy clothes and official-looking sunglasses marked him as an outsider. Michael watched the sheriff's big hand engulf the coffee cup as he swiveled around on the stool to look at the café full of regulars. Greetings were sent his way from around the room, and the sheriff nodded his response with a quick dip of his head. When his gaze fell on Michael, however, his smile straightened out and his expression turned serious.

Marcy came by with their sandwiches, breaking Michael's eye contact with the sheriff, and he was left wondering what that look had meant. When Marcy left, he again looked at the counter, but now the sheriff's broad back was turned to him as he talked to the deputy sitting beside him.

"That's the county sheriff," Michael said with a nod toward the counter. Luc was hunched over his sandwich, eating with the same passion Michael had observed the night before at his house. "Sheriff Marlon Fastwater and his deputy, Leonard."

Luc stopped chewing and looked up. "Fastwater?" he asked.

"Yup. Ojibwe, I think."

Luc looked at the two men conversing at the counter, then slowly resumed chewing and turned back to the plate in front of him. "That's the first Indian I've seen around here," he said. "I didn't know they lived here."

"It's mostly just his family. The Fastwaters have been here since before the first white settlers. They're even buried up on the ridge in the town cemetery."

Watching the sheriff's back, Michael saw him talking to Marcy. The big man pushed his cap back on his head, removed his sunglasses and rubbed his eyes, then laughed at something she said. He seemed at ease, and Michael wondered if he'd misinterpreted the sheriff's somber expression.

"Marlon has a sister down in Duluth," Michael continued. "She's a hotshot lawyer with the district attorney's office. You ever see the two of them together you'd never believe they were brother and sister. She works around the clock on liberal, cause-oriented issues, and wears these crazy, flowing dresses with bright jewelry. Where the sheriff is a big, quiet man, Arlene is simply loud and large. When she sweeps into a courtroom, everyone sits up and takes notice." He nodded at the young man sitting at the counter with the sheriff. "That's her son there, the sheriff's deputy. I don't know who that other guy is. The story is that Sheriff Fastwater served in the First Gulf War. Got a purple heart and who knows what all. Guess he was one of the first to enter Baghdad. Bottom line, he gets a lot of respect around here." Michael shrugged. "I haven't had much to do with him, but from what I've heard, I think he's a good man."

Luc was soon watching the three women again, and when Michael turned his gaze their way he caught the tall blonde looking at Luc. When she saw that Michael had spotted her, she blushed and started laughing.

It was quiet for a few minutes while Michael resumed eating, but when he next looked around the room, he again caught the sheriff's eye. This time the big man eased himself off the stool, hitched up his trousers, and slowly wound his way between the tables to their booth where he towered over them like an encroaching thundercloud. His shoulders spanned the width of the table, and Michael figured he had to weigh close to 250 pounds. His unknown counterpart edged up beside him.

"Afternoon there, Sheriff," Michael said, feigning a sense of good humor.

"How you doing today, Michael?" the sheriff asked.

"Fine. Just fine."

Fastwater nodded at the man beside him. "Sergeant Jepson here and I just stopped out for a visit with Anna and the little guy. What's his name again?"

"Charles. Charlie." Michael started to get up. "What's going on? Why did you want to see Anna?"

The sheriff held his hands out to calm Michael. "It's okay. Anna's fine. Everyone's good."

Michael sat down again but his worried frown lingered until the sheriff continued. "I bought a sack of her beans and some carrots. It's getting that time of year again for slow-cooked comfort food."

An audible sigh of relief escaped Michael. Attempting a lighter mood, he said, "Well, you better get your pumpkin soon if you want a local jack-o'-lantern."

The sheriff smiled, but then leaned closer and gently rested his two thick paws on the edge of the table. He swung his bear-like head once toward Luc, who seemed oblivious to the sheriff's presence, then looked at Michael. "Let me ask you: you seen anything out of the ordinary out your way lately? Maybe a stranger hanging around, or a sick animal or something?"

"A sick animal?" Michael sat back, turning a puzzled expression up at the sheriff. "What do you mean, 'a sick animal'?"

Ignoring Michael's question, the sheriff asked, "Has Anna mentioned seeing anything odd out there? She spends a lot of time in her gardens; has she said anything about strangers or animals hanging around?"

Michael thought about Anna's scare the day before. Could all this be related to the presence of the rescue squad he'd seen out on the county road? But he shook his head. "No. No, she hasn't." He set the BLT down and looked from the sheriff to the clean-cut man standing beside him. If they'd already spoken to Anna, why were they questioning him? "What's this all about, Sheriff? I saw your car up the county road yesterday. Is there something we should know?"

Luc surprised all of them by suddenly speaking up. "She saw wolves yesterday."

"Wolves?" Jepson repeated.

Luc glanced briefly at the out-of-place man in the sport coat, but when he answered it was to the sheriff. "Perhaps not a real wolf."

The sheriff straightened up and hooked his thumbs into the front of his gun belt. Luc was already taking another bite of his sandwich when Fastwater swung his full gaze at him. "What do you mean 'a real wolf,' and who are you, anyway?" he asked, making no attempt at cordiality.

"I'm sorry, Sheriff," Michael interrupted. "I should have introduced you. This is Luc Trembley, a friend of mine. He's doing some work for me this fall. Luc, this is Sheriff Marlon Fastwater."

For a moment, neither Luc nor the sheriff said anything, and Michael thought their silence resonated with an uncomfortable mutual distrust.

Then Fastwater said, "I asked you what you meant."

Luc hesitated even longer, and when he finally spoke, Michael was surprised by what he heard.

"You are very large for Anishinaabe, monsieur. Your fingers are wide and your nose is broad. I can see you come from a race of great warriors. Your people are Dakota, non?"

Michael saw the sheriff step back in confusion. Had he just been ridiculed or given a compliment? In a ponderously slow reply, the sheriff said, "My people have been the law in Black Otter Bay for fifty years." He bent over the table again, but this time he leaned toward Luc. "Now, just who the hell are you?"

"It is as Michael says, monsieur. My name is Luc Trembley. I'm visiting from Canada."

"Trembley," the sheriff repeated. "French-Canadian?"

Luc shook his head.

"No? Then you must be Métis."

"He's French," Michael interjected again. "From France."

Fastwater didn't take his eyes off Luc as he considered Michael's words. Then he asked, "Don't you need a green card or a work permit or something?"

"He's mostly just visiting, sir," Michael said. "He's only working for me because I need a hand to get this last job done before the snow flies." Michael smiled. "So you see, actually, he's kind of doing me a favor."

The sheriff slowly straightened up again while returning his attention to Michael. "I don't care why he's here, or where he's from." He gave a quick glance over his shoulder, as if to confirm that no one was listening, then, lowering his voice, he said, "A problem turned up yesterday. A couple miles up the Black Otter Trail." He hesitated long enough to be sure he had Michael's full attention. "Some backpackers from the Cities found a body."

Michael sat back, stunned. "Do you know who it is?"

The sheriff paused, nodding. "I think you know that real estate woman, Nichole Nielsen, who moved here a few years ago?"

Michael threw his napkin on the table. "You can't be serious. You mean Niki who drives the black Volvo? What happened?"

"Can't say for sure. The autopsy will answer that. The hikers found her not far off the trail. There was blood splattered around a wide area, so I figure her body was dragged into the woods by wolves—or the murderer."

"The murderer?"

"Shhh!" The sheriff looked over his shoulder again, and then back at Michael. "Let's not go upsetting people just yet. You keep this under your hat, Michael, until I find out for sure what happened. I just thought you should know since she died out your way."

"But you think she was killed, don't you?"

The sheriff looked down at the table and drummed his fingers a couple of times. "That's my guess." To Luc, he asked, "What did you mean when you said it might not have been a real wolf?"

Luc shrugged. "You know of Manitou, monsieur?"

"Manitou? What's that got to do with wolves?"

Luc looked at his friend across the table for help. After a long pause, Michael finally said, "Luc found wolf tracks out at our place last night. And Anna felt something watching her yesterday, but couldn't see it, so Luc thinks it could have been a passing Manitou."

Now Jepson stepped forward. "Are you kidding me?" he scoffed. "Come on, Sheriff. Do you hear this? Are we supposed to believe a ghost killed her?"

"Not a ghost, monsieur. And not murder."

"Then what?" Jepson barged closer. "And where were you when all this was happening?"

Fastwater stuck his arm across Jepson's chest, but the detective pushed it away. "This is crazy talk, Sheriff. First you tell me about old ladies with powers, and now we have invisible wolves and ghosts. Come on, are you listening to all this?"

But Fastwater was thinking, remembering all the wolf prints where Niki died, and now picturing more tracks out at Michael's place. He'd always had an open mind about the spirit world, but Manitou didn't get spoken of much these days. So, while he'd concede that his grandmother's "medicine" could reach into the spirit world, he wasn't ready yet to accept Manitou passing through the forests behind town.

Fastwater straightened up and sighed. "You still working up the Moose Lake Road?"

Michael was slow to reply, thinking about the woman suffering an awful death all alone in the woods. Finally, he looked up at the sheriff, and said, "Yeah. But if the weather holds, we'll be done by tomorrow. Then I'll help Anna put the gardens to bed for the winter."

"Well, keep your eyes open. I'll let you know what we find out." Then he turned his dark eyes on Luc again. "How long you plan on hanging around these parts, Mr. Trembley?"

Luc shrugged.

"I'm hoping he'll help me set up a trapline," Michael said. "Luc's done a lot of trapping up in Canada."

"Well, come and see me before you leave town. I might want to ask you a few questions."

Luc nodded, picked up his coffee cup, and let his gaze wander out the window, away from the sheriff. Fastwater lingered at the table, though, slowly rocking on the balls of his feet. It looked to Michael as if he had something more to say, but didn't know how to begin. Studying Luc's averted eyes, the sheriff finally said, "I don't know how you knew about the Dakota blood. No one else in town has any idea." Luc flicked his piercing gray-blue eyes up at the big man, and the sheriff continued. "Many generations ago the Ojibwe pushed my people out of the territory. Down south and onto the prairies in the Dakotas. But some of my ancestors stayed behind, here along the shores of Superior. We became part of their tribe, just as we're a part of the white community now. But we've always stayed here." He studied the longhaired Frenchman for a moment while Luc again made a point of avoiding his stare. "What I'm trying to say, Mr. Trembley, is that this is my home. It always has been, and it always will be, because I take care of it and protect it."

Michael watched Luc to see how he'd react to this thinly veiled warning. Luc didn't flinch. It was like he hadn't even heard the sheriff's words. A few tables over the three women burst into laughter again and, as Fastwater walked away, the glimmer in Luc's expression turned sour.

As the backpackers got up to leave, Michael became aware of them watching his booth, making no attempt to hide their surveillance. They probably think we're a couple of troublemakers getting a lecture from the town cop, he mused. As they filed past the booth, the tall blonde let her hand trail along their table for a moment, her shapely fingernails clicking against the wooden tabletop. She giggled as they moved on, and Michael had a chance to admire the long, thick braid hanging down her back past her waist. He watched as Luc's gaze followed her, too, first with his eyes, then by turning his whole body to watch her as she left.

"Come on, Luc," Michael said with a laugh. "She's fifteen years younger than you." His words snapped Luc around, and Michael thought he detected a blush of embarrassment. "Let's get out of here," he said, reaching for his wallet. Dropping some bills on the table, he thought about the news the sheriff had just related. If he was wrong, and Niki hadn't been murdered, could there be a rabid animal out there? Or a pack of wolves that had lost their fear of humans? Bear hunting season had started a couple of weeks earlier, so there could be an old, wounded bruin wandering around looking for revenge. A prickle of anxiety jabbed at him as he thought of Anna and Charlie working the gardens alone. He shook his head, trying to reassure himself with the knowledge of Anna's capabilities. But the sheriff had just spoken to her, so she knew about Niki, and the fact that she was all alone played on his deepest fears.

He spotted Marcy behind the counter watching them as he and Luc headed for the door. He threw her a confident smile and an energetic wave, an attempt to cover up his misgivings about the sheriff's words. But at the last moment he changed his mind and turned toward the counter. Over his shoulder he said to Luc, "Wait for me outside. I'll be there in a minute."

Stepping to the end of the counter, he said, "Hey, Marcy, any chance I can use the phone?"

"Don't you have a cell phone yet? My God, Michael . . ."

"Yeah, yeah. Just hand me the phone."

From a shelf under the counter she retrieved the cafe's old black landline and set it in front of him. "Do you even know how to use this thing?" she asked, laughing.

Michael's grin was still pasted to his face, but he hardly heard her words. Now that he'd given in to anxiety, he was focused solely on the need to reach his wife. His fingers fumbled over the touchtone numbers, his impatience mounting with the wait.

The connection was finally made, and he heard the phone ring on the other end. "Come on, Annie," he silently exhorted. "Please be home."

A second ring, and Michael racked his brain trying to remember what she'd planned to do today. I know she told me, he thought, why didn't I pay closer attention? After the third ring he concluded she must be outside working and couldn't hear the phone. If everything's okay, he thought. By the fourth ring he'd decided to make a detour home with Luc to check on her. Could there be a connection between her intuitive misgivings and the body found less than a mile from their house? A fifth ring and suddenly she was there, panting and gasping for breath. "Hello? Hello?"

"Anna! What's going on? Are you okay?"

"Oh, Michael, it's you!" Then her voice aimed away from the mouthpiece and she laughed while catching her breath.

Michael's anxiety vanished with the sound of her laughter. "What's going on out there?" he asked. "Is everything okay?"

"Of course everything's okay. Charlie and I are baking pies. You wouldn't believe the mess we've made." She hesitated for a moment and it sounded to Michael like she was licking something off her arm or hand. Then she asked, "Why did you call, honey? And why did you ask if everything's okay?"

"Well, I don't know. I was worried, you know, it took a long time for you to answer."

"Oh, gosh, Michael, I have blueberries and flour up to my elbows. I had to rinse off before I could touch the phone." Then she was laughing again. "You should see Charlie. He has a blue nose and white streaks all over his hair. Charles, honey, come here. Let me wipe you off. Bring Mommy the dishrag."

Michael emitted a feeble chuckle, but what he mostly felt right now was relief. Relief and admiration. He should have known there was nothing to worry about with Anna. They were baking pies, for goodness' sake! There were no rabid animals or wounded bears or wild packs of wolves besieging their house.

In a hushed tone, she said, "Sheriff Fastwater stopped by. Did you hear about Niki?"

"Yeah. We were just talking to him. I can't believe it."

"I know. But let's not talk about it right now. Charlie is trying to climb up my leg."

"Okay. I'm just glad you're all right."

"The sheriff said not to talk about it, but is that why you called?"

"No. I mean, yes. I mean, I don't know. No special reason. We just had lunch in town—thought I'd check in with you." He looked over to see Marcy still hanging around the counter, probably wondering why he needed to call home, and if it had anything to do with his conversation with the sheriff. Fastwater had been adamant about not leaking the news about Niki, however, and if Marcy got wind of it, it would be all over town.

"Well, it's really sweet of you to call," Anna said. "How is your friend working out?"

Michael laughed. "He's a horse, Annie. Luc was on the roof working before I even got there this morning. We hauled the old roofing to the dump, and now we're going to start shingling. "

"Well, I'm glad he's such a good help."

Michael released a silent sigh of relief. Anna's usual self-assurance had returned. Her easy laugh was back, and the common sense stability he admired so much. He concluded that the panic she'd endured yesterday was finally gone. Looking down, he noticed the phone cord twisted around the fingers of his right hand; he must have done it while anxiously waiting for her to answer. Marcy was still watching him, giving him no privacy, so on a whim he made a face at her, to which she immediately stuck out her tongue in return.

"I better get going, Annie. We may be a little late tonight. I want to get as far as I can on that roof. We might even finish today." They said goodbye, then Michael freed himself from the phone cord, thanked Marcy while grabbing a toothpick from the counter, and headed for the door.

Outside, Michael looked up the street to see the three women backpackers come out of the liquor store and walk north through town, apparently headed for the Superior Hiking Trail. So, it was just as Marcy said—they came into town to eat, maybe find a shower or do some shopping, then headed back into the woods to continue their hiking tour. And, he thought, Marcy had probably been right about another thing—those girls wouldn't last a week living out in the country like Anna.

Standing near the truck cab, Luc asked, "Where are they going?"

Michael followed Luc's gaze to the coeds crossing Main Street. "Well, they're carrying only daypacks, so they must have a campsite nearby. Probably up the Black Otter River somewhere out on the Superior Hiking Trail. Can't be too far."

As he pulled himself up into the truck, a sense of pride and renewed respect for his wife welled up inside him. Anna was so strong and capable. He figured the news about Niki would get out soon enough, but he hoped to have this last job done by then so he could stay home and help with the gardens. The change of seasons was always a busy time for Anna, and he didn't want her worrying about rabid animals or marauding wolf packs. For that reason, bringing Luc home for the winter might ease her workload, as well as help keep her and Charles safe. He figured it was the least he could do for her.

Chapter 7

*I*t was remarkable, Eileen thought, how much the moon illuminated the woods when you got away from city lights. Peering into the forest around their tiny campsite, she easily distinguished the shadows cast by bushes and trees. Sprawled out near the campfire, she'd unbound her long blond hair from its customary braid, and after resting her head on a bunched-up goose-down vest, her hair splayed out behind her like a frothy wake trailing a ship. Long legs stretched toward the fire, pointing her stocking-clad feet at the warmth.

"Watch the clouds floating past the moon," she suggested to her friend, Caitlin. "If you look long enough, it almost seems like you can feel the Earth rotating under you."

"That's just the wine you drank, dummy," Caitlin giggled. But she lay down beside her friend near the campfire to watch the celestial spectacle. A broad band of glittering water reflected the moonlight across Big Island Lake. Even at midnight there was enough light to reveal the Superior Hiking Trail and the girls' campsite set back twenty-five yards from the water.

The two girls had been friends since childhood. They'd grown up together on the same block in Duluth Heights, a suburb just over the hill from Duluth. It had been a dreary sort of place to grow up, a sprawling expanse of strip malls and one and two–story office complexes. The forests had been clear-cut and bulldozed in the haste to build houses. In an effort to compensate, city planners had dotted the town with treeless open areas—parks with baseball fields and outdoor hockey rinks.

Every summer of their childhood Caitlin and Eileen had played baseball, first with the boys in the neighborhood, and later in high school on the girls' fast-pitch softball team. Eileen was the better athlete of the two, but Caitlin had worked hard to master the physical abilities that came naturally to her friend. After years of playing ball together, there was still no doubt that Eileen was the more talented of the two, but all the hard work had made a pretty solid ballplayer out of Caitlin, too.

They'd shared a dorm room in Griggs Hall on the campus of the University of Minnesota in Duluth. Both of them had made the varsity women's softball team their sophomore year. But even though they'd played organized ball all their lives, they'd never seen a player dominate the field the way their new friend Jenny had.

From inside the tent came exclamations of frustration and the sound of gear being shoved around. "Jenny," Caitlin called. "What are you doing in there? Come on out and look at this moon. It's not that cold, forget your stupid sweater."

"There's no room to move in here!" came the disgruntled reply. "And most of this mess is yours, Cait." More shuffling of equipment and then the tent flap flew open and Jenny's robust frame crawled through the doorway. "I'm using your jacket because I can't find mine." She carried a nearly empty bottle of zinfandel and stood swaying over her friends, looking from Caitlin to Eileen while draping the Duluth Bulldogs letter jacket over her shoulders. She tipped her head back to look at the stars, and a second later stumbled backward under the influence of the wine. When she tripped on a tree root and sprawled on the ground, her friends burst out laughing.

"Hey, easy on the jacket," Caitlin said when she was sure her friend was okay.

Nightwatchers

Jenny crawled over to sit beside them. Looking up at the sky, she said, "It looks like somebody turned on a big lamp up there. Can you believe how bright that sucker is?"

Jenny's size and weight didn't generally lend itself to being a standout athlete, but in softball there were two things she could do as well or better than anyone else. On the mound she was a dominating pitcher, glowering at batters half her size and humiliating them with her blazing sixty-five- to seventy-mile-per-hour fastball. What made her pitching even more effective was the fact that she often threw wild. She'd laugh derisively when a batter dove out of the way of one of her pitches. Even the really good hitters found it intimidating to dig in and concentrate when they knew the next pitch might come humming along head-high and inside.

The other talent Jenny brought to the ball field was exhibited in her twenty-eight-ounce aluminum bat. When she swung into a belt-high fastball and got her upper body weight and strength into it, the resulting towering fly ball would inevitably land somewhere in the soccer field beyond the left-field fence. While it was true that Jenny couldn't run very fast, and she wasn't regarded as being any too quick with her glove, she could sure pitch and hit. Her fellow teammates had chosen her as their player-captain each of her last two years at UMD.

Unlike Caitlin and Eileen, Jenny came from a small farming community southwest of Minneapolis. She chose Duluth for her college career because of its proximity to the northwoods. The hills and forests of northern Minnesota were a complete contrast to the flat farm fields where she'd grown up. She told everyone that going to school in Duluth was like visiting a foreign country. "You even talk different up here," she often told her friends.

After their sophomore year in college, the three friends had taken a week-long backpacking trip on the Superior Hiking Trail outside of Duluth. The next year they'd celebrated winning the conference title with a canoe trip into the Boundary Waters Canoe Area Wilderness. Now, after graduating the previous spring, they'd had to postpone the annual excursion until fall because of summer internships and work commitments. The delay had worked out well because this late in the year there were no mosquitoes, and they'd had the spectacular beauty of the trail mostly to themselves. They had only a few days remaining, however, before they'd hike out to the nearest town and call Eileen's parents for a ride back to Duluth.

The girls were quiet for a while as they studied the starlit heavens. Then Jenny pointed out the Big Dipper and showed them how to find Polaris, the North Star, by following the outside edge of the dipper straight up to the next brightest star in line.

"And look," Caitlin added, "the Superior Hiking Trail is headed in the same direction." All of them looked where Caitlin pointed, at the path from their campsite to the water. A stone's throw down the trail it turned to the right to skirt the edge of the lake. But from studying the map they knew it eventually headed off into the woods again, roughly in the direction of the North Star, once it left Big Island Lake behind.

A breeze whispered through the treetops and a loose branch disrupted the quiet as it clattered to the ground. All three girls looked at each other. Caitlin's eyes were wide and alert, but Jenny snickered and said, "Anybody know any good ghost stories?" Passing the bottle of wine to Caitlin, she added, "It's a perfect night for a scary story."

"No way," replied her friend, shivering in the cool night air. "That's about the last thing we need right now." She took a swallow of wine and handed the bottle to Eileen. Turning back to Jenny, she poked at her and said, "Don't you know there's monsters and bears and werewolves and stuff out there tonight? Just look at that moon."

"Jeez, Cait, you're scared of everything." Jenny smirked. "Every camping trip has a ghost story. It's tradition: a campfire, a bright moon overhead, and a ghost story. Isn't that right, Eileen?"

"Well, it isn't a tradition for me," Caitlin shot back before Eileen could respond. "It sounds stupid to me. It's like tempting fate. You're just asking for trouble." Caitlin looked up at the moon. "Bad things can happen if you push your luck telling scary stories on a night like this."

"What a wuss, Cait. You don't really believe that bears or wolves will bother us just because the moon is out, do you?"

"Of course not. I just don't want to tell ghost stories."

They turned their attention back to the night sky just as a large dark cloud passed over the moon, temporarily blackening the woods around them. Skittering noises in the brush betrayed the secret movements of little animals.

"Did you hear that?" Jenny asked, whispering to Caitlin. "I bet its Bigfoot. I heard they spotted him out here last summer."

"Oh, shut up!" Caitlin said, rolling over to slug her snickering friend on the shoulder. They all laughed, and the cheery sound of their voices seemed to push back the darkness and bolster their courage. They laughed longer and harder than was warranted, until the cloud moved beyond the moon and the eerie bluish-white moonlight once again hung over their little campsite.

Eileen sat up and pulled her hair off her shoulders so it lay in a long fall down her back. She reached for the stick they used as a campfire poker and pushed the logs around, building up the flames, then draped her arms around her bent legs and rested her chin on her knees. Her friends sat up, too, and for a while they studied the images flickering in the fire. Slowly they inched closer to the warmth, and closer to each other.

Finally, Caitlin looked at Eileen and asked, "What are you thinking about?"

"I don't know, nothing much. Remember those guys at the café this afternoon?"

"Oh, God," Caitlin said. "That guy with the long hair?" She nudged Eileen with an elbow. "He was checking you out, girl."

Eileen scoffed and acted like she wanted to disagree, but in the end she just shook her head and went back to staring into the fire.

Caitlin looked at Jenny. "See how she doesn't deny it? I think somebody has the hots for a certain longhaired jackpine savage."

"No way," Eileen retorted over her friends' laughter. She shook her mane of blond hair so it rippled along her back. "In fact, I thought he was kind of creepy." With these words their laughter died out, and when it was quiet again Eileen continued. "Did you see the way he stared at us? I felt like he could see right through me." She turned her thoughtful expression toward her friends and said, "Or maybe more like he could look inside me, like he was reading my soul."

Now it was dead quiet again except for the crackling of the fire. When the silence became too much for her, Caitlin shuddered and said, "Come on, you guys, I thought we weren't going to tell ghost stories."

Jenny snorted and said, "Jeez, Eileen, are you naïve or what? The man wasn't reading your soul. He was obviously undressing you with his eyes. He couldn't stop looking at you."

Grabbing the wine bottle, Eileen ignored Jenny's comment and took a drink, then handed it to Caitlin. Sometimes, she found Jenny's sense of humor irritating. Her friend wasn't usually this annoying; if anything, Jenny was an introspective, quiet person—until she started drinking. Having grown up on a farm, she was more knowledgeable about the outdoors than her friends, so while they looked to Eileen as their leader for campus life, Jenny made most of the decisions for them on these annual camping trips.

Eileen sprawled out again and silently resumed her contemplations of the night sky. The moon wasn't even full yet, but she thought it looked larger than she'd ever seen it before. The others lay down, too, and when all was quiet again, she asked, "Didn't the Indians have special names for the moon? Like each month had a different name?"

"What do you mean?"

"You know, like the Neil Young album, Harvest Moon."

"That sounds more like something old-timer farmers would say," Caitlin suggested.

"But this is October," Eileen persisted. "It could be a harvest moon. Farmers could work their fields at night with all this moonlight."

Jenny shrugged. "My dad used to talk about this, but I don't remember all the names. March is the Maple Syrup Moon, and August is the Blueberry Picking Moon." Quietly reaching over, she pinched Caitlin in the ribs and said, "Maybe this is the Werewolf Moon!"

"Ahhh!" Caitlin screamed and sat bolt upright.

"Shhh!" Eileen commanded, holding her hand up for quiet. Her friends immediately became still when they saw her sitting up straight and looking into the woods.

"What is it?" Jenny whispered. "Did you see something?"

Eileen continued her inspection of the woods behind their tent. Several utterly silent moments passed as all three women peered into the forest, mouths open, hearts pounding.

"Well?" Jenny asked. "What was it? Did you just hear a noise, or did you actually see something?"

"Neither—or both. I don't know." Eileen shook her head and blinked hard a couple times. "It just seemed like something was out there."

The northwoods solitude closed in around them as they sat in silent expectation, but nothing revealed itself, and finally Jenny said, "I think you had too much to drink, Eileen. There's nothing out there."

"Oh yeah?" Caitlin taunted. "You're so sure, why don't you go check it out?"

"Well, maybe I'll just do that," Jenny said, staggering to her feet with a drunken grunt. "Girls," she announced, "I have got to pee."

"I wouldn't go out there," Eileen warned, nodding at the forest.

"I'm so scared I could pee right here in my pants," Caitlin added, her voice quivering. Her fingers shook as she brushed wisps of hair away from her face.

"There's nothing out there," Jenny scoffed. "That's what you get for growing up in the city." She walked past the fire, and then stopped at the entrance to the tent. Away from the light of the campfire, the moon framed her figure with an eerie illumination. "Besides," she added, "I've got Ralph's gun, remember?" Reaching inside the tent flap, Jenny pulled out her father's pistol. Waving it in the air, she pantomimed some shots at treetop targets. She was enjoying the effects of the wine, and with a big cocky smile on her face turned to her friends again. "That reminds me of a ghost story from when I was a kid on the farm. It's a good one, too, because it's true. Build up the fire and I'll tell it to you when I get back." She grabbed the toilet paper from a stump outside the tent and walked into the shadows beyond the range of the campfire's glow.

Eileen poked at the fire again and sent a shower of glittering embers into the air. Caitlin hovered at her side, leaning over the rock fire ring as Eileen added the last of the firewood to the flames. Spruce boughs crackled and hissed and sent up a thick wall of smoke.

"I think we ought to go to bed," Caitlin said. "It's really late and we have a long hike ahead of us tomorrow."

The stick Eileen used as a poker now had a small flame on the end of it, and she held it out in front of her, watching as the flickering tongues of fire slowly died out. "We don't have that far to hike," she said. "In fact, we don't have to go anywhere tomorrow if we don't want to."

"I know, but we planned to get all the way up to the Confirmation River. We'll never make it if we don't keep moving."

"We'll make it; you just don't want to hear Jenny's ghost story," Eileen said, still staring into the fire. "But you know it doesn't make any difference if we sit out here or inside the tent in our sleeping bags." She set the fire poker next to the ring of rocks encircling the flames and slowly swung her gaze around to her friend. "Now that she knows you're scared, she's going to tell her story no matter what."

They looked across the campsite into the woods where Jenny had disappeared. "Well, I still say we should go to bed," Caitlin said, but neither of them moved. They huddled next to each other against the chill. Eileen thought the buzz she'd gotten from the wine felt more depressing than exhilarating.

"What do you think is taking her so long?" Caitlin asked, peering into the woods. "I'd be out there and back in a flash—and only if I couldn't hold it another second."

Eileen picked up the poker again and looked at the charred end. "I don't know," she said wearily. Laying the stick across the fire she added, "But you're right, let's get to bed. I'm too tired to sit out here any longer."

They stood up and stretched, both women watching the woods that had swallowed up their friend. "Jenny!" Caitlin called urgently, but not too loudly, as if trying not to give away their position. She was surprised how her voice seemed amplified in the wooded darkness. "We're going to bed, Jenny, come on."

A rustling in the brush near the water caught their attention, and Caitlin grabbed Eileen's arm and whispered, "Did you hear that? Down by the lake?"

Eileen didn't bother to answer, but took a couple of tentative steps toward the lake and the Superior Hiking Trail, pulling Caitlin along behind her. "Jenny?" she said timidly. "Is that you?"

They heard a commotion in the bushes just out of sight in the dark, then a heavy-bodied scuffling on the ground. Caitlin pulled back on her friend's hand and harshly whispered, "Jeez, Eileen, do you hear that? I think it's a bear!"

"Jenny?" Eileen called, more loudly now. "Jenny!" They crouched in unison, like sprinters toeing the mark, ready to run to their tent and it's façade of safety. It was quiet again, but they had no doubt something was coming up the trail toward them. They waited, holding their breath, eyes big and round in the moonlight. The fire that Eileen had stoked up snapped and popped behind them, the forest full of shadows lurked all around them, and the sparkling, moonlit waters of Big Island Lake glistened down the path in front of them.

"Damned tree roots!" Jenny exclaimed as she burst into view on the trail. Caitlin almost collapsed from relief, and Eileen grabbed her arm to steady her. "That's the second time tonight I've tripped over roots," Jenny said. "I almost broke my rear end back there trying to brush my teeth!"

Behind her, Eileen heard Caitlin suck in her breath and suddenly her friend jumped out in front of her to yell at Jenny. "What the hell were you doing out there? Why didn't you answer when we called?"

"Hey, settle down, will you?" Jenny approached her friends and displayed her toothbrush and toothpaste in one hand, the half-roll of toilet paper and handgun in the other. "It's hard to yell when your mouth is full of toothpaste." She looked directly at Caitlin and grinned. "Guess I should have taken the flashlight."

"Damn, Jenny, you scared the hell out of us," Eileen said, anger boiling over in her voice. She stepped in front of Jenny and faced her with feet planted wide apart. "Don't go wandering off like that without letting us know. We were worried about you."

Jenny swiped at dirt smudges on her hip, ignoring Eileen's comments. When she again looked up at her friends, she displayed a wine-induced, pleased-with-herself smile. "Where were you guys going?" she asked.

"To bed," Eileen answered, still mad. "But first, promise you won't ever do that again."

"To bed?" Jenny swayed as she tried to see the watch on her wrist. She gave up with a shake of her head, and asked, "What time is it? I suppose it's pretty late."

Eileen looked over her shoulder for Caitlin, but her friend was already crawling into the tent. "Come on, Jenny" she insisted. "You scared Cait half to death."

"Okay, okay. Lighten up, will you?"

They headed for the tent and Jenny slapped a hand on Eileen's shoulder to steady her stumbling shuffle. "That was some good wine, wasn't it?" she stated. "Is it all gone?"

"Yeah, it's gone." Eileen let her eyes roam around the woods behind their camp, trying to read the shadows, looking for a shape that didn't belong. Jenny's little escapade had put her on edge, and an alcohol-induced headache throbbed over her eyes. But she couldn't put away the feeling that something was out of place in the woods nearby.

She grasped Jenny's arm and supported her as her friend knelt to climb into the tent, then she straightened up for one last look around the perimeter of the campsite. Like Jenny, she felt the urge to pee coming on, but she had no intention of going out into the woods alone. It was comforting to see that the fire was a huge blaze now that she'd piled on the last of the firewood. It cast an undulating glow around the little clearing, and the moonlight pushed the shadows even further back into the woods. The few remaining aspen leaves gently whispered in a soft breeze billowing across the treetops.

She looked up at the moon again and tilted her head to better see the silhouettes of the king and queen playing cards that her father had shown her as a child. The whimsical memory spread a smile across her face as she realized Jenny was probably right. There wasn't anything out there. She admitted that the wilderness was a little alien to her and her suburban upbringing, but even at night she saw that the woods could be a beautiful place. Sure, it was dark, but it was the same setting they'd considered so peaceful and serene in the light of day. Just because she couldn't see the beauty now didn't mean it was malevolent, or something to be feared. Smiling at this newfound confidence, she knelt down, pulled the tent flap open, and joined her friends in their little shelter under the trees.

• • • •

"I think I was seven or eight years old," Jenny began, "and my brother was about twelve. One Saturday night our parents were going to a wedding reception in town. It was like the biggest event of the year and all the grown-ups were going. Well, at the last minute our babysitter called to say she couldn't come over, and our parents were going to have to stay home because no other sitters were available on such short notice." Jenny sat hunched over under the sloping wall of the dome tent, sitting on her butt while tugging at her boots. The flashlight on the sleeping bag beneath her threw garish shadows around the tent as it rocked about in her struggles. Both Eileen and Caitlin watched from their bags, and outside they could hear the crackling of the campfire.

"You want some help with those boots?" Eileen asked from her position in the middle of the tent. She was in her bag but sitting up, loosely braiding her hair. It hung over her left shoulder down to her lap, while her long fingers wound the three thick strands together. Her hands worked blindly in the dark, years of experience directing her nimble fingers.

"Just a minute," Jenny said. Grimacing and grunting, she finally managed to free her feet. "There," she said, tossing the boots toward the foot of her sleeping bag. She took off her flannel shirt and reached behind her under her T-shirt to unsnap her bra. This was the way they'd been sleeping all week: socks, shorts and T-shirts. Then, if they had to step outside during the night, they didn't have to grope around for something to put on. Besides, they'd decided it was just too cold in the morning to crawl out of a toasty sleeping bag and put on underwear that felt as cold as the air around them.

Jenny smoothed out her flannel shirt and laid it inside the sleeping bag to keep it warm. Then she crawled in herself, zipped up the cover, and shut off the flashlight.

"Are you finally in bed?" Caitlin asked. "It must be close to morning by now."

"Oh, shut up, Cait," Jenny said with a laugh as she scrunched down deeper in her sleeping bag. When she was finally settled in she let out a long, tired sigh and said, "So anyway, my brother and I convinced our parents that we were old enough to stay home alone. After all, they'd been looking forward to this wedding party for weeks, and most of their friends would be there."

"Oh, God," Caitlin quipped with all the sarcasm she could muster. "Here comes the old 'home alone' story. Forget it, Jenny, we saw the movie."

"I told you this is a true story, smarty pants. It really happened."

They lay quietly for a few moments after that, and Eileen squinted into the dark as her eyes slowly became accustomed to the lack of light. She could just make out the shape of the rounded tent ceiling and the faint shadows of trees cast against it by the moonlight. The fire sizzled and popped outside.

"They finally decided to leave us home on the farm by ourselves. Remember the first time you got to stay home alone? It's like, if you pass this test we'll maybe let you stay alone more often. And, staying home alone is like the most important thing you've been wanting for years. We knew the neighbors' phone number, and the dance was just in town at the union hall, so it was no big deal, but they warned us to behave and get along."

"That was their first mistake," Caitlin interjected. "Expecting you to behave."

"Hah!" laughed Jenny. "We thought we were pretty cool. And like I said, my brother was older—it's not like we were scared or anything."

"So what did you do, burn the house down?"

"No, we started out watching TV, and I think we made popcorn. Everything was just fine. After a while we'd even forgotten that we were home alone." Jenny hesitated for a moment, like she was trying to remember exactly how the story went.

In the quiet, Eileen studied the shadows on the tent ceiling. It was easy to discern the low-hanging branches of trees outside, but another form had slowly appeared right above her. It was impossible to be sure, but she didn't think this particular shadow had been there when Jenny first turned off the flashlight. The blob of darkness didn't move, just hovered above her head. The longer she looked at it the more she envisioned a person outside leaning over the tent. Her heart began to race. "Cait, Jenny, look," she said, but before she could say more the shadow suddenly disappeared.

"What?"

"On the ceiling," Eileen stammered. "There was a shadow right above me. It's gone now."

"Jeez, Eileen," Jenny said. "We're in the woods, you know. There's lots of shadows out there."

"But I could have sworn . . ."

"I didn't see anything," Caitlin volunteered too quickly. It sounded more like an attempt to convince herself that nothing was out there.

"Forget it, you guys," Jenny said. "Close your eyes and let me finish my story." Her voice softened to where it was barely audible. "So there we were, watching TV and minding our own business."

Eileen didn't close her eyes, but lay in the dark with the sleeping bag pulled up tight under her chin. She studied the ceiling, ready to yell at the first sign of movement outside. In the meantime, the urge to pee was getting stronger. Sighing to herself, she decided it was going to be a long, uncomfortable night.

"All of a sudden," Jenny continued, "we heard this awful wailing outside. It was kind of like a moan, like something in a lot of pain, but it didn't sound human. At first it seemed kind of far away, so we shut off the lights inside and looked out the front windows. We couldn't see anything, and we didn't hear it for a couple of minutes until suddenly it wailed and moaned really loud, right by the side of the house. Oh, God, did we jump! My brother quickly flipped on the outside yard lights, but we still couldn't see anything."

Jenny paused again in her story and they lay quietly listening to the night. Eileen strained to hear the campfire outside and was puzzled by the complete silence that enveloped their tent. She thought she should have been able to hear it, as it had been a small bonfire just moments ago, but before she got too far with these thoughts, Caitlin timidly spoke up. "So, what was out there, Jenny? Or was it just the wind?"

"Well, it sure wasn't the wind, I can tell you. We were looking out the front window when suddenly there was a heavy bump against the side of the house, and loud huffing and puffing noises. It banged against the wall like the Big Bad Wolf wanting to get in, and then it made that horrible moaning, bellowing sound again."

"Weren't you scared?"

"Scared? Hell, we were terrified," she replied with a laugh. "We were so scared we ran upstairs into our parents' bedroom and locked the door."

"Why didn't you call the neighbors?" Caitlin asked. "You said you had their phone number—or I suppose the phone just didn't happen to work, either," she added with a smirk.

"We did call the neighbors, but they weren't home. We figured they were probably at the wedding dance, too. Besides, on the farm, our nearest neighbor was a quarter of a mile away, and this thing sounded like it wanted to come in right now."

Side by side the girls lay together, Jenny spinning her tale, Caitlin acting skeptical and trying hard not to believe her, Eileen only half listening as she wondered what had happened to the campfire. Then she felt a slight nudge against the top of her head. Absent-mindedly she swatted at it, just a gentle brush of her hand, as if shooing away a mosquito. Her head was several inches from the wall of the tent, but when she swiped her hand over her hair she felt the tension of the tent wall tightly pressing in, almost touching her. When she made contact, the nylon wall immediately sprung back into position. Eileen sat up and spun around.

"Oh my God," she whispered as she felt along the tent wall. "Something's out there, you guys! It just touched me."

"Eileen . . ." Jenny began.

"Didn't you feel it, Cait? It was pushing against the tent."

"Stop it, Eileen," Caitlin pleaded. "You're scaring me."

"I'm telling you, there's something out there! I saw the shadow, and now it touched me right through the tent."

"Come on, Eileen, get a grip," Jenny sneered, but she reached out to feel along the wall, too. When neither of them could find anything, Jenny said, "I know, let's just say you're right. Pretend something is out there. Remember the raccoon that came in the tent our first night out? Remember how scared we got over that? And that was nothing. But, even if a bear is out there, it isn't going to bother us. We don't have any food in here. Besides, we have the gun," and even though Eileen couldn't see it, she could feel her friend retrieve the handgun from under her sleeping bag.

For a long time they listened to the stillness around them, the presence of the gun in Jenny's hand bolstering their nerves.

"Good golly," Jenny finally said sarcastically. "I didn't know my story was going to scare you so much. If you want, I'll quit telling it."

Eileen had to admit that Jenny was probably right again. A bear wouldn't bother them in the tent. It was probably just some critter sniffing around, looking for food. She was overreacting. After all, she'd seen earlier how the moon could cast bizarre shadows everywhere, and even the softest noises were amplified in the cold night air. It had been a long day, and a very nerve-racking evening.

"No," she said quietly. "Go ahead, finish your story. I guess I'm just overtired."

"You don't have to finish it for me," Caitlin interjected.

Ignoring her, Jenny asked, "Are you sure, Eileen?"

"Yeah, go ahead. It's okay."

"Well, all right, then. So, anyway, I wanted to call the cops, but my brother said we had to deal with this ourselves, otherwise our parents wouldn't be able to count on us. He said we couldn't act like scared little kids. He was sure there had to be a logical explanation. Outside, it sounded like the huffing and puffing monster was circling the house, so we snuck back downstairs. Boy, was I scared! We peeked out a couple of windows but didn't see anything, so then my brother said we had to go outside. He figured that would be the grown-up thing to do, and the only way to find out for sure what was out there."

"It was probably a bear," Caitlin suggested.

"My God, girl, are you dumb or what?" Jenny said. "We don't have any bears down there."

"Well, no way would I go out there to find out."

"That's what I told my brother, so he said he'd go first, but I had to stay right behind him. We each found a flashlight, and he grabbed a hatchet from Dad's tools. At the last minute I picked up a butcher knife from the kitchen rack."

"You mean you actually went outside?"

"We sure did! The growling moans were coming from the side of the house. My brother went first, and I grabbed the waist of his pants and followed right behind. We snuck along the front of the house, shining the flashlights all around us. It was really dark when we got to the corner because the yard light didn't reach that far, so we stuck the flashlights around the edge of the house first, then poked our heads around the corner."

Jenny stopped again, and in the silence Eileen listened for sounds outside the tent. There was nothing—no fire, no breeze. She thought this must be how the astronauts feel when they're orbiting the Earth, their little space capsule, just like this tent, shielding them against the dark alien worlds outside. But the protection was just a state of mind, she realized. That spaceship could be annihilated by the slightest mishap, and this tent she hid in was, after all, just a thin sheet of waterproofed nylon. "Can you guys hear the fire burning out there?" she asked.

It was quiet as all three girls listened. Then Jenny said, "It must have burned out. I don't hear a thing."

"It couldn't have burned out," Eileen said. "It was burning like crazy just a few minutes ago." She unzipped her sleeping bag and crawled to the tent opening. An unexpected apprehension sucked the breath out of her as she slowly lifted the flap. Tentatively sticking her head through the opening, she saw that the fire was completely burned out. Not even a wisp of smoke from the ashes was visible. Then she looked around and noted how the stars still shone benignly above them, and the three-quarter moon hung silently over everything. But she felt an uncommon stillness in the woods, like creatures were holding their breath in anticipation. Looking from side to side in the moonlight, she tried to shake the creepy thoughts from her mind. She took a last look at the dead campfire, then backed into the tent. "I don't get it," she said. "The fire is totally burned out. There isn't even a hot coal left."

"Just goes to show," Jenny said with a laugh. "City girls don't have a clue about building a campfire."

"You saw how it was going when we came in. There's no way it could have gone out already."

"But it did. Sometimes they do that—just flare up big and bright, then go out. You have to have the firewood stacked in there just right."

Eileen didn't bother responding. Too many weird things were happening. She found herself on edge again, upset, and the need to go to the bathroom was becoming more urgent. She barely heard Caitlin ask, "So what did you see around the corner of the house, Jenny?"

"Well, the first thing that happened was my brother's flashlight burned out. Can you believe it? Then he wanted me to go first, but I said, 'No way!' So he started sneaking along the back of the house, and I stayed right behind him, shining my flashlight over his shoulder. For a while we didn't hear anything, then suddenly there was a loud, bellowing roar nearby in the dark. Oh, man, was I scared! I turned to run but dropped the flashlight. I threw the knife in the direction of the noise, then my brother began wailing."

"Oh, my God, Jenny! What was it?"

Jenny rolled onto her side and propped herself up on an elbow. Even Eileen was listening now, her misgivings temporarily set aside.

"My brother just stood there while I felt around on the ground for the flashlight. I guess it turned off when I dropped it. He kept repeating, 'Oh no! Oh no! Oh no!' The monster was coming closer. We heard it shuffling along—we even heard it breathing. I finally found the flashlight and stood up and turned it on. It was horrible, Cait. You wouldn't believe what happened."

"What was it? What happened?"

Jenny's voice went soft again, but she kept the intensity in it, enjoying the rapt attention of her friends. "Well, my brother kept up his wailing. Oh, he was yelling and cussing up a storm. Then I pointed the flashlight out into the dark. Not twenty feet away stood the neighbors' huge brown bull. Hanging from his neck and wrapped around his head were long strands of barbwire he'd torn out while escaping. His head swung back and forth while he stomped his big fat hooves at us. I screamed and started to run. 'Come on!' I yelled at my brother, but he just stood there crying. I let the flashlight shine at his feet and what I saw was horrible! The most disgusting thing I've ever seen."

"Oh my God, Jenny," Caitlin gasped in a voice full of awe. "What was it? More barbwire?"

"I tell you, Cait, it was terrible. You see, because we'd been in such a hurry, my brother hadn't worn any shoes or socks when we went outside.

Now he was stuck in the thickest, grossest pile of warm bullshit I've ever seen!" Jenny turned on the flashlight and aimed it at Caitlin's face, then broke into fits of laughter. "Bullshit, Cait. Get it? A big pile of BS!"

"You mean to tell me you made up that whole story?"

"It's all bullshit, little girl, and you fell for the whole thing!"

Caitlin pulled the sleeping bag cover over her head, partly to get away from the annoying flashlight, but mostly to hide her embarrassment.

"You're crazy, Jenny," Eileen said, but she was chuckling at the joke, too. "Turn off that stupid light, will you?"

The tent immediately became pitch-black, and the silhouettes of trees and branches returned to the ceiling. "Nothing like a good campfire story," Jenny said as she settled back down in her sleeping bag. "And you guys are so easy!"

"Okay, okay, so maybe we're easy," Caitlin said, poking her head out of the sleeping bag. "But we're also tired. Let's get some sleep."

Sitting up again, Eileen said, "I think I'll take a quick timeout before turning in. Otherwise, the wine will wake me up in another hour." Turning to Caitlin, she prodded her hopefully. "Come on. Let's go outside before you get too comfortable."

"No way am I going out there! I'll just wait until daylight or drown in my own pee, whichever comes first."

"There'd better not be any flooding in here tonight," Jenny commented, but she was the only one to laugh at her joke. In a quieter voice to Eileen she said, "I left the toilet paper on the stump outside. You want to bring the gun?"

"No, I'll be fine. It'll just take a second."

Chapter 8

*E*ileen *crawled outside and, with the help of the moonlight, located* the roll of toilet paper. Looking around the edges of the campsite, she searched for an easy access into the bushes. For a moment she considered going back to get the flashlight, but climbing in and out of the tent was so awkward. Besides, she didn't intend to be outside very long.

She took a closer look at the pile of wood in the fire ring. It was obviously out cold, the charred and sooty logs no longer adding light to the campsite. She held her hand over the ashes and was surprised to find no heat at all. And the logs almost looked wet, as if a rain shower had snuck through unseen and doused them. She'd have to ask Jenny about that—about how the coals could have cooled so quickly, and why the logs seemed to shine as if damp.

Her fears and apprehensions were subsiding, a fact she attributed to the humor in Jenny's story. She giggled softly at the thought of how easily she'd been taken in. But now, looking around the campsite, she noticed again how the woods seemed so still and silent, like an audience sitting on their hands with an air of expectant waiting.

Near the opening where the Superior Hiking Trail wandered off to the north were two large pine trees. Standing side by side, the giant white pines looked like sentinels guarding the trail access. In her stocking feet she gingerly made her way over to them. Their lowest branches were several inches above her head, and when she stepped underneath them she noticed how they blocked out the moonlight, how all the shadows here mingled together in darkness.

The chill of the night raised goose bumps on her bare arms. Her long T-shirt wasn't much protection against the midnight chill, and for a moment she crossed her arms in front of her, hunched up against the cold. Looking back at the campsite and the tent just thirty feet away, she decided this little cave-like recess under the pine trees would serve her purpose well.

While the branches here obscured the moon, its light still clung softly to the objects in their campsite: the tent and trees and even the rocks around the campfire pit. She yawned deeply, but then arched her back as a sudden bone-chilling fear sucked the breath out of her. Something was next to her; she could feel the bulky presence behind her. She didn't dare turn to look, but in the pitch-blackness under the pines she knew she wouldn't be able to see anything anyway.

In the next instant a thousand images flashed through her mind: the dead campfire and the light of the moon just a few feet away. The raccoon raiding their snack foods last weekend, and the bulky, bearlike shadow hovering over their tent. She heard breathing behind her and smelled a slightly tangy odor of body sweat. Panic locked her breath in her chest while cramping spasms rippled along her thighs. She was frozen in place, and a moan of pure terror came out of her, surprising her with its inhuman quality. But the sound of her own voice jogged her brain into action, pushing her away from the tree, hurtling herself away from the presence behind her. She'd barely moved, however, before a large hand wrapped around her face and clamped down hard over her nose and mouth.

• • • •

Because of the miles she'd hiked on the hilly, rocky trail that day, not to mention the effects of drinking most of the half-gallon of wine they'd shared that evening, Jenny fell asleep just moments after Eileen left the tent. But Caitlin was awake, stretched out like a corpse in her sleeping bag, her body rigid and straight as she listened to the quiet outside. The silence rang in her ears like the aftershock of a loud noise. It reminded her of the first two or three seconds after being startled awake in the middle of the night by a booming thunderclap. It wasn't tangible, it couldn't be, but it had a certain aura of substance to it nonetheless.

What kept her awake now was the feeling that Eileen had been gone too long. Or does it just seem like a long time, she wondered, because I'm sitting here waiting and worrying? One thing she was sure of, however, was that Eileen had had more than enough time for a quick stop in the bushes. Holding herself completely still, Caitlin strained to hear a familiar noise from her friend outside, but other than the deep breathing emanating from Jenny's side of the tent, there was nothing.

Slowly, she eased herself to a sitting position and looked around the dark tent. Jenny had their only flashlight, but it was out of sight somewhere in the bulging folds of her sleeping bag. Caitlin thought she'd never felt so alone as she did sitting here in the dark, listening for the return of her friend, the minutes slowly ticking off while her nerves wound tighter and tighter. Finally, mustering her courage, she got out of her sleeping bag with the intention of looking outside. When she grasped the flap to the doorway, however, her resolve suddenly deserted her, and instead she looked at the heavy form sleeping peacefully along the far wall of the tent.

"Jenny," she said. No response. She called a little louder, but thanks to the wine, her friend had crashed into a deep sleep. Caitlin crawled across Eileen's sleeping bag and on hands and knees perched over Jenny's covered head. "Jenny," she whispered stridently. "Wake up!" She grabbed the sleeping bag and pulled it back, revealing her friend's thick tangle of hair. "Come on, Jenny, wake up." She shook her, rattling her roughly back and forth. "Jenny, Eileen hasn't come back yet."

She finally got a response, in the form of muffled snorts and groans, but soon Jenny rolled over to face the wall of the tent and resumed her slow rhythm of deep breathing. Caitlin shook her again and said, "Jenny, Eileen is still outside. I'm worried about her."

With a groan, Jenny rolled back to face her. It was dark, but Caitlin's eyes were adjusted to it, and she could see Jenny looking at her with a dazed expression. "Eileen's gone, Jenny. She's been out there too long."

Jenny blinked several times and looked at the sleeping bag Caitlin crouched on, as if she suspected their friend could be hiding somewhere inside it. She brushed hair away from her face and cleared her throat. When she spoke, her voice sounded sticky and dry. "Maybe she's doing something else. Brushing her teeth or something."

"She's not brushing her teeth," Caitlin retorted, exasperated by her friend's nonchalance. "Come on, get up. We have to find her."

"You go find her," Jenny said, snuggling deeper into her sleeping bag. "I tell you what, she's probably doing to us what I did to you guys. Hiding out there so we'll worry about her and get scared. She must think we're really stupid." Jenny pulled the cover up under her chin. "I'm not going out there, it's time to go to sleep." Then she raised her voice and yelled, "You hear me, Eileen? We ain't coming out. It's time to go to bed!"

• • • •

The pressure around Eileen's face slackened when Jenny called out, and she gasped a mouthful of air. But instead of letting go, her attacker pulled her to the ground next to one of the sentinel pines. She struggled against a second arm wrapped around her chest, tried to kick out or bite, but the lack of oxygen left her too weak to defend herself.

The brutal strength of her attacker sent more images flashing through her mind: Jenny's story about the neighbors' bull, and Caitlin's fear of bears. Frantic, she reached behind her and grabbed a fistful of hair. But no, this isn't hair, she thought. It's fur! It was long and coarse, thick and bristly. Jenny's reference to Bigfoot came to mind. She yanked and pulled, causing the arm wrapped around her chest to let go. A hand grabbed at her fist, but she yanked it away, still clutching the handful of dark fur. She twisted and spun, but her strength and will were slipping away. She flung the fur aside and eyed the tent perched so peacefully in the moonlight just a few yards beyond the darkened campfire ring. Eileen's pulse pounded in her neck. She had to breathe, but when the tent flap finally moved, she felt herself being dragged further into the covering darkness under the pines.

• • • •

Caitlin dug around in the folds of Jenny's sleeping bag until she located the flashlight, then crawled back to the tent flap and listened. "Eileen?" she called softly. "Are you out there?" She sat completely still, straining to hear an answering word from outside. Then she began fingering the tent flap, slipping her hand through the opening. "Eileen?" she called again as she pulled it apart. With just a narrow slit to look through, she peered into the moonlit campsite outside their tent. The fire was out, she noticed, just like Eileen had said. "Come on, Eileen," she called through the doorway. "Quit fooling around and come to bed."

Opening the flap wider, she crawled halfway out and stopped to turn on the flashlight. She passed it over the dead campfire, then quickly into the woods on each side of the tent. "Eileen," she yelled. "It's not funny anymore. Come on, you're scaring me."

Saying it out loud helped her realize just how frightened she really was. Eileen didn't usually joke around like this, and the notion that something was indeed very wrong caused Caitlin to wriggle backward into the tent. For a moment she sat inside the doorway, breathing hard while her heart pounded in her chest. She shined the light on Jenny, but the sleeping bag was pulled over her head. Working to calm herself, Caitlin got her breathing under control, and then steadied her resolve for another look outside. Ultimately, it was fear that finally gave her the courage to do what she had to do, and after nodding an affirmation to herself, she inhaled deeply, held her breath, and grabbed the tent flap.

"Eileen!" she yelled as she stuck her head through the opening. "Where are you?" She crawled through, stood up on shaking legs, and aimed the flashlight into the woods. The beam of light instantly found Eileen in the darkness under the tree. Shadows flitted through the brush, and Caitlin dropped the flashlight while her terror-stricken screams, coming out in gasping spasms of shock, shattered the stillness of the midnight woods. She stood frozen in place, and didn't feel or see when Jenny staggered to her side.

Jenny quickly retrieved the flashlight and located the place where Eileen lay sprawled on the ground. Something cowered behind their friend, but she couldn't see much more in the darkness. Then Caitlin grabbed at her and the light swung wildly around the woods. Pulling herself free, Jenny again pointed the light at Eileen while raising the handgun in her other hand. More shadows flitted around the perimeter of the campsite. Next to Eileen crouched a bundle of fur, it's sightless eyes directed up at her. There was no fear in the animal's eyes, just a lifeless cold stare. Then she fired. Once, twice, three times. Low and wide to avoid hitting her friend. The shots exploded into the night, the barrel flash temporarily blinding her. When the ear-shattering echoes of the gun subsided, the wolf with no eyes was gone.

Jenny stepped away from the tent with Caitlin wailing and crying and hanging onto her arm. Swinging the light around them, Jenny searched the woods with her eyes and ears, but Caitlin's whimpering distracted her.

"Shut up!" she commanded, and Caitlin immediately dropped to the ground in spluttering submission. Jenny was scared, terrified, all her senses on high alert. Now she drew upon her fear to feed her will to survive. Slowly, she walked toward Eileen, flashing the light around her, looking and listening. Something was out there, moving through the brush, but she couldn't fix it in the beam of light. She spun around at the sound of a growl in the woods beside her, a growl that extended into a drawn-out snarl.

Wolves, she thought, circling the campsite. She could imagine their eyes glinting in the moonlight as they slunk through the bushes around them. The growling faded away, but Jenny heard more rustling in the brush behind the tent, more snarls and movement off to the sides.

Slowly, she lifted the flashlight to the spot where Eileen lay. She walked across the open campsite toward her, grateful to see her friend moving, trying to get to her feet, coughing in rasping breaths.

This can't be happening, she thought. And where is that animal with no eyes? Did I hit him?

She marched back to Caitlin, a collapsed wreck on the ground in front of the tent. Jenny directed the flashlight like a weapon at the noises in the forest. She decided that if they had to fight, they'd be better off sticking close together. By the time she reached Caitlin's side the area of the forest nearest around them had gone quiet. In the distance she heard the yipping and howling of the receding wolf pack. Caitlin sat on the ground crying, mumbling an incoherent barrage of words.

With the wolves gone, the forest seemed to be brooding in its silence, like an unwilling witness. She'd never heard of a wolf pack attacking campers before, but whatever it was that had been out there had probably been there all night, just as Eileen had suggested, watching them and waiting. And Jenny knew it could still be out there, just beyond the thick trunks of white pines, in the heavy underbrush hidden from the moonlight.

With the gun clasped firmly in her right hand, she bent down and grabbed Caitlin under the arm. Propelling her to her feet, Jenny dragged her along as she followed the light from the flashlight back to Eileen's side. She found her friend hiccupping for breath, her eyes open but dull, a recent vacancy revealed in them. Jenny knelt beside her wounded friend, brushing hair away from her face. "It's okay now, Eileen," she said softly. "We're going to get you out of here." She called for Caitlin to come closer. "We're going to stay together," she promised her friends, "and go for help." And as the three huddled together under the stoic stand of pines, the last pair of stalking eyes faded into the night.

Chapter 9

Gitch *stood at the window, paws on the sill, wagging his tail at the* black SUV pulling into the headquarters parking lot. He knew this vehicle and looked forward to seeing the occupant. Behind him, Sheriff Fastwater jotted a few more notes, slammed several manila file folders shut, and quickly stashed them aside.

"He's here. Let's go, Leonard." With surprising speed and agility the sheriff pushed away from the desk as his nephew stepped to the door, zipping his woolen field jacket.

Gitch let out a whimper before crowding up against Leonard's knee. "I know, big guy," the deputy said. "Your best friend is here. Come on."

When the door opened, Gitch bounded outside and cruised around the sheriff's squad car to meet up with Captain Phil Simanich. From the doorway, Fastwater and his nephew heard the captain's greeting. "Gitch! You big overgrown mutt. How's my best four-legged friend?"

Gitch stood on his hind legs trying to reach the captain's face with a slobbering tongue, but the big man used both arms and a bear hug to wrestle the malamute into submission. "How's my buddy? Huh? How's my pal?" Simanich had been prepared for the overzealous greeting and produced a huge dog biscuit for Gitch, who reverently mouthed the gift and trotted back to the door to savor the treat in privacy.

Vincent Wyckoff

Fastwater opened the trunk of the squad car and deposited a small daypack of supplies and a heavier coat. A front had moved in overnight, causing frost warnings to be issued just before dawn. "Let's take my car," he said, slamming the trunk.

Offering the front seat to the chief of the Special Investigations Bureau, Leonard opened a back door of the squad car and whistled for Gitch.

"Where's Jepson?" Simanich asked.

"Haven't seen him," Fastwater responded. Opening the driver's door while looking out at the predawn horizon over Lake Superior, he added, "He's probably still sleeping."

"He said he was on his way," Simanich countered. He pulled a thick wool cap on his head and looked at the sheriff over the top of the squad car. Phil Simanich was a big man, nearly as large as Fastwater. Growing up in a rural setting over on the Iron Range, he was used to starting the day early, not afraid of long hours of manual labor, and not particularly picky about his attire, as evidenced by his tattered wool cap and faded canvas barn coat. The two men had played high school hockey against each other, entered Baghdad together with the US Marines in the First Gulf War, and clocked their careers in law enforcement side by side. But where Fastwater was satisfied staying home policing his own community, Simanich had larger goals, as well as a huge office and staff in the police department building in Duluth.

"Let's give him a few minutes," Simanich said. "He should be in on this."

"We've wasted enough time," Fastwater argued. "It will be full light by the time we get up there."

"It's okay, Marlon. No one will be out there this early."

Simanich stood by the passenger door. He glanced at Gitch and Leonard climbing in the back seat, and then looked over the roof at Fastwater. "Did you get anything else out of those two girls?" he asked.

The sheriff leaned into the open door, one boot resting on the doorframe. He was a master at concealing his emotions, but Simanich had spent enough time in his company to recognize his friend using a long pause to swallow his frustration.

"Not much," Fastwater finally replied, choosing to look at the pinkish glow on the lake's horizon rather than his boss. "Both of them mentioned seeing or hearing wolves, but it was the one with the gun that actually described one of them." Now his gaze found Simanich. "She said it looked like the eye sockets were empty. Like it was blind. But it was gone after she fired the gun, so she isn't sure. You have to wonder how it could run off in the dark of night without any eyes."

Simanich nodded. "Well, she could have been mistaken. It was the middle of the night and she was half-drunk and scared; she might not have had all her wits about her."

Fastwater shook his head. "She's a big farm girl, Phil. She calmly defended her friends with a .357 Smith & Wesson. She remembers how many rounds she fired. She aimed low and wide so as not to hurt anyone. Then she guided them out of there to get help. Believe me, she had her wits about her."

Both men gazed out over the brightening horizon. The fresh pink line of dawn was slowly turning orange. Fastwater said, "She couldn't be sure of anything because it all happened so fast, and it was dark and hard to see. Her friend wrestled with the attacker on the ground, and in the shadows and confusion it was impossible to make out one from the other. That's why she fired so far wide. She admitted the sightless wolf could have been something else, like maybe a man's head and ponytail as he rolled on the ground. That would explain its disappearance afterward. She just couldn't see."

Simanich frowned. "Okay. But the victim? She really didn't see anything?"

Fastwater's expression almost revealed his exasperation. He took a deep breath, the cold, dry air tweaking his senses. Looking at the horizon again, he noticed how quickly the sun was rising. "She never saw him. He grabbed her from behind and she almost suffocated. Strong guy. She says she ripped a clump of hair off his head, but it looked more like fur than human hair."

"And that's when she mentioned Bigfoot," Simanich concluded.

Instead of responding, Fastwater looked at Leonard and Gitch in the back seat. "We have to go," the sheriff said. He wasn't suggesting or asking anymore. "Get in, Phil. The café should be open by now. We'll get a cup of coffee to go. Then we're heading out there with or without your detective."

• • • •

Red Tollefson was once again dominating conversation at the café. "I'm telling you, I heard gunshots. At least three of them."

Marcy scrunched up her nose. "How come you only hear these things at night? You sure it wasn't some kind of brain fart or something?"

Owen Porter stifled a laugh, but Red threw a puppy dog look of hurt across the counter at the waitress. "It was the middle of the night, Marcy. Woke me up from a dead sleep."

The kitchen door swung open and Abby Simon emerged with two plates of pancakes, one large and one small. She wound her way around the counter, and everyone watched as she delivered the aromatic platters to the table where her father and brother sat. Ben's head rested on his arm draped across the table. He would have been asleep in another thirty seconds if the food hadn't arrived.

"This looks great, Abby," Matthew said. But then her father stood up, adding, "How about you start on this for me? Keep your brother company. I need to talk to Marcy for a minute."

When Matthew reached the counter, Marcy's hand instinctively stretched out to grab his. For a moment they stood there, the rare public display of affection reddening Matthew's cheeks above his beard. He leaned back, but their fingertips maintained a solid connection. Marcy said, "I wasn't expecting to see you and Ben this morning. What's the occasion?"

Matthew shrugged. "I don't know. Sometimes I just want to see Abby in her world. They grow up so fast." He looked at Marcy and squeezed her fingers. "You okay with running her up to school later?"

"Of course. And don't forget we're having dinner tonight. We have to discuss Halloween plans."

Matthew nodded and smiled. "Good. We need to talk about that Raggedy Andy costume. Deer season is coming on and I'm not shaving my beard off for a Halloween party."

Marcy laughed. "Just remember, Andy was a doll, not a lumberjack. Besides, you look so cute in bib overalls and that sailor hat."

That was a little too much for Matthew, so he swiveled on the stool to look at Red and change the subject. "Gunshots in the middle of the night, Red? Where?"

"How should I know? A way off, I guess." Red leaned forward on the counter now that he had an audience. "I know a thing or two about guns, though, and I can tell you it wasn't no shotgun. Sounded like a handgun to me." Now he looked at Marcy. "And no little .22, either. Probably bigger, like a .38 or something."

"You're crazy, Red," Marcy said. "No one around here would be shooting off guns after midnight in the middle of the week."

"I didn't hear anything," Matthew said. "And we don't live far from you."

"Well, I'm a light sleeper. But the missus heard it, too. At least she said she did after I woke her up."

Marcy shook her head in disbelief. "You should hear yourself sometime, Red." She pulled her hand away from Matthew's and reached behind herself for the coffeepot.

Owen Porter said, "Too early for deer hunting unless poachers are working over spotlights."

Red opened his mouth to respond when the front door opened and Sheriff Fastwater strode in. His nephew, Leonard, followed close behind. Phil Simanich stood just outside with Gitch, rocking on the balls of his feet while watching the vacant highway for signs of his lost detective.

Marcy hoisted the coffeepot and Fastwater held out his thermos.

"What, no time for a cup today?" she asked.

The sheriff gave the briefest wag of his head before looking at the row of men seated at the counter. Marcy turned to rinse out the thermos, giving Red the opening he needed to engage the sheriff.

"You investigating those shots I heard last night?"

Fastwater pivoted to scan the room, pausing for a moment to watch Abby and Ben eating pancakes. Then he turned his attention to Red. "What shots?"

"The shots I heard. Middle of the night. At least three of them."

Fastwater looked away, his gaze traveling from Marcy at the sink to the big lake trout mounted above the cash register, and finally outside to his friend Simanich. As soldiers behind enemy lines on the advance into Baghdad, they'd learned to communicate with just a look, and now Simanich instinctively reached for the door and stepped inside.

Leonard leaned in close beside his uncle to address Red. "We're heading out there now. You heard three shots?"

"Well, yeah, I guess so."

Simanich soon joined them, leaving Gitch to sit outside the door. Red looked at the Special Investigations Bureau chief and an uncommon shyness overtook him.

Fastwater turned to Matthew again. "You folks hear anything last night?"

"No, sir."

There was impatience in the sheriff's demeanor, and while Leonard leaned his lanky torso against the counter, Phil Simanich approached with an officious swagger, ears tuned to the conversation. Owen Porter leaned back, keeping Red between himself and the three lawmen, but Red had nowhere to hide, so he directed his attention at the coffee cup in front of him. Matthew looked about to speak again when the door swung open and Mrs. Virginia Bean's voice clattered over the tension in the room.

"Well, of course you can come in, Gitch," she trilled. Looking at the trio of men at the counter, she added, "Did these mean old guys leave you outside in the cold all by yourself?" With a challenge in her eye, she sauntered up to the sheriff's elbow, Gitch sticking close to her side. She greeted Leonard, and just about the time it occurred to her that it was too early for the sheriff's nephew to be up and about, she noticed Phil Simanich reaching for an offered cup of coffee from Marcy. It might be too early for Leonard, but it had to be important if the bureau chief was here, too. She focused her challenging expression at the usually taciturn sheriff and asked, "What's going on?"

Fastwater looked at Marcy, hoping to grab his thermos and leave, but Red finally found his voice again. "They're investigating those gunshots I heard last night."

"Gunshots?" Mrs. Bean clutched the sheriff's arm. "What's he talking about? I didn't hear any gunshots."

Marcy said, "No one did, Mrs. Bean. It was just Red rolling around in his sleep."

The postmistress eyed Simanich. They'd met before, and now his face softened in recognition. She returned his smile, saying, "Phil Simanich, Marlon's dear friend. It's nice to see you again." She paused to shake his hand, and then added, "As wonderful as this place is, I don't think you drove up here to experience the café's breakfast. It's about those gunshots, isn't it? What happened?"

Simanich was leery of revealing anything to the postmistress, but even more so in front of the sheriff. But as it turned out, he didn't have to.

"I heard the shots, too," came a voice from behind them. Everyone turned to see Abby stacking dishes at her table. She stood and walked toward them, returning her father's questioning look. "I was studying last night, but fell asleep for a while at my desk. I woke up when I heard the shots and looked at my clock. It was just after midnight." She paused as she rounded the corner with the dishes. "I was awake by then, so I worked some more on my algebra." She shrugged before continuing into the kitchen. "I didn't hear any more shots after that."

The swinging kitchen doors hardly moved before Red blurted, "Well, there you go. I knew it. Shots fired and I heard them."

Everyone's attention turned to Fastwater, still waiting for Marcy to hand him the thermos. Mrs. Bean jostled his arm. "What's going on,

Marlon? What brings your friend up here, and why is Leonard in town so early?"

Marcy tightened the rubber stopper in the thermos and handed it over the counter, but with everyone looking at him the sheriff knew he had to give them something. Simanich offered the briefest nod, and Fastwater exhaled a mighty sigh of frustration. "Some campers were attacked last night out by Big Island Lake. One of them had a gun and scared off the attacker."

Then everyone was talking.

"Was anybody hurt?" Marcy asked. "Did someone get shot?"

"Anybody from town, Sheriff?" asked Red.

Matthew stood up. "Big Island? That's where we go shore fishing."

Fastwater put his hands out to stop the onslaught. "Nobody got shot," he explained. "Nobody got seriously hurt."

It was quiet for a moment, so Simanich used his authority to step up and take command. "We're headed out there now. It was three young women from Duluth. Backpackers. Only one was physically hurt, but she'll be fine. Sheriff Fastwater escorted them to Duluth earlier this morning. No one has any reason to be afraid."

Fastwater used the stillness in the aftermath of the captain's words to grab his thermos of coffee and turn for the door. Marcy stopped him. "It was those three college coeds that were in here yesterday, right? You saw them. They were here for lunch."

The sheriff paused, but then nodded. Pandemonium broke out as the three men and Gitch headed for the door. Fastwater gave Mrs. Bean a look. "I'll get word to everyone when we know more. There really isn't anything for anyone to worry about."

"Be careful, Marlon. I'll be over at the post office waiting."

He nodded, and then pushed through the door to the gray light of dawn.

• • • •

The drive up the Moose Lake Road started quiet enough, but the sheriff's restlessness crowded the big squad car with tension. Even Gitch felt it, and sat like a statue in the back seat looking out the window.

Simanich said, "You know, they were going to find out sooner or later."

Fastwater hurled the car around a curve, and when the hood gobbled up the centerline, Simanich was grateful for the early hour and complete lack of traffic.

From the backseat, Leonard said, "In a way, it could even be a good thing."

The sheriff shot him a glower in the rearview mirror, but Simanich turned to look at him. "How so?"

"Well, you know they're going to talk about it. And because it just happened, one of them might remember seeing something—or someone. Like Marcy, she mentioned seeing the girls in the café. When they talk about it, maybe one of them will remember seeing something else."

Simanich looked over at the sheriff. "He has a point, Marlon." But when Fastwater didn't respond, he added, "Anyway, I can't see where any harm can come from it."

With a dismissive shake of his head, Fastwater said, "Everybody saw them in town. And not just in the café. They were in the liquor store, too, and walked right down Main Street." He looked at Leonard in the mirror again. "Pretty much everybody saw them. But that's not the point. I don't believe anyone from around here attacked them, so I'm wondering who else knew they were here." Fastwater took his foot off the gas and studied the ditch ahead for the abandoned entrance to the Big Island Lake boat access.

With the car slowing, Gitch stood up in anticipation of getting out. Leonard said, "Well, maybe someone will remember seeing a stranger hanging around town."

Fastwater pulled the squad car to the side of the road across from the access point. It was easy to see that driving the rock-rutted road with a big sedan would be impossible, but that wasn't what attracted their surprised attention. Parked across the road in the access entrance was a shiny black Mustang. Early morning sunlight glinted off the chrome dual exhaust pipes.

"Humph," Fastwater muttered.

"What's he doing here?" Simanich asked.

"Did you tell him to meet us here?"

"No. I may have told him about the Big Island campsite, but I'm sure I told him to meet us at your headquarters."

And then, as if on cue, Detective Bryce Jepson walked up the access road and waved at them across the highway.

"That stupid—"

"It's okay, Marlon," Simanich interrupted. "It was just a communication breakdown. I should have been more clear."

"If he went out there and ruined the site . . ."

"He didn't ruin anything. He's a professional. He knows protocol."

Fastwater turned on Simanich. "And when does protocol let you tramp solo through a crime scene?" He abruptly yanked the keys out of the ignition and opened his door. Once again, his nephew was surprised by the big man's speed and agility.

"Hey, Sheriff," Jepson called from across the highway. "Where you guys been?"

Fastwater went to the trunk of the squad car while Simanich, Leonard, and Gitch walked over to meet the detective. Gitch didn't seem particularly happy to see the young man, and watching from across the road, Fastwater bit back a smile when the big dog lifted a leg against the Mustang's rear wheel. Strapping the daypack over his shoulders, he joined the others, gratified to hear Simanich lecturing his detective. Without greeting, Fastwater plunged down the steep access road while Gitch sauntered to the edge of the gravel searching for an appropriate rock to carry.

They hiked without words, the only sounds in the early morning light coming from their heavy breathing and stones dislodged underfoot. Even the birds were quiet, and the farther they went the more uneasy the sheriff felt. At the old, discarded boat landing on Big Island Lake, he finally turned around. The others drew up close behind. Leonard, as he often did on these excursions, was ten feet off the road, eyes on the ground, looking for signs of anything passing through. Since the closing of the boat landing several years earlier, virtually no one came through here, but if someone did, Leonard would find the evidence of it.

Fastwater looked at Jepson, and with the prospect of a looming blow-up, Simanich stepped closer. It took a moment for the sheriff to find his words, a moment for the men to catch their breath while Leonard stepped from the woods onto the path hugging the lake. A couple of hundred yards around the shore and they'd hit the Superior Hiking Trail, just steps from the girls' campsite.

Fastwater looked from Jepson to Simanich, and finally back to the detective. Surprisingly calm, he asked, "You came down here this morning alone? How did you find this place?" His voice may have been calm, but Simanich heard the accusation in the words.

Jepson smiled. "GPS, Sheriff." He held up his smart phone. "I downloaded the whole Superior Hiking Trail. The captain said the campers were out on Big Island Lake, so I looked at the map and decided this was the closest access."

Fastwater saw the hint of a smile emerge on Simanich's face while Leonard politely turned to look out at the lake. Even Gitch started off along the trail again, and with nothing more to say, the sheriff turned to follow. Jepson rolled his eyes, calling after him, "I thought it would be faster if I just met you up here. Whether you went in this way or the longer route from town, I figured it would be best to come straight here. I didn't mean any harm, Sheriff."

Fastwater didn't respond. He strode quietly along the trail while Leonard worked his way back into the woods.

Simanich asked Jepson, "So, you've already been out there?"

"Yeah. But there's nothing to see. It's just a deserted campsite."

"You didn't walk through it?"

"Of course not. But you can see it from the hiking trail."

And in just minutes they were there. A short spur trail broke away from the lake, and a bright orange tent stood at the far side of a small clearing. Fastwater paused beside a pair of towering white pines and, calling Gitch to him, had the big dog sit and stay at the edge of the campsite. He watched Leonard slowly approaching through the woods, moving silently in a half crouch, eyes intent on the ground. His long braid hung over one shoulder, while his hands gently moved branches out of his way.

When Fastwater stepped close to one of the pine trees, the uneasy feeling that had kept him on edge mushroomed like a darkening thunderhead, growing into a storm of anguished emotions. He reached for the tree trunk, bracing himself against the onslaught of panic. Simanich saw his distress and moved closer. "You all right, Marlon? What is it?"

Fastwater, eyes shut, leaned his weight against the tree. He drew a hand over his face, as if wiping something away. His mouth opened for a gasp of air, but when Leonard called to him he snapped to, swiveled away from the tree, and stood up straight as if nothing was wrong.

"Marlon," Leonard said. "Look at this."

Fastwater and Simanich stepped through the underbrush to Leonard's side. His nephew pointed to a clump of hair or fur on the ground.

"Oh, yeah," Jepson said, drawing up behind them. "I found that earlier. It's just an old wad of wolf fur." Everyone turned to look at him. "It looks like it's been there a while," he added with a shrug.

"You didn't touch it, did you?" Simanich asked.

"Well, yeah, sure. But just to look at it. It's just an old pile of fur."

"It's evidence," Simanich barked. "This is a crime scene."

"But he may be right," Leonard interjected. "This isn't new." Gathering around him now, the men squatted to look at the ball of fur on the ground. "I'm not even sure it's fur," Leonard offered. "At least, not a natural fur. Could be man-made."

Fastwater took off his daypack and removed latex gloves and a ziplock plastic bag. "We'll take it with us," he said, handing the equipment to Leonard.

"That's evidence, Marlon," Simanich said. "You can't just take it."

"It's a ball of fur, Phil. Your evidence team, if they even find this place, will never spot it on the forest floor." Standing again, and all business now, he looked at Jepson. "Is this where you found it?"

Having just been chastised by his boss, and expecting more of the same from Fastwater, the detective looked around as if studying the ground for more clues while avoiding the sheriff's gaze. "Well, I think so. Probably. I may have carried it a little while."

Simanich interrupted their conversation by stepping closer to Fastwater. He nodded at the nearby pine trees and lowered his voice. "You had one of your visions, didn't you? What happened?"

The sheriff watched his nephew collecting the ball of fur, and then reached out to run his fingertips over the big flakes of gray-colored bark lining the trunks of the white pines. "Not really a vision, Phil." He paused, thinking. "I felt it. The girl was really scared. So scared she thought that dying would be better."

The two friends stood in the secluded spot under the old growth pines. Even if the girl hadn't said so, Fastwater would have known that this quiet little shaded oasis had been the site of the attack. Simanich nodded. "I see. But why? I mean, I don't understand why someone was trying to kill her out here."

Leonard joined them as the men slowly moved through the campsite. "A jealous boyfriend?" he suggested. "Or some sort of crime of passion?"

"Okay, but again, why? He's bigger and stronger, so why try to kill her?"

Jepson stepped forward, emboldened by Leonard's interaction with the older men. "Maybe it was a robbery gone bad."

Fastwater answered. "Assuming the attacker didn't know about the gun, if it was robbery, why not just come in and take what he wanted? The victim said he was a powerful man." The men stopped near the cold campfire ring and tent. "Besides," he continued, "they were campers. Two of them had credit cards, but there wasn't much cash on them. Even less jewelry. You going to murder someone for their sleeping bag?"

147

Leonard squatted near the campfire ring and used a stick to poke around the ashes. "Marlon?" he said. "This fire isn't only out cold, it's been doused with water." He slowly spun on his heels. Noting the empty gallon jug of wine next to the campfire stones, he leaned over to sniff and look. "They probably hauled water from the lake in this to put out the fire."

"Don't touch it," Fastwater commanded. "We may find prints." He looked at the shiny black coals. "The farm girl didn't say anything about putting the fire out."

"You think the attacker did it?" Jepson asked.

"Humph. Maybe. But if he was worried about the light, there was a bright moon overhead last night."

"Well, I suppose he thought every little thing would help him hide."

Simanich turned in a slow circle, taking in the whole campsite. "So, if it's not about sex, and not a robbery, I guess that kind of brings us back to Bigfoot, doesn't it?"

Fastwater stuck his head inside the tent and saw the three sleeping bags lined up. Backpacks and clothing lay strewn about. Outside, Leonard made his way around the backside of the tent. To Fastwater, Simanich asked, "You think this attack and the death of the jogger are related?"

The sheriff paused, watching his nephew systematically studying the ground around the tent. "I do," he said. "At least, they're related in the fact that no one from around here is involved."

"So, it becomes a question of who knew the jogger would be out there at that early hour, and also knew these campers were here last night." Then he shook his head. "But I still don't understand why. And for that matter, we don't even know if women were the specified targets. It could just be random."

"Hey, Marlon," Leonard called from behind the tent. "Check this out."

They made their way around the tent and leaned over Leonard squatting in the dirt. Using an index finger, he outlined the slight impression of a shoe print close against the tent wall. Looking up at his uncle, he said, "I believe all the women were wearing hiking boots with deep treads. No treads here. Someone wearing dress shoes, or maybe cowboy boots, stood out here yesterday or last night."

Fastwater nodded, stood up straight, stretching his back, and looked around the campsite again. Drawing a deep sigh, he said, "Okay. Phil's crew from Duluth should be arriving soon to take a closer look." From his daypack he removed a small digital camera and handed it to Leonard. "Get some shots of the shoe prints and campfire ring, and whatever else you think is important." Then he turned to Jepson. "I need you to expand your research in Duluth. All three women went to UMD, so check with instructors, administration, their softball coaches, and members of the team. Go wherever the investigation takes you. Interview current employers, and talk to all the families. We're looking for connections, especially if we can attach someone to these women and Niki, the murdered jogger." He stepped away, but immediately turned back. "And Detective Jepson, I need you working this around the clock. I'm convinced you'll find the link we're looking for, so I want to know what you learn as soon as you learn it. Got it?"

Jepson nodded, once again scribbling notes in his notepad. Simanich said, "I don't think you should completely disregard the local element, Marlon. This connection you're looking for may be right under your nose. And didn't you already ask the detective to follow up on that young man you encountered on the highway a few years back? If these incidents are the acts of a crazy man, we may never understand the connections."

Jepson asked, "How did you find these girls, Sheriff? They didn't walk to town in the middle of the night, did they?"

The sheriff crossed his arms and Simanich and the detective stepped closer. "The Selstad brothers found them. A couple of old guys living not far from here." When Simanich raised an eyebrow in question, Fastwater continued. "They heard the shots and went outside. The girls were making a lot of noise with their yelling and crying. The brothers started up their tractor to maybe go investigate, but when the farm girl heard the tractor engine, she led the women to them. The brothers called me, maybe about one o'clock this morning."

Jepson asked, "They were going to drive a tractor through the woods in the middle of the night?"

Fastwater looked away, but not before noticing the glimmer of a smirk on Jepson's face. Leonard continued snapping photos, but stopped long enough to say, "The Selstads collect aluminum cans to sell to the recycler. They drive the tractor along the ditches and around campsites looking for cans. Neither one has a driver's license, so really, they take that thing everywhere."

"Well, I think we should talk to them," Jepson suggested. "Don't you think their story is a little far-fetched? And, come on, who collects aluminum cans by tractor?"

The sheriff's silence made him a little uncomfortable, so to bolster his argument, he added, "If the brothers regularly drive the back roads and trails, they probably knew the girls were nearby. You asked the question yourself, Sheriff; who knew they'd be out here?"

Simanich gave the briefest nod and stood back to listen to the exchange. Fastwater shook his head, but then looked at the detective and said, "Listen, son, the Selstad brothers are eighty years old. Don't ask me why they collect aluminum cans on a tractor. I have no idea what eighty-year-old think about, and no idea why they act the way they do. But I'm reasonably certain those two old boys had nothing to do with harming that girl. The only role they played was finding them and getting help."

"Okay," Simanich interjected. "Fair enough. But let's not dismiss the possibility of someone local being involved."

Not wanting to rile his elders again, Jepson asked Leonard, "Have you noticed anyone new around town?"

Leonard looked at his uncle, held up the evidence bag of fur, and with a grin, replied, "Not unless you count the new pack of wolves moving in."

Jepson laughed, but Simanich asked, "You think this is sign of a pack expanding their territory?"

"It looks that way. But it is a weird coincidence. Two attacks in two days, and wolf prints at both sites."

"Well, obviously a wolf didn't try to strangle that woman last night," Jepson said.

Simanich nodded at Fastwater. "It is odd about the wolves, though."

The sheriff looked at him. "You mean like coincidences? Like the fact that a delusional young man comes through town years ago and now two women are attacked? Or that Leonard wears cowboy boots that match the prints out behind the tent?"

Simanich shook his head. "No, Marlon. Come on. I'm just . . ."

"There are no coincidences, Phil. You know that. Things happen. Wolf packs expand, people get hurt."

"Okay, fine. Send Jepson down to Duluth to open that end of the investigation. But I think we should go back to the café and start there."

No one else saw the sheriff flinch, but Simanich knew his friend's behavior probably better than anyone. "What is it, Marlon? What are you thinking about?"

Fastwater looked at him. "Wolves."

Simanich grimaced. "Well, like the sergeant said, I really don't think a wolf attacked that woman last night."

Fastwater nodded. "Wolves and Manitou," he said, drawing blank stares from everyone. "Remember that longhaired fellow we talked to in the café yesterday?"

Jepson jumped forward. "Yes! That guy from Canada, or France, or wherever."

The sheriff looked at Simanich. "He explained how Manitou could take the shape of an animal—like maybe a wolf."

"I have no idea what you're talking about."

Jepson added, "He said he ran traplines in Canada."

"Exactly. He's a hunter and trapper." Then Fastwater looked at all of them. "But he has the eyes of a wolf."

Chapter 10

*T*he *post office in Black Otter Bay sat back from the road, boasted five* towering flagpoles, angled street parking out front, and was generally considered the ugliest building in town. It used to be worse, however, with faded-to-gray siding crosshatched with woodpecker and chipmunk holes, until a few years ago when Sheriff Fastwater and his nephew volunteered to patch and paint the structure. Unfortunately, the federal government supplied the paint, sending it over from Fort Ripley in central Minnesota. It consisted of five-gallon buckets of Vietnam War–era paint in pea soup green and olive drab. Originally used to camouflage equipment in the jungles of Southeast Asia, the military no longer had a use for it in the wide-open landscapes of the Middle East and Afghanistan.

Positioned as it was between native stone- and cedar-clad structures, Michael Hagen had once commented to Mrs. Virginia Bean that the post office stuck out in town like high heels at a picnic.

"What do I care what it looks like?" she'd responded. "As long as I have enough firewood to keep the place warm, they can paint it plaid for all I care."

And sure enough, when Michael pulled the door open early on this suddenly brisk morning, warmth from the woodstove rushed past him as if trying to escape its own confining heat. Good golly, he thought. It must be ninety degrees in here.

Piles of letter trays and mail tubs were strewn about the back room, with a hamper full of packages parked amidst the clutter. "Mrs. Bean," Michael called over the counter. Discarded mail sacks lay scattered across the floor and draped over her desk. He spotted her then, on the far side of a tall metal shelving unit housing pigeonholes of addresses. Mrs. Bean sorted letters like a machine, stuffing them one after another in their proper slots without seeming to even look. So engrossed was she in her work that when Michael called a second time, even louder, she jumped in surprise.

"Michael," she said, coming around the corner of the shelves. "You're in early today."

"Good morning, Mrs. Bean. I had to run into town for a load of mulch and thought I'd grab what mail we have while I'm here."

"Well, it's not quite ready yet," she said, handing him a few pieces. From her other hand she plopped a thick stack of letters on the ledge and began fingering through it.

Glancing at his mail, Michael said, "It's starting to feel like winter out there. That wind off the lake is cold." Noting her thick postal sweater, he added, "But it sure is warm in here."

Mrs. Bean looked at him over her reading glasses. "Helps my joints loosen up," she explained. "I'll be going through two or three thousand pieces of mail by noon, so my fingers have to be nimble."

"Wow. That's a lot of mail. I had no idea."

"That's on a light day, like today. You should see the mess in here around the holidays." She finished fingering through the stack of letters and then tapped the stack on the counter like a deck of cards. "Nothing more for you. How's Anna?"

"Anna's fine. Just fine."

Mrs. Bean pulled off the reading glasses and let them dangle from their beaded chain. She inspected her fingernails and straightened her sweater before assuming a more serious expression. "It's kind of frightening about what happened to that young lady."

Everyone in town had been talking about Niki's death, so Michael said, "I know. Anna was getting to know her pretty well. It was quite a shock."

"Know her?" Mrs. Bean retorted. "There wasn't much time to know her. I guess she'd spent some time in the café, but . . ."

"Of course she was in the café. It's the only place in town to eat."

"Well, I can't even imagine how frightening that must have been."

Michael studied the postmistress and the deep furrows of concern wrinkling her forehead. She said, "The sheriff will figure out what happened, I'm sure of that."

"Mrs. Bean?"

"He has help today from Duluth. Not that he needs it, or even appreciates it."

"Help from Duluth? Mrs. Bean—"

"They're out at the campsite right now. They were in the café first thing this morning."

"Wait a minute. Campsite?"

"The sheriff says she'll be okay, but can you imagine—"

"Be okay?"

"It was the middle of the night, Michael. I don't think she even saw him."

"Mrs. Bean—"

"Out there by Big Island Lake. It was just lucky she had some friends with her."

"Mrs. Bean!" Michael interjected more forcefully. The postmistress stopped talking and squinted at him. "Mrs. Bean, seriously, she's not going to be okay. Niki died out there, and she was all alone."

"Well, of course, Michael. I know that. And it's tragic. But I'm talking about those young ladies last night." And as Michael stepped back, startled, she told him what little she'd learned earlier that morning. She spoke in rapid, emphatic phrases, making it clear she considered Michael's interruption to be rude. Standing straighter now, and employing a haughty stare, she concluded by saying, "The sheriff said he'd stop by later to tell me what they find."

Clearly upset, Michael asked, "This was just last night? What time? And how did the sheriff find her? There's no cell service out there."

"Nels and Ingvald called it in on their landline."

"The Selstads?"

A prickling anxiety stole his breath away. First Niki, and now this. Was it just coincidence that he'd been working out there yesterday? Thankfully, this attack was farther from home than the first one. And he felt a little relief when he remembered he'd be working with Anna now, and helping out with Charles.

He suddenly felt an urgent need to leave, to tell Anna the news. "Well, thank you, Mrs. Bean. I better get going."

"But I haven't sorted all your mail yet. I haven't even looked at the packages."

"That's okay. Maybe we'll stop in later."

She saw the fear and confusion on his face. "It's going to be okay, Michael. Sheriff Fastwater is right on top of this thing."

He nodded, attempted a half-hearted smile, and turned for the door. Pausing outside to zip his jacket, he looked up at the ancient ridge behind town where majestic white pine and spire-like cedar trees climbed the steep slope. A shiver tickled his spine, only partially due to the damp, cold breeze off the lake. He peered up at the darker recesses under the trees and wondered, What the heck is going on out there?

• • • •

Most of the bite had been taken out of the wind by the time it reached Anna's Gardens and Toolshed, but it still felt raw, even with the sun showing low in the sky. Michael and Anna bent over their shovels, turning under dead plant stalks and roots in their flowerbeds. The big red pickup truck stood nearby with bags of manure mulch stacked on its lowered tailgate. The mulch, rich in nitrogen, was spread on the ground and mixed in with the plant detritus. Charles played nearby in the dirt with Anna's small gardening tools. Today he was free to dig anywhere he wanted.

With Luc's help, Michael had reroofed the small Selstad farmhouse in just one day, finishing the peak as darkness descended the night before. Luc had worked hard right to the finish, and then crammed Michael's cash payment in his backpack without bothering to count it. He'd smiled and shrugged at Michael's offer to join him and Anna for a late dinner and homemade pie. The last Michael had seen of his friend was his receding form entering the darkening woods surrounding the Selstad property.

Looking up from his digging to scan a low bank of thick gray clouds amassing to the north, Michael observed, "Just look at those clouds, Anna. I think we better wrap this up today. Looks like Old Man Winter plans to pay an early visit."

Anna knelt to pull out another rock that had been baffling her shovel. She carried it to the pile stacked near the side of the garden. Come spring they'd use these rocks to repair existing flowerbeds and hopefully line a new one. After dropping the stone she placed her hands against the small of her back and stretched, then looked at the sky off to the northeast where Michael was looking. "That's not snow," she said. "Just a front building up over the lake. When the wind dies down tonight those clouds will move out to sea."

Upon his return from town earlier this morning, Michael had told Anna about the attack on the campsite. Coupled with the death of her friend Niki just a couple of days ago, the news had come as a shock. Michael sensed her anxiety in the quiet intensity she brought to her work. She wasn't scared, he knew, just reflective, her thinking deliberate. They discussed it whenever Charles was out of hearing range, but there really wasn't much to talk about. He suspected she connected it to the scare she'd experienced the other day, and he tried to reassure her. "I bet the sheriff already has this thing wrapped up. After all, who would dare pull something like this in Fastwater's jurisdiction?" He laughed. "Remember what happened to Randall and his boat? The sheriff blew that thing right out of the water."

Anna looked at him but didn't return his smile. For a few minutes they stood together taking a break from the digging, each lost in their own thoughts. Then out of the quiet came the sound of crunching gravel as a car slowly wound its way up the road. Even Charles stopped his playing and they all watched the nearest curve. A moment later Sheriff Marlon Fastwater's big county squad car came into view. The sheriff's elbow stuck out of the window as he idled the car along the road, examining their groomed plots while taking in the woodland scenery.

Michael and Anna walked out of the garden beds, slapping dirt and mud from their jeans. Charlie ran over and grabbed his mom's hand, and together the three of them waited for the squad car to pull up. Michael noticed the way the sheriff looked around, as if searching for something. There was a big fellow riding in the passenger seat, and the sheriff's nephew peered out from the closed rear window, where Gitch paced back and forth across the back seat.

"Well, isn't this the hard-working family," Fastwater said as the car came to a stop. Michael leaned on his shovel, leery but grateful for an excuse to take a break. "Hello, Sheriff," he said, bending over for a better look in the car. "Leonard, good to see you." The deputy got out on the far side and smiled at Michael and Anna, then sauntered around to the front of the car to lean against the hood.

Fastwater said, "This is Captain Phil Simanich from Duluth."

Michael looked at the stranger, feeling Anna pressing up against him. Right from the start the conversation was strained. They mentioned the weather, and how quickly it had turned cold. Simanich walked around the car and joined them at the sheriff's window. When talk slowed down, Fastwater asked Anna if she planned to hunt deer this year.

"Probably a few hours on the opener," she replied. "We're pretty busy right now, though. As long as the weather holds, I have to keep at it."

With big, round eyes, Charles studied the uniformed sheriff as he got out of the county cruiser with the rack of colored lights on top. Leonard continued to lean against the hood, arms folded in front of him, seeming out of place in his deputy's uniform and traditional Native American braid. Michael thought Anna appeared nervous. She gripped his arm and pressed up tight against him. Then she gave Simanich a hard stare, looked the sheriff up and down as if suspicious of his motives, and in her straightforward manner asked, "What brings you guys out here today? I'm sure you didn't drive all the way up here to talk about the weather and hunting."

Fastwater smiled at her candor, and then turned to Michael. "Actually, I was hoping to have a word with your friend. That Canadian fellow working with you."

Michael thought the sheriff's stare a little too intense. Obviously, the friendly chatter was over. "We finished up at the Selstads' last night," Michael said. "I paid him cash. He walked off into the woods, and I have a feeling he's on his way home to Canada."

Fastwater stood up straighter and looked past Michael at the neatly laid out plots of dug-up earth. His usual blank expression tightened into a thoughtful grimace. Little Charlie pulled Anna closer to the squad car for a better look. The silence was becoming awkward until Leonard took out his handcuffs to show the youngster. He squatted in front of the boy and held them out for his inspection. The adults looked on, finding an escape from their stalled conversation by watching as Charlie handled the cuffs with great ceremony. A pair of woodpeckers hammered at a tree in a stand of black spruce across the road.

Anna had known Leonard all her life. They'd grown up together, were the same age, and as youngsters had attended the now deserted and closed two-room schoolhouse in Black Otter Bay. Together they'd explored the woods and fields around town, fished for trout and walleye in nearby rivers and lakes. Leonard was quiet by nature, sincere and loyal, and he'd been like a brother to Anna—except for several months during their senior year when she'd attempted to make something more out of their relationship. Leonard hadn't responded to her overtures, however, and avoided all the school-sponsored social gatherings, especially dances. Anna had finally abandoned her romantic efforts when he announced his intention to spend the summer after high school in the Black Hills of South Dakota.

Sheriff Fastwater finally broke the silent ruminations when he said to Michael, "Well, I need to have a talk with that friend of yours. I thought he was staying out here with you."

"He was camping up by the Black Otter headwaters," Michael replied. "I'm not sure just exactly where. But again, for all I know, with our work done, he's probably headed back to Canada by now."

Anna spoke up. "How come you want to talk to Luc?"

Fastwater retrieved a notepad from his shirt pocket, ignored Anna's question by looking at Michael, and asked, "What's his last name?"

"Trembley," Michael said, spelling it for him.

"Do you know where he's from? I mean, whereabouts in Canada he came from?"

Michael looked at Anna, and then shrugged. "I don't think he ever said. I can't imagine that it's very far, though. I mean, he doesn't have a car. As far as I know, he walked here."

"You're saying he walked all the way from Canada?" Simanich asked. "You've got to be kidding."

"Are you going to tell us what's going on, Sheriff?" Anna asked.

Fastwater looked at his nephew unlocking the handcuffs for Charles. "Leonard," he said. "How about you show this little fellow how the squad car works. We need to have a talk with his mom and dad."

"Sure thing," Leonard said, standing up. "Come on, little buddy, let's take a look inside the police car."

"Can I work the lights?" Charles asked excitedly.

"Sure you can. Come on."

Michael led the way up the road, moving at a slow amble that reflected their thoughtful moods and tired bodies. Sheriff Fastwater went over the few facts he had about the latest attack in the woods, and the death of Niki Nielsen. "But I see no reason for you folks to worry," he said.

"So just one of the coeds was attacked last night, right, Sheriff?" Michael asked.

Fastwater stopped and they all looked at each other. "How do you know that?" he asked.

Michael blushed and looked at his feet. "Well, down at the post office, you know, Mrs. Virginia Bean—"

"Mrs. Bean," the sheriff interrupted. "Good for her." He looked at Simanich. "If a person wants information spread around this town, all you have to do is tell Marcy in the café, or Mrs. Bean at the post office. Half a day, that's about all it takes. Half a day and the whole town knows about it."

Fastwater took off his hat and worked his fingers through his hair. Michael studied the smirk on the sheriff's face and realized the leak of information had been intentional. Fastwater wanted the town to know what was going on.

As they resumed walking, the sheriff went on. "If the attack on the real estate agent was random, I'm sure the culprit is long gone by now. But last night—I just don't know. We have a man in Duluth working that end, looking for a disgruntled boyfriend or some other motive. I mean, why else would he pick out just one of the girls?"

"That still doesn't explain why you want to talk to Luc," Anna said. "Do you think he may be involved?"

"Oh, come on, Annie," Michael said. "For goodness' sake, we've had him over for dinner. We shared a meal in our home." He wagged his head in denial. "Nope. There's just no way Luc could be involved in something like this."

"But you invited him for pie last night," she countered. "Remember? You paid him off, invited him over, but he never showed up. Where was he?"

"I told you, Anna, he's so shy I barely got him into town for lunch."

"Well, Michael," Sheriff Fastwater interjected. "That's one of the reasons why I want to talk to him."

Michael stopped and faced the sheriff. "What do you mean?"

"The girl that was attacked was in the café when I talked to you guys. Remember the three backpackers sitting near you?"

Michael did remember. But he shook his head. "No way, Sheriff. If anything, Luc was kind of taken with them, if you know what I mean. I don't think he's used to seeing young women around. There's no way he could do something like that."

The sheriff shrugged and held out his hands. "I'm not accusing him of anything, Michael. It's just a routine step in the investigation. But if you're so sure of this guy, tell me how I can find him."

The woods suddenly resounded with the amplified voice of a laughing youngster. They turned around and looked back at the sheriff's car. "Mommy! Mommy!" they heard, then peals of laughter came at them through the squad car's loudspeaker. The roof lights were flashing, and Charles had the door-mounted spotlight pointed at them. Even in broad daylight the piercing search lamp was hard to look at.

For a moment they stood watching, hands jammed self-consciously in jacket pockets, while Michael emitted a nervous laugh. When Anna started walking back to the car, the sheriff said to Michael, "The other day you told me this Luc fellow was born in France. But you're sure you don't know where he lived in Canada?"

Michael shook his head. "I'm sorry, Sheriff. He never said."

Anna yelled up ahead to her son. "Charles, shut off that spotlight. It hurts my eyes." They could see Leonard reach over to help him. Charles bounced behind the steering wheel, laughing, having the time of his life.

Fastwater studied the gravel at his feet, nudging stones with his boot. Anna returned and started telling him about Luc's visit for dinner, and how convinced she was that someone had been watching her in the woods that day. How Luc startled her at the kitchen window and led them to the wolf print in the woods. The sheriff gave her account his complete attention. She knew he was listening to every word, even when he kicked at stones in the road. When she started describing Luc's discussion of Manitou, the sheriff's head snapped up and the focus of his dark eyes narrowed. "Luc said they can take the shape of any animal," she explained. "Like a wolf or bear."

"I know what Manitou can do," Fastwater said.

"Come on, you guys," Michael interjected. "I can't believe this. Now you're going to start talking about ghosts and spirits again. Snake magic, or whatever Luc called it."

"Snake magic?" Simanich asked.

Michael sighed and mumbled to himself, then stalked off, returning to their work site and the squad car. The sheriff, Simanich, and Anna stood in the middle of the road watching him walk away.

Anna said, "Luc talked about an evil spirit taking the form of a snake." When neither Simanich nor the sheriff responded, she added, "But it wasn't a snake watching me. It was big, and definitely fast and terrifying." Simanich looked at Fastwater, but the sheriff's face revealed nothing. Anna asked, "Does that mean you believe in them? Manitou, I mean?"

The sheriff paused before replying. "In my experience, there are many mysteries in this world. And I have found that some of them are better left alone. What else did he say about Manitou?"

"He only suggested that maybe a roaming spirit had passed by our place. I guess it would account for my fear, the way I knew something was out there even though I couldn't see it."

"Humph," the sheriff grunted. It would account for a few other things, too, he thought. They began a slow saunter back to the squad car.

Simanich said, "Well, apparently this 'spirit' wears hard-soled shoes."

Anna looked at them, confused, so Fastwater explained. "We examined the campsite this morning. There were wolf tracks everywhere, but Leonard found a couple of smooth scuff marks from shoes. The girls didn't leave any tracks because they wore socks around camp."

Anna studied the expressionless face of the sheriff. He seemed lost in his thoughts, stuck in the confusing puzzle confronting him. "You know," she offered, "Luc doesn't wear shoes. Only moccasins."

She noticed a new glimmer in Fastwater's eyes when he looked at her. "Is that right," was all he mumbled, but the significance of his stare was not lost on her. In silence they finished the short walk back to the squad car, where Michael rejoined them.

"Come on now, Sheriff," he said. "With all due respect, these tales about Manitou are just ghost stories. They've got my wife scared half to death."

Fastwater ignored Michael's comment and said, "So, you're sure he isn't a full-blood or Métis."

"I don't think so," Michael said. "But he lived with Indians in Canada."

The sheriff turned away and walked to the edge of the road. With hands buried deep in his pockets, he looked out at the garden plots and the woods beyond. The chill from earlier in the day gripped him again, causing an involuntary shiver, but this time he couldn't pretend to blame it on a wind off Lake Superior.

Michael retrieved his shovel and strode out to where they'd been working. He found all this talk about Manitou and spirits irritating, and he resented the sheriff's obvious suspicions regarding Luc. As he walked, his boots kicked through the overturned garden bed with an angry resolve. He let everyone know how annoyed he was by turning his back on them and thrusting the shovel into the ground with an indignant fury.

Anna took Charlie's hand and helped him out of the squad car, then thanked Leonard for entertaining her son. Gitch jumped out of the car and licked Charles's face, knocking him down while eliciting squeals of laughter from the boy. Soon the two of them were running down the road together, the big dog bouncing around the boy with giant leaps and bounds.

Anna saw Leonard smiling at their antics. She asked, "What do you think about these attacks, Leonard? Does the sheriff know more than he's telling us?"

The deputy smiled and looked down at his clasped hands in front of him. He had huge hands, with long fingers decorated with half a dozen turquoise, onyx, and silver rings. His skin was very dark, a Native American brown, made even darker by all the time he spent outdoors. His nose was long and straight, his lips full. "Uncle Marlon doesn't confide in me, Anna. You should know that. I'm just along for the ride."

Simanich stopped near the squad car's passenger door, and Anna turned to glance over her shoulder at the sheriff. She saw Michael digging with more energy and force than necessary. Fastwater stood nearby, rocking on the balls of his feet, also watching Michael but lost in his own thoughts. Probably something about the case, she figured, maybe even the information she'd given him about Luc's moccasins.

And Anna was right. Fastwater was thinking about moccasins, which could leave marks much like hard-soled shoes in the soft dirt. He also considered Luc's ponytail, long and thick like the tail of a wolf. Luc had seen the victim on the day she was attacked. Also, there was the fact that he was an outsider. The sheriff wondered what had brought the stranger to town. Why on foot and all alone? Was he on the run from something? But really—on foot? Maybe Michael is wrong, he thought. Perhaps the Canadian had arrived by bus. He admitted that all this evidence was circumstantial, but it certainly afforded plenty of reason to justify a visit.

He'd considered and dismissed these ideas quickly, and Anna would've laughed if she knew the sort of thoughts his serious expression pondered now. The sheriff looked at his watch. There was plenty of afternoon daylight left for an excursion up the Black Otter River headwaters. Besides, he knew that area well. He'd hunted and trapped out there many times as a young man. But tending to his duties would mean passing up a potential offer for a piece of fresh berry pie from Anna. And even worse, he'd told Mrs. Bean he'd check in with her later, their private code for dinner together at the post office.

With a deep sigh he looked up at the few remaining colored leaves, and in his mind said farewell to Anna's pie. It would have to wait if he was going to get back to town by dinnertime. Right now, he really needed to talk to that Frenchman.

He looked across the garden at Michael while estimating how much time it would take to find this wildman and get back to town. He didn't like being rushed. If he had to, he'd simply haul him back to headquarters and let him sit until after dinner.

He asked Michael, "You suppose your friend is camping at the base of the ridge on the north end? You know, past the duck marsh and beaver pond? There are some shallow caves out that way, gives plenty of protection from the weather."

"Beats me," Michael replied. "But it seems like a waste of time. Luc wouldn't hurt those girls."

Fastwater's patience had worn thin. "Well, somebody sure did. We've got a woman left in the woods with a shattered skull and another one nearly scared to death while her friends slept nearby." He stepped closer to Michael. "Tell me how all that happens just when your friend comes to town." He glanced over his shoulder at Leonard and Anna laughing at Charles's antics. "Leonard and I are going out there, Michael. But I'm warning you. You see that Frenchman, you get his ass into my office. Understand?"

Michael returned the sheriff's glare. He opened his mouth to respond, to speak out for Luc's innocence, but the fire in Fastwater's eyes backed him down. He knew the sheriff was tough and tenacious, a thorough police officer. There wasn't much that shook him, so why this sudden outburst? The sheriff's frustration surprised Michael, leaving him feeling uneasy and leery of starting an argument with the big man.

Fastwater finally tore his glare away from Michael. "Let's saddle up, Leonard," he called to his nephew. "Phil, we'll drop you at headquarters to get your car." Anna tried to offer them pie and coffee, but the sheriff declined. He had the car door open for Gitch before she could finish asking. Leonard looked at her over the roof of the car, rolled his eyes and shrugged his shoulders, bringing a smile to Anna's face. They said their goodbyes and left Michael and his family standing by the side of the road. Michael put his arm around Anna and laid a hand on his son's head.

This whole thing is just too weird, he thought. It reminded him of the day when Anna was frightened and acting paranoid. That was the same day Luc came for dinner. Now the sheriff was acting strange. All this odd behavior by normally strong, steady people—and it all centered on his friend Luc.

After manhandling the big car back and forth on the narrow road, Fastwater got turned around and accelerated back toward the county highway. Michael shook his head. No leisurely sightseeing drive for the sheriff this time. He thought about the discussion they'd had. There was one other common ingredient in all this fear and anger and confusion.

Manitou.

He turned his attention from the choking eruption of dust following the receding squad car and looked at the silent forest surrounding them.

166

Trees without leaves, stark and nearly naked. Grasses and brush turning brown in the long fall nights. Everything withering and dying. His eyes continued moving across the forest landscape. No color anywhere, just a million gray shades of black and white. Under a low, cloudy sky, everything in a state of death and decay. Could it be that another form of death stalked these woods? Something unnatural and evil that operated outside the laws of this seasonal transformation?

Michael found himself shuddering at the idea. He thought that now he could understand Anna's fear and the sheriff's apprehension. "Come on, you guys," he said. "Break's over." He looked at Anna and forced a smile. "We still have a lot to do . . . before it snows," he finished. He was pleased to see her return his smile, even as she shook her head in denial of his forecast of snow. As she walked over to retrieve her shovel, Michael let his vision linger for one last moment on the woods. For the second time that day he wondered, what the hell is going on out there?

Chapter 11

he *Superior Hiking Trailhead near Big Island Lake, where the* tractor-driving, aluminum-can-collecting Selstad brothers had found the girls' terrorized campsite, was not even a mile past Nels and Ingvald's house on the Moose Lake Road. Six miles farther down the road was a seldom-used footpath that follows the Black Otter River to its source. This stretch of the Moose Lake Road was narrow and shoulderless, hemmed in tightly on both sides by deep drainage ditches and dense walls of cedar and spruce. The gravel road was rough, suffering annually from the ugly blemishes of frost heaves and washouts. Discarded tires, rusted car parts, and in some places whole exhaust systems lined the washboard roadway.

Deputy Sheriff Leonard Fastwater drove the county squad car as fast as he dared along this treacherous, car-eating strip of road. His uncle sat in the passenger seat, reading glasses perched on his nose, struggling to manipulate his cell phone. Thick fingers, small buttons, and the bouncing ride made it a frustrating task. Finally, he got through.

"Jepson? Fastwater here. I need you to run a name for me."

The sheriff flipped through pages of his notebook with one hand. After spelling out Luc's name, the detective interrupted him. "I remember that guy, Sheriff. We met him in the café yesterday."

"That's right. But all we really know about him is he grew up in an Indian community in Canada. Just run the name. See what comes up."

"You think this is our guy?"

"Just a hunch. But he may have left the area already, so get in touch with the RCMP, and make sure the border authorities have his name."

"Got it."

"Look for similar cases up there. Probably not too far; focus within a hundred miles or so of the border. If nothing shows up, expand your search farther out." Fastwater could hear Jepson typing notes into his computer. "Don't bother with big cities," he added. "Keep it rural, especially Indian communities. See what you can find. We'll want a list of names, dates, and offenses." Almost as an afterthought, he added, "Did you get in to see the girl?"

"She's a wreck, Sheriff. Her family is with her around the clock. They won't let me talk to her, but they say she doesn't remember anything anyway."

"Well, just be available. When she wants to talk, you be there." He paused for a moment, thinking, then said, "We're probably going to lose cell service. You need to find that kid, too. What was his name? Benson?"

"Yeah. We're getting close. He was released from the psych ward down in St. Peter over a year ago. Supposed to be in a follow-up program, but they haven't seen him in months now. He was homeless for a while, then they hooked him up with a job in a Duluth lumberyard, but he hasn't been to work in weeks. No one knows where he is, but Captain Simanich hit up some contacts and we'll find him soon enough."

Looking at the passing gray and brown colors of the fall forest as they drove deeper into the wilderness, Fastwater nodded and said, "All right. Good job, Jepson. Stay with it."

"You're breaking up, Sheriff."

"Push the DNA samples and fingerprints from the campsite."

"I can't hear you."

Almost shouting into the phone now, Fastwater said, "I asked about DNA."

No reply. Out of range. Fastwater threw the phone on the dashboard and pointed at a spot up ahead at the side of the road. The path to the Black Otter River headwaters began at a ninety-degree angle to the road, in a rocky, overgrown spot of weeds just large enough to accommodate a single vehicle. Leonard eased the squad car off the gravel and parked at a precarious sideways angle. In the backseat, Gitch paced back and forth in anticipation of a run in the woods. When the sheriff let him out, the dog eagerly sniffed his way up the hillside to the road and the bridge spanning the Black Otter River. Fastwater and Leonard joined the dog on the bridge and stood for a moment looking over the wilderness setting.

"Remember when I brought you out here fishing when you were just a kid?" the sheriff asked.

Leonard smiled and nodded, scrunched his hands deep into his jacket pockets, and looked upstream at the boulder-strewn whitewater racing at them. The sky was overcast, and he felt a clinging dampness in the air. Apparently, the sun hadn't shone over this stretch of forest today, while it had been windy but bright and clear down by Lake Superior. Not a breeze stirred, and Leonard figured up here, where the cold night air still lingered, it was twenty degrees colder than back in town.

Leonard's long black braid hung thick and heavy over his blanket-lined woolen coat. For the trek upstream he'd changed into his well-worn logging boots. Now he gently rocked in place against the cold while looking at the mad dash of water.

At this point, the Black Otter River was less than a third of the width it developed by the time it reached Lake Superior. The wooden bridge, originally built a hundred years ago by long-gone and forgotten homesteaders, spanned the fifteen-foot-wide stream. Repairs and upkeep of the bridge were performed by anyone having the time and inclination to do so. The local snowmobile club regularly used the Moose Lake Road for their winter runs, and they'd put as much work as anyone into maintaining the bridge. Over the years it had been rebuilt several times, one broken or sagging log at a time. The present structure consisted primarily of discarded creosote-soaked railroad ties. However, while sportsmen and townsfolk performed basic repairs to keep the bridge passable, no one had attempted to improve it, and the wooden deck itself was still no more than the original ten feet wide.

Sheriff Fastwater noted that the caution signs on either side of the bridge were still standing, warning drivers that vehicles must not meet on the bridge. Not that there was much chance of that happening, he thought. There were no longer any permanent dwellings beyond the bridge, and the entire landscape for miles around was state forest. The only traffic coming through here now was an occasional grouse hunter or fisherman. He thought it amazing, though, that the bridge could support any sort of traffic at all. He considered the fact of its continued existence to be a credit to the ingenuity and engineering skills of the early settlers.

Fastwater strolled the length of the bridge, stretching leg muscles already tightening up from the earlier hike into the campsite. He casually kicked at the bridge lumber, looking for loosened boards or weakened supports. Many years ago there'd been a two-by-four wooden railing on each side, but floods, ice, and logging trucks had long since removed them. In the summertime, when the sun beat down on the creosote-soaked logs, they emitted an acrid odor of tar and pitch. Bees nested in the rotting boards, and birds raised their broods under the cover of the bridge deck. But everything was still and quiet today. Frost clung to low-lying boards, and sedge grasses along the banks of the river were turning brown and drying up. Fastwater, ever vigilant of the natural progression of the seasons, could see that winter's stranglehold had already begun on the isolated bits of life existing around the bridge.

Fastwater hated this time of year. November depressed him. This was the season when life shut down. Animals hid away in hibernation, lakes froze over, plant life shriveled and died, and the thick canopy of tree leaves fell to the earth to decay. From his standpoint here in October, Fastwater thought the emerging buds of May seemed too far away.

Walking back across the bridge, he saw his dog sniffing his way down the hill to the path that began near the river on the far side of the ditch below the car. Fastwater watched as Gitch paused to inspect several rocks lining the edge of the streambed. The rocks were pieces of bedrock, heavy chunks of granite broken off over time by the slow processes of erosion. Wind, water, and ice had smoothed off their edges and tumbled them into various sizes. Finding one to his liking, a softball-sized, three-pound chunk of solid rock, Gitch carefully fitted his mouth around it and extracted it from its perch in the sand. Hefting the load, he stood still for a moment, as if making sure he'd selected just the right one, then turned and headed off along the path at an easy trot.

"Well, come on, then," Fastwater said to Leonard, striding past his nephew to follow Gitch down the hill. "I never did much like this place," he added. "It's too damn bleak and desolate out here."

Winding over gradually rising terrain, the path was easy to follow for the first couple of hundred yards. A few fishermen hiked this stretch each summer, stopping every now and then to cast dry flies for native rainbow trout, so the first part of the trail remained open and visible. But soon the path climbed over a low ridge of bedrock and the men plotted their course by following the sound of the stream on their left. With most of the foliage down, picking a passage through the forest wasn't difficult, and for twenty minutes they made good time. They hiked silently and efficiently, Fastwater occasionally emitting a short whistle to keep Gitch nearby.

The loose-fitting trousers of his sheriff's uniform suited this sort of walking. His jacket, with the embroidered sheriff's patch on his left shoulder and heavy metal badge pinned to the front, was lightweight yet warm enough for see-your-breath fall weather.

Leonard stopped at a natural opening beside the stream and the sheriff walked over to join him. The melancholy he'd felt back at the bridge had gradually left him. Walking was always a good tonic, he thought, and now he smiled as he watched Gitch splash through the shallow water near shore. Fastwater threw his head back and sucked in the earthy aroma of white cedars lining the riverbanks.

"Remember when we came up here and caught all those brookies on red worms?" Leonard asked.

"Sure, I remember. You couldn't have been more than nine or ten years old."

"Must be at least a hundred times I've been back here on my own," Leonard continued, "but I've never caught fish like we did that day."

"You remember to sneak up to the shoreline so you don't spook them?"

"Yup."

"Tip the barb with a kernel of corn?"

"Yup. Sometimes two."

"Well, the fish are still out there. It's not like they've migrated off somewhere. I bet you've forgotten the secret I showed you."

"And what secret might that be?" Leonard asked.

The sheriff grinned at his nephew. "Don't you remember how I showed you to spit on the worm? Works every time. Fat and sassy brookies can't resist it."

Leonard laughed. "That was just a trick an old man used to make fun of a kid," he said.

Fastwater smiled and looked at Gitch sniffing his way along the water's edge. Apparently, the dog had grown weary of hauling his rock around. "You say you've been out here a hundred times?"

"Sure. Not always fishing. There's good diamond willow back here."

Fastwater nodded, thinking of the furniture his nephew crafted. The last piece he'd seen was an end table with a half-inch-thick slab of beveled glass for the top. Epoxied to the underside were a couple dozen pieces of tumbled, colored beach glass scavenged along the Lake Superior shore. "Come on, Gitch, let's keep moving."

"I've been out here several times lately," Leonard said, falling in behind his uncle.

"And you never saw the Frenchman?"

Leonard shook his head. "My guess is he's probably back up north getting ready for trapping season."

"And maybe he isn't," Fastwater shot back. Why is everyone so eager to defend this guy? he wondered. "Michael Hagen said he was camping out here somewhere."

"He also said there's no way his friend hurt those girls."

"Oh, yeah? Well, what did Anna have to say about it? I saw you two talking back at their place." He was sorry as soon as he said it. He knew Anna and his nephew had been friends since their school days. He thought about the Frenchman again, and with a resonating impatience, blurted, "He matches the physical description the girls gave me. He's young, he's strong, and he knew they were in the area." Turning to leave again, he added, "Besides, I just don't like him."

Leonard guffawed. "Now there's a unique physical description: young and strong. And how do you know you don't like him? You don't even know him."

"I've talked to him. He's belligerent." Suddenly Fastwater stopped and turned to face his nephew. "He's got a look about him I don't like," he explained. "He's wild, like an animal. He's smart. No, he's clever. He's clever in a way that reminds me of a predator. Like a wolf."

"Well, I don't know," Leonard replied. Looking at the forest around them, he said, "I've been all over this area and haven't seen any sign of him."

Fastwater turned to lead the way again. "I wish you'd carry a gun," he said. "You never know what you'll run into out here. And it's not like you don't know how to use one." The sheriff stopped and rested his hand on the holster at his hip. "There's the beaver dam up ahead."

They took a moment to scan the woods around them, and then moved forward along the water's edge. The end of the dam on their side of the stream was entangled in alder thickets. Gitch slid through underneath, but the men had to twist and contort their way before stepping out on the animal-engineered walkway. The exertion left Fastwater a little short of breath, made his heart beat a little harder. For a moment he stood very still, letting the absolute silence restore his composure. He looked out over a long, narrow, shallow backwater spreading out behind the dam. Cattails and decaying wild rice stalks lined most of the shore. At the far end, however, about a quarter of a mile across the slough, the gentle topography changed drastically. The land rose sharply over bedrock outcroppings, climbing ever steeper to the summit of a birch- and aspen-covered ridge.

"I figure he's up there somewhere," the sheriff said, pointing at the jumble of rock and ledges at the far end of the marsh. "There are a few shallow overhangs and caves that would give a fellow some protection from the weather."

Gitch now stood beside the men on the beaver dam, his four paws gingerly planted on the tangled mass of mud and branches. For a moment they looked at the stark, gray view across the marsh, and the calm water of the pond reflecting the dull heaviness of the cloudy sky.

"What do you think, Gitch?" the sheriff asked while stroking the dog's head. "Do you think our man is up there?" In reply, Gitch brushed his head against Fastwater's leg. His tongue flopped out in a panting sigh of contentment.

"How come he's living out here?" Leonard asked. "Not too many young folks these days would choose to live out in the open like that."

"Maybe you would if you had something to hide. Or if you're on the run."

Then the quiet of the surrounding woods was abruptly shattered by the piercing howl of a wolf. It started with a shrieking, high-pitched yap that extended into a drawn-out wail. The sound stabbed through Fastwater like a knife. Startled, he almost lost his balance on the uneven surface of the dam. He reached down and grabbed a fistful of Gitch's fur to steady himself and the dog. The howl echoed off the ridge rocks and resounded down the valley behind them.

Another howl, this time with an insistent sharpness to it. Then a series of answering yelps from lower on the ridge. Fastwater scanned the forested heights. Through the leafless tree cover he saw movement, flashes moving horizontally across the length of the ridge. Gitch tugged away from the sheriff's grasp and stumbled off the dam into the cover of the alder thicket. Then, as quickly as it had begun, the primeval chorus ended, the last eerie vestiges reverberating downstream to be swallowed in the splashing of the rapids.

The men followed Gitch into the thicket and hunkered down out of sight. Fastwater looked at his nephew and was relieved to see the young man's calm expression. Hearing a pack of wolves wasn't that uncommon.

But this particular pack seemed large, and they were much closer and louder than any the sheriff had encountered before.

"What was that all about?" Leonard asked in a hushed voice.

Fastwater didn't answer right away, but shifted his position to find a better view of the ridge a quarter of a mile ahead of them. The woods seemed in a state of shock after the sudden outburst of howling. Not a breeze blew, and the only sound was the tranquil lapping of water over rocks in the stream.

Leonard said, "My guess is the wolves have a deer trapped against the wall of that ridge. Maybe they've even brought him down."

Fastwater shook his head. "You ever heard them set out howling like that at a kill? They'd have every scavenger for miles around coming in to steal the meat."

"Well, what else would set them off like that?"

The sheriff studied the forest another moment, and then said, "It has nothing to do with deer. It sounded like a security alarm to me. Come on."

Fastwater began a hunched-over escape from the alder thicket. When he was clear, he stood up, patted his leg to make Gitch heel, then turned to Leonard. From inside his jacket he removed an old Blackhawk .357 from its shoulder holster. With one hand he popped the cylinder open to make sure it was loaded. Satisfied, he whipped it shut, then handed it butt-first to his nephew. With his other hand he dug in his jacket pocket and retrieved a speed loader of six rounds and shoved that at Leonard, too.

"Take this," he said. It was an order, not to be questioned, and Leonard quickly obeyed. The speed loader cylinder went into his pocket, and the .357 hung comfortably in his hand.

"Those wolves aren't going to bother us," Leonard protested.

"It ain't wolves I'm worried about," Fastwater hissed. "Now listen, we're going up there, and I want you to stick close. Keep an eye out for sign. Tracks, old campfires, garbage, anything that doesn't belong."

"I can get across on the dam if you want. Come around the other side of the marsh and meet you at the ridge."

Fastwater considered. "No. Stay on this side. What we're looking for is right up ahead."

The men moved out, slowly at first, Leonard paralleling Fastwater about twenty feet to the sheriff's left. Gitch seemed to understand that the hunt had begun. He worked back and forth in front of them, his nose inches off the ground.

Fastwater focused on the details around him. Clear black eyes scanned the openings through trees and brush, quickly flicked over the forest floor as he passed, then searched up ahead in the treeline where he'd seen the wolves. His ears reached out for unfamiliar sounds, while his footsteps touched down silently beneath him.

His mind searched, too. It's not often that the woods are this quiet, he thought. No birds, no breeze rattling the naked tree branches. He expected to smell a campfire, but there was nothing. The silence was like an invisible wall, he thought, hiding the secret movements of a fleeing adversary.

He became aware of his pounding heart. It banged hard enough to interfere with his efforts to listen. He concentrated on his breathing, relaxing his involuntary body functions. Something was wrong. He knew it, felt it. Stealing a quick glance at his nephew, he was encouraged to see the young man moving silently, the .357 buried in the huge paw of his right hand. Leonard looked calm, relaxed but alert.

Fastwater approached the beginning of the ridge outcropping while Leonard continued straight ahead into a thirty-yard-wide swath of flat terrain between the marsh and the ridgeline. The sheriff paused to inspect this closest wall of rock and timber. Twenty feet above him on the slope was where he'd seen the wolves running and howling. Must be an animal trail up there, he thought, to allow the wolves to dart so quickly across the face of the ridge.

"Marlon," Leonard called softly. Fastwater spotted his nephew bending over something on the forest floor. One last glance up the hillside, then he worked his way over to Leonard, his eyes and ears never stopping their search.

Leonard squatted over an old campfire. He burrowed his fingers deep into the ashes, then looked up at Fastwater and shook his head. The sheriff bent down and moved a charred hunk of log. "An awful lot of ashes," he said quietly. "More than one fire here." He looked around the open, level area in the woods. "Maybe many fires. Like someone's been camped here for a while." Again his eyes roamed warily over the forest ahead of them. Nothing. "It's too darn quiet," he said, standing up.

"The woods always get quiet after wolves move through," Leonard offered.

"It's not that kind of quiet," Fastwater said, his eyes never leaving the woods up ahead. "It's a stillness. Reminds me of overseas. After a while you get so you can feel the snipers watching you. Then, just about the time you realize something's wrong, the world explodes in muzzle flashes and automatic gunfire." He gave Leonard a hard look, his brow tightening into a frown. "And I'll be damned if I don't feel those eyes on me right now," he muttered earnestly.

They took a few moments to scuff their boots through the damp leaves around the campfire. "Seems like we'd turn up something," Leonard said. "But with all these leaves down there isn't even a track. It's almost as if this campfire could be a hundred years old."

"Come on," Fastwater commanded. "Let's keep moving. I want to check out the overhangs up there by the ridge."

They resumed their slow trek through the narrow band of ground between the marsh and the ridge. Occasionally, Fastwater noticed disturbances on the forest floor, presumably made by the passing wolf pack. At the base of the ridge he found another campfire, but this one, too, was cold. Several leaves had fallen or blown into the ashes, giving it the appearance of having been unused for weeks or months.

Then Gitch emitted a barely audible, low growl. He's picked up the scent of the wolves, Fastwater thought. Following his nose, the dog slunk across the opening toward Leonard. Gitch moved slowly and carefully, his body low to the ground, as if stalking his prey. With a nod to Leonard to watch the dog, the sheriff let him go, let him follow the scent.

Vincent Wyckoff

Fastwater worked his way up and down the lower parts of the ridge. The sheltered overhangs were vacant, and most had accumulations of leaves and forest debris scattered about them. He could see places where animals had bedded down out of the weather, but he detected no sign of human occupation.

Pausing in his search, he looked at his nephew, now twenty yards ahead of him and to his left, about halfway between the ridge and the marsh. Gitch was moving quicker now, the excitement of the hunt showing in his stiff-legged helter-skelter dashes back and forth in front of Leonard.

Fastwater came across a broader, deeper opening in the rock formation. The floor consisted of a fine-grained, dark sand. With little or no exposure to the sun, the rock walls and floor were damp, the gritty sand providing a tamped-down, solid base for the floor. At the outside edge of the opening was another old campfire site. This one was long and narrow, cutting across the opening like a door off its hinges. He could see how the flames would reflect off the surrounding rock walls and warm the inside of the den. Fastwater found several clear wolf prints in the sand.

He turned around at the sound of Gitch barking. It was more of a baying sound, a noise Fastwater had never heard from his dog. Gitch lunged from side to side on the hot scent. Then, with a growling snarl, he suddenly darted ahead, making a run for the brush line bordering the marsh.

Fastwater thought about calling him back; after all, they weren't here to chase a pack of wolves. But he figured they were long gone by now. He watched as Leonard stepped quickly after the dog, following Gitch's thick bush of a tail into the dogwoods near the marsh.

The sheriff turned away from the ridge and studied the surrounding forest. The den was perfectly located, giving an unobstructed view down the streambed for a couple of hundred yards. And, he discovered, with the ridge behind it, there was no easy access from that direction. It would be virtually impossible to approach this spot undetected. If the Frenchman had been camping out here like Michael said, this was where he'd been. Fastwater was sure of it.

He slowly turned in a circle, scrutinizing tree trunks, the leaf-covered ground, and the boulders at the base of the ridge. There had to be something, he thought. Something to show human activity: a soda-pop can, or a mark left by an axe.

Gitch's barking faded away. He glimpsed Leonard disappearing into a thick copse of ground-covering brush. It sounded as if the dog was already at the far end of the marsh, with Leonard pursuing at an ever-increasing distance. Deciding he'd better follow them, Fastwater took one last look at the ash-blackened, cold campfire and the deserted den behind it. Then he saw it. Hanging from a branch on a small balsam tree near the campfire was a short piece of leather. Quickly, he stepped over to it and pulled it off the branch. Then he saw more pieces, narrow strips draped over branches, as well as smaller chunks discarded on the ground.

He worked the six-inch piece of leather in his fingers. It was supple and soft. Deer hide, he thought. Or maybe rabbit. Squatting down to study his find, he realized he was standing in the midst of several footprints between the balsams and the campfire. With an exasperated huff he jumped back. Bending down, he inspected the prints. Lugged soles had left deep indentations in the soft ground. The tread lugs were cut deep, with a distinctive design. He'd seen that style of sole on the heavy boots that loggers traditionally wore. He held his foot over the rounded end of a print and estimated the boot to be about his own size—a size twelve, maybe a little narrower. He made a mental note to call Jepson as soon as they got back in cell phone range. That psycho kid from four years ago had used the same type of ragged, homemade strips of rawhide to make his necklace and a collar for Gitch. He remembered how that incident, just like today, had involved an unseen but obviously present wolf pack. And the kid had recently been working in a lumberyard; Fastwater would love to see what kind of boots he wore now.

In the distance he heard Gitch's frantic, baying barks. Something was going on out there, and to Fastwater it sounded like more than simply chasing a hot wolf scent. He gave one last look around, studied the boot prints again to remember the tread design, then turned and headed off in the direction his companions had taken.

He moved swiftly, sliding over and around the few boulders deposited at the base of the ridge. While stashing several pieces of the leather remnants in his jacket pocket, he scanned the woods ahead to pick up Leonard's trail. Gitch's baying was soon replaced by a staccato of desperate barks. Fastwater could tell he'd caught up to the wolf pack. He'd stopped moving and was either fighting or in a standoff with the wolves. Fastwater heard their vicious snarls and eager yaps. It was a blood-hungry howling of predators.

Then a yelp, like a cry of pain or shock, and once again the woods went silent.

Where the hell is Leonard? he wondered.

A gut-wrenching spasm of fear wormed through him at the thought of his nephew. Chastising himself for letting them split up, he hit the dogwoods near the marsh at a dead run, immediately getting slapped by a faceful of wiry branches. He crashed on, no longer looking for sign, moving as quickly as possible through the whip-like thicket, ducking and dodging while using an arm to protect his face.

Fastwater fought his way out of the dogwoods, raced across an open area of mature forest with little underbrush, and then plunged full speed into an alder thicket with several inches of water underfoot. Catching his toe on a tangle of surface roots, he stumbled, reeling and splashing while grabbing at alder saplings to steady his headlong flight. Regaining his balance, he paused to catch his breath, started to run again, and then stopped. He felt cold water squishing around his feet as it seeped into his boots. In confusion he looked around, unable to see beyond the dense thicket. The only sounds here were his gasping breath and the pounding of his heart in his ears.

He moved forward more slowly, bending branches out of his way, listening. At any moment he expected to hear the sharp report of Leonard's .357.

"Leonard?" he called. No response. He finally emerged from the alders and stepped onto drier ground. He saw a lot of trail sign here. Scuff marks in the leaf-covered ground showed where the animals had passed. More loudly, he called, "Leonard!"

After listening to the silence for a moment, he headed out at a brisk walk, following the tracks on the forest floor. Walking became much easier here away from the lower, wet ground near the marsh. He unsnapped the leather thong over the hammer of his .44 and pulled the big piece out of its holster. No need to check the cylinder; this one was always loaded.

"Leonard!" he called again, moving forward quickly. The tracks entered a thick patch of blue spruce and tamaracks, abruptly shortening his vision to just a few feet. Not so many tracks here; a thick mat of pine needles, moss, and lichens covered the ground. He crept along, hunched over, senses on high alert. He was still out of breath, and his heart continued pounding to the sickening rhythms of fear and worry. His tongue was a sticky mass wallowing in the dried-up cavern of his mouth. He followed the .44 in his outstretched hand as he wound his way through the maze of small conifer trees.

Then he saw him. As Fastwater rounded another thick clump of trees he saw Gitch, sprawled out on his side at the base of a tall bedrock outcropping. The sheriff dropped into a crouch and grasped his handgun with both hands. From beneath the cover of overhanging branches he swung the gun around the small clearing where Gitch lay. All was quiet. Nothing moved, not even his dog.

Advancing in a crouch, Fastwater skirted the opening and approached his companion sprawled beneath the face of the steep cliff. He knelt next to Gitch and put his hand on the big dog's shoulder. A moment later he whirled at the sound of movement on the rocks above. Looking pale and in shock, Leonard leaned over the precipice only to be confronted by the gaping hole of the barrel of Fastwater's .44.

Scrambling down and around the edge of the short cliff, Leonard approached his uncle with weary steps and slumping shoulders. He dropped the .357 and muttered, "He's dead."

"No, he's not," Fastwater replied curtly. He worked his hand up under Gitch's front leg and felt the dog's chest. "There's a heartbeat here. Faint, but he's alive." At the sound of Fastwater's voice, Gitch opened his eyes. "It's okay, boy," the sheriff soothed. "You're going to be all right."

The dog whimpered when he tried to lift his head. Fastwater rolled him just enough to inspect for wounds underneath him. No blood. Gently, he ran his hands along the length of Gitch's body. When he felt behind his shoulder, the dog flinched and groaned with pain.

"Broken ribs," Fastwater said. The dog labored to get a breath. Muttering soothing words to calm him, the sheriff continued his search for wounds and broken bones. A gash running the length of his snout looked ugly but wasn't bleeding. He slid closer to stroke Gitch's head, all the while uttering words of encouragement.

"It's okay, big fella," he said. "Leonard and I are going to get you out of here." For several minutes the sheriff sat quietly with his dog, all thoughts of the Canadian and further pursuit set aside. Gitch's blue eye stared intently at Fastwater's face, and the sheriff was gratified to see the dog's legs and paws twitching, giving him hope that there was no damage to his spine.

Finally, Fastwater looked up at Leonard. "What happened?"

His nephew shook his head. "I don't know. I didn't see anything." Leonard stepped forward to kneel near the dog. "It happened so fast, and I couldn't see a thing in those pine saplings." He paused to look above them. "He caught the wolves up there and they attacked, but I was too late to help. I'm really sorry, Marlon."

"Did you see him? The Canadian?"

"No. When I got here, Gitch was lying on the ground. He didn't move; I figured he was dead. I tracked up ahead a ways, but the wolves are gone." He stood up and sighed, looking at the cliff face and the direction the wolf pack had run. Swinging his gaze back to the sheriff, he added, "I'm just so sorry about Gitch."

"It's not your fault, Leonard, but we have to get him out of here." Fastwater looked around as if help would somehow be lingering nearby. A big Canadian gray jay, emitting his characteristic croaking call, swooped through the clearing and landed above them in a twisted cedar bush hanging precariously from the lip of the cliff.

Fastwater noticed the bird, but when Gitch whimpered he returned his attention to the dog. Leonard asked, "How are we going to get him out of here?"

The sheriff jammed his handgun back in its holster. From his jacket he took the pieces of leather he'd found and stuffed them in his trouser pockets. Taking off his jacket, he said, "Give me that gun."

Leonard retrieved the .357 while Fastwater spread his jacket on the ground next to Gitch. He took the handgun from Leonard and returned it to his shoulder holster, then motioned for Leonard to help lift from the tail side of the dog.

"Okay, old buddy," he said to Gitch. "We're going to move you now." Looking across at Leonard, he said, "We'll lift together and lay him on my jacket. Move slowly; keep him level. I don't think his lungs are punctured, but one bad move could kill him." He paused to stroke the top of Gitch's head. From above he heard the crackling call of the gray jay. Gitch licked his master's hand. Slowly, Fastwater worked his hands under the dog's shoulder while Leonard prepared to lift the hips.

"Here we go now. On the count of three. Remember, slow and level. Ready?"

Leonard nodded while scrunching in tighter to the dog's rear.

"Okay. One, two, three."

They lifted. Gitch whined and tried to kick free, but with little effort the big hands gently set the dog on the jacket.

"Good boy!" Fastwater said, patting Gitch's head. Again he sat with the dog, calming him with soothing words.

"Marlon . . ." Leonard began.

"Forget it, Leonard. It's my fault. We never should have split up." After a pause, he added, "Just help me get him out of here alive. We're going to use my jacket as a litter." He looked around, as if taking a mental picture of where they sat. "There's still plenty of daylight left, so we'll take it slow, get him some water to drink down by the river."

Way off to the north a wolf howled. It sounded innocent and lonesome so far away. Above them, the jay squawked.

"Come on, let's do it," Fastwater said, standing up and grabbing two handholds on the jacket. They hoisted their load, and the sheriff was pleased to see that Gitch seemed content to lay still. Fastwater looked at Leonard, who nodded to indicate he was ready, and they started across the clearing into the jumble of spruce and tamarack trees. As they entered the twisting passageways through the conifers, the gray jay dropped from his perch in the scrub cedar and sailed north. His screeching cackle could be heard for a great distance, but the men, trudging south toward the river with their ninety-pound burden, paid him no mind.

Part II

Chapter 12

Sheriff *Marlon Fastwater awoke to a wet, slobbery tongue splashing* across his face. Squinting his eyes open, he reached out, grabbed Gitch by the neck, and playfully yanked him back and forth. The dog let out a yip, loud in the early morning quiet, deafening just six inches from the sheriff's face. Fastwater laughed. Still holding Gitch's neck, he looked into the strange contradiction of blue and brown eyes. "What is it, buddy? You have to go out?" The gash on the dog's nose had healed over nicely, but it would always be visible, a jagged white line running the length of his snout.

The sheriff rolled over in his sleeping bag to look out the window of his office. Another Monday morning, two weeks since Niki's murder. The sun was up, a large red ball glowing just above the horizon of Lake Superior. Far out on the lake a misty fog lingered, but the sky was a brilliant blue, and the water was an even darker, richer shade of midnight blue.

Gitch yipped again, and Fastwater said, "Okay, okay, I'm coming. Just hold on, will you?"

The sheriff kicked off his sleeping bag, almost tipping over the old army cot in the process. In his underwear, barefoot, he walked over to the door to let Gitch out. For a minute he stood there, rubbing sleep out of his eyes while watching the dog. Ten days after cracking ribs in a fight with wolves out at the Black Otter River headwaters, Gitch's recovery was almost complete. Most of his former speed and enthusiasm had returned, and about the only change Fastwater noticed was that his dog now walked with his hind legs canted slightly to one side, like a car with a bent frame angling down the road.

The sheriff watched as Gitch sniffed a couple of the rocks he'd carried back from various hikes, then slowly worked his way around the edges of the parking area, finally stopping to look down the hill at the rooftops of buildings in town. Under the veterinarian's supervision, the sheriff had kept a tight wrap around Gitch's torso for the first week to support the ribcage while the bones mended. Fastwater admitted that the ordeal had probably been as tough on him as the dog. Not usually one for sitting around, Gitch had lain on his special braided rug for days on end, either sleeping or watching the sheriff work around his office. Now he casually turned to look back at Fastwater. Satisfied that the sheriff was watching, the dog sauntered over to the squad car, sniffed one of the rear tires, then lifted his leg and let loose a stream that sent up puffs of steam in the cold air.

Fastwater couldn't stifle a laugh. "Okay, wise guy, now you can just stay out there until I'm ready to let you in."

He slammed the door, but snuck another peek out the window. He was grateful that Gitch was feeling his old self again. Apparently the dog wasn't too upset about being banished to the cold morning air. He happily trotted off, continuing his inspection of the parking lot, conscientiously marking his territory on various bushes and rocks. Fastwater shook his head and turned away.

The mess in his office surprised him. Stopping at his desk, he shoved the clutter around until he found his glasses. Mrs. Virginia Bean had been spending more time here, too, fussing over Gitch but attending to the sheriff as well. She brought food and games, and when Fastwater hauled in his television, they spread a blanket on the floor next to Gitch and watched old movies together. They never mentioned the extra hours they spent together, but Mrs. Bean's company had meant a lot to him. And as the days passed, the sheriff noticed when she added colorful dangling earrings to accent her floral-print dresses. He'd picked up on her subtle perfume when they sat together next to Gitch. And then just last night she'd leaned into him and they'd kissed. He stepped back at the sudden memory.

After the kiss, and maybe a second or third one, they'd toasted each other with a glass of wine. With a smile threatening to blush his face, he looked at the desk again, at the glasses and half-empty bottle of wine. He almost laughed when he thought how awkward it would have been if she'd spent the night on his narrow army cot. At their age!

Afterward, Gitch accompanied them as the sheriff walked her home, the two holding hands like shy high school sweethearts. It had all felt just right, although he had to admit he was glad no one was out that late to see them. Later, sprawled out in his sleeping bag on the cot, rest hadn't come easily. His thoughts went back to the postmistress. They'd played several games of cribbage last night, her rambling dialogue a distraction. Of course, he couldn't very well blame his losses on her nonstop chatter.

"I think it's just terrible about that Aasen boy," she'd said at one point in the evening. "You know the youngest son, Roger? Angie was in the post office the other day and told me he was the one who painted graffiti all over Hank's boat. Now, why would anyone want to hurt a dear old man like Henry?"

Before she could ramble on, Fastwater said, "Roger will be just fine, Mrs. Bean." He studied his cards for a moment until he realized she wasn't going to let it go that easily. She opened her mouth to speak again, but Fastwater cut her off. "First thing next spring," he said, "before Henry takes his boat out of dry-dock, Roger is going to help him repaint the whole thing. Including scraping and sanding the hull." He looked at Mrs. Bean across the desk from him. "Roger is going to heating and air conditioning school next year. He'll be just fine."

She'd smiled at him then, a smile of fondness and adoration. Despite the endless prattle, Fastwater liked it when she looked at him that way. He couldn't imagine a more faithful or loyal friend than Mrs. Virginia Bean.

Being with her was like spending time with an old best friend, but he had to admit that last night threw a whole new dimension into their relationship. Maybe it was odd, he thought now, that they weren't an actual couple, married and living together in her old clapboard house, tending her sparse and dreary little garden.

Fastwater rubbed his face and wormed his fingers through his hair. Gitch startled him when he stood up at the window and barked to come in. Ignoring the dog, the sheriff straightened small stacks of paper on his desk and finished brushing crumbs onto the floor. At the edge of the desk he found Mrs. Bean's nearly empty crockpot. It was still plugged in, turned down low. He lifted the lid and with two fingers plucked out a tiny meatball in barbeque sauce. Popping it in his mouth, he savored the tangy flavor while making faces at Gitch in the window. The dog watched him intently, all signs of his earlier impudence gone. They'd discovered late one night last summer that Gitch loved Mrs. Bean's meatballs. The sheriff snorted and went to the door.

"Get in here, smart-ass," he said, grinning as Gitch trotted in the door. The sheriff grabbed the broom and began sweeping up crumbs from the concrete floor. When he got around to the crockpot, he snatched another meatball and flipped it to Gitch. With a laugh, he said, "You really like those meatballs, don't you, old buddy?"

He paused to pet Gitch on the head, then looked at the garbage can containing the remains of last night. He'd had a good time. A flutter in his chest suggested that perhaps the quiet, domestic evening with an old friend had taken a sudden turn. Mrs. Bean. Now that Gitch was better, he'd promised to stop by the post office later for lunch. Maybe they'd have dinner together, too. He shook his head to clear the persistent thoughts of her from his mind.

"Let's finish these meatballs so I can clean out Mrs. Bean's crockpot," Fastwater said, dropping another dripping wad of meat into Gitch's mouth. The sheriff wiped his fingers on his boxer shorts, reached for the broom, and jumped at the sound of the cell phone vibrating across the desk. Before he could think of who'd be calling him so early, he grabbed the phone just to stop the annoying buzz.

"Hello? Sheriff's office," he said, suddenly realizing how ridiculous he looked standing in his underwear. Wedging the phone between his shoulder and ear, he stubbed his toe on a leg of the desk while reaching for his chair. With a grunt his big body fell sideways into a sitting position, and he silently winced at the pain in his big toe.

"Marlon? What are you doing?"

"I just sat down at my desk." Fastwater scanned the mess in front of him, shoving paper plates and the cribbage board aside, looking for his shirt and trousers. He finally spotted them on the floor next to the cot.

"You're at the office pretty early, aren't you?"

Not wanting to struggle with getting up again, the sheriff scooted his chair toward the cot and reached out with his toes to snag the shirt. "I've been sort of camping out here with Gitch. You know, so he wouldn't have to stay home all alone." He shoved an arm into one sleeve, but then stopped. Something must have happened; there was no other reason for Phil Simanich to call so early. He slid the chair back and shoved aside the clutter on the desk. Other than threats from the Feds to swoop in and take over the case, nothing new had come to light in the last week and a half. "What is it, Phil? Did Jepson finally run down our Halloween vagrant?"

"No. But he's getting close. You've been hounding the poor guy every day since Gitch got hurt, so he came to me for help. Turns out the kid was locked up off and on for almost three years in St. Peter. Some sort of schizophrenia. He has medications to help, but a long history of not taking them. We hit a lot of dead ends trying to track him down: a job here, an apartment there. Nothing lasting more than a month or two. Jepson thinks he's about two weeks behind him, so if he hasn't left the area we'll find him any day now."

Fastwater nodded understanding at the phone. So why the early phone call? And what about the Frenchman? "Anything from the Canadian authorities?" he asked. "What about the border patrol?"

There was a pause, and Fastwater used the break to slip another arm in the shirt.

"We had a visitor down here last night, Marlon."

The sheriff didn't understand, and shook his head at the phone. "What do you mean? What visitor?"

"It seems Mr. Luc Trembley walked out of the woods into the latest victim's backyard last night and sat on her back stoop to chat until well after dark."

Fastwater lunged to his feet, the chair rolling back across the room. "He did what?"

"Yup. The young lady was sitting on the back steps after letting her little dog out to pee. The dog trotted off into the woods and wouldn't come back when she called, so she got up and started to walk across the yard when Luc suddenly emerged carrying the dog. And get this: her dog is a rescue animal and very antisocial. He especially dislikes men. But he was a whimpering ball of fur in Luc's arms."

"You're kidding. What the . . . ? What did he do?"

"That's just it. He didn't do anything. He was very polite and cordial. Eileen's parents even came out after a while and they all sat and talked."

"This is the same guy Jepson and I met in the café? How did he find her?"

"Well, we don't know. He never said exactly. But he told the girl he'd heard the screaming and gunshots out at the campsite. Now get this: he explained that he sort of travels with an adopted pack of wolves. The night of the attack, they all ran off together to investigate the racket. The wolves found the campsite first, but by the time he got there the girls were gone. He heard the Selstads' tractor and followed them back to the farmhouse. The girls were obviously shook up, but when he heard that you'd been called he decided to leave."

"And the parents heard this story? And they believed him?"

"They believed him, Marlon. I interviewed them earlier this morning. They had tears in their eyes. They only called because they know it's still an open investigation."

"So he hears that the sheriff has been called and he runs away. Doesn't that sound a little suspicious?"

"If you want to look at it that way. The parents claim he's unaware of being a suspect. And they thanked him for trying to help their daughter."

"Did he tell them where's he going?"

"Nope. He just walked off into the forest the way he'd come."

Fastwater retrieved his chair and sat down, piling the wad of trousers in his lap. "It still doesn't explain how he found the girl in Duluth."

"It doesn't explain a lot of things. But the girl talked to me. It seems Mr. Trembley eased her mind. And the whole time he sat holding and petting her paranoid dog."

A flicker of anxiety wormed into the sheriff's guts. "What do you mean 'he eased her mind'? What does that mean?"

"They talked for a long time. Like I said, the parents came out and they all sat around. He told them about being deserted as a child, first by his mother, and then his father. He explained how he'd turned inward and become self-sufficient to protect himself from hurt. At some point the girl started talking. She went over the whole night of the attack. She remembered everything. The way she explained it to me was that he seemed to draw it out of her, like sucking poison out of a victim. Afterward, she told me she felt calm but worn out, like you sometimes feel after a fever breaks."

"And they have no idea where he went?"

"Nope. He set the little dog on the steps, gave a little bow to the girl and her mother, and walked off into the woods."

"But—"

"Believe me, Marlon, when I heard all this I got all hands on deck. We've scoured the countryside, but he's gone."

The knot in Fastwater's stomach cinched tighter. "I don't understand how he just showed up like that."

"He told them he didn't socialize much, that he'd never learned how. But living inside his own head all the time taught him how to observe. He's always watching. Oh, and get this, while he's sitting out there talking, all of a sudden they hear wolves howling up in the hills behind town. They've never heard wolves so close to a big city before. And this was a whole pack of them. Soon after that he was gone. He wished the young victim well and then disappeared into the woods. Almost like a mirage."

"Or Manitou."

"What?"

"Nothing. Just thinking out loud." Fastwater looked at Gitch on his rug over by the door. He shivered and reached down to button his shirt.

Simanich said, "What do you make of this wolf thing? Can they really adopt someone like he said?"

Fastwater shook his head. "Not that I'm aware of." But he was thinking of other things, like shapeshifters and Manitou and the evil snake magic.

"Marlon? You still there?"

"Yeah," Fastwater replied, standing up while his trousers fell to the floor. "Listen, Phil, we have to get word to the border agents. He's probably going to try heading home again. And I'm not so sure he's walking. He may be hitchhiking, or riding a bus across the border."

"Marlon—"

"What about dogs? Can't you track him? It's only been a few hours; he couldn't have gone very far."

"He might be a person of interest to you, Marlon, but he's not a suspect. He has his rights. We can't just go running him down like that. Besides, from what the parents say, he doesn't even know you're looking for him."

"But he was at the campsite. And after finding all the wolf tracks up the Black Otter River, I bet he was at the scene of the murder, too."

"If he'd intended to hurt the girl, he could have done it last night."

"I know, I know. But he was out there. And so were the wolves." Fastwater rubbed a hand over his face. "And that reminds me. The fur Leonard recovered at the campsite was real, from a wolf. But it was several years old. How does that play into all this?"

"Maybe it was just there, you know, randomly, like Detective Jepson suggested."

"I told you I don't believe in coincidences." Fastwater's thoughts raced back to the conversation in the café when Luc brought up his Dakota ancestry. Was he supposed to believe the Frenchman figured that out just by observation? He shook his head. There were simply too many strange facts piling up.

Simanich said, "Well, we're putting everything we have into it on this end. What are you going to do?"

The sheriff looked down at his toes sticking out from under the pile of trousers. He felt a headache coming on. Maybe a cup of coffee would divert it from becoming a migraine. "Right now I'm going to head down to the café for coffee. But I may put a couple people out on the Superior Hiking Trail in case he comes this way. And we have a big Halloween dance coming up next weekend." He paused for a moment before adding, "Keep after your detective. I really need to talk to that missing kid."

"You just told me you don't believe in coincidences, Marlon. But now you're asking us to track down a missing person you last saw four years ago . . . and at Halloween. Talk about your long-shot coincidences."

"I know, I know, but—"

"Listen up, Marlon. Nothing is breaking our way down here. You may think differently, but I have my doubts about that Canadian as a suspect. You need to start shaking some trees up there and see what falls out."

Fastwater nodded. "Yeah, okay." But his mind had wandered elsewhere, bouncing from coincidences to evidence to timelines. Maybe the Frenchman wasn't their guy, but if he were, it sure would answer a lot of questions. But with all the factors they had to work with, he knew there was one big piece missing. It was right there in front of him; he could feel it, he just couldn't quite see it. "I'll call you later, Phil. And let me know as soon as your detective finds that kid."

He threw the phone on the desk and grabbed his trousers. Full daylight had broken over the horizon, but a light frost still clung to bushes and trees. Not a killer freeze yet, but getting close. He'd bet that up over the ridge, however, the gardens out at Anna's place were done for the year.

"Come on, Gitch," he called. "I need some coffee. Let's go for a walk."

• • • •

Once outside, with his breath billowing and dissipating around him, the sheriff snugged his SOO cap down tight over his ears. It was downright cold this morning, although Gitch seemed to revel in it. After ten days cooped up inside, he was ready to move, and the brisk morning air only added to his perky enthusiasm. Fastwater watched the dog hurrying down the hillside, grinning at his newly acquired crooked amble. But mostly he looked at the lake and the steady stream of whitecaps rolling past. He was sure that just fifteen minutes earlier the sky over the eastern horizon had been pale blue, with frigid dark waters rolling beneath. Now bands of color, from purple to turquoise, played across the lake, highlighted by the regular swells of froth-capped waves racing by.

It wasn't until he reached the bottom of the hill that he glanced at the café. A white van sat outside, a telescoping antenna on the roof, and "4 NEWS" painted large on the door panels. The sheriff's headache thudded, expanding from one eyebrow to both.

Speaking to Gitch, or just muttering out loud, he said, "What are they doing here?" He paused at the door, looked back at the van, and then noticed Gitch watching him in expectation. He had to admit that having only the sheriff for company over the last ten days couldn't have been much fun for the dog, either, so when he said, "Come on, buddy, let's see what's going on," he laughed to watch Gitch lunge for the door.

The café was usually quiet this early in the morning, the loudest sounds generated by coffee cups clunking on tabletops or silverware rattling against plates. But a clamoring din of voices met his arrival this morning. In the back of the dining area he saw the news crew setting up cameras and running extension cords for lights and microphones. The sheriff spotted

Abby Simon and her younger brother, Ben, in a booth near the windows. When not spying on the camera crew, they were cutting out Halloween decorations for the upcoming party and dance. Black cats and witches were taped to the windows, and they had an array of various-sized pumpkins lined up on the table.

Several voices suddenly called out greetings to Gitch. Fastwater stood aside as the big malamute made a pass along the counter to receive well wishes and friendly pets from the regulars. "Abby!" Marcy called. "Abby, look who's here." Marcy set the coffeepot down and scrambled around the counter to kneel in front of Gitch. She grabbed him by the neck and rubbed noses. "You know you're not supposed to be in here," she cooed. And then Abby and Ben joined her and soon everyone was fussing over the dog. Abby gently touched the scar along Gitch's snout and gave him a hug. Everyone had heard about his injuries, and the sheriff grinned to see how much Gitch meant to the townsfolk.

Abby looked up as the sheriff stepped closer. "I saw you walking through town last week and didn't recognize you without Gitch. I'm so happy he's feeling better."

"Thank you, Abby. I think he's nearly good as new." Over the past few months Fastwater and Abby had developed a special bond, ever since last summer when her brother had been kidnapped and the sheriff struggled to coax information out of her. He understood and respected her family allegiance and dependability. They related to each other from a place rooted in community and small-town loyalty. So he appreciated her candor regarding Gitch and returned her smile, nodding at the booth covered in construction paper, scissors, glue, and tape. "Looks like you have quite a project going on over there," he commented.

"Oh, believe me, we've only just got started," she said.

Ben looked up at the big lawman and added, "We're going to make jack-o'-lanterns after school today. And Marcy and Dad are going to help us make giant spiderwebs." The sheriff smiled and started to say something when he felt a familiar presence beside him. Turning, he saw Mrs. Virginia

Bean giving him a quick once-over. "You still sleeping at the office?" she asked. Startled, he looked down, saw nothing out of place, but smoothed a hand over his shirt anyway. "You look fine, Marlon," she added with a chuckle, standing in close to him. He felt her arm around his waist and settled in against it.

When Marcy stood up to return to work, the sheriff looked over at the camera crew and asked, "What are they doing here?"

Marcy glanced over her shoulder at the news journalist standing by a bank of windows overlooking the highway and Lake Superior beyond. From across the room they heard her say, "No, we can't have the windows behind me. I know it makes a better backdrop, but then my face will be in the shadows." Somebody answered her, and she replied, "I don't care about the lights. I don't want the windows behind me."

Marcy said, "They're here to do a story about our Halloween dance and party. You know, something about our recent troubles and Niki's death, how we persevere or something, I think she said."

Marcy marched off to work and Red Tollefson called out to Fastwater. "Hey, Sheriff. Owen here has some ideas for your investigation. You should listen to what he has to say."

Fastwater looked down the counter at Owen Porter, but the tall young man had his back to him as he watched the television journalist at work. The sheriff's gaze pivoted to the object of Owen's stare. Christine Anderson was a popular news reporter. Even out of the studio and without makeup, her upper Midwestern good looks were apparent. She wore her straight blond hair cut short at the shoulders, and her thick blond eyebrows indicated that her hair color was real. Her skin was clear and soft with a slight rosy-pink glow in her cheeks. Dark eyes studied the screen on her smartphone, their scrutiny revealing a keen intelligence at work.

"Owen," Red snapped, knuckles rapping the counter in front of him. "Owen, tell the sheriff some of the stuff you've been reading."

Mrs. Bean rubbed Fastwater's arm with affection and said, "It really is kind of interesting, Marlon."

Owen Porter finally swiveled on his stool and looked at the sheriff. His usual shyness returned, and he fumbled with the coffee cup in front of him. Fastwater, with Mrs. Bean in tow, took a couple steps toward the counter. Owen waved a hand of dismissal and muttered, "It's just some stuff I've been reading." He looked at Marcy as if asking for help.

"Tell him about these split personalities," she said.

"You mean schizophrenia?" Fastwater interjected, remembering his conversation with Simanich.

"Exactly," Owen responded, showing interest for the first time.

Red said, "But tell him why you were reading about it." The retired highway foreman looked from Owen to the sheriff with an expression that said, "Wait until you hear this."

Owen suddenly went shy again. He turned away to look at the news reporter. Marcy said, "He thinks someone from around here attacked those girls and killed Niki."

Owen immediately swung back and said, "I never said that, Marcy. Don't go saying what I said when you don't know what I said." Everyone paused to think about that, until Owen continued, "It just seems to me that whoever did this must have known those girls were camping out there, and also that most mornings Niki ran the trails behind town. With two incidents occurring so close together I don't think they're random, or crimes of opportunity. Someone planned them."

This got the sheriff's attention. It poked at the jumbled pieces of evidence rattling around in his head, and aligned with his mistrust of coincidences. "Okay," he offered quietly. "Go on."

"Well, to have knowledge of the victim's presence would seem to indicate a local, but that's not my point." He looked at Marcy, but then realized everyone at the counter was studying him. He took a sudden interest in his hands in his lap, so when he spoke again everyone had to lean in to hear. "If it is someone from around here, they're doing an incredible job of hiding their guilt. I haven't seen anyone acting any stranger than usual."

Red said, "Why are you looking at me? Who are you calling strange?"

Marcy snapped her dishrag at him and said, "Be quiet, Red. Let him talk."

Owen shrugged. "Well, I did some reading on sociopathic behavior." He looked at Fastwater. "Anyway, sir, many of these guys have no idea that they've committed a crime. Most of the time they're just like you or me, living normal lives and doing normal stuff. But they have this other personality, like a person they don't even know, living inside them. For some reason this other personality is triggered to act out. Then afterward, the normal person experiences something like a time warp. They can't account for whatever time was lost to the other personality. Sort of like an alcoholic having a blackout. They have no memory of what they did until the next day when someone tells them about it."

Red burst out laughing and slapped Owen on the shoulder. "That reminds me, remember the time old—"

Now Mrs. Bean, Marcy, and Abby all yelled at him in unison to be quiet. Red sat back on his stool looking like a chastised puppy. Fastwater thought about missing pieces and coincidences and how schizophrenia had manifested itself in that young man four years ago on Halloween. But the idea of Owen Porter being the one to reveal all this was the biggest mystery of all. "Where did you say you heard this?" he asked.

"Like I said, I did some reading. Google 'sociopath' and it will take you down a rabbit hole."

"A rabbit hole?"

Mrs. Bean said, "He just means there's a lot of information to read about." Fastwater looked at her and she patted his arm again. "I can show you later if you want."

Then Owen said, "Some of these sociopaths have multiple personalities."

The sheriff reached for the counter and the cup of coffee Abby poured. The girl asked, "What causes these other personalities to act out?"

Owen looked from Abby to Marcy, and said, "Could I get that corned beef hash?"

"Sure," Marcy answered, but made no move to place the order. Instead, she rested both forearms on the counter and studied the angular, awkward young man.

Owen squirmed for a moment and looked at everyone watching him. "I don't know," he blurted. "I guess it's different in each instance. I recently read some case histories, though. Actually, it's kind of interesting," he added, finally warming up to being the center of attention. "There was this one guy who was kind of odd, very timid and quiet."

"So, are we talking about you now?" Red asked.

Marcy slapped a palm against the countertop. "Shut up, Red!"

Owen rearranged his long legs and scrawny rear end on the stool. "Anyway," he continued, "this guy was in therapy. He always acted very shy and polite. Then one day, in the middle of a group session he stood up and began yelling like a crazy teenager. His voice even cracked when he talked. He called the psychiatrist every name in the book. Cussed up one side of the room and down the other. Then, just as suddenly, he stopped. He looked around until he spotted his customary chair and quietly walked back and sat down. He had no recollection of what he'd said or done, and no idea why he was suddenly standing in the middle of the room."

"Wow," Marcy muttered. "That's so bizarre. Could they do anything to help him?"

"It takes a while, but sometimes they make a little progress. It sounds kind of weird to me, but the dominant personality can actually become aware of and get to know the stranger inside. They might not be able to get rid of him, but they can know when he's acting out."

Fastwater asked, "If they know about this other personality, why don't they just ignore it?"

"Well, sir, it's not that easy," Owen explained. "It's not so much ignoring it as just trying to prevent anything bad from happening. Like this one man who was suicidal. He lived in a big city and walked his dog every day. He knew he had this other personality trying to get him to kill himself. So one day he's walking his dog and they pass a subway entrance. A train is coming, and suddenly a voice in his head is telling him to walk out on the tracks. He goes down the stairs and buys a subway token. Somehow, he knows he's doing the wrong thing and tries to fight it. Finally, at the edge of the tracks he makes a personal breakthrough. He ties the dog's leash to a bike rack and calls his therapist. The doctor immediately dials 9-1-1 and sends the police out to retrieve him."

"Oh, that's wonderful," Mrs. Bean said, lightly clapping her hands.

"So the guy was okay?" Marcy asked. "He learned how to deal with this other personality?"

"Well, not exactly," Owen Porter replied, looking down at the counter again. "The police got there within minutes, but all they found was the dog leashed to the bike rack."

"Oh no," Marcy said, stepping back.

Mrs. Bean knelt down to give Gitch a big hug.

"So what's that got to do with us?" Fastwater asked, a note of disdain in his voice.

"Probably nothing. You guys wanted to know about split personalities, that's all."

"Are you saying someone from around here blacks out and attacks women and then doesn't remember it?"

Marcy wrote out a ticket for Owen's order and clipped it to the kitchen window. To Abby, she said, "Take the coffeepot around and make sure everyone has what they need." When her young helper was gone, she looked at the sheriff. "I can't believe anyone from around here would kill Niki. Everyone liked her."

Owen Porter shook his head. "I never said it had to be someone from around here. I was just explaining how a mind can block out memories. What I would say is that the person had to know about the girls camping out at Big Island Lake, and have an idea about Niki's running schedule."

Christine Anderson silently appeared behind Owen. "That was a horrifying tragedy, wasn't it?" she said, placing a well-manicured hand on Owen's shoulder. "Did you know the unfortunate victim?"

Owen Porter melted under her touch, curling into himself as if trying to disappear on the stool. Sheriff Fastwater knew the young man wasn't going to be able to respond, so he maneuvered behind Red to stand next to Owen. Totally ignoring the reporter, he asked, "This person living in someone's head, is it always the same character? Could it be an animal, like, say, a wolf?"

Owen wasn't ready to look up yet, but the sheriff's thoughts kept rolling. "Since these personalities are imaginary anyway, could they come from the paranormal, like a spirit or ghost or something?"

At this point it was apparent that the newswoman's close proximity would continue to render Owen mute, so the sheriff sighed, finally looked her in the eye, and said, "I'm Sheriff Marlon Fastwater, and you are?"

She took her fingers off Owen's shoulder to shake the sheriff's hand. "Christine Anderson," she said. "Channel 4 News."

"And what brings you to Black Otter Bay?"

"They're doing a story about Halloween," Red Tollefson said.

"Well, yes," the reporter responded. "Your big Halloween party, and, of course, the recent tragic events in town."

"Does that really warrant a news team driving all the way up here?"

"I think it does, Sheriff. It's a human-interest story of loss and resiliency." Now she put both hands on Red's shoulders, and while looking along the line of patrons at the counter, she sculpted a broad, warm smile on her lips. "I heard some of your conversation about schizophrenia. Do you think there's a sociopath running loose around town?"

Fastwater took a closer look at the reporter and the shrewd intelligence whirring behind those sparkling dark eyes. He sipped his coffee and shrugged. "I'd have to say the notion has merit. It would answer some things." He stretched an arm out to place the coffee cup on the counter.

"You mentioned a ghost. Do you suspect a ghost attacked that girl out at their campsite?"

Red burst out laughing, but when Fastwater looked back he saw the phone held out in the reporter's hand, obviously set to record.

"What's that?" he asked. "What are you doing?"

"Just making sure I get the interview right."

"Interview?" Fastwater turned to face her. "This isn't an interview."

"Well, of course not, Sheriff. Not like a real question-and-answer session. I'm just collecting bits and pieces for a story."

"You're not using any bits and pieces from me. Shut that thing off."

"Some folks wonder why it's been two weeks and you haven't arrested anyone yet."

Fastwater's scowled darkened. "Which folks are wondering?" he growled.

Christine's smile was a taunt as she scanned the regulars at the counter. "Why, I think everyone would like to know."

Fastwater rocked on his feet, searching for words. Mrs. Bean hooked an arm through his and pulled him back. "Marlon, it's okay. She's just doing her job."

Christine directed her voice at the phone in her hand. "So, exactly what is going on with the investigation, Sheriff? Do you have any suspects? Are you close to making an arrest?"

Fastwater made a grab for the phone but missed. "This isn't an interview," he hissed. "I never agreed to speak on record."

"It's just background information," she said, calmly stepping back. Owen and Red sat up, and even Gitch seemed agitated by the sudden tension in the room.

Fastwater pulled away from the postmistress and said, "Come on, Gitch. Time to get back to work." He squared himself up to the reporter. "There's no story here, Ms. Anderson."

"It sounds like quite a story to me, Sheriff. I mean, wolves and ghosts. It all fits with Halloween, doesn't it?"

Mrs. Bean grabbed his arm again and forcefully turned the sheriff toward the door. "Let's go, Marlon. We both have jobs to do."

"We'll be making an arrest any day now," Fastwater said as he walked away. "Come back then and we'll have a story for you."

A smirk rippled the edges of Christine Anderson's mouth as she slipped the phone into a sweater pocket. "Why, thank you, Sheriff. Thanks for the invitation."

When he looked back at her she grinned, a broad, open smile, as if they were now best friends. And as the door closed behind him, he heard her parting words: "We'll be back for the party next Saturday, and I'll look forward to speaking with you then."

Chapter 13

rs. *Virginia Bean held the sheriff's arm the entire time on* the walk to the post office. Gitch stuck close to the sheriff's side, seeming a little out of sorts, but they didn't know why for sure. It could have been due to a lingering stiffness from his injuries, or maybe he missed having his customary rock to carry. Mrs. Bean decided it was because he sensed the sheriff's wrath, which clung to them like an irritating, itchy burr.

"It'll be okay, Marlon," she said when they left her at the post office door. "You know how it is with those big city folks; they always have to be pushing and prodding. My advice is to not even think about her anymore."

He tried to give her a smile, even waved an arm as if brushing it all aside, but the intensity in his cold black eyes betrayed him. As the man and his dog continued their walk around town after dropping off the postmistress, Mrs. Bean would have been relieved to know the sheriff wasn't thinking about Christine Anderson at all. Instead, it was the discussion with Owen Porter that so unsettled him.

They crossed the highway and walked through the gravel parking lot of the municipal liquor store and bar. Protruding from the corner of the building was the butt end of a straw broom, as if a Halloween witch had flown into the wall. Her pointed black hat hung from the stick. Fastwater wondered if patrons understood the irony of a crashed broomstick in the parking lot of a bar.

With the roadway behind them, he could finally hear the surf on the rocks along the shore less than a hundred yards away. He paused for a moment to breathe deeply of the frosty fresh air. He ambled past the eighteen-foot open fishing boat on display in front of the bar. The same storm that sunk the Edmund Fitzgerald had hurled this heavy wooden boat up on the rocks just north of town. The Bengstons had been among the last of the commercial fishing folk working out of Black Otter Bay, and the destruction of their boat had marked the end of their story on the big lake.

Sheriff Fastwater passed a hand along the well-worn gunwale as they walked by. He stopped at the stern, thinking maybe to head up to his office, but the sound of the surf called him back. They walked down the wide trail to the shore and looked out across the cobblestone beach to the water beyond. He was surprised to see a clear coating of ice on some of the rocks and steam rising from the lake, indicating the air temperature was indeed very cold this morning.

With hands sunk deep in his pockets, he hunched his shoulders against the chill and looked at the deserted landscape around him. Part of an old pier still jutted out of the water, but commercial boats had stopped docking in Black Otter Bay years ago. A few old boathouses were scattered around the harbor, but other than one or two that had been restored for use as artist's quarters, they stood in various degrees of disrepair and neglect. Turning to follow the shoreline, he quickly discovered that ice coated more of the rocks than he'd first thought. As he sorted through pieces of driftwood looking for a suitable walking staff, he noticed Gitch nosing through the rocks looking for the appropriate cobblestone to carry.

"Good boy, Gitch," he said, finally allowing himself a smile. "I think we really needed this." The big dog looked up at him with eyes of contentment and a mouth full of granite.

They hobbled along the shore, following the tree line on one side and the rolling surf on the other. Twenty yards along they passed an old wreck of a fishing boat overturned on the rocks, pressed up hard against the trees. It had been there for decades; in fact, the sheriff couldn't remember ever not seeing it there. Made of white cedar and weathered to a smooth gray finish, the old relic had become a part of the landscape, like the huge driftwood logs or giant boulders protruding from the beach.

Eventually they made it to the mouth of the Black Otter River. The only sound here came from the surging torrents of crashing water. The deafening roar even drowned out the noise of waves coming ashore. Covered with foam, the river thrashed and bawled as it sought freedom from the confining bedrock-lined riverbank. Every time he came here, each of the thousands of times he'd hiked this shoreline, the river had presented a different facet of its character. There'd been times in the summer when he jumped from boulder to boulder over the narrow chute of water in the main channel. And for as rough and tumultuous as the cascades were now, by spring they'd be twice as dangerous. Whole trees would be carried downstream and set afloat in the big lake, coming to rest perhaps months later as driftwood on a remote shoreline in Wisconsin or Upper Michigan.

His thoughts wandered back to the stories Owen Porter had shared. In some ways it only made sense that someone with a deranged split personality would be responsible for the attacks in the woods. He wished he could talk to his grandmother, Floating Bird. Despite the fact that she'd passed on before he was born, he felt a strong connection to her and the old ways. She would have known about the workings of Manitou and the spirit tricksters, probably even the ancient snake magic, a concept that seemed so alienated from the real world but nonetheless resonated with him. Instead of simply wandering the countryside aimlessly, could Manitou inhabit a person and hijack their personality? Could it find a home in a mind that was raised to believe in such things? Perhaps the impressionable mind of a young boy exiled to live in a culture not his own?

Fastwater shook his head. It didn't feel right. While all these musings would fit the puzzle he struggled with, he knew there was still a piece missing. He watched the river tumbling past, looked out at the brown water deposited in the blue lake by the rain-swollen river. It felt so close; he was sure the missing piece was right there in Owen Porter's words. The sheriff had evidence and suspects, but none of it quite added up.

He exhaled a breath of frustration while looking upstream at the Highway 61 bridge spanning the falls at the edge of town. From the mouth of the river up to the first major falls was a wild run of water, but a patient angler could catch trout and steelhead here. Presenting a hand-tied fly in these rapids, or a hook baited with salmon eggs, took finesse and experience. And traipsing over the slippery, wet rocks while manipulating a fishing rod took athletic agility. Many times he'd heard the excited call, "Fish on!" from an angler along the shore, and then everyone would reel in their lines to get out of the way, for the hooked fish invariably tried to run back to the lake. Leaping and twisting, the fish would alternate tail walking and diving in a mad rush downstream. The angler had to keep up, climbing over rocks and around trees while keeping his line away from the sharp edges of submerged boulders and sunken tree limbs. Spectators would cheer, yelling advice while making room for the combatants fighting their way downstream. It was an exhilarating spectacle to watch, and an experience never to be forgotten by the angler—win or lose.

But fishing this wild stretch of river was more than just exciting. It could also be dangerous. One missed step, one slip on a wet rock, could hurl a person headlong into the thrashing whitewater. Fastwater had seen huge boulders, some as large as cars, torn loose from the shore and rolled downstream. The river didn't care what it hauled: trees, rocks, or humans. Its sole purpose, it seemed to the sheriff, was to smash its way free to join the freezing waters of Lake Superior.

The town had installed one safety precaution, however. Years ago, a one-inch-thick steel cable had been strung across the mouth of the river. Bolted into solid bedrock on each side, the cable was stretched tight just above the high-water line. As hopelessly inadequate as it appeared, it offered one last desperate handhold for anyone swept into the current.

And it worked. Several anglers over the years had found themselves hurtling downstream in the clutches of the ferocious river. Heavy waders filling with ice-cold water made it impossible to fight their way out against the current. In the back of their minds they knew the cable was there, and no matter how the river tossed them, spinning forward or bobbing along backward, they fought to keep an arm extended to make contact with the wire.

Of course, some weren't so lucky. Dragged beneath the current or battered against boulders, every year a handful of anglers perished on North Shore rivers. Many of their bodies were never found. The current continued for a hundred yards or more into Lake Superior, where the bottom quickly dropped off to hundreds of feet deep. Most of these unfortunate folks were never seen again, for Lake Superior clutched them with a tenacious resolution, burying them deep in her ice-cold womb.

Fastwater eyed the steel wire. At least once a year the rescue squad came down to inspect it. They tested the anchor bolts and checked the cable for fraying. The wire took quite a beating in the spring from tree limbs and ice floes hurled against it. Standing alone down here this morning, the sheriff thought the cable looked like a forlorn, deserted sentinel. A puny, man-made device overshadowed by the immense forces of a mostly untamed wilderness.

Looking around, he discovered that Gitch had already started back across the rock-strewn beach. With all four feet clawing and slipping over the stones, he looked like an ancient apparition slowly tottering away. With a heavy sigh and a last long look out to sea, Fastwater turned to begin his own trek back. To his dismay, he found that when he left the river mouth behind, he left his short-lived tranquility behind, too. Even the soothing rhythms of surf on the Lake Superior shore couldn't untie the knot in his stomach. He wanted to believe the parting words he'd thrown at the reporter in the café—that he'd make an arrest any day now—but until that actually happened, he knew he wouldn't feel any peace. After all, he thought, if Manitou had hijacked the Frenchman's personality, how was he supposed to stop that?

• • • •

"Why the long face, Marlon?" Mrs. Bean asked. "What's the matter?"

After the walk along the shore, the sheriff and Gitch had hiked up to Fastwater's house, where he took a container of venison stew out of the freezer and put it in the microwave to defrost. He showered, put on a clean uniform, and then heated the stew in a covered pot on the stove. Gitch watched the food preparations from an oversized dog bed in a corner of the kitchen. To the sheriff, the big dog appeared stiff and sore from the morning's activities, but when Fastwater hoisted the steaming pot of stew and headed for the door, Gitch was right beside him, determined to not be left behind.

Now the sheriff took another spoonful of stew and looked at the dog on his braided rug beside the desk. Gitch chewed on a huge rawhide bone, using his front paws to steady the snack.

"Marlon," Mrs. Bean said again. "You're not still upset about that reporter, are you?"

The sheriff frowned, but finally looked at her. "No. No, I'm not. In fact, I'd forgotten all about her, so thank you for reminding me."

She patted his hand on the desk across from her. "Well then, what is it? You haven't uttered two words since you got here."

"I'm sorry." Fastwater set the spoon down and leaned back. His gaze roamed around the cluttered mess of the post office before returning to the inquisitive stare of the postmistress. "Actually, I've been thinking about my grandmother lately."

"Your grandmother? You never knew her, did you?"

He shook his head. "No. But I've heard many stories about her. I think I'd really like to talk to her."

"Well, of course, Marlon. Who wouldn't want a chance to meet with a grandparent, or a lost sibling or friend, for that matter?"

Fastwater nodded in agreement with the sentiment. "I just think she knew some things that might be of use."

"Like what?"

He shrugged. "I'm not even sure. But in her world, there were creatures and powers that don't exist in the land of computers and space-age technology."

"Okay . . ."

The sheriff slowly sat up but wouldn't look her in the eye. He straightened his silverware, wiped his mouth with a napkin, and again looked at Gitch. "I've been wondering about spirits and how they might interact with a sociopath." When he finally looked at Mrs. Bean, he was grateful to see her serious expression rather than the one of derision he expected. He added, "I think my grandmother knew about this stuff."

"I see. You mentioned ghosts or something like that this morning."

Fastwater nodded. "There was a stranger in town a couple weeks ago, a Frenchman who grew up in an Indian village in Canada. He talked about Manitou, a spirit that wanders the forests, or sometimes lives in a lake or river."

"And you think that maybe this fellow from Canada lives in the same world your grandmother lived in? What was her name?"

"Floating Bird. The stories I heard said she understood the natural forces around us, and that she could communicate with spirits."

"She talked to ghosts?"

Even Fastwater had to smile at that. "I doubt she carried on conversations, Mrs. Bean. But she felt their presence and understood their intent. Most spirits are benign, but others . . ." Fastwater shrugged. "Who knows?"

"So if an evil spirit passed through the area, she'd know about it?"

Again he shrugged. "I don't know. That's why I'd like to talk to her."

It was quiet for a few moments then. The postmistress contemplated her stew while the sheriff studied his dog curled up napping on the rug. Finally, Fastwater cleared his throat. "I've been thinking about something," he said. "I want to get your opinion."

"Go ahead, Marlon. I'm always happy to help."

"Well, a thought occurred to me while I was walking down by the lake. If something doesn't break our way soon, I'm thinking about canceling the Halloween dance."

The words were barely out of his mouth when she responded. "Oh, Marlon, you can't. You just can't do that. Think of all the work the town has put into it."

"It just seems like we'd be asking for trouble."

Mrs. Bean put her spoon down. "You'll be asking for a lot more trouble if you cancel the dance," she said sternly. "Think of the tradition—one hundred years."

"What I'm thinking about," he responded, irritation blossoming in his voice, "are all the people coming to town. If a sociopath is on the loose, how can we possibly keep everyone safe? If something bad happens, how will the townsfolk feel then?"

"Well," Mrs. Bean replied, determination highlighting her words. "We'll just have to make sure nothing happens." Fastwater could see her mind reeling along, a tenacious bulldog not about to let go. "We already have support staff volunteering as greeters around town. Let's just add a few more people out there. No one will know the difference." A spark flashed in her violet-blue eyes and she grabbed Fastwater's hand. "I know, Marlon. Station some of your people from Duluth around town. And I don't mean in uniform," she added, nodding in agreement with her own thought. "But they'll have radios and can keep in touch with each other."

"I don't know . . ."

"Come on, Marlon. They're professionals. They'd know what to look for. They'd recognize right away if someone looked out of place."

"Everyone will be in costumes and masks. They won't even know who they're looking at."

"Marlon, please."

The sheriff went quiet. The last thing he wanted was an argument with the postmistress. He hadn't anticipated such a strong response. Mrs. Bean usually went along with everything he said. He'd expected her to say something more along the lines of, "Whatever you think best, Marlon."

"At least give it some thought," she encouraged. "I'll talk to the dance organizers and see what else we can come up with." She gave his hand an affectionate pat. "Talk to your police buddies," she said. "See if they can spare some people next weekend. Have them dress in civilian clothes, but bring two-way radios."

Fastwater withdrew his hand. "I'll give it some thought," he said, without much conviction.

"I hope you will," she replied as if chastising a child. "Just think of it, Marlon. One hundred years. Your grandmother was just a child then. You don't want to be the one to break that tradition."

"I suppose not," he said, turning to look at Gitch again. The dog was watching them now, his blue and brown eyes registering the tension between them.

The conversation stalled. Fastwater sought something to say to change the subject while looking at the dingy old walls and equipment in the backroom of the post office.

"Did you see that Anna will be back working in the café?"

"Of course I know that," was Mrs. Bean's terse reply, her tone indicting that she was still upset. "It's the best thing for her. Cooped up out there in the woods all day . . ."

"She likes it that way," he argued. "Besides, Charles will be starting school next year, so she'll have even more time to work in her gardens. That's quite an enterprise she—"

They jumped when the phone on the desk rang. Mrs. Bean kept the ringer on the landline turned up loud so she could hear it while working in the back room. Holding a hand up to let him know she wasn't done with the conversation, she grabbed the receiver before it could ring again. "Post office," she answered.

Then it was quiet while she listened, her eyes never leaving the sheriff's. "Why, yes, Phil, he is here. Just a moment please."

She reached the phone across the desk and whispered to Fastwater, "Why is he calling you here?"

He didn't respond but grabbed the phone, and with a twinge of hopeful expectation, said, "Yeah, Phil. What you got?"

"Where's your phone, Marlon? I've been calling you for the last couple of hours."

Fastwater slapped a hand at his trouser pockets and stood up. He tried to step away, but the corded receiver held him back. "My phone . . ."

"I tried you at the office, too. Where have you been?"

The office! Of course. He'd left the phone there when he walked down to the café, and later to the lake. "I accidently left it up at headquarters. I've been out all morning."

"And eating lunch with Mrs. Bean. Marcy told me I'd probably reach you there."

"Marcy?"

"I need to talk to you, Sheriff. Now. I'm at the café."

"In town here?"

"Yes, Marlon. I'm in town, which you would have known if you had your phone with you. Get over here before my coffee gets cold."

"Sure. Okay. Wait, what's going on?" Fastwater snuck a peek at Mrs. Bean. "We just spoke on the phone this morning. What happened?"

"Just get over here. And let me talk to Mrs. Bean again."

He handed the phone across the desk and said, "He wants to talk to you. I have to run." Gitch stood at attention, ears pricked forward, and when Fastwater turned for the front counter and door, the dog bounded to his side. "You'll have to wait here," the sheriff said. Fastwater looked at the postmistress talking on the phone. "Okay if Gitch stays here with you until I get back?"

Mrs. Bean nodded and waved him away. He heard her say into the phone, "Yes, of course, I understand. It's not a problem. He's on his way."

The sheriff walked Gitch back to his rug and told him to stay. "I'll be right back, buddy. You keep Mrs. Bean company for a while."

Fastwater looked back one last time as he opened the door. Mrs. Bean offered him a tentative wave, but all he saw was the worry in her eyes. "I'll be back in a bit," he said, forcing a smile her way.

. . . .

As it always did, conversation in the café dried up when the door opened. For a moment Sheriff Fastwater stood in the doorway, his eyes roaming over the lunchtime crowd. He nodded a greeting at Marcy and raised a finger for a cup of coffee before sauntering among the tables in the direction of the man in a suit and tie sitting near the windows.

Phil Simanich had a faraway look as he stared out the window at the highway and forests beyond. He was just a little bit worried about the sheriff. Whatever had transpired that day out in the woods when Gitch got hurt seemed to have shaken the confidence of the big man. He'd been uncommunicative ever since, seemingly doing nothing else while caring for Gitch. But that didn't fit with the Fastwater that Simanich knew. From their long history together in state high school hockey tournaments and, later, Desert Storm, he knew his friend didn't rattle easily. On the drive up here he'd rehearsed a strong dress down, a reprimand the sheriff couldn't ignore. Words to poke at raw nerves, to awaken the sleeping spirit in his old comrade. But now, watching the sheriff in his clean, pressed uniform approaching his table, the words of rebuke left him, and he stood up with a smile and an outstretched hand to greet his friend.

"Have a seat, Marlon. I was just sitting here thinking about the old days."

"What's this all about?" Fastwater asked. "What happened?"

"Remember when they dropped us over the border into Iraq before the war? What a mess."

Fastwater looked at him, an eyebrow raised in question.

"Remember how everything was screwed up?" Simanich continued. "Guys getting lost in the dark. Whole units getting mixed together in the confusion." Simanich chuckled and eased forward, working into the memories. "I don't think I've ever seen it so dark. And in all that wide-open space, you couldn't see a damn thing; absolute blackness stretching out forever in all directions." He watched for a reaction out of Fastwater, but the sheriff just sat across the table from him, back straight, eyes passively watching his counterpart. "We'd hunker down out of the wind next to the bombed-out ruins of an old building," Simanich went on. "Blowing sand everywhere. If you sat in one place too long, you'd be buried alive."

Marcy walked over and set a coffee cup in front of Fastwater. "Hello, Sheriff," she said, a little too brightly to suit his obviously sullen mood. "Twice in one day; you must like my coffee." Getting no response, she produced the coffeepot in her other hand and filled his cup, then topped off Simanich's.

Fastwater shook his head when she asked if he wanted anything else. "I won't be here that long," he said.

For another moment she stood there, looking from one set of dark, brooding eyes to the other. "Well then," she said, sounding a little put out by their reticence. "You boys just let me know if you need anything else." With that, she turned and stalked off, her annoyance revealed in her stiff-legged swagger.

After another awkward minute of silence, both men looked out the window at the windblown leaves along the roadway. Simanich hoped that if he just kept talking he could get Fastwater to open up. He saw it like chipping away at an old ice fishing hole; sooner or later you'd break through.

Simanich grinned. "Remember how hot it was over there? Hot and dry. Blistering heat all day, and sand gritting up the guns and machinery. You were always going on about how cold and snowy it was back in Minnesota. I think it was like a daydream to help you cope with the desert. Most of the time we would've killed for an ice cube, and you kept going on about lakes freezing solid and snow falling for days on end."

"That was a long time ago, Phil," Fastwater said, his eyes finally leaving the highway to look across the table. "You didn't come all the way up here to talk about the war, did you? I've got things to do."

"What, like luncheon dates?" Simanich studied his friend and decided it was time to get down to business. "You know, Bowers has been up twice from Minneapolis. The Feds are going to be all over this thing any day now."

With the threat of the FBI getting involved, Fastwater pitched an ice-cold glare at the captain.

Simanich continued, "I haven't heard anything from you in a week and a half. It's not like you, Marlon, just sitting around doing nothing. I have no more excuses for Bowers, so tell me, what the hell is going on around here?"

"I thought that's why you wanted to see me," Fastwater replied lightly, mock innocence on his face. "To tell me your high-tech boys have solved my case for me."

Simanich shook his head in frustration and shifted in his seat. "What were you thinking when you bullied Detective Jepson around like that? He told me that the first time he came up here you asked him if he'd ever shot a man before. What's the matter with you? I sent him up here for you to mentor. I thought you'd show him the ropes like you've done for Leonard."

Fastwater opened his mouth to argue, but Simanich wasn't done yet. "But no. You never need any help, do you, Sheriff? You like being that lone Indian up here in the woods." Getting worked up now, the captain punctuated his tirade with emphatic gestures and somber head wagging. "You're a real badass, Sheriff, with your big gun and that little magic thing you do."

Moments passed while the two men studied each other, and then Fastwater's hand left his coffee cup to rest splayed out on the table, as if bracing for impact. "What about Jepson?" he asked. "What happened?"

"He was looking for that guy you hauled in a few years ago, that kid who had Gitch as a puppy. You know, about the only time we'd hear from you was when you'd call the detective to harass him about that." Simanich sipped his coffee, cold now, and looked around the room. Marcy stood at the counter, obviously watching them while acting like she wasn't. "It might have been luck," he continued, "but Jepson spotted the guy in the lobby of the library early this morning." Simanich sat up with a haughty expression. "You know, Marlon, the detective wasn't even on duty today. He was just doing anything he could think of to impress you. He said that finding this kid was really important to you. Jepson had a hunch that if the guy was homeless, had no money, and was still in the area, he'd be using public spaces to keep warm."

The captain finished off the last of his coffee, held Fastwater's stare and, satisfied that he still had the sheriff's attention, went on with his story. "Detective Jepson called it in shortly after I spoke with you this morning. I told him to hang back, just keep an eye on the guy. I tried to reach you, but you never picked up." Simanich lowered his voice, shook his head, and said, "You big fool. You don't even have voicemail."

Fastwater sighed, tried to look out the window, but Simanich caught him again. "Jepson followed him when the guy left. He called me and I told him to not engage without backup. Just follow him, see where he goes."

Fastwater nodded. That sounded like standard procedure, but he had a feeling it wasn't going to work out that way.

"So the kid ran down to the shipping yards; actually, to that vacant industrial area near the docks. Lots of transients and drunks hang out there. By that time Jepson was pretty sure the guy knew he was being followed. He crisscrossed through a couple of deserted warehouses and then jogged across an open field to an old unused utility shed. Before going in he looked back, right at Jepson. The detective told him to stop, but the guy ducked inside."

"Probably destroying evidence," Fastwater offered, but then paused as a bad feeling rolled over him. While studying the captain he added, "Or getting a weapon."

Simanich nodded. "Jepson pulled his own gun and approached the door. Seconds after going in, the guy charged back out, yelling and looking all crazy and wild-eyed. He ran right at Jepson. There was no time to think, so the detective reacted and shot him twice in the chest."

Fastwater sat back, releasing the breath he hadn't known he was holding. Simanich pushed his coffee cup away, giving the sheriff time to mull this over, time to get as uncomfortable as possible.

"Did the guy have a gun?"

Simanich shook his head.

"Not even a knife?"

Simanich continued shaking his head. "Nothing."

The sheriff's gaze wandered back outside. After several moments of uneasy silence, Simanich cleared his throat. "The detective is on administrative leave. That's just SOP when shots are fired. From what he says he didn't really have an alternative, but I don't know how this will work out. He didn't follow orders. If he had to engage, he should have waited for backup." The captain thrust his chin out at Fastwater. "But we both know he wouldn't have been in that situation if you hadn't pushed him."

Fastwater opened his mouth to protest, but thought better of it.

"Jepson went in there trying to prove himself to you." Simanich scowled. "You know, Marlon, the kid isn't stupid, but at this point, even if he loses his job, I guess he's lucky he didn't get hurt or killed."

Angry at the sheriff's lack of response, he threw his napkin at the table and took a deep breath. "Okay, listen to me, Fastwater. We've spent some hard times together. For the rest of my life I'll be grateful to you for sitting with me that last long night in the desert." Locking eyes with the sheriff, he growled, "But it's like you said, that was a long time ago. I'm the boss now, and when I call, I expect you to answer. Enough of this John Wayne bullshit."

Simanich became aware of the silence in the café. He realized he'd been very loud, and the "John Wayne" comment seemed to resonate around the room. He reached for his empty coffee cup as the door hinges creaked open and Leonard Fastwater walked in. The deputy paused in the doorway, the unusually quiet café revealing that he'd stumbled into an awkward moment. He spotted Marcy and flashed her an embarrassed smile. As much as he may have wanted to join her at the counter, he nevertheless walked over to the sheriff's table, pulled a chair over, and, straddling it backward, joined his uncle and the captain next to the window overlooking Lake Superior and Highway 61.

After exchanging greetings, Simanich said, "Marlon was just about to recount for me the incident in which his dog got hurt." Turning his still-angry stare on the sheriff, he prompted, "Weren't you, Marlon."

Fastwater tapped his empty coffee cup on the table, surprised at the sudden turn in the conversation.

The stare-down lasted several moments before Simanich forced a smile in Leonard's direction. "Remember the morning we investigated the campsite? Later, you and Marlon went out to the headwaters. What did you guys find out there?"

Leonard knew his uncle got ornery about outsiders butting into their business, but this obvious hostility had to be about more than just that. He didn't know how to respond. He felt caught in the middle and wished he'd never come into the café. Leonard wouldn't generally be considered a talkative man, but with some prodding from the captain he related a brief account of their foray up the Black Otter River. "Really, about all we found," he concluded, sneaking a look at the angry sheriff, "besides the wolves, were a few old campfires."

Simanich sat back, and then pushed his cup forward when Marcy returned with the coffeepot. She offered Leonard a cup, but he declined. "I just stopped in to see if I could borrow Marlon's electric brush cutter." To his uncle, he said, "Remember that pile we stacked up behind my garage?"

"Help yourself. I thought you were going to cut it up weeks ago."

Leonard smiled. "Better late than never." Satisfied that he'd extracted himself from their head-butting discussion, Leonard got up, shook Simanich's hand, and then wandered over to the counter to sit for a minute with Marcy.

When they were alone again, Simanich said, "Okay, Marlon, what's the deal? What's the story on this Canadian you want to talk to? Sergeant Jepson couldn't find anything on him, but you know we have no authority in Canada."

"He's just a stranger that passed through a couple of weeks ago. I think he was around when the real estate agent died, and I know he saw those girls in here."

"And then he shows up in Duluth to help the one who got hurt."

Fastwater didn't respond.

"Any other reason why you think he's involved?"

The sheriff paused to look out the window, and then Simanich jerked forward. "Wait a minute," he said. "I see now. You had one of your visions, didn't you?"

Fastwater continued his surveillance of the road outside, but muttered, "I didn't have any vision, Phil."

Simanich ignored the comment and said, "I didn't know you still got them." He sipped his coffee, and in a quieter tone said, "I'll always remember that premonition you had in the war. It saved my life. Probably saved both of our lives."

"I told you, Phil, I didn't have a vision. I only get them when there's deep trouble."

Simanich swirled the coffee around in his cup and wagged his head at the memories. Maybe this was the way to get the sheriff talking. "I hurt so bad that night. A bullet hole in my shoulder, the bullet still stuck in my back. Another round through my leg, shattering the bone. And all night we lay there. We couldn't make a sound because we were in such a forward position. Remnants of Saddam's army were all around us."

Fastwater grunted. "I filled you up with gauze and tied you up with tourniquets."

"Then you stuck the handle of my knife in my mouth to keep me from yelling. You said the knife would be handy in case they found us."

Even Fastwater grinned at that. "We were just kids, Phil."

Simanich said, "It hurt so bad I don't think I cared if I lived or died."

Fastwater nodded. "What a miserable night. I thought for sure you were a goner."

"No way was I going to die in that god-awful desert." Looking outside at the leaf-strewn highway and bare branches of the trees along the shore, he added, "Maybe I didn't care about dying, but I didn't want it to happen over there. I had to get home."

The sheriff nodded. "A couple times during the night a sentry came so close I had to lay over the top of you to keep him from tripping on us. You kept passing out. Half the night you were in and out of consciousness. Then you'd begin muttering and I had to put a hand over your mouth to keep you quiet."

The men continued talking. It was an easy, quiet conversation, one they'd had many times before, although they'd never shared it with anyone else. It was their own tale of horror and survival, the lines they spoke so familiar they seemed almost scripted.

"Close to morning I dozed off, too," Fastwater said. "The Iraqis were everywhere. Sometimes they walked right up to the shell crater we hid in. To this day I don't know which times were real and which ones I dreamt."

Simanich added, "And then shortly after dawn you sat up and said our men were nearby."

Fastwater nodded. "All night I'd seen dim forms sneaking through the rubble, and I knew they were enemy soldiers. In hindsight, they were probably withdrawing in front of the American advance. But then, as if in another dream, I saw a patrol on the same road we'd been ambushed on the day before. I couldn't make out the unit, but one of them had this bright red cross on his steel pot. The whole dream was in black and white, but that red cross was glowing red. I didn't know who they were, but I knew for sure that that one guy was an American medic."

"You left me to go get them," Simanich interjected as if on cue. "I thought I'd never see you again. I thought, 'because of a dream he's going to walk away and leave me here.' I would have cussed you out if I'd had the strength to say anything."

Fastwater smiled. "I headed straight through a maze of bombed-out buildings and vehicles," he said, remembering. "There wasn't an Iraqi soldier anywhere. It was like, poof, they'd all disappeared. But I'd seen all this in my vision, so I knew where to go, and when I stepped out on the road, I turned just in time to see the patrol approaching."

"I still don't get that red cross thing," Simanich said. "Why a vision of a medic?"

Fastwater shrugged. "Because of fear, I guess. We'd been out there for hours in the dark desert night. You needed help badly, and I was desperate to get you out of there. Seems like the vision came along just in time. Otherwise, that patrol could have walked right by us."

Simanich drew in a deep breath. "And now you've had another one."

Fastwater shook his head, pausing to look out the window. "I told you, Phil, I didn't have a vision." He was getting tired of all the questions. This was his jurisdiction. He was in charge. He considered this meeting to be nothing more than a lack of faith in his abilities. Finally turning to face the captain again, he said, "It's like I told your man Jepson. No one from around here hurt those girls."

Simanich slowly twirled his coffee cup, thinking, and then stared into it for a while as he considered the sheriff's words. "Okay, fine," he said. "You know your people up here. You'd be aware of a violent character like this guy." He looked across the table at Fastwater. "So, it's your contention that this Canadian Frenchman wandered through here a couple weeks ago, attacked these women, and now he's gone?"

Fastwater looked his friend in the eye, no change in his expression.

"The man disappears, there's no more trouble, and so you're just going to let him walk away?"

"Hey, he sauntered right through your backyard last night."

Simanich rapped the empty cup hard against the table. The sharp crack got everyone's attention, but this time he didn't care. His eyes bored into the sheriff's as his previously rehearsed reprimand came to mind. "Listen to me, Fastwater. I've been talking to some friends over the border. Made some inquiries of my own. There is no Luc Trembley. Officially, the man has never existed, although, granted, many of the small village populations aren't documented very well. We got nothing from DNA samples, and now your Halloween psycho won't be talking to anyone ever again." His anger mounting, he hissed, "So cut the crap. You know what I think? I think this killer scares you. You don't want to find him because he just might be tougher than you. Is that it? Are you scared, Marlon?"

Fastwater steamed but kept his silence.

"Okay, then," Simanich said, his argument sounding preposterous even to himself. "I didn't think so. But you don't think that kid from Duluth is our guy, either, do you? You were using him to keep Jepson out of your hair. And now the kid is dead." Simanich held his hands up in question. "So, what are you going to do, Sheriff? Sit around here and hope the killer has gone away?" Simanich threw his glower around the room before sticking Fastwater with his piercing glare. "Come on, Marlon. What else do you know that you're not telling me?"

Once again, Marcy returned with the coffeepot, but Simanich waved her away. He sat up straight, stuck his chest out, and then adjusted the knot in his brightly colored tie. Eyeing Fastwater, he noted again his friend's professional appearance and well-cut uniform. But he wasn't about to cut him any slack.

When Marcy strutted off, her long, loose skirt swirling around her, Simanich said, "Come on, Marlon. I've never seen you so timid before. You act like you've seen a ghost."

Fastwater's eyes snapped up with surprise, a reaction that wasn't missed by Simanich. "What is it, Marlon? What happened out there at the headwaters?"

The sheriff looked down at his cup. The gleam in his eyes glazed over as he retreated into himself. Simanich waited, watching the big lawman wrestling with something. Finally, growing impatient, he decided to prod the sheriff along. "Leonard said you came across a pack of wolves and some old campfires. You mentioned the pieces of leather. What else, Marlon? What happened to Gitch? Was it really the wolves that hurt him?"

When Fastwater swung his gaze up, Simanich watched his friend's journey back to the present through the light returning to his eyes. The sheriff cleared his throat and said, "I found some tracks out there. Boot prints. Like logging boots."

With a loud sigh, Simanich showed his disappointment. The sheriff was playing him. He gave him meaningless tidbits while avoiding the real issues.

Simanich turned to look at the counter and the brassy young waitress with her flamboyant gestures as she talked to Leonard and some of the regulars. He almost grinned thinking of how she always showed up with the coffeepot whenever his discussion with the sheriff became heated. His gaze wandered past the regulars and came to rest on the sheriff's nephew. Standing to leave, Leonard said something that made Marcy laugh. Straight-backed like his uncle, he stood tall and rocked on the balls of his feet.

Without looking at the sheriff, Simanich asked, "Are you talking about boots like those?"

Fastwater followed Simanich's eyes and glanced at his nephew. "Yeah. But that style isn't exactly rare around here. Guys wear them for cutting wood. Steel toes and all that."

Simanich continued watching Leonard as the young man walked to the door. "Didn't that one girl say their attacker might have had a ponytail?" Now he looked at Fastwater. "And didn't you say in your report that he must know his way around these woods?"

Fastwater nodded a goodbye to his nephew. His thoughts went to ponytails and tufts of fur, about logging boots and diamond willow. After Leonard left, he let his vision linger on Marcy, and then his eyes slowly worked their way over the patrons, finally coming to rest on Simanich's face. Sparks seemed to emanate from his suddenly glittering black orbs. In his calm monotone, he said, "You're out of line, Phil. Leonard doesn't go in for violence. He doesn't even carry a gun."

"All I'm saying is that maybe you should broaden your investigation. Kick up some dust around this place. Let everyone know you're going to find this guy. Maybe someone will get nervous and a new lead will pop up." He looked hard at the sheriff, overcoming Fastwater's glare. Jabbing a finger across the booth, he added, "And you better keep in touch with my office. Bowers is nagging me every day for updates. You keep giving me the silent treatment and I'll turn him and the Feds loose on you."

While staring at the sheriff, Simanich worked his way out of the booth and stood up. He could see Fastwater retreating into his shell. "I want daily reports, Marlon. In person or by phone, your choice. The Feds have gone through all our paperwork, but so far there's nothing to match up with other cases out of state."

He leaned over and dropped a five-dollar bill next to his coffee cup, and then rested his hands on the table. Fastwater watched the ugly tie swing out and brush over the tabletop. In a quieter voice, Simanich continued, "Maybe your killer is gone, Marlon. But maybe he isn't. Maybe he's right here in town, ready to strike again." He looked behind him—at the counter, the customers, the door. Then he turned to face the sheriff again. "Here's something else Bowers told me. Once one of these serial killers gets going, they tend to increase the frequency of their attacks. If you don't squash it now, this little village of yours could look like the highway into Baghdad." Simanich straightened up and aligned his tie. "See you, Sheriff. Keep in touch."

"Phil," Fastwater called, stopping his friend as he turned to leave. When Simanich looked back, Fastwater asked, "Remember when we visited Anna at her garden store?"

"Yeah. And then you went out to the headwaters and Gitch got hurt."

Fastwater nodded. "Anna mentioned Manitou, remember?"

Simanich furrowed his brow, put his hands on his hips, and asked, "So, what are you trying to say, Marlon?"

Fastwater smiled and waved his friend off. "Forget it. Have a safe drive home. I'll talk to you soon."

Simanich hesitated for several moments while scrutinizing the sheriff. "Okay, full disclosure, Marlon. I did some research after that conversation, and I have to tell you there isn't much information out there about Manitou, and even less about stopping one."

Fastwater broke eye contact and looked outside again.

"Is that what's bothering you, Marlon? You don't know how to stop Manitou?"

Fastwater returned the question. "And you don't really believe in it, do you?"

"You're the Indian, Marlon. You tell me."

Fastwater thought about this. Finally, he shrugged and said, "In the old stories they used magic. But I seem to be running a little low on that these days."

Simanich shook his head and turned to leave. "You worry me, Fastwater. You really do."

After he left, the sheriff sat quietly with his thoughts for a couple more minutes, thoughts about logging boots and ponytails and an array of relatively unknown passageways through the woods, corridors that were rarely used and never spoken of. He thought about narrow strips of leather like the ones tucked in his desk drawer. And, of course, he thought about Manitou.

Chapter 14

Temperatures *along the North Shore dropped steadily leading* up to the day before Halloween. Bright yellow aspen and birch leaves combined with the red and orange hues of maples to create a rustling explosion of color on the forest floor. Days grew shorter, and during the long, still nights stars glittered overhead, appearing close and friendly like cheerful little campfires, but for all their brilliance giving no more warmth than a scattering of sparkling diamonds. And, because it sat ever lower in the sky this time of year, the sun was hard-pressed to warm things up during the day. Meanwhile, Lake Superior rolled along cold and deep, its surface a glittering expanse reflecting the dazzling sunlight overhead. Like the old-timers were fond of pointing out, it would have been even colder if the voluminous body of forty-degree water in the big lake didn't moderate the temperature.

Just as Sheriff Fastwater had predicted, however, there was no moderation five miles outside of town beyond the cedar- and white pine–covered ridge. At Anna's Garden and Toolshed, heavy frost clung to bushes and branches. The few remaining plants in the garden beds were drying up or dead, awaiting the spade and shovel to dig them into the earth. Most migrating birds had left for warmer climes, while the native bird populations hunkered together at night in the cover of cedar and pine boughs.

Vincent Wyckoff

Deer huddled up in small herds, their thick winter coats beginning to show in a dark gray bristling along their necks. Billowing wafts of vaporized breath formed eerie clouds over their heads in the predawn darkness. All around, the forest lay silent, as if holding its breath in anticipation of the impending demise of those creatures not strong enough to survive.

Into this forbidding setting a silent figure trekked up the frozen gravel lane toward the house at the end of the road. It was the darkest time of the night, an hour yet before the first gray light of dawn. A waning crescent moon had long since set. From beneath the cover of a small copse of cedars, half a dozen deer watched the trudging upright shadow pass. Their haunches twitched and flexed at the prospect of having to flee their covered shelter. Nostrils flared, and long, furry ears flicked back and forth while their eyes remained riveted on the moving creature on the road.

Without needing to look, the passing figure was aware of their presence, too. He felt their uneasiness and fear. He knew there were six of them, five bedded down and one sentry standing behind the trunk of an old white cedar. The man knew if he stopped walking they'd be up and gone in an instant. But he had no desire to disturb them, for he was nearing the end of his journey.

Moose-hide moccasins stepped along the gravel road in silence. The braid of his long hair curled over his shoulder to mingle with the thick beard at his neck. He carried a canvas Duluth-style pack on his back, and walked with a minimum of extraneous movements. His hands were balled up and shoved deep in the pockets of his flannel shirt-jacket. He didn't bob or lurch as he hiked, but glided ahead with little apparent effort, like the giant iron-ore freighters out on the big lake slicing through the darkness and cold with an irrepressible momentum. He'd been traveling for a few days now, preferring the privacy of hiking after dark. Besides, in his experience it was during the last few hours before dawn, especially on these cold, clear nights, when the spirits of the old ones preferred to move about. He could sense an unsettling restlessness in the forest. For him, it was a tangible feeling, like an odor that anyone should be able to smell, or a succulent herb ready to burst open with flavor. That's what brought him back.

It wasn't like the first time he'd passed through here, when he thought he'd finally found a place to call home. Instead, chaos had been loose in the forest, drawing the attention of the big Dakota sheriff. There was a powerful aura about the lawman, a mystical energy that had temporarily suppressed the evil. But the Nightwatchers were once again on the prowl, leading the hiker to believe the sheriff was away, or, perhaps more significantly, suffering from a spiritual ailment of his own.

It was this sense of an impending confrontation that drew him back to this dark patch of woods, to this lonely stretch of frozen road, in the certain knowledge that his fate would be played out here. Ultimately, it didn't matter why the old ones had risen. Malevolent forces wandered this land, and the bearded, flannel-clad figure had come to confront them.

Silently, past the last of the turned-over garden beds, the shadow-like figure slid along to the end of the road. The old Chevy pickup was parked here, its red paint and rust blending together in the dark. Pursing his chapped lips, he ducked around the corner of the house and moved through the shadows along the length of the building to where the hand-hewn log walls began. He stopped, listening, and then withdrew his hands from his pockets and cupped them against a window. The thick stone fireplace and chimney stood in silence at his side. He paused for a moment, everything quiet and still around him, then he pressed his face against his cupped hands and peered through the darkened windowpane.

• • • •

Registering more than twenty degrees below the Fahrenheit freezing point, icy tendrils of arctic air infiltrated the isolated house at the end of the road. Through cracks in the log walls it crept, around window and doorframes, unseen and uninvited. Into the darkened corners and across the hardwood floors it settled, methodically usurping the heat so doggedly produced by the hardworking woodstove. The interior woodwork contracted under the influence of the brittle, cold air, with studs and joists creaking and groaning, sounding like ghostly footsteps in the dark.

Vincent Wyckoff

When Anna awoke at dawn on the day before Halloween, she was shocked at how cold it was in their bedroom. The house had an open floor plan, and the woodstove in the fireplace generally did an adequate job of keeping them warm. It was their separate bedroom and bathroom that didn't get the full benefit of the stove's radiant heat. The bathroom had an auxiliary electric heater, but when it got this cold, they usually just threw an extra blanket or two on their bed.

Snuggling next to her husband, she lingered for a few moments under the pile of blankets. Charles would be fine in his loft, she mused. The warm air held out against the cold up there longer than anywhere else in the house. She exhaled deeply across Michael's blanket-covered chest, half expecting to see her breath in the gray dawn light. Blinking her eyes to focus around the dim interior of the bedroom, Anna let her thoughts wander through the upcoming day. Most of her gardening chores were done, the vegetable and flower beds put to sleep for another six months. Her indoor work could now begin in earnest, including the few hours she'd work in the café over the Halloween weekend. A lot of folks came to town for the dance and parties, so she'd offered Marcy a hand. It would be fun to go back; after all, she'd worked there for several years over a decade ago. And that was where she'd met Michael. She smiled to remember the excitement in Marcy's voice when she talked about the costume party at the bar. "Wait until you see Matthew," she'd said, laughing. "You won't believe his costume."

She thought about the pies she planned to bake with Charles today. Either blueberry or raspberry, or probably a couple of each, from the berries she'd put away last summer. Anna especially enjoyed baking in this frosty, cool weather, filling the house with wonderful aromas, not to mention the added luxury of all the heat from the oven.

But it was the thought of a hot cup of coffee that finally roused her to the task of braving the cold wooden floors. Moving slowly, so as not to disturb Michael, she lifted her robe from the bedpost and slipped it on over her flannel nightgown. Her feet found her slippers, the big furry ones

Michael had given her last year at Christmas. Hugging herself against the cold, she left the bedroom and marched straight to the woodstove. Hot coals still glowed inside, so she added some heavy kindling to reignite the fire, then stood stoically waiting for the flames to rise.

Her gaze wandered over to the framed portrait on the wall beside the stone chimney. Gilbert and Anna, her great-great-grandparents, looked back at her from over the years. Gilbert's big, reassuring hands, and Anna's stern, work-worn countenance. "How did you ever do it?" Anna asked them. "How did you manage to survive out here all alone?" With a self-conscious smirk she thought about her indoor plumbing, the telephone, and electricity. Even the woodstove was a huge improvement over the open fireplace they'd had in the old days. Studying her great-great-grandfather's eyes, the eyes she was convinced were as blue as her own, she was once again filled with an admiration for her pioneering ancestors.

After stuffing a couple split logs of maple in the fire, she stood with her back to the open stove doors and let the heat gently caress her. She could see Charles in his bed next to the railing up in the loft. His mouth hung open, and he'd thrown off all his blankets during the night. Charlie's chubby stomach protruded from his dinosaur-print pajama tops. He's always warm, she thought with a smile, just like his father. Nonetheless, after closing the stove doors, she made a quick trip up the ladder to tuck a blanket over her son.

Back downstairs, she could feel the woodstove slowly reclaiming its domain throughout the house. She went into the kitchen, and with a feeling of contentment started up a pot of coffee. She extracted two bags of frozen berries from the freezer and set them on the counter to thaw. Looking out the kitchen window, she paused to study the frost-laden forest along the road leading to her garden beds and the blacktopped county road beyond. Before turning back to begin preparations for rolling out piecrusts, she glanced at the red pickup truck and, almost as an afterthought, hesitated to take a closer look. Leaning over the counter, she examined the truck and woods. It was early, but there was more than enough light to see, so it was disturbing when her view fogged over, cleared, and then went fuzzy again. Shaking her head and squinting, she saw a tiny puff of smoke drift out from the far side of the cab. She blinked her eyes and looked again. Over the rear fenders now she spotted faint wisps of smoke, looking like exhaust plumes, except they came from the far side of the truck rather than from under it.

"Michael?" she called as she turned to run to the bedroom. "Michael, you'd better get up and come see this."

• • • •

Even wearing his quilted coveralls and a stocking cap pulled low over his head, Michael thought the frigid morning air would suck the breath out of him. He stumbled toward the truck on legs that weren't quite awake yet. The smell of woodsmoke hung low against the ground, but he knew it wasn't coming from the chimney. It seemed to linger around the truck. At the driver's door, he peered inside. Seeing nothing disturbed in there, he turned around, his nose wrinkling up in confusion as his gaze searched down the road for an explanation. The narrow band of gravel looked lonely and small in the vastness of the woods. In the stillness of dawn, the cold, heavy air seemed to press its deadly weight against the Earth, as if trying to squash the life out of anything on the surface. Pivoting his view across the parking area, he noticed a thin column of smoke rising through the brush at the forest's edge. Absolute silence shrouded the woods like a blanket draped over the landscape.

"Hello?" Michael called softly toward the plume of woodsmoke twenty yards off the edge of the road. "Anybody there?"

Getting no response, he followed an opening through the brush, using an arm to push aside stiff, frozen shafts of dogwood and sumac. His mind spun in a bewildering whirl, but the notion of fear hadn't wedged its way into his sleepy consciousness yet. When he broke through the tangle of branches lining the parking lot, he paused and called softly, "Hello? Who's there?"

He smelled the fire, just yards ahead of him, beyond a thin strip of alders. He proceeded cautiously, still following a faint opening through the brush. Halfway through the alder thicket he finally spotted the campfire. A man sat cross-legged on the far side of it, facing back out toward the road, a blanket draped over his lap and tucked underneath him. It looked to Michael as if the man was asleep.

Slowly moving ahead, all the time watching the lone figure across the fire, Michael became aware of a shortness of breath as the first wave of apprehension hit him. But it didn't occur to him to turn back. After all, this was his land. Someone had snuck in during the night and built a campfire, mere yards from his wood-sided house, and now the culprit sat sleeping in his patch of forest. For a moment he considered his shotgun, readily available in the house, but his curiosity urged him forward to discover the answer to this early morning mystery.

Michael stopped at the fire's edge, directly across from the sleeping form. The stranger's chin and full, thick beard rested against his chest. The only way Michael could tell the man was alive was from the thin whiffs of breath vaporizing out of his nostrils at slow, regular intervals. A tall fur hat perched on his head, a stuffed backpack supported his sitting position, and a walking staff stood nearby, propped against a tree. When Michael squatted down for a better view, he saw the man's thick braid of hair wound around his neck and into his beard. The hair was light-colored and looked familiar. "Luc?" he said softly.

The man didn't move or alter his breathing pattern. Michael scanned the ground to find his footing around the fire. After a couple of silent steps, he looked over at the sleeping man's face and drew up with a gasp. For the briefest instant he'd caught the man's sparkling gray eyes watching him. Without moving a muscle, the eyes were cocked up at Michael, flashing with a fierceness so primeval and wild they stopped Michael in his tracks. The man's mouth split open in a frozen grimace, cracked lips revealing bared teeth that flashed like fangs.

The predatory leer lasted only an instant. Narrowed eye slits quickly widened to reveal the large, clear, gray-blue eyes inside. The man rocked forward in his sitting position and extracted his balled-up fists from under the blanket. Just the slightest groan could be heard with the movements.

"Luc?" Michael asked, stepping around the fire to approach his friend. Now that he knew who the stranger was, the leer of animosity he'd received quickly dimmed in his memory. He bent over Luc's stiff form and inquired, "Are you okay? What are you doing out here?"

Luc reached his hands out toward the fire. His whole upper body seemed to move in unison, as if frozen in place, or wrapped in a straitjacket.

"Have you been out here all night?"

Luc clapped his hands together to get the blood pumping, and then crossed his arms, shoving his fingers up under his armpits.

Michael reached out a hand to help his friend get up. "Come on," he said. "Let's get inside and thaw you out."

• • • •

From her spot at the kitchen sink washing up cooking utensils, Anna asked, "What I'd like to know is, what brings you back here? I thought you'd be long gone by now, headed home for the winter."

The question irritated Michael. Why couldn't she just accept him? Due to her natural sense of hospitality, she'd insisted on making a big breakfast for their guest, but Michael knew she was keeping her distance by firing off these innocent-sounding questions from across the room.

For his part, Luc was in a festive mood. He hadn't eaten this well in a long time, hadn't sat at a table in a warm house for weeks. Earlier that morning, after Michael helped him inside, Luc took a hot shower to thoroughly warm up. And then later, while retying his long braid, Anna served up a breakfast of eggs, hashbrowns, slabs of ham, and toast dripping with her raspberry preserves. Accenting the mouth-watering aromas were the warm, hearty smells of homemade pies baking in the oven.

Standing by the sink, Anna looked Luc in the eye and in her matter-of-fact, straightforward manner, asked, "So what is it, Luc? Why did you come back here? Where have you been?"

Luc shrugged. "Just traveling. The woods are beautiful this time of year." When Anna opened her mouth to say more, he held a hand up to stop the questions while wiping his mouth with a napkin. "And I almost forgot. I have presents for you. For my good friends. So that is why I am here." Michael laughed, relieved to hear this simple response.

"Mommy, is it Halloween yet?" came a timid voice from the entryway to the living room. Everyone turned to look at Charles, barefoot and wide-eyed, studying the stranger sitting at the kitchen table. Charles's pajama top was still cinched up above his belly. Paper cut-outs of pumpkins and ghosts festooned the wide entryway around him. Charlie's hair was mussed and adorned with cowlicks, and sleep still hung heavy around his eyes, but his fingers were wringing with anticipation and wonder.

Going to kneel in front of her son, Anna said, "No, honey. Halloween is tomorrow." Then she stood and waved an arm at their guest. "Do you remember Luc? He worked with Daddy a few weeks ago and came over for dinner." After reaching down to straighten his pajamas, she picked him up and brushed a hand through his hair, pulling it across his forehead and out of his eyes.

Charles kept a steady watch on the bearded man. "He brought the wolves," he said.

Michael laughed, and even Anna had to smile. "I don't think he actually brought them," she said, but looking back at Luc with a smirk, she added, "You didn't, did you?"

Luc said, "I think wolves go where they want, not where you tell them."

Anna used her fingers to smooth out cowlicks in Charles's hair. Walking toward the sink and stove, she deposited him in Michael's lap, and asked, "How about some eggs? I'll scramble them up with cheese just the way you like them." He nodded and settled back against his father, but never broke his wary vigilance of the wild man sitting at their kitchen table.

"Mon petit ami," Luc said, his tenor voice soft in the awkwardness of the moment. His eyes sparkled with fun. He leaned forward, pushed his plate away, and rested his forearms on the edge of the table. "It is true, my little one, as your mama says, that I did not bring the wolves. But," and now he winked at Michael and leaned closer toward the boy, "I have been to the deepest forests in the north country where the magic little folk live, and they gave me something to give to you." He pointed at his backpack leaning against the wall near the outside door. "If you will bring me my bag," he said, "I'll show you what they have made."

Charles craned his neck around to look up at his father. In a loud whisper, he asked, "Are the magic people real?"

"I think so, Charlie," Michael whispered back with a grin. He helped his son slide off his lap and watched him scramble over to the backpack.

Anna threw the heavy iron skillet back on the stove and found a couple more eggs in the refrigerator. She was too busy today, not to mention confused and worried by the sudden return of Luc, to play the happy hostess much longer. Charles grunted and groaned as he dragged the heavy backpack across the floor. When Luc began unfastening the straps on the top of the bag, Charles stood next to Michael's knee, anxiously rubbing his hand over his father's thigh.

Michael caught Anna's eye and gave her a warm smile, but she wouldn't return it. She was wearing her old bib overalls, the ones she sometimes wore for cooking and baking, so she wouldn't have to bother with an apron. The denim was faded and soft, and Michael had always found them sexy in a rustic sort of way. He still wore his insulated coveralls, even though the house was more than warm by now. The cuffs were unzipped to the knees, and the front was open to reveal his checkered pajama tops underneath. Watching Anna working at the stove, Michael noticed how she kept turning to look at Luc, to keep an eye on what was going on. But she wouldn't sit at the table with them and join in. He thought she was overreacting, maybe even rude, with the way she smashed open the eggs and vigorously whisked them around with a wooden spoon.

"In Canada," Luc began, "there is a little bird that is very special." From his backpack he extracted a small leather pouch secured with a rawhide drawstring. The bag looked fresh and new, supple and soft. Plush rabbit fur lined the inside. Opening the cord, Luc stuck his hand in and fingered the contents while speaking to Charles. "This bird has much spirit, and spends even the coldest winters in the north country. The older people call him Waabishki Gondashkway. White Throat. Sometimes in the evening you can hear his call." He paused for a moment and licked his lips, then in a high-pitched whistle he mimicked distinctly, "Sweet, sweet, Canada, Canada, Canada."

Luc pulled his hand out of the homemade pouch and produced two life-sized carvings of white-throated sparrows. Offering them to Charles, he smiled to see the awe on the boy's face, and the reverence with which he reached for the birds. Taking the wooden carvings in his two chubby hands, Charles solemnly held them up for his father to see. Michael grasped one of the tiny birds between his thumb and forefinger. Hand-rubbed with a light oil, the wood was dun-colored and as smooth as silk. On the head, wings, and tail feathers were small, black highlights smudged into the wood. Fine lines of detail were etched into the feathers, which were shaded from black to light gray. Across the throat was a fingernail-sized splash of white, and over the top of the head were narrow stripes of white shading. The belly had been slightly flattened so it sat upright on the table.

Anna was the first to speak. From her vantage point at the stove, the carvings looked like nothing less than real birds crouched on the table. "They're amazing, Luc," she said, stepping over for a closer look. "Did you . . . ?"

Charles piped up, "The little people in the woods made them, Mommy. And they sing, too." Scrunching up his nose, he peered at Luc. "How do they sing?" he asked. Once again, Luc performed his sparrow call. Michael pushed the two birds together on the table and noticed how they were different. One held his head up as if looking around, while the other one had his face directed toward the ground, about to pick at some seeds or fruit.

"There is a pair of them," Luc explained. "They live together, as it should be." He tousled Charles's hair and said, "When you are not here to play with them, they will have each other to keep them company."

"They're really wonderful, Luc," Michael said. "They look so real." To his son, he said, "Charles, can you thank our friend for the gifts?"

"Thank you," Charles responded softly while pushing the birds around the table like toy cars. He made small cackling noises, and it took a minute for the others to realize he was trying to imitate Luc's birdcalls.

Anna served a plate of eggs and ham and toast, then sat down next to Charles to cut up his food for him. When he started eating, she picked up one of the birds to inspect it more closely. "This is really marvelous work, Luc," she said.

Luc began rummaging through his backpack again, pulling out clothes and equipment and setting them aside. "It is quiet work," he said. "Relaxing exercises for around the campfire."

Charles scooped eggs into his mouth while using his free hand to walk one of the birds across the table. Between bites he made little birdcalling noises. Anna glanced at Michael, but then turned to Luc again. She said, "You know, the sheriff was here a couple weeks ago. He wants to talk to you."

Luc didn't look up, didn't stop his distracting rummaging.

"He went out to the headwaters to look for you," she continued. "His dog got into a fight with some wolves and got hurt pretty badly." She glanced at Michael and noted his frown, but she was determined to see this through.

Finally, Luc sat up and placed another bag on the table. This one was larger, and by its soiled, tattered appearance seemed to be much older. His expression was passive, easy and carefree. Very casually, he said, "It is not me the sheriff is looking for."

Anna took a bite of Charles's food. "Well, then," she countered, "just who do you think he is looking for?"

Luc picked up one of the hand-carved birds and studied it. Without being broad or heavy, he was still a big man. He was tall, and his beard made him look even larger. His forearms and hands were thick with muscle. So when he spoke, his soft, tenor-range voice was always a surprise. "I heard about the woman who died near here. Then, in the middle of the night, when the restless spirits feel free to roam, a campsite of young girls was visited."

"Come on, Luc," Anna interrupted. She wiped her mouth with a napkin and threw it on the table. "Don't start this talk about spirits and ghosts again."

Luc's gray-blue eyes focused on her. Even as she watched, a shadow seemed to pass over his face and his eyes turned dark and narrowed. "And you saw the Manitou," he said. "You saw it with your mind, if not with your eyes. You felt it." He paused to let her catch up to his words. She held his gaze, but at the mention of the scare she'd had a few weeks ago, her face visibly paled. He lowered his voice to say, "You saw the evil, madame. That is what brings me here."

Charles began squirming and she let him get down. He grabbed his birds and ran into the other room, zooming the woodcarvings along at arm's length as if they were capable of flight. His squawking birdcalls rattled around the kitchen.

Again she met the intensity of Luc's stare. "How do you know what I saw or felt?" Luc shrugged, sat back, and seemed to relax again. "You are a brave woman, madame. A good woman to your husband and son. These woods do not frighten you. But you ran. You ran from something you couldn't see. If it was an animal, or a person, you would have known it."

Anna sat very still, one hand drumming on the table, staring at Luc. Finally, with a touch of sarcasm, she said, "So you're telling me I encountered Manitou."

Luc simply nodded.

Anna exhaled with a huff. She was too pragmatic to go along with Luc's story. It didn't fit with her experience of reality, and she wasn't about to let him off that easy.

"You said you're here because it is evil," she said. "How can you see it if no one else can?"

Luc thought about this for a moment. When he spoke, he seemed even more shy than usual. His voice even softer. "I have a gift. I've always had it. I can see those mysteries that others only feel." He looked at his hands in his lap, at the dirty dishes on the table. In his discomfort he even squirmed around to look at the kitchen sink and window. He paused to collect his thoughts, gave Michael a quick glance, and finally managed to look Anna in the eye again. "The sheriff also has this gift, and it is Manitou that he seeks."

Michael's guffaw came out louder than he'd intended. Embarrassed, he looked into the other room where Charles's birdcalls had morphed into guttural quacks. "I'm going to check on Charles," he said, pushing away from the table. Anna didn't know what to say. Luc sounded so sincere, so humble about his self-proclaimed powers. But the story—was she supposed to believe this? She began to wonder if Luc's mind was a little off-center, and her eyes darted over to the kitchen door.

To Michael's back, Luc said, "You must understand me. I don't mean to frighten your family. You are my good friend, and I hope you know in your heart that what I'm telling you is true." Michael nodded, more in agreement with the friendship concept then the Manitou story, but then left to join his son in the living room.

When he was gone, Luc leaned forward, returned his attention to Anna, and continued his explanation in a more casual tone. "Manitou has always existed, you see. But he roamed the Earth more often in the old days. Sometimes as a giant, sometimes in the form of an animal. But he is not suited to this new world." Luc held out his hands in a gesture meant to emphasize his point. "Automobiles, airplanes, so many people everywhere. These days no one has respect for the old ways; no one fears the spirits of the old ones. Comprendez-vous?"

Anna couldn't disagree. After all, the present state of society was one of the reasons she chose to raise a family out here. But Manitou?

"Something is disturbing the balance in the forces of life," Luc continued. "The world we walk in is no longer in step with the world of death, the land of spirits. Remember, I told you about Matche-Manitou, the most evil and powerful of the spirit gods. The elders in our village in Canada performed the ancient rituals to resurrect him. To call him back among the living, like in the old days. The old people, they see how the young ones have lost respect. How they honor money and television, laugh at the old ways—the ways of living in spiritual harmony. The elders have called upon Matche-Manitou to bring balance back into the world."

Despite her wariness, Anna found herself enthralled with Luc's tale. His French accent, his sincerity. "Why not a benevolent spirit?" she asked. "Why call on a devil of death and destruction?"

"There is much more power in evil," Luc replied.

"It sounds like all they're going to get is fear and death."

"Fear is another form of respect, madame."

Anna considered Luc's words for a moment. Her instincts told her he was relating the truth; at least, the truth as far as he understood it. "So, why are you here? If the tribal elders called upon Manitou, why have you come to meet him?"

"Manitou is also known as a trickster. The elders thought he would perform a powerful magic to bring the world back into balance, to lead it back toward the old ways. But Matche-Manitou was very angry to have his sleep disturbed, and now his anger will last forever. So you see, the trickster has already performed his magic. In his anger, he has turned against the elders, and now he's directing his wrath at the innocent." Luc shrugged. "I have been chosen, like the warriors of old, to match my powers against him. To return him to his world of spirits and death."

Luc's expression suddenly changed as he aimed a jovial grin across the room and called to Michael standing in the doorway. "And for you, mon ami," he said, "I also have a gift." With a broad smile he pushed the big leather bag across the table.

"For me?" Michael asked, slowly walking in to retrieve the bag. He looked at Anna, but she had already begun stacking dishes on the table.

Michael opened the bag and pulled out two pairs of moccasins. They'd been stitched together by hand, big looping swirls of rawhide around the soles and heel. With a look of surprise blushing across his face, he stuck a hand inside one of them to feel the leather. "These are just like the ones we talked about," he said. "The moccasins you wore for roofing the old farmhouse."

Luc nodded. "I promised to make them for you." He pointed at one of the shoes on the table. "Moose-hide soles. They're tougher than store-bought. And this pair I lined with rabbit fur for warmth."

Anna set the dishes in the sink and came over to look at Michael's gift. Completely unadorned, the leatherwork was primitive and basic. But when she pulled at the stitching, she found it tight and solid. Over the rawhide loops and knots was a thick coating of wax to keep water out of the seams. When she secretly glanced at Luc, she saw him smiling with pleasure.

Michael asked questions about the moccasins while trying them on. Returning to the sink, with her back to the others, Anna replayed to herself the conversation she'd had with Luc. He really did have a warrior aura about him, she thought, just as he'd said. But he was also a lone wolf. And even though she wasn't ready to let go of her apprehension, she had to admit that there was a certain allure about the man. The way he survived outdoors, the obvious pleasure he took in giving a gift. Even the way he'd said "store-bought," she thought with a tremor of a smile on her face.

From the other room she heard Charles singing out his birdcalls. He didn't know how to whistle yet, so he sounded like an immature crow. "Caw, caw, caw." While it had been very generous of Luc to make the moccasins for Michael, he had, after all, promised to make them. But the woodcarvings—how many hours had he spent working the wood, making the colored stains, oiling the finished product? To show up here and give the bird carvings to Charles, now that was truly thoughtful and generous. This was a side of Luc that was new to her, a part of his character that revealed a kindness and serenity, a side to balance the warrior and lone wolf.

But she still had her instincts, and to win her over would take something more.

"Hey, Anna," Michael called. "Look at this."

Anna snapped out of her reverie, rinsed her hands, and wiped them on a dishtowel. More exclaiming over the moccasins?

She turned around to find Luc standing up, holding out a large wreath thickly woven in a complex pattern of twigs and branches. "For you, madame."

Anna's eyes registered astonishment as she looked from the wreath, up to Luc, and then to Michael. Walking over, she gently grasped the gift and held it up. Luc's whole face seemed to glow with his smile.

Michael was so excited he could barely stand still. "He made it, Annie. Wove the whole darn thing together himself."

Michael's childlike enthusiasm finally broke through her restraint. Before she could stop it, a quivering slash of smile squirmed across her face. Words wouldn't come. She stuttered something, and then became aware of the earthy smell of cedar and smoky campfires.

Holding the wreath close, the wild aromas caressed her senses. Supple branches, some as much as half an inch thick or more, looped around and twisted together to form the basic circular shape. Short lengths of cedar boughs were woven into the branches, giving the wreath its piney smell. Rawhide cords lashed around the branches at the four quarters held it together and gave it strength. The green of the cedar contrasted sharply with the bare brown branches.

But there was even more color than that. Looking closer, Anna found tiny clumps of dried flowers stuck in the wreath. Small white daisies, bright orange Indian paintbrushes, and sprigs of red mountain ash berries.

"It is made in the old way," Luc said. "I thought you would be one to appreciate that."

"It's beautiful," she finally stammered. Tearing her eyes away from the wreath to look at Luc, she said, "I can't believe this. It's incredible."

Michael burst into laughter, and Luc's grin of satisfaction couldn't have been any broader.

Vincent Wyckoff

Again Anna studied the gift. Now she found dried mushrooms lashed to the rawhide strings. A spray of wild mint lent its aroma to the display, and the whole thing smelled of campfires and sage and the outdoors.

"The branches are from the rowan tree," Luc explained. "In the old days, tribal people hung wreaths of rowan over their lodges to keep evil spirits away. So you see, madame, you need not fear Manitou anymore."

"I don't know what to say, Luc. I've never seen anything so beautiful."

"You could start by saying 'thanks,'" Michael offered, smiling and stepping closer for a better look at the wreath.

With a studious fervor, Anna said, "This must have taken hours to make. And even more hours to collect and dry all the flowers and berries. Look at this, Michael. There's an owl feather tied into this rawhide strap."

"I burned sage over my campfires to purify the pieces," Luc said. "The owl feather was given to me one evening, just before dark."

"Who gave it to you?" Michael asked.

Luc raised an eyebrow in confusion. He merely shrugged his shoulders and said, "Why, the owl, of course. The owl gave it to me."

"Oh, the owl just flew up and plucked out one of his feathers and handed it over."

Luc smiled his timid grin and stuck his hands in his pockets. "No, no," he replied, laughing. "Not like that. Monsieur owl, he sat on a branch of a huge maple tree. The owl, he often sits near an open area, like a meadow, because that's where they like to hunt. So, when I look for a campsite, if I hear an owl calling, I follow the sound to find a good open camping spot."

Luc used his hands to gesture how he'd seen the owl in the tree. "Maple forests have a thick cover of branches," he explained, waving his arms over his head. "So there isn't much brush or undergrowth. When I came near to the place where the owl sat, he watched me, thinking I would move on. But I stopped. It was a wonderful place with many of the flowers you see in the wreath. I thanked the owl for his kindness in showing me his beautiful home."

Once again, Anna found herself mesmerized by Luc's story. His rugged physical appearance, the odd accent and strange way he put words together, all added to the exotic quality of his tale. Luc looked at her, a shy, downward glance that said he didn't think they'd believe what he had to say.

"So, when did he give you the feather?" she prodded.

"Owls are very smart," Luc said. "Maybe not wise like everyone thinks, but certainly very clever. An owl can know what's in your heart." Luc tapped his chest, then sipped his coffee and hesitated, as if waiting for one of them to laugh at his words. But they sat quietly, waiting for him to continue. "I unpacked some of my bag, then I showed him the moccasins I'd made, and the bird carvings for your son." Luc pointed at the wreath Anna held. "I showed him the wreath I'd started making, and thanked him for leading me to the flowers and berries you see there. It is late in the season, so they are hard to find. When the owl left, he dropped the feather for me to use."

"Amazing," Michael said. "Only you, Luc. Only you could get an owl to give you one of his feathers."

They continued talking about the gifts as Luc began repacking his backpack. Anna took the wreath over to the kitchen window to study it more closely before washing the dishes. The woven branches and primitive style had a classic look to it, like something you'd find in an antique shop or museum. Something you'd expect to pay a lot of money for. It was put together with such care, and she had no doubt that Luc was sincere when he said he'd used burning sage to cleanse the pieces. He obviously believed in its ability to ward off evil spirits. Somehow, Anna felt a power residing in the homemade gift, an essence of sorts, consisting of both natural and spiritual components.

Gently touching the flowers and berries, she became aware of a sadness settling over her, a brooding that was slowly insinuating itself in what should have been a happy family time. It had to do with the man who'd created these traditional presents. In his own way, Anna could see that Luc had an incredible eye for beauty. And he knew so many interesting things about the woods. He had a sensitive side to him, and a loyalty to his friends. She'd seen how genuinely thrilled he was to give the woodcarvings to Charles.

But for all his wilderness experience, his layers upon layers of spiritual knowledge, he had no one to share it with. Anna shook her head and pressed her lips together in a pout. That wasn't the way it was supposed to be. It was that no-good lone wolf thing, she thought.

Anna placed the wreath out of the way on the counter and turned to look at the two men at the table. Michael still had his childlike enthusiasm glowing on his face, and Luc was busy rearranging his backpack. She leaned back against the sink, telling herself that she didn't want this wild man getting any closer to her family. But her mind replayed the image of the owl dropping a feather into Luc's hand. She saw again his shy smile of joy and pride when he'd given her the wreath. It was getting so cold outside—where would he go now?

Before consciously thinking of a reply, she found herself saying, "Stay here for a day or two, Luc." With a sense of purpose she strode across the room, bent forward to lean her hands on the table, and said, "It's getting really cold out. Tomorrow is Halloween. Stay here and come to town with us tomorrow."

Luc grabbed his backpack with both hands and shook it to compact the load. Setting it on the floor again, he folded the top over and began cinching it down.

Anna looked at Michael and nodded for him to say something.

The jovial expression was gone when Luc looked at Michael. Anna could see he'd already decided to leave. She'd bet he didn't want to, though. She'd seen how happy he'd been, how much he enjoyed spending time with their family.

A series of questions popped through her mind. She wondered why he had become such a sad, aloof character. Why wouldn't he let anyone get close? And why couldn't he allow himself to stay for a while? Well, what did she expect? Luc had told them that his mother had been a prostitute. He probably never even knew her. And his father had sent him away to a wild country, to be raised in the woods by complete strangers with an unfamiliar language. No wonder he'd grown up a lone wolf. No wonder he'd learned to rely solely on himself, to keep others at a distance.

"You have to give us a chance to repay your gifts," Anna said with a heart full of sincerity. "I have pies baking in the oven."

Luc held up a hand to stop her. "Do not belittle my gifts by asking to repay them," he said. "You are my friends. I received much enjoyment from making them."

Anna was mortified. "I didn't mean to be rude, Luc. I just thought it would be fun to share the day together. I thought you'd like some companionship after all the time you've spent alone."

"I must go, madame. Your family has filled me up with wonderful food and laughter and friendship." Luc got to his feet and walked over to the door where the coats were hung on pegs.

"Come with us to town, Luc," she called after him. "Let us talk to the sheriff for you."

With his back to them, Luc seemed to hesitate for a moment, but then he hefted his flannel shirt jacket over his shoulders and shrugged his arms into the sleeves.

Again Anna looked at Michael, but he had nothing more to offer. Watching Luc's fingers buttoning the heavy shirt, she said, "You need to talk to the sheriff, Luc. We can help."

Luc didn't respond, but his agitation was obvious in the firm, resolute manner with which he yanked the collar tight under his beard. When he finally turned his glance at her, his stern countenance caused Anna to blush with embarrassment. He nodded at her, turned and bowed to Michael, and in his quaint and formal way of speaking said, "Thank you for your generous hospitality. You have a wonderful family. I feel fortunate to call you friends." Looking at Anna, he said, "But for now I have much to do." He let his glance linger on her, as if to say, "You know what I mean."

Michael and Anna walked with him to the door. Luc found his big fox-skin hat and using two hands, pulled it down tight on his head. Words were scarce; they all felt awkward, and then Charles came running into the room with his birds.

Spotting Luc at the door, he yelped his "Caw, caw, caw," and ran up to throw his arms around Luc's legs. Everyone laughed, and to Anna's great surprise Luc bent down to pick up the boy. He cleared his throat, licked his lips, and softly emitted his sparrow call. Charles lit up with laughter.

"Remember, little one," Luc said. "Waabishki Gondashkway is a bird of much spirit. He is small, like you, but unafraid."

"I am unafraid, too," Charles concurred. "Wabash Gondash!" he exclaimed, bringing a round of laughter from everyone.

"I will see you again, my little friend," Luc said to Charles as he set him back on his feet. He knelt on one knee and held Charles's hands. The twinkle of fun had returned to Luc's eyes. "Like you, I am unafraid, too. White Throat will be our secret," he said to the boy. "When you hear the White Throat's call, you will know that I am near."

The dried skin of the fox head on Luc's hat caught Charles's attention. The empty eye sockets bobbed around as Luc spoke. The boy carefully reached out a finger to touch one of the small openings. "He can't see," Charles said solemnly.

"Oh, yes, he can," Luc replied. "He sees many things." He stood up and reached for his backpack. Charles stood nearby, quietly watching the big man sling the pack over his shoulders. Luc paused when he noticed the boy's downcast, somber expression. "You don't believe me, little one. You think my furry friend can't see because he has no eyes." He flashed his white-toothed grin, aimed it at Anna, and then Michael. Touching his hand to Charles's head, he said, "Just ask your papa. This morning he learned how well the fox can see."

He winked at Michael, nodded a bow toward Anna, and then opened the door and pushed off into the sunny but frigid mid-morning air.

Chapter 15

*L*ate *in the afternoon on Halloween, a fire burned low in the mouth* of a shallow opening in the rock wall. A thick bed of white-hot coals gave off a gentle hiss in rhythm to the shimmering glow of heat. The hunter sat cross-legged before the fire, his back facing the cooler interior of damp, dark rock. He leaned forward slightly, giving his long body a short, hunched-over appearance. All his edges were sharp angles, from his knees and elbows jutting sideways, to his long, crooked nose and wide shoulders. At first glance, from the way the man sat leaning forward, a passerby might think he was preparing to stand up. In reality, however, the hunter was in a stage of waking sleep. A place where dreams were free to come, but conscious thoughts still manipulated his senses.

A handmade leather "possibles" bag laid open at his side, on top of it a stiff-bristled brush. The hunter's long blond hair was unbound and freshly combed out into fine, wavy strands. In his dark beard, which had also been brushed out, several flakes of ashes from the fire had settled. His weather-beaten skin gave off a yellowish glow from the flames, like the well-oiled leather of the bag containing his personal items. Even in this semi-conscious state, the hunter remained tuned into the workings of his body. The familiar odors of dried sweat, wet clothing, and old leather were like a lullaby to his senses. Clutched in his hand was a small silver locket attached to a short length of delicate chain. The clasp was open, and the man's thumb gently stroked a tiny black-and-white photograph of a young woman. Over the years he'd memorized every line of the photo, every nuance of shading. Sometimes, when he sat quietly like this, he could almost smell her, the combination of rosewater and glycerin his mother had used as a bath oil. He knew it was unlikely that he could actually recall an aroma that he attributed to his mother; after all, he had no real memory of her. But he'd been told one time that the sense of smell was the strongest of the human senses, that it fixed itself in one's memory and lingered there for years. So in times of quiet reflection like this, he basked in the sweet feminine memories while gently stroking her cheek.

His father hadn't been the sort to talk much about his mother. A hard-working, heavy-drinking commercial fisherman, his father had spent most of his time either chasing fish around the outer banks of the Bay of Biscay or chasing wild times from one seedy wharf-side bar to another. And the young boy had gone everywhere with his father.

The hunter's breathing became slow and even. His muscles relaxed in a physical meditation, almost to the point of suspended animation. With eyes closed, his senses roamed freely through the nearby woods and became one with the trees and brush, even the small skittering animals on the forest floor. He watched the woods through the eyes of a Canadian jay overhead. From the alder thicket down below, he heard the gentle dapple of trickling water over the narrow slot in the beaver dam.

Once the liquor got into his father, the old man became loud and quarrelsome. As a boy, the hunter remembered bouncing on his father's shoulders while they careened around the bar in drunken fits of dancing. Sometimes, when the raucous behavior turned violent, he took refuge under tables. Other times, he'd found himself sitting in a stranger's lap as he watched the old man climb the back stairs with some woman from the bar. The strangers bought him food and candy, and he seemed to have the recollection of them talking about him. What they'd said he couldn't remember, although in his memory their comments often contained an edge of pity. He did recall, however, the praises regularly spoken about his father. "A great, good guy," they'd said of him. "Generous and fun-loving. The best fisherman in the whole fleet."

His uncle once told him that his mother was many years younger than his father. While the old man had been rough and calloused, in the hunter's memory his mother had been soft and genteel. His father had been the toughest and loudest of the cadre of fishermen and dockworkers that made their living by the sea. And he knew his mother had been one of those who'd made their living secondhand off the workers.

The hunter's chest expanded with a deep, shuddering inhalation. His brow wrinkled slightly with the recollection, and his lips tightened into a sorrowful scowl. Ghostlike images passed through his mind. Fleeting glimpses that could've been her: a woman standing at a distance from the docks, clasping a threadbare shawl against the freshening sea breeze. He could see her melancholy smile as she watched the young boy load fishing equipment into his father's boat.

A ribald laugh from the far end of the bar. Bloodshot eyes leaning over the counter, gawking at him through the smoky haze while he sat in the safety of his father's lap. The sweaty face smudging caked-on makeup into frightening clown-like aberrations. Sweat glistening in the bright lights reflected off the tiers of fancy bottles lined up behind the bar.

The hunter's breathing became ragged as he pinched the tiny locket photo under his thumb. He calmed himself with deep breaths, envisioning the small seaside town of his youth. Holding his father's hand as they walked along the cobblestoned street. The old man, in his boisterous style, shouting greetings to friends they met along the way. Big stone buildings crowding in upon the narrow street. Across the boulevard, a young woman turning to watch as they passed. Slender and tall, a modest scarf pulled close around her head. While having to jog to keep up with his father's long strides, he leaned back to look at the dark-eyed woman watching him, her full lips revealing a wistful smile.

Vincent Wyckoff

A coy backward glance as she led another young man up the rickety wooden stairs at the back of the bar. High heels and a swagger at the hips. A playful slap at the groping hand reaching for her from behind.

Picking up his brush again, the hunter continued his reverie while making several more swipes through his hair. Gently closing the locket with one hand, with the other he separated a wide swath of hair and began the braiding process. The enclosed photo returned to its prominent location in the tightest twist of hair at the top of the braid, nearest his scalp.

It was all about honor, he told himself. Like his father, the biggest and strongest man working the fleet. Generous to his friends, a scourge to his enemies. The hunter jammed the hairbrush back into his "possibles" bag and cinched the rawhide strap closed. With a brooding intensity, he looked out over the dammed-up headwaters pond. Silence reigned here. Everything was pure and clean, the way the earth had been created and intended. It was the only place he felt at ease. Out here, where the spirits of the old ones lingered before passing over.

But it hadn't always felt like home. His father had sent him away— thousands of miles away to a wild land. At first, he'd never known such fear. To cope with the strange surroundings he'd adopted what he could of his father's fearless behavior. The hunter remembered back to those early days in his uncle's village. Subsistence living and government handouts. Poverty and a ruthless climate always barking at the door. But through it all, even those first terrifying weeks and months, he'd never cried. Never given in to the fear or the ache at the loss of his parents.

During the long winter months the Indian elders told stories and related the legends of their ancient heroes. He remembered being mesmerized by the tales of Manitou. Here was a powerful spirit that could transform the evils of the world. As a youngster he'd latched onto this mighty force. He'd learned all the stories, accepted into his being the hope they conveyed. Manitou could change the behavior of people as easily as it changed its own form. As a life force, perhaps in the guise of a bear or wolf, Manitou could strike down its enemies.

Matche-Manitou, an evil spirit and trickster. A snake lying in wait beside the path. Quick to strike, and often deadly. An avenging serpent, preying on those who would upset the purity of creation. Withdrawing in silence into the depths of the forest, an unseen spirit in search of honor.

The hunter pulled his braid tighter. The yanking at his scalp interrupted his meditative visions, so he abandoned the memories and they quickly fled to their secret places in his subconscious. Without untangling his crossed legs, he deftly pushed himself to his feet. His movements were silent, but when he stood up the big male wolf got to his feet, too. When they were all in camp together, the alpha male made his bed just outside the cave opening. He slept far enough away from the fire, however, to remain completely concealed when darkness fell. If one of his brethren wandered in too close, he'd emit a low snarl of warning to emphasize his place as leader. When they were at rest like this, the pack dispersed themselves farther out along the base of the ridge and in narrow niches in the cliff face just above the opening.

The hunter accepted their presence as a matter of course. Kindred spirits drawn together. At some level his instinctive nature communicated itself to them. The wolves were outcasts roaming the fringes, staying out of sight. He was a loner sharing their distrust of humanity. As a pack, the wolves retained their own identity, leaving for days at a time to hunt the remotest regions of their forest kingdom. Searching out the weakest and most vulnerable. Returning to this safe haven beneath the solid rock bluff.

Looking around, the hunter contemplated the cozy, cheerful fire, and his few belongings stacked around him. It was past time to return home. He shivered at the thought of the dismal existence in the tiny village in the far north. For years he'd considered returning to his boyhood home in France, but he knew there was nothing for him there. He'd heard nothing from his father since being dumped in his uncle's village. And he preferred to think of his mother the way she existed in his childhood memories.

No, there was another reason why he lingered: the words Anna spoke to him yesterday. She'd said they were friends. And Michael had given him work. With the boy, they'd been more of a family to him in the few hours they'd spent together than anyone else in his life.

You lied to her. The one person you truly respected. The only woman to show a willingness to be your friend. You told Anna you had returned to stop Manitou. But you don't have that kind of power. And the elders didn't call on you for help—you used them as an excuse to leave the village.

Sneaking away from his uncle's home on a starlit night had left him feeling cowardly and more alone than ever. For days and weeks he'd wandered, generally heading south, living off the land the way his uncle and the old ones had taught him. But now he realized that the very act of avoiding towns and roadways, of eschewing the company of others while prowling through the forest like a ghost, threatened to turn him into the very monster everyone feared.

The alpha male suddenly jerked his head around and looked downstream. In the same instant, from a protected place curled up below the cave opening, another wolf leapt to his feet to begin a low-slung, furtive lope toward the heavy cover of brush around the north end of the headwaters.

Someone was coming.

With shaking hands, the hunter stashed his belongings into the oversized backpack. Above him he heard the clattering of dislodged pebbles as the wolf pack moved across the face of the bluff. After jamming the rest of his things into the pack, he buckled the flap down tight and forced his senses back out to the surrounding wilderness. His eyes roamed over the silent landscape, peering intently into the alder thicket near the beaver dam where the big Dakota sheriff had appeared a couple of weeks ago.

Nothing moved. But in his experience the wolves were never wrong. Something indeed approached his camp in the rock wall. Something to be avoided.

Manitou.

The hunter buried his fire under sand and rocks, and then scattered leaves and forest debris around the opening to cover any marks he'd made in the sandy floor. After looking around to ensure he hadn't forgotten anything, he hoisted the backpack and slung the straps over his shoulders.

The long gray tail of the fox-skin hat curled over the pack and around his shoulder when he slapped it on his head. The open walkway along the rock wall provided a track-free, narrow passageway to the edge of the dense conifer cover. The wolf pack was gone, but he spotted the alpha male just inside a fringe of dogwoods near the pond.

Honor. It was an intangible thing, a character trait developed and grounded in one's personal story. Like the sheriff and his ancestry, or Anna and her work and family. But what did he have? A prostitute, a drunk, and ages-old tales of tribal heroes conquering mighty enemies.

Outside the cave opening, standing on solid, windswept rock, he paused for one final look around. This little patch of forest had felt like a good place to call home. He didn't really want to leave, but the persistent urge to escape was even stronger. The hunter set a determined grimace on his face and settled the backpack more squarely on his shoulders.

A last look downstream. Over the silence a soft sigh floated on the breeze: Matche-Manitou passing through the late afternoon shadows. Following the rock ledge, the hunter soon entered the covering safety of a dense stand of conifers. He darted forward, headed north, his thick flannel shirt quietly shoving aside the soft young balsam branches reaching out for him. The wolves had disappeared. A gray jay called from the top of a dead cedar.

The hunter stopped.

Honor. It was indeed an intangible commodity. Sure, it resided in personal stories and mighty deeds, but to most folks it simply consisted of decisions rendered in the face of fear, and behavior conducted with integrity. To stand rather than run.

The hunter looked over his shoulder as a quaking shudder rattled his chest. He let his mind's eye follow the trail down past the beaver dam, out to the Superior Hiking Trail and the girls' campsite, and eventually to the little town by the sea. And from there, up over the ridge to the square-logged house at the end of a gravel road, and the little boy who wasn't afraid.

Chapter 16

*I*t was already full-on dark outside by late afternoon when Sheriff Fastwater met with the law enforcement personnel assembled in his headquarters office. Phil Simanich had recruited a handful of volunteer officers from Duluth and brought a box of police radios to hand out. He'd also allowed Detective Bryce Jepson to ride with him. Jepson had been reinstated that morning on a probationary basis after a legal panel inquiry into the shooting along the Duluth waterfront. There'd been no witnesses, so the detective's testimony and clean record had carried the day. Simanich figured this would be a good opportunity to guide the young man back into action. For his part, Jepson sported a homemade costume to help him blend in with the local party crowd.

Fastwater had also called in all available county personnel, and now he looked over the group as the radios were handed out. They were all professionals, but he'd requested no uniforms, and the casual attire and easygoing joviality didn't inspire a lot of confidence. They split up afterward, some leaving individually, some in groups of two or three, to meander the streets monitoring the crowd.

Jepson approached the sheriff while Simanich handed out the last of the radios. "Do you really think all this is necessary?" he asked, waving an arm at the departing crew. "I mean, that guy in Duluth . . ."

"Listen, Detective, I'm sorry about what happened down there." Fastwater stepped closer. "I had no idea it would turn violent like that."

"But he was the guy you wanted to talk to," Jepson argued. "I found him, and he ran. Case closed."

Fastwater nodded. "The kid had a lot of problems. He was really messed up. But he didn't attack these women up here."

"How do you know? How can you say that?"

With just a glance the sheriff looked over at Simanich and asked for another minute. Turning back to the detective, he said, "I'm sorry for what you're going through. I'm sure it's hard. But that kid had no way of getting up here. No job, no money, no car."

"But still," Jepson interrupted, "he had some serious mental issues. Delusions. He could have found a way up here if he wanted. It seems obvious he was guilty by the way he ran."

"He didn't know anyone from around here," Fastwater countered. "He had no idea about the girls' campsite or the real estate agent's running schedule."

"But you met him. Four years ago today you met him, and he was covered in blood."

Fastwater nodded. "It was his own blood. He was a very disturbed young man. And you're right, he was totally delusional. But in all the years he spent in the state hospital he never exhibited a penchant for violence."

"A penchant for violence? The guy was nuts, Sheriff!"

Fastwater's voice acquired a harder edge. "If you think this is such a waste of time, Detective, why are you here?" He looked at the costume the young man wore: a tattered fur coat, like something from a second-hand store, and a ridiculous coyote or gray wolf hat. The hat was threadbare and dried out with age, with a newer, fluffy raccoon tail attached with hair clips.

Simanich eased up beside them. "We should probably get out there," he said, a tone of caution in his voice. "I'm going to run through some radio checks in a few minutes."

In response, Fastwater turned toward the door.

"What about that French guy?" Jepson asked. "The one we met in the café a few weeks ago."

Simanich placed a hand on Jepson's shoulder, directing him to follow the sheriff. "If that fellow from Duluth isn't our guy," he said, "then we have every reason to be here tonight. The town is packed with people."

• • • •

Activity around town had been increasing all week, and most of the tourist gift shops were open once again. Variations of Indian flute music emanated from one shop after another. Out-of-towners wandered the short streets of Black Otter Bay, bringing with them an injection of outside energy as well as pocketbooks full of cash. They strolled past the café and gas station and the mini mall consisting of old stone- and cedar-sided buildings, with the ugly pea soup–green post office across the road. The angled parking slots were full today, and visitors wouldn't have recognized the place a few weeks ago. After Labor Day the sidewalks had been deserted and the gift shops closed for the season, but the annual Halloween bash filled the village with revelers, so that even the café would stay open through the dinner hour tonight.

"What I'd like to know," Phil Simanich said to the small cluster of folks sitting at the counter, "is just exactly who this Bernie Hofstad is . . . or was."

Simanich and Sheriff Fastwater had stopped in for a cup of coffee. Detective Jepson had left them to wander around town, no doubt chasing after that young reporter, Fastwater thought. Christine Anderson had returned with her camera crew to do a follow-up story. Probably one of those sappy feel-good pieces, he thought, the type showing resilient townsfolk, but highlighting panoramic images of Lake Superior in the background.

"I remember old Bernie from when I was a kid." Red Tollefson spoke up like a resident expert on the subject. "His real name was Bertrand," he informed them, as if that would be the next logical question.

Anna Eskild sidestepped along the length of the counter freshening everyone's coffee cup. She'd been working since noon, and while the physical aspects of being on her feet all day were not a problem, the socializing and constant commotion wore her down. Michael was out trick-or-treating with Charles. Later, they'd stop in at the dance while she closed up the café, and then they'd all leave for the peace and quiet of home.

Anna said, "His name was Bernard, Red. Bernard Hofstad."

Red arched a husky eyebrow under his Northern Hydraulics cap. "Don't you think I'd know what his real name was?" he asked, incredulous. "You weren't even born until thirty years after he died. I was there, Anna. I may have been a kid, but I knew the man. His real name was Bertrand."

"Bernard," Anna said quietly to Simanich.

"Now listen here, little Miss Know-Everything—"

"If his name was Bertrand, why didn't they call him 'Bertie'?"

Red sat back on his stool as if slapped, an expression of absolute confusion and dismay contorting his face.

Anna wore her ten-year-old Black Otter Bay Café t-shirt from when she used to work there. This one was red, which drew out the highlights in her strawberry-blond hair. It was warm in the café, causing a rosy glow in her fair-skinned cheeks.

The café had been busy since it opened before dawn. Marcy had worked most of the day, only leaving a short time earlier to work on her costume with Matt. A constant drone of conversation filled the room, with bursts of laughter erupting from time to time among the costume-clad patrons.

Fastwater fingered the portable radio clipped to his belt. Every now and then the static increased in volume and he had to turn it down. After a while, when the airwaves had been too quiet, he'd slowly turn it up again, just to ease his mind that no one was calling for help.

Simanich leaned into the counter, and to Anna, said, "You know, it really doesn't matter to me what this guy's real name was. I just wanted to know how your Halloween party got tied up with him."

Owen Porter cleared his throat and sat up straighter. "Bernie was a trapper in the old days," he explained. Anna nodded encouragement and turned to prepare the coffee maker for another batch. "He lived in town here," Owen continued, "but ran a trapline extending up the shore. That was back in the days when a fellow could still make a living off fur."

Anna looked at them over her shoulder. "Most everyone else around here fished," she said. "Some cut timber, until all the big forests were gone. Bernie was a lifelong bachelor, so he wasn't missed much when he took off for several days on his trapline."

"Must have been about nineteen twenty-five," Red commented. "The day after Halloween, when a big November gale blew in off Lake Superior."

"It was nineteen twenty," Anna corrected. "And it started on Halloween. Haven't you seen the posters around town? It's the one-hundredth anniversary."

"Nope, nope. Couldn't have been that early," Red replied, shaking his head. "My dad was working—"

Owen interrupted. "It was nineteen twenty, Red. Do the math."

Simanich laughed. "I don't think it really matters what year it was. Just tell me what happened."

Anna pulled her order booklet from her back pocket and retrieved her pen from over her ear. Walking out from behind the counter, she said, "You tell him what happened, Owen. I've got customers waiting."

The men sitting at the counter turned to look at the lanky young man perched on his stool. "Well, it's like Red was saying," he began. "A huge storm blew up on the lake. Of course, in those days there wasn't any radar, or even telephones. A lot of boats were caught out there when the weather turned bad. Most of the fishing fleet from Black Otter Bay got home safely—those old-timers were pretty good at reading the sky."

Owen looked at Phil Simanich sitting two stools away and seemed pleased to find the big man paying close attention to his story. After taking a sip of coffee, Owen sat up straighter and turned to face his audience.

"There used to be a lot of schooners that ran along the shore, hauling supplies from one village to the next. Even the mail came in on boats. You have to remember that there weren't any roads back then, so everything traveled by water."

"Barges, schooners, steamers. Anything that would float," Red commented, adopting his voice of a higher learner again. "But they stayed along the shoreline. Not too many captains dared to venture out there beyond the sight of land."

There was a pause while everyone looked at Red. Fastwater fiddled with the radio again, and Simanich asked, "So what happened?"

Red sat back and nodded at Owen, apparently giving his okay for him to continue.

"The storm raged for two full days," Owen went on. "Close to two dozen boats sank from Canada clear down to Wisconsin. Now, Bernie, he had a small log hut he'd built up the shore. He'd stay there sometimes when out on his trapline. It was a tiny place, no bigger than a good-sized closet. It was on top of a tall cliff overlooking the lake."

Fastwater glanced over at Owen. It always startled him to see how tall the man was. With his hair cut a little longer in back, and wearing a tight-fitting navy blue turtleneck, he looked even taller and more gangly than usual. Like some kind of giant spider, the sheriff thought, all arms and legs, hunched over the counter.

Owen continued. "The way the story goes, it all started in the middle of the night. Bernie had hunkered down that first day in the cabin waiting out the storm. He was suddenly jerked awake on Halloween night by a thunderous crash. The cot and cabin shook beneath him. He said he thought it was the end of the world. He ran outside but the wind howled all around, and icy sleet pellets slashed against him. Tree branches snapped off, and debris crashed through the air. From out on the lake, a fading yellow light was glimpsed through the fog and rain, but when he went closer to the cliff edge, there was just the black, windswept sea."

Owen paused for a sip of water, licked his lips, and went on. "From out of the dark a terrified voice arose. 'Help me!' it called, but in the noise and confusion of the storm Bernie couldn't tell where it came from. When a brief lull in the wind occurred, he heard the new foghorn down at Split Rock bellowing into the night and fog. And then the voices again, 'Help! Help me!' Later, because of the howling winds and crashing waves, he described the voices as coming from all around him; out on the lake, up in the night sky, and from deep in the forest. He became convinced that the Earth had opened up and all the demons of Hell were coming for him. He scrambled back into the cabin, bolted the door, and hid under the warmth of his fur robes and blankets."

Owen had a reputation for telling tall tales, especially about the women he allegedly dated in Duluth. But Fastwater had to admit, even if he did tend to exaggerate from time to time, the kid could still tell a good story.

"Okay," Simanich said. "I get the Halloween connection now."

"And it gets better," Red exclaimed. He backhanded Owen's shoulder, adding, "tell him what happened next."

"Well, by first light Bernie was on the trail to town," he explained. "The storm at sea still raged, but he had the fear of the Devil in his pants, so he raced the shoreline back to town. And he came right here," he said, slapping the counter. "There wasn't a sheriff's office back then, or even a cop in town. Bernie stumbled into the café here and told his story. Of course, they fed the poor man plenty of hot food and coffee, but you have to remember this was a village of hard-nosed lumberjacks and fearless seamen. When Bernie told them about voices calling for help, and lights out on the lake, they laughed at him. They said the goblins of Halloween had gotten into his head. The woodsmen said nobody would be fool enough to venture out into the forest in that storm, and the fishermen said no one could survive the wrath of those twenty-foot seas."

Red guffawed. "One guy told him to get a wife if he wanted to hear voices in his head."

This caused a brief chuckle along the counter, with Anna simply rolling her eyes.

"It got so bad for old Bernie," Red added, "that he just up and left. Hiked all the way back up to his cabin."

Owen nodded. "By late in the day the storm seemed to be blowing out. Oh, it was still wicked nasty in the woods, and the sea still slammed against the rocks, but it wasn't as frightening in the light of day."

Simanich asked, "So, Bernie made it back to the cabin safe and sound?"

"Yup. Built up a big fire in the stove and settled in for the night. Believe me, by the time darkness settled in the old trapper was hidden away, tucked under the folds of his furry blankets. But deep in the night he awoke. Once again, he heard voices on the wind. Men crying out for help. For a while he thought it was just a trick of nature, you know, the sound of the wind in the pines and the waves against the cliff. He remembered the ridicule he'd received in town. But the harder he listened, the more convinced he became that there were real voices in trouble out there, so he lit an old lantern and went outside."

"That's braver than anything I would have done," Red proclaimed.

"Be quiet," Anna admonished, swatting at Red with her dishtowel.

Everyone laughed, but attention soon reverted to Owen. "Bernie fought his way against the wind and rain toward the cliff's precipice. In the dark, tree branches buffeted him, and the wind snuffed out his little oil-fed lantern. But now that he was outside, he could definitely hear the shouts of men out on the water. Finally, crawling the last few yards, he peered over the edge. Fifty feet below he saw an old steamer barge bashed against the cliff face. After shoving it up on the rocky coast, the waves were slowly grinding it to pieces."

"It was a Canadian steamer packet out of Fort William and Port Arthur," Red interjected. "Hauling supplies down to Two Harbors and Duluth."

Owen paused while his small audience looked at Red. Nobody seemed ready to argue with his facts, so when Simanich returned his attention to the young storyteller, Owen continued. "There were seven men on board clinging to what remained of their boat. There isn't any shoreline to speak of along that stretch, just some jagged boulders and the cliff, so there wasn't any place for the men to go. Bernie hurried back to his cabin and retrieved a long coil of stout rope. He lashed one end of it to a tree nearest the cliff, then looked down at the men. Waves washed over them as the storm slowly disintegrated their boat against the rocks. In the noise and mayhem it took a while for Bernie's shouts to be heard, but finally one of the sailors looked up. Bernie threw the rope down, and one by one the men made desperate lunges to grasp the lifeline and climb their way up the cliff."

"Wow," Simanich whistled. "That must've been one god-awful climb."

"You bet it was," Red said. "They all had frostbitten fingers. And the waves pounded against them even as they climbed to safety. But every single one of them made it," he concluded with obvious pride. "Thanks to Bernie Hofstad."

"So where does this party and dance come in?" Simanich asked.

"Well, after Bernie got the men into his cabin," Owen said, picking up the thread of his story, "he saw that they were in pretty rough shape. Half frozen, all their clothes soaked through. He built up a roaring fire and tried to make them as comfortable as possible, but the place was so small they barely fit everyone inside. And he didn't have dry clothes or enough blankets to go around. So, once they were sure that everyone was accounted for, Bernie once again made the trek to town to get help."

"He walked all night," Red added, "and showed up here at first light."

"Later that day," Owen continued, "when the storm abated somewhat, a couple fishing boats took off to rescue the crew. They brought with them dry clothes and food and blankets. They had to land far short of the wreck site and walk overland to Bernie's cabin. They found the men hungry and cold. Some had frostbite, and a couple had broken bones, but they all survived. Not a trace of their ship was ever found, though."

"Lake Superior ate that old boat like a picnic lunch," Red spouted. "And I bet she was mad that she didn't get the men, too. Sort of like having a hot dog without the ketchup and mustard."

Another pause while everyone aimed quizzical frowns at Red. "What?" he asked, sitting back defensively.

"Anyway," Owen said, "Bernie became somewhat of a celebrity around here. Even had his picture in the Duluth newspaper. The photo showed him dressed in his big fur hat and coat. The next year, just for fun, a couple of locals hiked up to his old shack to commemorate his heroics. It became kind of an annual event for a while. Each year, more people would make the trek, some even camping out at the cabin. A few years later, however, when the highway was put through, the old shack was lost."

"They used to commemorate Bernie's story the day after Halloween," Anna interjected. "But eventually the two were combined. Because he always wore fur, popular Halloween costumes around here often involve fur hats, gloves, or even coats."

"Werewolves are popular," Red commented. "Or the Big Bad Wolf."

Fastwater peered at Red, a sudden intimation floating into view, but before he could think it through the door flew open and Bryce Jepson came in, a broad smile lighting his face. Soon the sheriff saw why. Following close behind was Christine Anderson and her two-man camera crew. She turned a giggly face up to Jepson as he held the door for her. They paused a moment while their eyes adjusted to the dimness inside, then Jepson led them over to the counter, where they gathered behind the row of seated men. The young detective made some brief introductions as Red's open-mouthed grin threatened to dislodge his false teeth.

To Anna, Christine asked, "Do you mind if we take a few shots in here?" Before she could respond, Christine put a hand on the cameraman's shoulder and pointed across the room toward the windows. "Let's put the tripod over there. With the windows behind you, we'll have enough natural lighting so we won't need the spots." The men walked off to do as she requested, bumping their way among the tables with their armloads of equipment.

"How are preparations for the dance coming?" Simanich asked, looking at Jepson.

The young man shook his head and laughed. "There's about a million people out there," he reported. "And it seems like half of them are copying my Big Bad Wolf costume." Jepson stepped closer to his boss and lowered his voice. "Our people are spread out all over town. They're up on the streets, in the gift shops, and down by the bar and harbor. Hey," he added, digging in his pocket. "They're giving out these commemorative patches. Look at this," he said, holding out a colorful cloth patch with the words "100th Annual," and the date sewn on it.

Fastwater noted the excitement in Jepson's voice. He'd bet it wasn't just the patch that made him so animated. Glancing at Christine, he was again struck by her stunning, simple beauty. Today she wore a powder blue beret. Her thick blond hair curled gently over her shoulders. A tight-knit, authentic Norwegian wool sweater, dark blue with a white woven design, kept her warm.

Christine saw the sheriff looking at her and stepped forward to speak. "It's so good to see you again, Sheriff." She bestowed on him one of the warmest smiles he'd ever seen. Just how sincere it was, he couldn't tell. When he didn't respond, she looked at Simanich and said, "I understand from the sheriff here that you're close to making an arrest." Again, the too-warm smile. Fastwater was pleased to see his old companion refrain from commenting. Holding his coffee cup up in front of his face, Simanich turned a wary eye on the sheriff.

Almost imperceptibly, Fastwater nodded an acknowledgment of his friend's loyalty. To Christine, he said, "It's kind of dark out there for photojournalism, isn't it?"

Christine turned to face him, the smile gone now, replaced by a determined smirk. "I heard your nephew may soon be a suspect," she said.

Fastwater stepped back. "Where did you hear that?"

"Just some talk around town."

The sheriff looked at Simanich still hiding behind his coffee cup, but his friend simply rolled his eyes and turned to watch Anna pick up a tray of food from the kitchen window ledge. When he glanced at Jepson and the young man looked away, however, he knew the origin of the rumor. Probably an attempt to impress the reporter, he thought.

Completely redirecting the conversation, Christine said, "You have some pretty spirited folks around here, Sheriff. I mean, just a few weeks ago they lost one of their very own young citizens. Then there was that brutal, ugly attack out at the campsite, and now they're hosting this big event. I can tell you there are no glum faces out there. And we did, by the way, get some splendid footage of the harbor and crowd. Even a close-up of your nephew. You know, just in case we need it."

Fastwater cast his glance along the line of men at the counter. Owen Porter stared open-mouthed at Christine, and even Red seemed offended as he turned to look away at the crowd of customers in the café.

Before the silence became awkward, Jepson piped up, "Boy, that food sure looks good. Want to join me for dinner?" he asked Christine.

The reporter looked at her crew setting up in the far corner of the cafe. "I think I'll go see how the boys are doing with the equipment," she said. "Maybe I'll get a bite later."

Owen stood, and to Christine asked, "Mind if I watch them set up?"

Christine smiled and led the way through the tables. Owen ambled along behind her like an overgrown teenager, not quite comfortable with his long feet and arms, ducking his head out of habit even though the ceiling was several feet above him.

Jepson took Owen's seat, looked around for Anna to place an order, but then noticed Fastwater's dark-eyed glare. "I don't know what you and Phil have been talking about," the sheriff muttered through clenched teeth, "but it should be pretty obvious that Leonard is not a suspect. He never will be."

Jepson nodded. "Okay, I'm sorry. I didn't mean any offense. But you've ruled out the crazy dude from Duluth, and now you took Leonard's name off the table, so what about that French-Canadian guy? Are you done with him, too?"

Fastwater paused. He drew himself up and took a deep breath. "Phil says he couldn't find anything on him in Canada. There's no record of him."

"But he was just searching for a name. Official records are really hit or miss in those small villages. And what if he had a different name in Canada?"

Fastwater's eyebrow went up.

"You know," Jepson said, "at one point I thought I might be onto something."

"What was that?"

"Well, about a year ago a Canadian Mountie was dispatched to investigate some acts of violence against Cree women living in a little village out in the bush, out in the middle of nowhere. Apparently, one of the women even disappeared."

Fastwater sat up with interest. His hand dropped to his side to turn down the squelch on his radio. "What happened?"

"That's just it," Jepson responded. "Nothing happened. They were mostly all Natives in the village, and none of them wanted to talk to this white policeman. The women in question were mostly prostitutes. They didn't exactly make a habit of talking about their customers."

Anna returned with the coffeepot and poured a cup for Jepson. "What's this about prostitutes?" she asked.

"About a year ago some Cree women were attacked by one of their customers," Jepson informed her. "Way up in Canada, some little hole-in-the-wall place. I don't remember the name."

"No one was arrested?" Fastwater asked.

"Nope. There really wasn't much to it. After the Mountie left, there wasn't any more trouble."

Fastwater jumped ahead. "Which means their perpetrator could now be down here."

"Hey, Marlon," Simanich cautioned. "That's a pretty big stretch you're making."

"Is it?" Fastwater asked. "He said one of the women up there disappeared. We never would have known what happened to Niki if those hikers hadn't found her body."

Fastwater's mind raced along. It all tied together, even his previous talk about Manitou. The Cree were big into all that superstition stuff. If the Frenchman had grown up in a Cree village, he'd have heard all their legends.

Jepson said to Anna, "The sheriff here thinks it's a French-Canadian who's responsible for Niki's death."

"You mean Luc?" she asked. "It couldn't be. We just saw him yesterday."

"He was here?" Fastwater demanded.

"He just stopped by," Anna said defensively. "He'd made some presents for us." Anna's brow furrowed. Looking at Jepson, she added, "You know, speaking of prostitutes, he told us that his mother had been a prostitute."

"I wanted to talk to him," Fastwater said. "You were supposed to send him into town."

"I told him that," Anna responded. "We even said we'd go with him. But he said it wasn't him you were looking for."

Fastwater's glare raced around the room. "Well then, just who does he think I'm supposed to be looking for?"

Anna didn't answer, but didn't back down from the sheriff's stare. When he reached for the coffee cup, she turned to leave, but in a calmer voice, he asked, "You say he made some gifts for you. What kind of presents did he make?"

Everyone looked at Anna. "He carved some little wooden birds for Charles," she answered. "And he made two pairs of moccasins for Michael. Used moose hide for the soles, and sewed them together with strips of rabbit hide." Her gaze wandered over the crowded room before settling back on the sheriff. "For me, he made a beautiful wreath out of dried flowers and branches he'd gathered in the forest. It even has an owl feather in it. He told me he'd followed an old Indian custom in making it. Said it would protect me—that it would ward off Manitou."

The men at the counter were staring at her, and again she looked away. "He said he was just passing through," she explained, trying to lighten her voice. But the light in her eyes clouded over as she pondered their recent encounter. As an afterthought, she added, "My guess is he's on his way back up north."

Fastwater's stare once again intensified. "What else did he say about Manitou?"

Anna refocused on the sheriff. "He said that Manitou had been called upon to do good in the world. But the spirit was angry, so instead he was using his strength to hurt people. He told me the village elders had sent him out to stop the evil. He said he had some special powers or something that would help him."

"Okay, now you're creeping me out," Jepson said with a laugh to break the tension. Then he looked at the sheriff as he added, "This has got to be our guy."

Simanich looked at Fastwater. "What did he mean when he said he'd been sent to stop Manitou?"

Owen Porter had sauntered back up to the counter, and now he cleared his throat. "Ahem. Maybe this Manitou character is his other personality." Now everyone's attention turned to Owen. He shrugged. "Sounds like he even knows about it. And his mother could be the trigger. It could even be that he made up the story about the Native elders to convince himself and others, like Anna here, that it's not him."

Fastwater looked at Simanich. "We need to get word up to the border."

The captain frowned. "I doubt he'll try passing through a border checkpoint, Marlon. Without an ID or anything they'd never let him through."

Jepson got off his stool and pulled his phone out. "I'm on it, Sheriff. I'll make a couple calls," he said, walking toward a quiet corner of the room.

Then the café door swung wide open and Mrs. Virginia Bean strolled in, her hand resting on Abby Simon's arm. Dressed in a royal purple floor-length gown, the postmistress held her head high and looked over the café crowd like a queen inspecting her entourage. It was a grand entrance, the only thing missing a quartet of trumpets to announce her.

Anna ran out from behind the counter and performed an awkward curtsy, after which Mrs. Bean giggled and offered her a hand up. Abby reached out to straighten the cumbersome, gaudy tiara on Mrs. Bean's head, then turned to the assembled regulars. "Ladies and gentlemen," she announced. "I give you the queen."

Applause broke out along the counter as everyone turned to look. A purple blush powdered on her cheeks highlighted the sparkle in Mrs. Bean's violet-blue eyes. Necklaces consisting of several strands of linked silver, gold, and white plastic baubles were looped around her neck. Mirrored pieces of glass and plastic in the tiara reflected the fluorescent lights in a dazzling display of fake opulence. She held her regal pose, enjoying the moment in the spotlight, while seeking out the sheriff's face.

Fastwater stood in place, still contemplating the discussion about Manitou, when Simanich grabbed his arm and pulled him toward the grinning and giggling Mrs. Bean. The sheriff looked lost as his friend bowed before the queen. "Your Majesty," Simanich announced, "I present to you the royal Knight of Law Enforcement, and your loyal servant, the Sheriff of B.O.B."

"To the Sheriff of Bob!" Red cheered, raising a coffee cup in toast.

Simanich bowed again, backed away, and left the two of them near the door. Mrs. Bean's smile radiated pure joy. The glow in her cheeks wasn't all brushed on, the sheriff noticed, and he thought she looked ten years younger.

She said, "Oh, Marlon, I always wanted to be a princess." She looked down at the necklaces and gown. "And now I'm a queen."

"Yes you are, Mrs. Bean," he said. "You look lovely."

"Abby helped me with the makeup."

Fastwater cleared his throat, but before he could speak Christine Anderson approached, wearing an expression of awe and reverence. "My goodness," she exclaimed. "I didn't know there'd be royalty in town." She edged her way in closer, bumping Fastwater aside. "We have to get some pictures," she said. "Would you mind stepping over by my camera crew?" She introduced herself while reaching for Mrs. Bean's hand. The postmistress looked at Fastwater, but the determined reporter pulled her away before she could say anything.

The sheriff watched them go, with Jepson following close behind, the cell phone still pressed to his ear.

Simanich came up and patted Fastwater on the back. "Don't let her get away, Sheriff."

Fastwater emitted a half-hearted grunt, then nodded toward the camera crew. "Seems like the detective is getting pretty chummy with that reporter."

Simanich looked across the room at them. "I guess they've gone out a couple times. I think he's way out of his league with that one."

"I didn't know they were dating."

"I wouldn't call it dating. She's always hanging around the police department, looking for stories. I think she goes out with him hoping to land a scoop. That's why I have to be careful what I say around him."

"You mean like Leonard being a suspect?"

Simanich turned to him. "Okay, I'm sorry about that, Marlon. I never should have said that. But he knows I wasn't serious." He looked over the sheriff's shoulder at the door. "Let's go outside. I need some air. It's getting a little too crowded in here."

They stepped into the parking lot, where the cold night air met them with a refreshing caress. Tucking hands into pockets, they stood side by side looking at the crowds streaming along the sidewalk. A raucous cheer erupted from the parking lot down by the municipal bar. Electric guitar music from the warm-up band could be heard every time the door opened.

Fastwater adjusted his radio and turned to his friend. "I've got a feeling it's going to be a long night."

"It's going to be fun," Simanich replied, a forced enthusiasm in his voice. "And I hope you plan to spend at least some of it with Mrs. Bean." When the sheriff didn't respond, he asked, "Are you still thinking about that Manitou stuff?"

Fastwater took a deep breath and nodded. "Manitou. Wolves. It's just a big mess."

"Why would that French-Canadian guy tell Anna he was sent to stop it?"

The sheriff exhaled and turned to face his old comrade. "Manitou is a trickster, Phil," he explained, as if thinking out loud. "He's got our minds all mixed up. He has us pointing fingers at each other while he's disguising the facts."

They stood in the glow from the café windows, the ebb and flow of street noises washing over them. "Disguising the facts?" Simanich asked.

"I just can't help feeling that I've missed something."

"You mean like a clue or something?"

"No. We have all the clues. The answer is right there. We have the parameters for the case, and all the information we need or will likely get, but I just can't see it."

Simanich studied his friend, wishing he could help by thinking of the correct words or phrases to unlock the mystery.

Fastwater shook his head in resignation. "I'm telling you, Phil, it's all there, but the pieces are mixed up. Manitou is playing a game—he's setting us up."

A moment later Simanich shivered, and the sheriff spun to look up at the darkened ridge behind town. A mournful howl drifted down the slope, disappearing into the crowd noise. Then another one, louder and closer, a sound full of anguish and despair. The pair peered up into the dark as more howls erupted from above, a yipping chorus that rained down on them like primordial drops of fear.

"Listen to that," Simanich said in a voice hardly more than a whisper.

The howls became louder and more distinct. A pack of wolves on the move. Fastwater rocked back on his heels. The wolves were on the run, getting closer. Excitement echoed in their howls. A pack on the hunt, looking for a kill.

The sheriff pursed his lips into a frown and nodded. "He's coming."

Chapter 17

*D*etective *Bryce Jepson finally got his dinner later that evening.* Christine hadn't joined him, opting instead to shoot footage of the townsfolk and costumed revelers carousing through town. The café dinner rush was over, but tourists still lingered in gift shops and down at the municipal bar where the Halloween dance was going strong. Michael had dropped Charles off at the café after trick-or-treating, and now was taking a turn himself to see the festivities at the bar.

With the dinner hour behind her, Anna posted the "CLOSED" sign in the window. Only two or three tables and booths were occupied, one of them by Mrs. Virginia Bean, still awaiting an escort to the dance. She sat in a booth telling little Charles an old folk tale about Benji the Beaver.

Finally pushing his plate aside, Jepson asked Anna, "What, no costume tonight? Aren't you going down to the dance?"

"I kind of doubt it, unless Marcy stops by to help me close up. Did you see her costume?"

"I did. Raggedy Ann. And her friend Matt is Raggedy Andy. I guess the big story is he shaved off his beard for the white face paint."

Anna smiled. "His daughter, Abby, told me that in her whole life she'd never seen her dad without a beard."

"Well, they were dancing up a storm last time I saw them."

Anna placed a stack of plates under the counter. "What's with that get-up of yours?"

Jepson looked down. "This?" he asked, holding out the lapels of his fur coat.

"It looks like something old Bernie Hofstad dragged in."

Jepson laughed and pulled a rubberized snout out of his pocket. He strapped it to his face with an elastic cord, and then plopped the beat-up wolfskin hat on his head. "There you go," he announced. "The Big Bad Wolf."

Anna smiled. "That's not what I'd call it. Especially with that raccoon tail."

"Well, maybe I'll sew on this '100th Annual' patch to commemorate the occasion."

Anna smiled, grabbed a tray of cups from the dishwasher, and began stacking them under the counter. Her expression turned serious when she said, "You know, our friend Niki, the woman who was murdered, had a costume of Little Red Riding Hood. She wore it last year."

"Is that right?"

Anna nodded. "That was one hot costume."

"I bet it was," the detective replied. "She was a good-looking gal."

"You knew her?"

Jepson reached for his coffee. "I saw a lot of photos of her during the investigation." He returned her serious look. "Were you two close friends? Did she ever talk about her life before she moved here?"

Anna laughed. "I don't think she was real close to anyone in town. It takes a while for folks around here to warm up to a newcomer." She grabbed more cups, and then paused again. "But she came out to our place regularly. She loved flowers, and did some gardening of her own."

"But nothing about her past?"

"Not really. I know she went out with a couple guys from the snowmobile club. She thought they were a refreshing break from the hotshot male egos in Duluth. Her words, not mine."

"I see."

"What about that reporter? Is she into your Big Bad Wolf thing?"

Jepson snickered. "No, I don't think it's her style. But a fellow can try, right?"

Anna paused to ring out a couple more customers. A welcomed quiet settled over the café when the door closed behind them. She looked at her son sitting with Mrs. Bean in the booth, and then, turning back to the detective, she placed her hands on the counter and leaned forward. "So tell me, Detective, what do you think is going on around here? Do you still think there's a threat?"

Jepson shrugged. "I don't know. But I think the sheriff is right; that French-Canadian guy is probably our man."

Anna snorted. "That's ridiculous. He may have some problems, but killing people isn't one of them."

"There's a lot of evidence."

"It's only circumstantial." Anna was surprised how her words of defense resounded in the empty diner. "He carved little birds for my son," she added, a little too stridently, while looking over at the booth by the windows. The edge in her voice had attracted Mrs. Bean's attention. The postmistress studied her, an arm draped around Charles's shoulder. When Anna looked back at Jepson, the detective's condescending frown poked at her anger.

Quietly, like speaking to a child, he said, "Look at the facts, Anna. His parents deserted him. He lives alone out in the woods."

"So that makes him a sociopath?" She couldn't keep her voice down. "He's been in my house. Twice."

"Oh, come on, Anna. The guy is a creep. He sneaks around in the woods—"

"A creep? Look at you with those flea-bag furs," she retorted, gesturing at his coat. "Talk about creepy."

Jepson's voice rose to match hers. "His mother was a prostitute."

"So what?" she exclaimed. "It's like you calling Leonard a suspect because he has a ponytail."

"I wasn't the one who said that. But you have to admit, the deputy certainly knows his way around these woods."

"So do I! Your arguments make no sense; you see a loner, you point a finger. You see a ponytail, well, that must be him." She leaned closer, jabbing a finger at his chest. "How about this? I see a Big Bad Wolf and Little Red Riding Hood."

Jepson glared at her. "That's preposterous." But the fury in his eyes caught her off guard, so that when the café door suddenly banged open, she gasped and stepped back, knocking a coffee cup to the floor.

Owen Porter and one of the cameramen barged in. "See?" Owen said to his new friend. "I told you they'd still be open."

Leonard quietly slipped in behind them. He scanned the empty room, noted the apprehension on Mrs. Bean's face, smiled at Charles, and went to sit with them.

"We're closing," Anna announced, a breathless quiver in her voice.

"How about a cup of coffee to go, then?" Owen asked. He appeared oblivious to the tension in the room. "We've been lugging that camera equipment all over town. How about a hot cup to take the chill off?"

"Might as well." Anna sighed. "I can't leave until everything is ready for the morning."

Jepson stood, plopped some cash on the counter, and turned to Owen. "Where's Christine?"

The cameraman looked at him from around Owen's back. "She took the handheld down along the shore. She wants to get some footage of the lake in the moonlight." He watched Anna pour coffee into a pair of to-go cups, and then turned back to the detective. "You folks sure have a pretty little town here."

Jepson grabbed his fur hat and headed for the door. Pulling his jacket open, he revealed the badge pinned to his belt. "I don't live here," he said, the cold edge still sticking to his voice.

"I'm real sorry about that young lady," the cameraman said. "I heard the sheriff is close to making an arrest."

Jepson stopped. Being recognized as a detective and fielding questions about the case by himself helped restore his sense of authority. He stood a little taller and, despite the worn-out coat and hat, mustered up his best look of official prerogative. "We're looking at a few people," he said. "We just don't have enough evidence."

"Not enough evidence?" Anna smirked. "More like not enough common sense."

Jepson gave her a parting sneer and left. Owen looked around the empty café, nodded at Mrs. Bean, and then turned to his new friend. "We should probably leave, too. Let Anna close up."

She said, "If you see Michael out there, send him over. The truck is in the parking lot. Tell him I'm heading home after closing up."

They made their way to the door, turning to wave goodbye while nodding thanks to Anna for the coffee.

Mrs. Bean, Leonard, and Charles soon joined her at the counter. "Leonard is going to walk me down to the dance," Mrs. Bean said, wrapping a sweater over her shoulders.

"Me too!" Charles proclaimed, grabbing Mrs. Bean's hand.

Anna came around the counter and knelt in front of her son. "Can't you stay to help Mommy? If you wipe off all these tables, I'll put the dishes away. And then we'll vacuum the floor. You like vacuuming." She held a dishrag out to Charles and they watched him grab it and run off.

Anna stood up and looked at Leonard. "The sheriff was in earlier. He seems kind of nervous, doesn't he?"

Before Leonard could respond, Mrs. Bean quipped, "The sheriff doesn't get nervous. He just has a lot of responsibility, that's all."

"Isn't that the same thing? Is he expecting trouble tonight?"

They both looked at Leonard. He paused, studying his boots while considering the question. "I think he's just being careful. There are a lot of people in town, and everybody's in a partying mood. There's no telling what might happen."

Mrs. Bean worked the buttons on her sweater. "Well, I'm sure he appreciates all the extra help tonight." She looked at Anna. "You know, those radios were my idea."

Anna smiled and grabbed her arm. "Are you meeting the sheriff down there?"

"Of course. We haven't missed a Hofstad Dance in years."

At the door, Leonard looked back. "Maybe we'll see you down there."

Anna smiled. Such a good man, she thought. But the memory of her words with Jepson brought the heat back to her cheeks, and when the door closed on the postmistress and deputy, Anna and her son were the only ones left in the Black Otter Bay Café.

• • • •

The sun had set hours ago, and darkness descended quickly on the little village. Mrs. Bean and Leonard strolled along the mini mall boardwalk, where he paused to look across the highway at the stands of cedar, spruce, and pine trees. Lake Superior was out there beyond the narrow swath of forest, a pitch-black rolling sea of ice-cold water. He shivered and said, "It sure got cold in a hurry."

"It's a damp cold," Mrs. Bean informed him. "That big ridge behind town holds the moist air off the lake next to shore. The air temperature isn't really that cold yet," she added. "It just feels colder because it's so damp."

Leonard grinned. "Okay, Mrs. Bean. But to me, it's just cold."

Lights from the gift shops shone with a cheery glow as tourists ambled by, their cars parked at regimented angles along the curb. By the time the two of them passed the post office, they could hear the noise emanating from the dance further down the street at the Black Otter Bay Municipal Bar. It sat alone on the lakeside of the highway, its huge gravel parking lot full of vehicles. A small crowd stood outside smoking and laughing, but many more people were visible through the rows of windows lining the building.

Mrs. Bean stopped to look at the scene before them. "You know, the bar used to be our town hall," she informed him. "There are still some city offices upstairs, but it's not like the old days, when everything went through that building. It warehoused goods brought in by boats. The fishing fleet sold their catches out of it. There was even a school there for a while. And every Saturday night they showed movies in the main hall, where the dance floor is now."

"I remember that," Leonard said. "Bring your own popcorn."

Mrs. Bean slowed, grabbed his arm, and turned to face him. "Something is bothering me," she said. "Before you came into the café, that detective fellow was arguing with Anna. He said you could be a suspect in that murder because of your ponytail. And because you know these woods so well."

Leonard laughed. "Well, you can tell him I don't have an alibi, either. I was here in town for both attacks." They began strolling again, and then Leonard asked, "What did Anna say?"

"She basically told him he was nuts."

Leonard laughed. "Well, that certainly sounds like her."

Mrs. Bean patted his arm and they continued into the parking lot. Sheriff Fastwater's squad car was parked near the door. Gitch sat in the front seat, watching people going in and out of the bar. Leonard stopped next to him when he saw the sheriff walking toward them, Phil Simanich at his side.

"Everyone behaving themselves?" Mrs. Bean asked.

Fastwater stopped in front of them, but his eyes continued roaming over the parking lot. When he finally looked at her, he smiled and reached to straighten the tiara wedged in her hair. "You should get inside," he said. "The band is about to start another set."

Simanich looked from the postmistress to the sheriff. "How about you take her in," he suggested. "You have a radio. Leonard and I will hang around out here."

Fastwater took Mrs. Bean's hand. "I'll be in shortly. I just want to take a quick loop through town."

Simanich shook his head. It seemed almost rude the way he dismissed her. He's too obsessed with this Manitou ghost, he thought.

"I'll save you a dance ticket," Mrs. Bean said to the sheriff, patting his arm with affection.

Simanich called after her. "And if he doesn't use it, I'll be along soon enough."

She turned to smile at him, and he awkwardly pantomimed the Twist, grinding his toes into the gravel.

When she was gone, the three men stepped over to the squad car and Fastwater let Gitch out.

"Seems like a pretty nice evening, Marlon," Simanich said, gauging the sheriff's temperament.

Gitch's nose stopped at the rear tire and he adjusted himself to lift a leg. At the last moment he noticed Fastwater watching him from only a few feet away. Thinking better of it, the dog dropped his leg and resumed sniffing. The sheriff wasn't wearing his trooper hat tonight, and his thick black hair gleamed in the lights from the bar. Simanich observed how straight he stood, with thumbs hooked in his belt. He seemed calm, but at the same time alert and wary.

"I saw Michael in there," Fastwater commented, nodding at the bar. "Did Anna go home?"

"She's closing up the café," Leonard informed him. "She said she might stop down in a little while."

Fastwater's eyes flicked over to his nephew. "She's alone?"

"Well, Charles is with her."

"Come on, Marlon," Simanich intervened. "Lighten up. The town is full of people. Everyone's having a good time. Your Manitou guy isn't going to come around tonight with all these people here."

Fastwater ignored his friend and strolled around the car to watch Gitch. It was that old tactical problem of having too many fronts to defend. He remembered allowing Leonard and Gitch to run off on their own a few weeks ago out at the headwaters. The outcome had seen the Frenchman get away, and Gitch seriously injured. He wished everybody would just stay together where he could keep an eye on them.

"Michael left her the pickup truck," Leonard offered, "so she won't be walking over here alone."

Fastwater opened his car door and whistled for Gitch. "I think I'll drive up to the café and see how she's doing." The dog bounded in the open door, but the sheriff hesitated when he saw Simanich shake his head and kick the toe of his boot against the gravel. "Phil," he said, willing his friend to look at him. When he did, Fastwater stepped closer and said, "It's one of those feelings. It's like an ambush about to happen, with no Black Hawks keeping watch overhead." He paused to cast his glance around the parking lot and the woods leading down to the harbor. "He's here, Phil. I can feel him."

And then the first cries for help shattered the evening sky around them.

• • • •

From the nearest corner of the parking lot, a stumbling figure climbed the gravel track leading up from the harbor. "Help!" he called, panting for breath. "Somebody help me!"

Sheriff Fastwater whistled for Gitch and the big dog leaped back out of the squad car. Together they led the charge past a row of cars to meet the distraught man staggering up the last few yards of the hill. Middle-aged and balding, he held his blood-covered hands out in front of him. Huge blubbering sobs rasped out of him as he grabbed the sheriff's arm for support.

"Back there!" he cried. "It's Christine. I think she's dead!"

Simanich and Leonard immediately took off down the hill, the captain grabbing for and drawing his handgun. "Where?" Fastwater demanded. "Where is she?"

"Near the beach," the man gasped, loud enough for the pursuers to hear.

Gitch seemed torn between following the men down the hill or staying with the sheriff. "Go!" Fastwater commanded, and Gitch wheeled and hurled himself after the men.

Fastwater snatched a quick look around. His thinking ran cool and deliberate, always clear-headed in a crisis. He grasped the stranger by the shoulders. Looking into his eyes, he detected a glimmer of rationality. To test it, he asked, "Are you one of the cameramen?"

The man nodded, still wheezing. "John Lerner. We just shot some background footage. We were all done, and Christine went for a walk while I packed up the equipment. When she didn't return, I went to find her." Now the tears and sobbing began again. "So much blood . . ."

Fastwater had all the information he needed. "Mr. Lerner," he said deliberately to the man falling apart in his arms. "Look at me." When the cameraman looked up, Fastwater latched the intensity of his own black-eyed stare onto the man's glassy eyes. "I need you to get yourself under control here, Mr. Lerner. You have to help me. I need you to walk over to the bar there and ask for Doctor Thompson." Fastwater turned enough to point out the bar. "See that building? Get somebody to find Doc Thompson for you and send him down to the beach. We'll take care of Christine until he gets there. Can you do that for me?"

The man nodded.

"His name is Doctor Thompson," Fastwater repeated. "I saw him in the bar at the dance. Everything's going to be okay here, Mr. Lerner. You just need to get the doctor."

The cameraman continued nodding as he broke free from Fastwater's grasp. The sheriff watched for a moment to be sure he'd follow his instructions, then turned and jogged down the gravel path, where he was quickly swallowed up in the dark. He knew it wasn't right to leave a man like that on his own, but the situation demanded his personal attention. Every second was crucial, and if anyone wanted to second-guess his actions when this was over, then so be it.

"Marlon! Over here!"

The sheriff reached the boulder beach at the bottom of the hill and turned left toward the voices. He spotted Simanich and Leonard kneeling over a form at the edge of the wood line. Gitch sniffed in ever-widening circles around them. The men stood up as Fastwater approached over the rocky, uneven ground.

"She's dead, Marlon," Simanich reported. "Looks like she hit her head on the rocks."

"It could've been an accident," Leonard said. "Maybe a wicked fall. It's mighty slippery down here."

Fastwater glanced at the body and recoiled at the amount of blood splattered across the wet rocks. The most obvious identifier was the blue beret that lay several feet away. With no sign of blood on it, he decided the hat had fallen off early in a confrontation. "She must have put up a fight," he said. "This was no accident." The sheriff never let his searching eyes rest. Light from the last quarter moon was dim, but he could see the rocky peninsula clearly against the black water and horizon. A couple of broken-down boathouses stood in silent silhouette against the beach. Not a breeze disturbed the brush at the edge of the forest. Looking behind him, he spotted the overturned, discarded fishing boat he passed on his daily walks. Gitch followed his nose away from the men, tracking along the tree line toward the boat and the mouth of the Black Otter River.

The sheriff spun around to face his compatriots. "This was no accident," he said again. He looked at the cobblestone beach and boathouses. "Phil, I want you to check out the harbor. Most of those boathouses will be open. And be sure you look at the pilings underneath. A man could hide under there with the lake so calm tonight."

The sheriff scanned the woods surrounding the narrow gravel track leading down from the bar. No sign of the doctor yet, but in the darkness it was difficult to see beyond the outermost growth of brush lining the trail. He pulled Leonard closer. "I want you to go back up to the highway. If this guy gets across the road into the forest behind town, we'll never find him. I sent the cameraman into the bar to get Doc Thompson. On your way, make sure he found him."

Simanich asked, "You left that fellow all alone to find the doctor?"

Fastwater looked back at Gitch slowly working his way along the beach. He began sniffing around the old Boston Whaler lying upside down next to the treeline.

"Marlon, that cameraman was in no condition . . ."

Fastwater ignored him. He watched Gitch make another pass around the boat. He thought about all the times he'd walked this beach and hardly noticed the old wreck. Now it seemed to stand out like a flashing neon light. It called to him out of the darkening gloom like some ancient, mystical sorceress.

With an abrupt change in plans, Fastwater ordered, "Follow me," and set out gingerly over the cobblestoned beach. Hobbling along close behind, Leonard and Simanich exchanged looks as the sheriff pulled the heavy .44 Magnum out of its holster. Approaching the boat, it occurred to Fastwater that the vessel had probably lain here for decades. Back in the 1940s and '50s, it had been among the largest and best of the one-man fishing boats. Eighteen feet long, with a deep hull for carrying hundreds of yards of netting, it was handmade from cedar planks and virtually unsinkable in the right hands. But time had worn it out, and the boulder-strewn shoreline had finally damaged the hull beyond repair. Now it lay here, a silent memorial to the hardy men who'd risked their lives on this temperamental, unforgiving body of water.

Fastwater didn't need to tell the others what he was doing as the three men lined up along the length of the boat. Handguns in one hand, they reached down with their free arms to grasp the gunwale. Simanich and Leonard looked at the sheriff, and when the big man threw his bulk and power into it, they lifted together and heaved the boat over against the trees.

A deafening crash of crackling ice and splintering boards broke the silence of the beach. They stepped back, Fastwater and Simanich leveling their firepower at the emptiness beneath. Simanich crouched with his flashlight app to inspect the thick carpet of decaying leaves that had accumulated under the boat. "My God," he croaked, jumping back. "Look at this, Marlon."

They huddled around the captain, trying to get a glimpse of what he'd seen. A twitch of movement caught their attention, and Simanich jumped back again.

"It's a snake," Fastwater said.

Now it was Leonard's turn to step back. "A snake? Come on, Marlon, it's too cold."

"Whoever saw a snake at this time of year?" Simanich demanded. "I mean, look at this, there's ice on these rocks."

"He's hibernating," Fastwater said. "This boat hasn't been moved in years." The sheriff's eyes picked up Gitch moving along the tree line again, but his thoughts lingered on the snake.

Simanich slid his sidearm back into his shoulder holster and exhaled loudly. "Well, I've never seen anything like that before. Have you ever seen a snake in the woods this time of year?" he asked again.

The sheriff ended his reverie and looked at his friend. Leonard stood a few feet away, looking out to sea, his hands shoved deep in his pockets.

"Nope," Fastwater said. "I've never seen a snake out this time of year." He looked down at the mound of leaves covering the serpent. "But then, I've never seen Matche-Manitou before, either." Time was getting away from them. Simanich quickly backtracked along the beach to investigate the boathouses. Along the way he communicated by radio with the remaining security team. Per the sheriff's orders, the primary focus now was an effort to prevent anyone from crossing the highway and escaping into the woods beyond.

The quarter moon ducked behind some clouds, turning the forest, water, and rocks into a cold, black cavern. The sheriff looked at Leonard. "You all right?"

Leonard nodded. "You really think someone killed her?"

Fastwater turned to keep his eyes on the swath of woods between the shore and highway. "I imagine that hitting her head on the rocks probably killed her, but I also suspect someone was responsible for making her fall." He paused to locate Gitch tracking toward the river, and then said, "I still need you to go back up top. Make sure the doctor has been notified. See if you can spot any of our security team in the bar. But keep an eye on the highway. If you find some help, have them spread out along the road. They have this guy's description. He'll try to get back into the forests behind town."

Leonard nodded. "Got it. Where are you going?"

Fastwater watched Gitch slowly sniffing his way toward the river mouth. "I'm going to follow the dog. He knows the guy's scent. He might be on it now."

Leonard started to leave, but the sheriff grabbed his arm. "Timing is critical. Just a quick stop at the dance, then work your way back through town to the café. I'll head along the beach here to the river and follow it up to the highway. The river is too wide and deep for him to cross, so I'll meet you up at the café."

Leonard hurried off to do as instructed. When his slender form melted into the dark of the surrounding woods, Fastwater was left alone on the beach. He looked back and spotted Simanich's solitary profile moving among the boathouse silhouettes. Fastwater slipped his .44 back into his holster as he carefully navigated the icy rocks at the edge of the woods. Gitch was nearly to the river, barely visible now even on the open beach.

Thoughts tumbled through his head as he concentrated on searching the forest shadows for movement. Again he was spread too thin. He should have asked the volunteer officers to stick around longer. Instead of turning in their radios and going their separate ways late in the evening, he could have had them posted around town, easily accessible with the push of a transmit button. But everyone relaxed after several hours without an incident. It would have been unfair to ask them to stay all night when they'd volunteered so many hours already. It was Halloween, after all, and they should be home with their own families. Several officers offered to stay, but, over Fastwater's opposition, Simanich released anyone else who wanted to leave.

In the end, Fastwater understood that it probably wouldn't have mattered. Thinking of the evil snake magic, he suspected there were forces at work tonight beyond the ken of radios and manpower. He gritted his teeth and let his senses take command of his body. He moved in silence against the edge of the forest, ears humming with an effort to locate a vibration of sound. His eyes peered deeply into the night, while his mind roamed ahead searching for evil lurking in the dark.

• • • •

Leonard met Doc Thompson and the cameraman on the dirt trail on his way up from the beach. He pointed out directions to the body, then continued up the hill to the gravel parking lot. Spotting a couple of security team members outside the bar, he gave them a brief description of what had happened and how the sheriff was working the manhunt, and then asked them to follow him up to the roadway.

Tourists continued their peaceful meanderings through town, unaware of the possible danger lurking around them, and ignorant of the savage scene that had played out on the waterfront. Leonard craned his head this way and that to see around them while reacting to every new movement on the street. The post office stood deep in the shadows, but the rest of the boardwalk shops were well lit. He paused to look back at one of the security team trailing him on the opposite side of the road. When she saw him, he nodded at the post office and she moved closer to investigate. Farther back, he spotted the second police officer standing watch by the highway above the bar's parking lot.

Leonard continued moving forward until, just beyond the lights at the other end of town, he spotted the café tucked up tight against the forest and ridge. Anna's old red pickup truck stood in the middle of the deserted parking lot. A couple lights inside the café gave off a cheery glow, and he saw Anna and Charles moving about, closing up for the evening. But outside a cold darkness, accompanied by a Halloween-inspired fog, had settled over the isolated building like a cold compress of dread.

Leonard shivered.

• • • •

Down on the shore, well away from the tree line, Fastwater found a narrow band of ice-free rocks. Sunshine during the day had melted the ice and dried out the stones covering this stretch of beach. The sheriff stumbled along in the darkness, but walking was less treacherous without the coating of ice underfoot. Most of the beach consisted of round, flat cobblestones, the largest about the size of a softball, held in place by a fine, gritty sand deposited by the waves over the years.

Gitch waited for him near the river mouth. "What's the matter, old buddy? Did you lose his scent?" Gitch whined and began sniffing around again. The river crashed and howled here as it leaped into Lake Superior.

Fastwater squatted to look at a wide patch of sand at his feet. Tracks everywhere, which only made sense considering all the tourists in town. Looking up at the woods between him and the highway, the darkness and shadows converged to form an indistinguishable black mass. Only the tops of trees could be faintly discerned against the backdrop of lights from town.

Leonard should be up there by now, he thought. In the far distance he could just make out Simanich's profile along the beach. Gitch came over to sit at the sheriff's side. "He's gone, isn't he?" Fastwater said. For some reason the trail seemed cold. He'd been so confident when they'd investigated the old fishing boat. He realized now that the trickster had played him by using the old boat as a ploy to slow him down.

Fastwater looked at the river. Not even the most powerful of spirits could cross a raging torrent like that. He spotted the steel safety cable stretched taut across the river mouth. A wide outcropping of rocks and boulders lined the shore. Not much chance for Gitch to pick up a scent there. The rocks gradually rose for a hundred yards, making an ever-deepening gorge for the river. Farther up, where the trees began, the terrain became even steeper, and a path wound up the hill at an angle to the highway and the café across the road.

In his mind he journeyed along the river's edge over rocks he'd hiked and memorized since childhood, with precipices jutting out over rapids, thinly cloaked in scraggly cedar trees and brush. All the way up to the well-worn path, used by sightseers and fishermen alike. There were a thousand places to hide, he conceded, and many spots from which to launch an ambush now that his few remaining officers were spread so thin.

He sensed more than saw the shadow climbing the trail, felt an image of fur and fear. This figure didn't move slowly because of the hill, but rather as a means to cloak his presence. Fastwater shook the apparition from his mind.

"Come on, Gitch," he called softly as he started upstream along the rocky bank. "I think we're close to the end of our journey."

• • • •

"Come on, Mom!" Charles whined, tugging on his mother's back pocket.

Anna shut off the vacuum cleaner and turned to face her son. "We're almost done," she said. "Just help me push all these chairs back under the tables."

"But I want to go now," he persisted.

"Just one more minute," Anna said as she unplugged the cord and wound it up on the old upright vacuum cleaner. Charles began shoving chairs at the tables with more force than needed. When a saltshaker tipped over, scattering granules of salt across the table, he turned a guilty face at his mother.

"Not so rough, honey," she said with a tired sigh. "Now we have to wipe off that table again." Anna stashed the vacuum cleaner in a corner near the door. In the kitchen she locked the back door, then stopped when she spotted another tub full of dirty dishes. Marcy never had come back to help close up. Not that Anna blamed her. The Halloween Dance was the one time of year Marcy legitimately let her eccentric side go wild. And this year she was sharing it with Matthew Simon. Anna grinned when she thought of the two of them in costume. They were older than she was, for goodness' sake! Old enough that Matt's daughter, Abby, had started high school this year. But tonight he and Marcy were acting like teenagers themselves.

Looking at the tub of dirty dishes, Anna decided she wasn't about to do them now. Whoever opened tomorrow could deal with it. On her way out of the kitchen she grabbed a dishrag and shut off the lights. A row of fluorescents along the back wall stayed on all night.

"Let's go, Mom," Charles called when she returned to the dining area. She wiped up the spilled salt and looked around. The big lake trout watched her from his vantage point high on the wall behind the counter. Marcy claimed that Agda's ghost resided here, and Anna was inclined to believe her, especially during these quiet, shadowy afterhours. Shivering from a sudden apprehension, she studied the big fish, half expecting the glass eye to wink at her.

She jumped when Charles grabbed her hand. "Mom," he complained, leaning his weight back from her.

"Okay." She took a last look around the room. For all of Charles's efforts, most of the chairs were still sticking out at odd angles where she'd pushed them while vacuuming. "I tell you what," she said, untying her apron. "You go out and get in the truck. I have to put away my apron and get the keys. I'll lock up and be outside in two minutes."

"Oh, boy!" he exclaimed, charging for the door.

She watched him run, watched him pulling on the heavy door. So much excitement and enthusiasm. She balled up the apron and tossed it with the dishrag into the laundry sack behind the counter. Reaching for the bank of light switches, she spotted Charles's coat lying on the floor. In his excitement, he'd run off without it. She walked over to retrieve it and again noticed the haphazard arrangement of chairs. One more minute, she said to herself, walking over to realign them. Then a dance or two with Michael and her son, and soon enough she'd be home and crawling into a soft, warm bed.

• • • •

Leonard jogged across the highway and paused near the café parking lot. Looking back, he saw the police officer returning to the street after searching around the post office. She ambled along the walkway like any other tourist, but her head swung from side to side as she watched the street. From inside the café he heard the muted drone of the vacuum cleaner go quiet. Now, in the far-off background, he heard the faint rumblings of the Black Otter River beating its way down the gorge to Lake Superior. He watched as a car backed out of a parking space in the mini mall and headed toward him, causing him to look away to preserve his night vision. It moved slowly, probably hauling tired tourists back home to Duluth. Across the roadway, the outer reaches of light from the headlamps illuminated a swath of trees along the ditch.

Leonard gasped. A man stood just inside the edge of naked brush, leaning his shoulder against a tree to conceal his profile. He seemed to be studying the café, apparently unaware that he'd been spotted. Leonard froze. As the car approached, he turned his face down and away from the lights. When it passed, he searched the darkened woods across the road again, but the silent apparition had vanished.

He stepped away from the parking lot and stood on the edge of the highway. Caution lights on the steel-girder bridge a hundred yards away flashed in the darkness. A fog hung over the river gorge, imparting a ghostly illumination from the lights on the steel girders rising high overhead at either end. Across the highway where the man had been standing, he spotted the opening to the path that angled down the steep hill to the river mouth and Lake Superior. With Fastwater coming up that path to the café, Leonard concluded that their man was effectively trapped between him and the sheriff.

Looking back into town, he saw the police officer pause in her scanning of the dwindling crowd. His thoughts raced. He'd been told to stay on the highway to keep the Frenchman from crossing the road and escaping into the woods beyond. On the other hand, his uncle was down there in the dark and might need his help. He considered using the radio to warn the sheriff, but the beeps and static of transmitting could give away his location. Then again, only a fool would confront his uncle and his .44-caliber cannon at night in these woods.

The trailing police officer was only half a block away. There were virtually no pedestrians in this dark end of town, so she'd easily see anyone moving around here. He looked up and down the highway one last time, and then made his move.

• • • •

Charles climbed up on the running board of the truck and reached for the door handle. Getting into the truck was easy. He'd done it hundreds of times before, all by himself. The best part, though, were all the knobs and dials inside. He knew how to turn everything on so that when his parents started the truck the radio blasted and the turn signals came on. It was fun to watch them jump. He even knew how to turn the heater fan on high, and last time he'd learned how the flashers worked.

He lifted on the handle but it was too awkward. He changed position and rose up on his toes. Sometimes he needed both hands to make it work. Then he stopped and listened. From nearby he'd heard a familiar sound. There it was again! That little bird that his friend had told him about. The brave little bird that wasn't afraid. Just like him.

Perched on the running board, he looked at the woods behind the café. The bird called to him in loud, clear whistles from across the deserted parking lot. He jumped down and ran toward the trees. Maybe he could

see it before it flew away. Such a brave little bird to live here all winter!
He wondered if the real thing looked like the ones his friend had carved
for him. While he ran he puckered up his lips to whistle, but all he could
manage was a hissing, spitting sound. As he neared the back corner of the
café, he gave up on whistling and resorted to his cackling birdcall. "Caw.
Caw-caw!"

• • • •

Huffing and puffing, Sheriff Fastwater pushed off the rocky
outcroppings and entered a narrow passage between trees high above the
river gorge. Pausing to catch his breath, he strained to hear any movement
from up ahead. Gitch stood by his side, unaccustomed to such a late-night
foray into the woods. The river rumbled like a living entity far below, and
the darkness here in the trees was absolute. With no discernable sounds
from the highway above it was like they'd been closeted in a sensory
vacuum.

Then, a light clattering of stones on the path. Deer? Gitch swung his
head up and stood at attention. Fastwater unfastened the hammer guard on
his holster while silently stepping to the side of the path. Something moved
up ahead, but in the dark it was impossible to know if it was moving up or
down the trail.

Another shuffle, closer now, and the .44 Magnum slid into his huge
hand. Gitch stepped back, well aware that something approached. The
sheriff's heartbeat drummed in his ears, and their tight little closet sanctuary
seemed to close in on them. For a full half-minute they strained to hear.
There was nothing from up on the highway, just the steady grumble of the
river far below. And then, as if uttered by the forest itself, "Marlon?"

The handgun slipped back into the holster as Leonard suddenly
appeared out of the dark. Gitch shoved his nose against the deputy's thigh
and Leonard scratched his ears.

"What are you doing down here?" Fastwater inquired, accusation in
his voice.

"I saw him. Across the road from the café."

"Saw who?" Their voices were hardly more than a whisper but carried a life-or-death urgency.

"I don't know. A man hiding in the brush near the ditch. He disappeared."

"What about Anna?"

"She was vacuuming and closing up the café."

Fastwater pushed past him. "She's all alone?"

Gitch bounded ahead and Leonard turned to follow. "I thought he came down this way. I thought maybe you'd—"

"I told you to stay up there." The sheriff crashed as quickly as he could through the trees. No more need for stealth. He felt it all getting away from him again. Like the chase at the headwaters and Gitch getting hurt. Chaos and loss of control.

The black void of the highway loomed just twenty yards ahead when the first scream blew past them in the dark. The terror in the voice hit a universal chord of distress, but he knew immediately to whom it belonged.

He sprinted for the top, heard a second scream, and then dove into the ditch when a blast from a handgun exploded into the night.

• • • •

Anna pulled the café door closed and rattled the knob. The cold air outside gave a refreshing boost to her flagging stamina. In addition to the kitchen fluorescents, the café had a few small lights that stayed on all night, but they did little to push back the darkness. The truck stood alone in the parking lot like a boulder sticking out in the vastness of the sea.

Beyond the truck she saw lights twinkling in the gift shop windows, not a common sight for this small town. It took a big event like the Halloween Dance to keep these folks out after dark. She smiled when she couldn't see Charles in the truck. He often hid inside to scare her when she opened the door. She almost laughed out loud when she remembered his latest innovation, turning on the radio and all the lights to startle her when she turned the key in the ignition.

She pulled the truck door open and stepped back, awaiting Charles's raucous greeting. When he didn't jump up off the seat at her, she threw his coat inside and leaned forward to peer down at the floor. With the door open the cab light was on, making it easy to see that Charles wasn't there. She looked in the narrow space behind the seat.

The unexplained apprehension from a few minutes ago blossomed. "Charles?"

A hand grabbed her shoulder and she jumped, banging her head against the metal doorframe. She struggled to maintain her balance while turning around, and when she did, Anna gasped in surprise at the furry apparition holding her tight. It glared at her with a sneer of anger.

"You!" she exclaimed, pushing against him.

Strong hands grabbed her shoulders but she continued pushing back. "Where's my son?" she demanded. "Where's Charles?"

The hands pulled at her, trying to yank her away from the truck.

She looked over his shoulders at the highway, but glimpsed only a dark stretch of vacant road. She screamed into the night. "Charles!"

She felt a hand release her shoulder, saw it raised in a fist, and she slammed at his chest with all her might, pushing away from the truck and driving him backward in her fury. When he stumbled away she saw the gun in his hand.

And then she heard the voice, close by yet sounding far away. "Mommy!"

Anna turned to look over the hood of the truck at the woods behind the café. In the faint glow from the kitchen fluorescents she saw her son running across the parking lot. The fur-clad man appeared at her side, the handgun clenched in both fists, leveled at a trajectory crossing the parking lot. Anna screamed, "Charles!" and then crashed sideways into the man and his outstretched arm.

The gun thundered in her ear, obliterating all sounds and knocking her senseless to the ground. From under the front bumper she opened an eye to see short little legs running toward her. Dazed, she fought to get up. Sensations slowly returned as the dizzying fog in her head loosened. Sounds popped back into place, and the parking lot quit spinning. And then she saw the little legs lifted off the ground. Rising up off her hands and knees, she careened like a drunken sailor against the truck. She saw her son thrown over the man's shoulder. She tried to yell but managed only an anguished howl.

The man turned and ran down the road toward the river with her son flailing and bouncing around his neck. Anna gulped deep drafts of the cold night air and violently shook her head in denial. Her faculties were returning. She saw her little boy punching the man's back, heard his grunts of effort, and felt her own surge of anger. She pushed away from the truck's fender and ran along the highway shoulder. The fear was gone now. No more screaming and frantic panic. Her son was right there in front of her. She opened up into a sprint down the middle of the highway, chasing the man with the struggling bundle as they disappeared into the fog and mist over the Black Otter River.

• • • •

Out of breath and gasping for air, the sheriff raised his head out of the ditch to scan the café and parking lot. He spotted the truck sitting all alone, the driver's door open and the cab light on. Beyond the truck, in the dim glow of the kitchen lights, a familiar figure sat on the café steps, obviously injured and unable to get up.

Fastwater took a deep breath and charged across the road, Gitch and Leonard at his side. Once again he pulled his handgun.

"Look!" Leonard yelled, pulling at his arm. The sheriff stopped at the edge of the parking lot to look down the highway where his nephew pointed. He saw Anna sprinting down the middle of the road, chasing after another figure near the bridge. Flashing yellow caution lights revealed the steel girders rising like a giant ribcage over the river gorge. In their murky golden glow he saw the fog rolling up off the river. Before the figures disappeared into the dark, the sheriff distinguished a fidgeting bundle thrown over the farthest one's shoulder. From this struggling heap came the helpless, faraway cries. "Mommy! Mommy!"

Fastwater turned back to follow his handgun into the parking lot for a quick look in the deserted truck, and then over the hood to the steps of the café. He cautiously approached the man sitting there, but spotting blood seeping between the man's fingers, he dropped his handgun into its holster and strapped it down tight in one fluid movement. He reached for Leonard's arm, but before he could speak, his nephew broke away to kneel by the injured man to lend assistance. Then another police officer ran up, panting hard and skidding on the sandy parking lot surface. "Who fired the shot, sir?" she asked, breathing hard. "Leonard doesn't carry a gun, and I know it wasn't that thing," she said, glancing at the sheriff's holster on his hip.

Fastwater spun back to look at the bridge and the retreating runners. Of course! The gunshot had been a regulation issue .38. That peashooter handgun he remembered from weeks ago when he'd seen it in his office. It all made sense now: the fur coat costume, the torn wolfskin hat with a new raccoon tail. He shook his head. That was the puzzle piece I missed, he thought. The original wolf tail was still tucked away in his desk drawer.

To the police officer, he quickly said, "Get on the radio. Get help over here. We have a gunshot victim." When he looked at his nephew, Leonard nodded up at him to indicate the wound wasn't too serious. Satisfied, Fastwater turned to look down the road into the dark and fog where the figures had disappeared. "And get Detective Jepson on the radio," he told the police officer. "Tell him I'm coming."

Chapter 19

*F*astwater *ran down the middle of the deserted highway.* Nearing the end of his endurance, he slowed down when he entered the pedestrian lane on the side of the bridge. There wouldn't have been any need to hurry at all if it weren't for Anna and her son. After all, Jepson didn't have a car here, and he wasn't going to find one this far outside of town. Maybe that's why he took the boy, Fastwater thought. A hostage and bargaining chip.

At the far end of the bridge he spotted Anna angling away from the highway and heading for the woods, her maternal drive still pushing her hard. Beyond Anna he caught a last glimpse of her quarry disappearing into the surrounding darkness at the entrance to the Black Otter Trail. The very trail where this whole saga began, he remembered, when he watched Niki set out for a run that fateful morning three weeks ago.

Fastwater slowed to a jog at the middle of the bridge. A series of waterfalls up here drowned out the sound of his steps. He peered over the edge as he passed. The steel girders looked solid enough slicing through the fog, but he felt a slight tremor as the structure vibrated beneath his feet. Below, a vast black void and an invisible roar of water leaped over falls and rapids.

Looking up, he saw Anna running for the darkness of the trail. He called to her, "Anna! Anna, wait!" But she never broke stride as she plunged into the woods. At the end of the bridge he slowed to a fast walk and stumbled down into the ditch behind her. A second later she was gone, a figure lost in the darkness of the forest. "Anna!"

Her only reply was a drawn-out wail. "Charles!"

• • • •

It was to no avail that Charles pounded his little fists on the solid back. Slung over the man's shoulder like when his daddy carried bags of fertilizer, he bounced along, his head hanging down over the man's back. He couldn't even yell for his mom anymore because his stomach was pinched over the man's shoulder. In desperation he bit into the back, but all he got was a mouthful of furry leather.

The man patted his rear end and laughed. "Stop it, young man. I'm not going to hurt you."

But Charles knew better. He wasn't supposed to go with strangers, and he'd heard his mother calling for him. He knew she was coming, knew from the sound of her voice that she was mad and scared. Again, with all his might he pounded on the furry leather tunic. He heard a chuckle, and then the man said, "Give it up, little boy. Don't worry, your mother is coming because of you."

Darting shadows appeared in the woods around them. As Charles craned his neck to see, two four-legged figures broke out onto the trail and quickly overtook them. Other than in storybooks or photos, he'd never seen a wolf before, but he knew instantly what these creatures were as they passed on either side of them to run up the trail ahead.

Charles thought of the birds his friend had carved. He remembered being told to be brave like the little birds that lived here all winter. When another ghostly four-legged creature loped into view beside him, Charles yelled, "Wabash Gondash!" and resumed his feverish beatings on the man's back. He grabbed at the thick neck, but when he felt the fur hat and tail, he clutched a fistful of fur and in a frenzy, pulled it free.

The jouncing ache in his stomach subsided when the man came to a quick stop. Charles felt himself hoisted roughly around the waist by two big hands. Then the upside-down forest spun around upright and he found himself standing on the ground. Fingers immediately dug at him, snatching at the hat in his hands. When he looked up he saw fear in the man's eyes. He watched him search the woods, eyes darting from shadow to shadow. Trembling hands fumbled with the fur hat. Had he seen the wolves, too?

In that instant Charles turned and ran. He didn't look back and he didn't scream. He just ran as fast as his little legs would carry him. For twenty yards he ran until a slick patch of mud took his feet out from under him. In desperation he scrambled to his feet, listening for the sounds of pursuit. But the woods were quiet, the four-legged creatures gone or in hiding. And so he took off down the trail again, shouting a triumphant "Wabash Gondash!" while flapping his arms like a bird in flight.

• • • •

Fastwater lumbered up the trail, out of breath and despairing for Anna and her son. He hadn't heard her yelling for the last several minutes, hadn't even seen her since she'd disappeared up the path into the forest. Gitch trotted beside him, his nose following an invisible scent on the ground.

The sheriff trudged up the slope as fast as he could manage. There had been a time when he'd jogged up these hills with little effort. When he'd run these rugged trails just for the joy of it. Even lugging a backpack and camping gear. . .

Out of the dark a hunkering form appeared in the middle of the path. He heard the sounds of crying and soft words. As he neared, he saw Anna down on one knee, her arms wrapped around her son. In silence he walked up to them and put his hand on Charles's shoulder. Anna didn't release her grasp, like she didn't even know the sheriff was there. She hugged her little boy with her whole body, gently rocking back and forth.

"Are you okay?" Fastwater asked.

Charles nodded his answer against his mother's tight embrace.

Anna stroked his hair. She pulled her face back and planted another splattering of kisses across his cheeks and nose.

"Wolves," Charles muttered, looking up at Fastwater. "I saw real wolves."

"Well, it's okay now, honey," Anna cooed. "There aren't any wolves here."

Fastwater squatted beside them and Gitch wandered over to join him. "How far away?" the sheriff asked.

Charles squirmed around in his mother's arms and pointed up the trail. "Just up there. I pulled his hair and got away."

This brought on a fresh round of crying from Anna, and she clutched her son with renewed vigor.

In a gentle voice, Fastwater asked, "Why did he take Charles?"

Anna snuffled back tears and replied, "Because I figured out who he was. The Big Bad Wolf, and Niki was Little Red Riding Hood. Talking to him this evening in the café, I realized they knew each other before she moved up here."

The sheriff nodded. Now he understood all of it. He'd put Jepson in charge of the Duluth investigation, so naturally the little fact of his previous relationship with the victim had never been revealed.

"He came back to keep me quiet. He didn't know Charles was with me."

The boy leaned back and his face became more animated. "I ran so fast, Mommy. I ran, and I fell, and I ran some more." Charles wiped tears from his mother's face. "And I yelled 'Wabash Gondash.' Remember the little birds, Mommy? I was brave like little White Throat."

"I know you're brave, honey," she said, pulling him close again.

Fastwater stood up and peered into the darkness up the trail. From the river gorge the constant background noise of churning water rumbled up at them. He slipped off his coat and draped it over Charles's shoulders. "Here," he said. "You folks take this to keep warm. Head on back to town now. I'm going up the trail to have a look around."

• • • •

Leaving his coat behind had been an easy sacrifice for Fastwater. He was warm from all the climbing and running, and the cool, cedar-scented air felt good. Even Gitch seemed to enjoy the slower pace as they walked up the trail. Fastwater conceded that if Jepson was merely intent on getting away, there was little chance of catching up to him tonight. The sheriff scrolled through the facts as they climbed the hill. He wasn't convinced that Jepson was looking to get away. After all, he had nowhere to go. Obviously, he'd taken the shot at the Frenchman, and he could have tried to blame everything on him, but with Anna figuring out the truth and getting away, he had nothing.

Near the top of the slope the sheriff paused. His heart still pounded from the exertion, and a light sweat cooled off over his brow and the back of his neck. He refused to consider the idea of going back for help. This was his job; these were his people to protect. If Jepson waited up ahead to challenge him, then he'd continue on and oblige him. Besides, he had only himself to blame for allowing all this to happen. The answers had been there all along and he simply hadn't seen them.

Fastwater sighed and let his body hang loose. His back, neck, and shoulders realigned as his mind relaxed. Jepson was confident of his physical abilities. Cocky and sure of himself. And by now he probably knew the sheriff was coming. He had the high ground and the element of surprise, but when it came right down to it, this was Fastwater's domain.

Gitch laid down on the path in front of him. The big dog's tongue lolled out of his mouth in staccato rhythms of panting. He turned his head to look back at the sheriff, and his odd-colored eyes watched Fastwater relax in a loose-bodied slouch, saw his head tip back and his eyes close.

The sheriff let his mind roam ahead up the trail. Within a quarter mile the path began its loop away from the river. Another mile or so ahead it intersected with the Superior Hiking Trail. The path was wide and easy to follow up here, flat and relatively rock free. There wasn't much of a river gorge along this stretch, just a short slope to the edge of the water.

He could feel Jepson nearby. He sensed the man's inner turmoil and fear. Waiting. In his mind, Fastwater wandered over the well-known path ahead. Seeking details, he pinpointed every jog in the trail, noted every tree hanging low overhead. Where the path turned away from the river was where Jepson waited, in the shadows beside the trail, near the hiker's bench where Niki's body had been found.

Gitch saw Fastwater's eyes pop open. The clouds parted and a sliver of moon glittered overhead. The dog stood up and came over to lean his frame against Fastwater's leg. The sheriff patted him on the head while looking up the trail through the foggy, moonlit shadows. "This is how it looked that night you came to live with me," he said to the dog. He continued stroking Gitch's head while studying the less turgid flow of water here. Still a lot of current, but not the rapids and waterfalls that lined the slope behind him. Deep pools of quiet water building up on themselves to begin the reckless headlong dash down to Lake Superior.

Open forest now on either side of the path. Deer trails crisscrossing in random lines of travel. He stepped off the path and out of the moonlight. A chill worked its way inside his shirt, and the need to keep moving to maintain his warmth helped Fastwater finally decide on a plan of action.

"I want you to stay here on the path, Gitch," he said quietly, scratching the dog behind his ears. "I'll need to know where you are if he decides to pull a gun." For a moment the two studied each other. He knew Gitch understood his instructions because he sensed the dog's disappointment. "I'm going through the woods," he said. "You stay here on the trail."

A final pat on the furry head and then the sheriff turned away from the path. In the moonlight he found the walking much easier than he'd expected, and the damp leaves underfoot made no sound as he passed. Still, it was slow picking his way over sticks and rocks littering the forest floor. He found progress a little quicker when he stepped out on a deer path. He tuned into the landscape around him, and blended his flowing movements into the shadows of the forest.

Anger waited just behind his cognitive thought processes. Like the river above the waterfalls, it quietly built on itself. He felt it there and let it grow. His self-assurance kept it contained, but if needed it would surge forth like a dam bursting, pushing everything out of its way. Unstoppable and unforgiving.

After a short time he changed course, found an alder thicket of shadows to follow, and aimed himself back toward the bench beside the Black Otter Trail.

• • • •

Phil Simanich jogged along the boardwalk in front of the mini mall. While searching the boathouses and harbor beach he'd heard the report of a distant gunshot, and almost immediately his radio came alive with accounts of gunfire, injuries, and even a kidnapping. On his way up from the beach he'd encountered Doc Thompson and some of the local rescue squad retrieving Christine Anderson's body. He learned that an ambulance had been dispatched to the café for a non-life-threatening gunshot wound. When he reached the highway he found a costumed security member who updated him on the ongoing crisis. And now, up ahead, he saw a police officer standing guard near Anna's pickup truck while the ambulance crew tended to a victim outside the café.

The whole time searching the waterfront he'd had the feeling he was working a cold trail, and then he began to suspect that Fastwater knew it, too. Sure, there were several good hiding places down by the harbor, but there wasn't any escape from there. The suspect needed room to run. So Fastwater had sent him on a futile mission. Why? The only reason that made sense was that the sheriff wanted to take this guy himself. He always bore the responsibility for the townsfolk's safety on his own shoulders. He considered it a failure to accept outside help, and didn't appreciate interference from others. The sheriff might be determined to resolve this case on his own, Simanich thought, but just look at the result.

He slowed to a fast walk as he entered the café parking lot. Leonard approached, a two-way radio in his hand.

"Who you are calling?" Simanich asked. "Where's Fastwater?"

Leonard clipped the radio to his belt. "I'm trying to reach Detective Jepson."

"Jepson?"

"He's the guy, sir. Anna figured it out and he came to get her. He ended up shooting the French-Canadian and taking Anna's son hostage. She and the sheriff are after him on foot now."

Simanich hardly had time to process any of that before they spotted Anna approaching out of the dark beside the road. She clutched Charles in a tight, protective embrace. Instead of walking up to the men, however, she turned into the parking lot and headed for her truck.

"Anna," Simanich called, falling into step behind her.

She laid her sleeping son on the bench seat of the truck and covered him with the sheriff's coat. Stepping back, she quietly eased the door shut, and then turned to face the men. Even in the dark Simanich could see the tracks of tears and signs of distress around her eyes. He thought she looked about ready to collapse.

"Is he okay?" Simanich asked, looking at the truck.

She nodded.

"Where's the sheriff?"

"He went after your detective. Across the river, up the Black Otter Trail." She choked off a sob, and added, "He took my son."

Simanich turned to the female officer standing beside him. "Use the radio to get someone to find Anna's husband. He's down at the dance. His name is Michael. Get him up here, now."

When the officer unhooked her radio and stepped aside, Simanich looked at Leonard. "Stay here until Michael shows up."

The deputy nodded. "What are you going to do?"

"I'm going after them."

When Anna turned away to look in the truck window at her son, Simanich pulled Leonard closer. "How's that French-Canadian fellow? Is he hurt bad?"

"He'll be all right. A flesh wound across his ribs. A lot of blood, but Anna deflected the shot and probably saved his life."

Simanich pulled out his handgun and checked the clip, then looked at Leonard. "You're in charge here."

The deputy nodded and walked with him to the edge of the parking lot. "Okay. Just get going. Jepson has lost all control. My uncle isn't a young man anymore. He's going to need your help."

"I doubt that," Simanich replied. But he was already stepping out on the highway. He spotted the flashing caution lights on the bridge in the distance and broke into a long-striding jog. He was soon isolated in the cold darkness as the lights of town receded, and his thoughts returned to his old friend up there on the trail. Deep in the forest, chasing a desperate, terrified foe. The setting might be different, but it wasn't unlike the war they'd fought together years ago. Fastwater had saved his life then. Maybe tonight he could return the favor.

• • • •

Inching along while carefully pulling branches out of his way, Fastwater neared the bench beside the trail. Moonlight cast a ghoulish glow over the silent forest. A man sat on the bench, the raccoon tail of his hat hanging over the back of the seat. One arm was stretched out along the backrest as he watched down the trail for pursuers. The sheriff knelt in the brush a few yards behind the broad back. Moonlight reflected a glint of gunmetal in the man's hand.

Fastwater sat and watched. As his eyes became more accustomed to the dim light, he noticed furtive shadows moving through the brush along the river. Jepson must have seen them, too, because his head darted back and forth trying to follow the movements. Once he even raised his gun and aimed across the trail, causing Fastwater to stiffen for the blast, but then the detective lowered the gun and resumed watching the trail behind him. The sheriff heard a quiet mumbling of words, and he thought perhaps Jepson was talking to himself until he realized it was the detective's radio.

Fastwater's right hand dropped to the holster at his belt. No hurry, just the need for absolute silence. The big .44 rose into view fractions of an inch at a time. When it was clear of the holster, Fastwater cradled it in his hands and resumed his surveillance.

The long-suppressed anger began to boil. He didn't need to conjure up images of the newswoman's broken body or Anna's terrified face to feel the disgust and rage course through him. This was where Niki had died, and now this man, sworn to uphold the law, sat in ambush awaiting the opportunity to take his life.

More secretive, sneaking figures on the far side of the trail caused Jepson to sit forward on the bench. He slowly rose to his feet, and when a trembling snarl and a scraping of branches erupted nearby, he suddenly hurled the radio into the woods at the dodging, evasive shadows.

Fastwater had seen enough, had waited too long to bring this tragedy to a conclusion. His thumb gripped the hammer of the gun and slowly eased it back. The "click" it made when fully cocked sounded like a thunderclap in the surrounding silence. He saw Jepson go rigid.

"Sit down, Detective," Fastwater said in a steady voice. "Put the gun on the bench."

Jepson ignored him. The man's breath swirled around in a vaporous cloud. When he spoke, his words were soft but carried easily in the silence of the night. "I never meant to hurt Niki, you know. I loved her. I just wanted to talk to her."

Fastwater was aware of the gun clutched firmly in Jepson's hand. "I said, sit down."

The detective continued to ignore him. "She thought she could leave the big city and make it all on her own up here."

When Jepson paused again, Fastwater spotted Gitch in a low crouch on the trail, approaching like a hunter closing in on its prey.

"Our first big date, other than just getting coffee or something, was a Halloween costume party."

Gitch was getting too close. Any second now Jepson would see him.

"We had so much fun. I knew we—"

"Sit down now, Detective!"

From just yards away a wolf snarled at the sheriff's harsh voice. Out of the corner of his eye he saw another wolf retreat up the path, and in that moment Jepson spun around, bringing his gun up while searching for his target in the brush. A blur on the trail and Gitch charged in, dislodging the gun and knocking Jepson aside. At the same time the wolf leaped out of the brush, slammed into Gitch, and the woods suddenly erupted in snarls and snapping teeth. In the commotion, Jepson scrambled across the trail and raced into the woods leading down to the river.

Fastwater sprang to his feet and yelled at Gitch. The dog stood on his hind legs, locked in a struggle with the alpha wolf, whose mouth was buried in Gitch's throat.

The sheriff swung the heavy .44 up, pointed it at the moon, and pulled the trigger just yards away from the fighting animals. The explosion was deafening, shattering the cold night air around them, causing the alpha wolf to disengage and chase his companions up the trail. The blast vibrated up Fastwater's forearm into his shoulder. A quarter mile away, near the highway and the entrance to the trail, the startling concussion of the blast made Simanich slip to his knees. The few remaining tourists still in town stopped in their tracks as shocked faces turned to look up at the ridge behind town.

The foot-long muzzle flash temporarily blinded the sheriff but he never stopped moving. Long, powerful strides carried him past the bench and across the trail into the woods. Fastwater automatically slid the .44 back into the deep leather holster as his momentum carried him recklessly down the hill toward the river.

Vincent Wyckoff

The slope was generally clear of brush, but hidden rocks and branches threw him off balance. He caught sight of Jepson leaping down into the tangle of brush lining the river. The sheriff followed right behind, his pent-up anger bellowing forth and sending him into a free-falling descent. He held his hands and arms out in front of him to deflect whipping branches as he crashed downhill.

Plummeting out of control, at the last instant he caught a passing glimpse of fur beside him hiding in the brush. Flinging out an arm, he grabbed a handful of the furry coat as he tumbled past. His body twisted sideways with the sudden resistance, but he hung on until he felt the weight behind him break loose. With his fingers dug in and clutching the coat, the sheriff pulled Jepson along as he crashed to the ground on his back. With a painful grunt he took the weight of the falling man on top of him, and then they rolled together through the last of the brush, soaring airborne and weightless off the short cliff before smashing into the frothy black river current.

Fastwater's chest constricted from the shock of the ice-cold water. After a frantic, desperate struggle, his feet finally found purchase on the gravel bottom. Using both hands, he manhandled Jepson into a standing position and began shoving and dragging the man to shore. He saw the sneering grin on the young man's face and realized Jepson was pummeling him with short jabs and punches. He knew they must be connecting, but because of the freezing water and physical exertion the impacts weren't registering in his mind. Still holding the fur coat with one hand, he used the other to punch back, and for several seconds they stood toe to toe in the waist-deep water, exchanging punches as fast as they could unload them.

Jepson's fur-clad leather coat had been doused in the river, and now the weight of the water-soaked leather impeded his ability to fight. Fastwater felt himself gaining ground, saw Jepson slowly giving way in front of him. Seeking escape from the sheriff's thick, heavy fist, the young man suddenly dove backward, and beneath the surface of the water the coat easily slid off over his head. Fastwater lunged after him, but when he reached into the water all he got was the heavy, empty fur coat.

The sheriff scrambled to regain his footing. It was deeper here, just on the edge of the stronger, faster-moving current. When he stood up, blindly wrestling the coat out of his way, a fist caught him square in the face. He reeled back, stunned by the blow. Another punch, and another, both landing solid on his face. The force of the blows staggered him, and then he felt Jepson grab his shirt and shove him down into the water. Before his head sank beneath the surface, he saw the leering face and gritted teeth just inches away. Bent over backward, Fastwater let the force of the current steady him while he regained his footing. With a renewed urgency he heaved his torso up with a mighty lunge against the weight pushing him down. At the same time, he ducked his chin against his chest and slammed the top of his head into the sneering face above him.

The impact was a solid, bone-crunching blow. The weight fell off him, and Fastwater struggled in the deep, black water to find his footing. He was moving, the current lifting and pulling him along. He felt his legs collide with a submerged boulder as he slid past. Picking up speed now. Gasping for breath while fighting to keep his head above water, the sheriff looked around. The main current had him; faster and faster it carried him downstream.

He spotted Jepson up ahead, also hurtling along on the tempest. Another boulder clipped Fastwater in the hips, spinning him around. The bone-numbing impact made him open his mouth, and the whitewater rapids threatened to drown him. Over the noise of the cascades he heard Jepson yelling. He looked ahead, but all he saw was a solid black void. Then, at the same time that he heard the crashing of the first waterfall, he felt himself flung into space. In a blind heap of water and noise he tumbled over the surging cataract, his cries of alarm erupting to join the thunderous roar around him.

Deep into the pool below the falls. Only a muffled din down here. Harder and harder he kicked, fighting the weight of his boots and waterlogged clothing. Desperation yielding one last kick after one last kick. Then he catapulted to the surface, frantically gulping for air. Backward in the current now, facing the waterfall already far behind him in the moonlight. All around him huge mounds of frothing whitewater.

Another boulder caught him square in the back, almost knocking the last of the wind out of him. He grabbed for the rock, felt a slender finger-hold, and then watched as it slipped through his numb grasp. The current was too much here, carrying his weight as easily as a leaf drifting on a stream.

He wrenched his body around, trying to twist himself face-first into the current. Over the noise of cascading rapids he heard Simanich calling to him. He tried to orient himself to the voice, caught a quick glimpse of the underside of the bridge as it swept by overhead, and then felt himself once again hurled out into space.

The lower falls, he thought. Higher and wider. A bottomless pool below. The river spit him out like a watermelon seed. Emitting a terror-stricken, "Whoa!" he sailed out of the waterfall and dropped twenty-five feet into the cold, black pool below.

As soon as he hit the water he started pumping his arms and kicking his legs. Even so, it was several seconds before he felt his downward momentum slacken. He cupped his hands and pumped his arms, not knowing how deep he'd sunk this time. No air left. His chest burning with the need to breathe. The silence underwater somehow calming. His kicks coming in easy strokes, matching the worn-out, slowing pumps of his arms. Everything peaceful and still. The image of fish in an aquarium. Languid movements of fins and tails. Deep silence everywhere.

Like waking from a dream, the noise of crashing water infiltrated the quiet around him, disturbing the dark serenity. Then he burst into the open, the roar of falling water accosting him even before he realized he'd come to the surface. He breathed, choked, and spit up water. Breathed some more. Flung water from his head and opened his eyes.

The waterfall had deposited him to one side of the pool like a piece of driftwood. Too deep here to stand, and the gorge too steep to climb out. Exhausted, he lay on the surface in a dead-man's float until his teeth began chattering like the keys of an old typewriter. Wearily, he lifted his head to look around. At the lower end of the pool he spotted flat boulders and ledges. A place to pull himself out of the water.

Fastwater eased himself along the cliff edge, grabbing for finger-holds with hands numb from cold. Sharp rocks and ice shredded his fingers. From high above him came another call.

"Marlon! Look out!"

A fist smashed into the back of his neck and he sank like a rock in the pool. A shooting pain coursed through his shoulders and neck, like electric jolts exploding inside him. His mind latched onto one thought: Don't lose consciousness! It became a repeating mantra in his brain. Don't lose consciousness!

Arms and legs pushed him underwater as Jepson climbed on top of him. In the bubbling darkness he heard the muted pop of a gunshot and a vibrating "zing" of a bullet spinning through the water. The sounds repeated themselves over and over, all merging to form a ringing in his ears. Then the weight rose off his back, and once again he pushed himself to the surface.

Gasping for air, he thrashed himself around to look behind him. Jepson was gone. Clinging to the rock wall with fingers he couldn't feel, the sheriff paused to consider whether one of the bullets had found the detective.

Escape from the river was only a few yards away. A chute gouged through flat bedrock at the base of the pool funneled the main torrent of water into its final descent into Lake Superior. If he could just work his way over to those flat rocks . . .

Out of strength and going numb in the freezing water, Fastwater struggled along the cliff wall. Behind him the waterfall crashed and pounded into the pool with a deafening roar. With his stamina wilting away, he crept along, handhold after bloody handhold. In the moonlight he watched the rocky ledges coming closer, saw and heard the main thrust of the river surging through the chute. Almost there. His feet hit on submerged boulders as the bottom of the pool rose up at the edge. Fastwater's numb feet scrambled up on an icy boulder, and to his astonishment he saw Jepson dragging himself up on a rock next to the main current.

Considering his present state, Fastwater was surprised to feel anger still churning inside him, but he used it to push himself forward off the boulders. Slipping and sliding, he lunged the last few feet over ice and rock to grab at the man lying on his stomach on the ledge. His fingers were too numb to grip anything, but by using all his strength, he heaved with both hands and arms to roll Jepson over on the rock.

"You're under arrest," he hissed through clenched teeth.

Blood flowed from a gash high on Jepson's cheek beneath his closed eyes, and moonlight illuminated the bruises and swelling covering his face. He looks defeated, Fastwater thought with a sigh of exhaustion. Ready to give up. But then Jepson's eyes opened and their glint of hatred took a stab at the sheriff. Fastwater felt the young man's body tighten, and then Jepson kicked out at him. When he missed, he used the kicking momentum to roll to his feet, and once again they stumbled together on the boulder-strewn bottom. The sheriff regained his balance and swung his whole arm like a club. He felt the solid impact on the man's head, and then he recoiled at the searing pain in his frozen fist. Glowing tendrils of agony shot up his arm. Jepson grabbed at him, but Fastwater's boot found a secure foothold and he thrust his weight forward at the man.

Over they went, with Jepson slammed on his back against the ledge. Fastwater grabbed the man's throat and tried to will his fingers to squeeze. Jepson struggled to pry the fingers loose, and then the sheriff felt an agonizing jolt as his adversary connected with a knee.

Their fingers still entwined at Jepson's neck, Fastwater rolled to the side, dragging the man with him. Solid rock beneath his back. Then another roll and they plunged into the rapids. The current racing through the chute was ferocious and sucked them along at breakneck speed. Fastwater fought to keep his head above water, but found his right hand still in Jepson's solid grasp.

Bounced and jolted by rocks and water, sometimes riding high on the rapids and other times dragged under the surface, Fastwater got himself upright in the current and clubbed at the detective with his balled-up left hand. He shook and yanked his right arm, trying to free himself from the man's relentless grip. The water deadened Fastwater's awkward blows as Jepson rode mostly beneath the surface.

Even as he felt the grip loosening on his hand, the sheriff continued kicking and clubbing at the man. Then a huge cataract of water raised him up as a giant boulder slipped by beneath him. He felt Jepson's impact with the rock, and then his hand was free. Fastwater fought to get his bearings in the river. Another frothing cascade lifted him up and hurtled him downstream. When he got himself oriented again he saw the moonlight on Lake Superior. A picture of peace and serenity; an endless expanse of cold, black water at the end of this thunderous maelstrom.

The river raced along, carrying him to a sure death in the deep clutches of the lake. He knew he'd never be able to swim to shore once the river current finally deposited him in Lake Superior. Frantic now, he looked for rocks or ledges, anything to hold him back from the lake.

Rapids crashed on either side of him as he flew face-first downstream. Then, in the moonlight, he caught a glimpse of the steel cable across the river mouth. Only seconds away, he kicked his legs to ride as high as he could in the water. At the last instant, he stretched out his torso and flung his left arm in the air. The tight cord bit into his forearm, stopping his downstream momentum. The river current lifted him higher as he held on with one arm to the cable. His body floated out toward the lake on top of the surging current like a bobber on a fishing line. For the moment he felt secure, his arm at the elbow wrapped in a vise-like grip around the cable.

He took several deep breaths, concentrating his remaining strength on the elbow joint holding him back from certain death. His body rocked near the top of the current, the cable swaying under his weight. Then a roar came from behind and Jepson crashed into him, grabbing at his body. Cold, wet arms wrapped around his head as Jepson climbed up on him. The cable yielded, sagging to the waterline under their combined weight.

Back underwater, Fastwater felt the man pounding on him, felt his gouging knees and stomping feet as the man climbed over him. He tried to hit back with his right arm, but there was no leverage, no room to swing with the heavy body crawling on top of him. He heard the anguished grunts of the man beating on him in a desperate effort to dislodge him from the cable.

Fastwater's strength was gone. He let his body go slack to hang in the water, his elbow locked over the cable in a frozen death grip. The blows raining down on him were weakening, in part due to the watery cushion above him, but mostly because Jepson was also at the end of his endurance. The thought came to Fastwater to let go of the cable, to take his chances with Lake Superior. He couldn't hold out here much longer. At least in the lake he'd be able to breathe; for a while, anyhow.

Then he felt a fresh scrambling of legs climbing over him, a high-energy assault of feet and claws digging into his arms and shoulders. He heard splashing and snarls from above as the cable sank deeper in the water. Jepson yelled louder in a voice full of anger and desperation. The cable went slack, and suddenly Fastwater was moving again as the current pulled him into the lake.

With the confining weight torn off him, he bobbed to the surface. Thrashing his arms to stay above water, he realized the cable was still wedged under his elbow. Snapped loose from the far side of the river, their combined weight and the river current had been too much for it to hold. Now he gently swung out of the river mouth, the long cable sweeping him across the current.

Looking out to sea, he spotted Gitch in the moonlight riding Jepson's body. They sank further under the surface, until Fastwater watched in horror as the moonlit waters filled in over the top of them.

Nearing the end of the cable, the sheriff slowly treaded water. There wasn't much current here where the river met the deeper water of Lake Superior. He wrapped the cord around him, securely tethering himself to the shore only twenty or thirty feet away.

"Marlon! Look!" Simanich stood on the cobblestone beach, pointing out to sea.

Fastwater turned to look. In the moonlight he saw Gitch swimming toward him, front paws slapping at the water, his big head cutting a beautiful wake across the surface. Behind the dog, Fastwater searched the spot where Jepson had disappeared. The man was gone. There would be no escape from the icy grave of Lake Superior. Fastwater shuddered.

Over the quiet surface of the lake, beyond reach of the river current, Gitch swam toward him. An easy dog paddle, as if he did this all the time, his blue and brown eyes riveted on the sheriff. He felt a tug on the cable, and Fastwater looked back to see Simanich gently pulling him in. Gitch caught up and swam beside him. Fastwater grinned and draped an exhausted arm over the dog's shoulders. He noticed a gaping tear in Gitch's ear, but if it was possible for a dog to smile, Fastwater would swear the upturned lips and sparkling eyes were doing just that. A big, wet, warm tongue slobbered across Marlon's face, and the sheriff laughed out loud.

Epilogue

*I*t *snowed the day after Halloween. Not much, just a gentle reminder of* the approaching change of seasons. But the following cold front that blew through Monday on a blustery northwest wind sent temperatures plummeting. By Tuesday morning, as regulars congregated in the café, it was obvious that the big fat snowflakes falling now would be sticking around for a while.

"This could be good for the deer hunt next Saturday," Red Tollefson offered from his customary place at the counter.

"You're going hunting?" Matthew Simon asked as Abby banged through the kitchen door with a plate of pancakes to share with her brother.

"Red hasn't hunted in years," Marcy said, walking up and throwing her arms around Matt's shoulders from behind. She held her left hand out in front of him to once again admire the engagement ring on her finger.

"I didn't say I was going hunting myself," Red argued. "But some folks will, and fresh snow is always good for tracking."

When Marcy left to go back behind the counter, Matt turned to look at his son and daughter. Ben had invited little Charles to sit with them, and between bites of syrup-laden pancakes, he helped the youngster color his placemat. Anna and Michael sat in the next booth with Luc Trembley. The French-Canadian sat up straight due to the heavy bandaging around his torso and ribs, but his expression was less guarded, as if he'd finally found sanctuary among these new friends and townsfolk.

Arlene Fastwater sat at a nearby table with her son, Leonard. She'd driven up late last night after her brother was discharged from the hospital. The hardest part of the whole trip was fitting Marlon into the front seat of her little hybrid sedan, the same car that had played a role in helping Marcy and Abby escape from a Chicago-based gangster in Duluth last summer. Sheriff Fastwater was expected to stop in any time now for his morning coffee.

"Is the sheriff going to be okay?" Anna asked Arlene. "I mean, no permanent injuries or anything?"

Folks turned to look. Next to Raggedy Ann and Andy's engagement announcement at the Halloween Dance, news of the sheriff getting evacuated by helicopter to the hospital in Duluth was the biggest story in months around here.

"Oh, sure," Arlene answered. "He'll be fine." She sipped her coffee and wagged her head before adding, "But I don't envy Mrs. Bean. I can't remember Marlon ever being sick, not even a cold, so hypothermia, frostbite, and stitches are going to make him a handful to be around." She set the coffee cup down. "But Mrs. Bean insisted, so there you go."

Arlene was the prosecuting attorney for the county in Duluth. She'd gathered information and talked to her brother while doctors administered to him in the hospital. Without a defendant, who was presumed drowned and lost at sea, she wouldn't be prosecuting anybody, but it was her natural curiosity to learn as much about the case as possible. Now she looked at Luc. "I hear you played a significant role in all this, too." She nodded at his ribs. "You going to be okay?"

Luc looked at his friends. Speaking in public wasn't his strong suit, so Michael said, "He should be fine. He was protecting our son, Charles."

Arlene studied the tall, bearded man. Luc might be averse to speaking in public, but that had never been a problem for Arlene Fastwater. Well aware that all eyes were on them, she swiveled on her chair to better face the French-Canadian in the booth. "And just how were you trying to help? I heard that the detective took the boy when he ran."

Luc sat up straighter and ran a hand down the length of his beard. In his quiet, tenor voice, he said, "I came down from the ridge because I felt an evil presence in town, madame."

"Oh, yeah, I heard about that Manitou story. Matche-Manitou."

"I saw the man hiding near the road when my young friend came out of the café, so I whistled to him."

"Actually," Anna interjected, "the detective was trying to get me. You see, I'd guessed at his involvement in Niki's death, so he wanted to keep me quiet."

Anna's voice quavered and Michael put a comforting arm around her shoulders. Turning to Arlene, he said, "The detective didn't know our son was here. So when Luc appeared with Charles, he took a shot at our friend and grabbed Charles, knowing that Anna would follow. He just didn't realize your brother would be coming right behind."

Luc cleared his throat. "Anna saved my life by hitting his arm when he shot at me."

Arlene looked at the young mother. Raw fear and worry still lingered in Anna's eyes. Michael held her close and tried to lighten the mood. "You know the old saying, when you save someone's life you become responsible for it? Well, Luc is going to stay with us this winter while he heals up. Then, when he's able, we're going to build a greenhouse out of a bunch of windows I salvaged over the years."

Everyone looked up when the door opened and Phil Simanich came in, Mrs. Bean close behind. She paused in surprise at the number of people inside, but quickly turned back to hold the door for the sheriff. In a creased and spotless uniform boasting shoulder patches, his nametag, and a polished badge, Marlon Fastwater stood towering in the doorway and looked over the gathered townsfolk. Their silent response was a little unnerving until he realized they were looking at Gitch standing beside him. When the dog heard Abby call him, he lunged past the sheriff and trotted over to join the group sitting by the windows. A cheer went up, and again Fastwater was surprised by the applause, until it became apparent everyone was clapping for the dog.

Marcy dashed out from behind the counter to greet the sheriff. Fastwater slowed her approach by holding up his bandaged hands. "Welcome back, Sheriff," she said, reaching out to him. Mrs. Bean stood at his side, pride glowing in her position next to him. He displayed his club-fisted hands for everyone to see as conversation in the café resumed.

"Looks like he's going to need a straw," Red called, eliciting a round of laughter.

The sheriff spotted Matthew at the counter and stepped in closer. "Congratulations on your engagement," he said. "I just hope you can take some of the edge off this one," he added, nodding at Marcy.

Red interrupted. "I still can't believe it, Sheriff. Marcy knew I was waiting for her."

The waitress cupped Matt's clean chin and cheek. "I'd say 'yes' to any man who'd shave off his beard to be my Raggedy Andy."

"Well, if that's all it would've taken . . ."

Folks laughed, and Mrs. Bean asked, "Is there a date yet?"

Matthew looked over at his children in the booth near the windows. Snow was sticking to the outside sill now, coming down in thick, wind-driven waves. "We'll probably go a little slow," he said. "Make sure everyone is comfortable. Maybe next spring or early summer."

Marcy held her hand out again so Mrs. Bean could see her ring while Marlon looked around the room. Abby had a new rug laid out for Gitch, and the children were scratching the big dog's ears. One of them had been chewed on in the fight with the wolves, but he seemed to like having it rubbed. Spotting his sister and nephew, Fastwater asked Marcy for a cup of coffee, and then headed over to their table. Simanich followed, pleased to hear the greetings and well-wishes thrown at the sheriff. Leonard pulled out a chair for his uncle, and Simanich joined them at the table. When Mrs. Bean arrived, Simanich gave her his chair and sat next to Luc on the edge of the bench-seat in the booth. Leonard looked at the sheriff's bandaged hands resting on the table, and asked, "Does the frostbite hurt much?"

Fastwater shook his head. Mrs. Bean patted his arm. "I think the stitches are worse for him. It itches, doesn't it, Marlon?"

His injuries were not topics the sheriff cared to discuss, but he offered a brief nod before looking over at Anna. "How are you, Anna?" he asked. "And your son?"

She gave him a timid shoulder shrug, and Michael said, "That was a pretty scary night. For all of us. It's going to take some time."

Fastwater nodded, and then Marcy appeared with a tray of cups and the coffeepot. "I still don't know how you figured it out," she said to Anna. "He had this stupid Big Bad Wolf costume, and you figured it out from that?"

"Don't you remember Niki's Little Red Riding Hood costume?" Anna asked.

"Of course, but they didn't even live in the same town. How'd you make that jump?"

"They used to live in the same town. Before Niki moved here." Anna seemed to loosen up a bit, leaning forward on the table as Michael withdrew his arm from her shoulders. "Besides," she continued, "the detective was making all kinds of absurd accusations. It was making me mad."

"Like what?" Arlene asked.

"Well, he had all these reasons he suspected Luc."

Arlene laughed. "Yeah, right. Sure, there was some circumstantial evidence, but he made up that stuff about the attacks on women in Canada. He figured if he put together a convincing story, which, by the way, no one would be able to disprove because of the complete lack of records up there, Marlon would eventually arrest the man." She looked at her brother. "And you almost did."

Fastwater ignored her by studying the snow falling outside the window. Luc leaned toward the sheriff. "It was the trickster, monsieur. Everything got confused."

Anna said, "You know, what really got to me was when he said it could be you, Leonard, because of your braid."

Leonard sat back, smiling. "Yeah, I heard about that." Then he shrugged.

"Well, it really made me mad," she continued, "so I told him that was as ridiculous as calling him the killer because of his costume. I wasn't actually accusing him. I was just trying to make a point. But then he gave me this terrible look and I realized I'd hit a nerve. Then he asked me if Niki ever talked about her past in Duluth. He wondered if she'd ever mentioned old boyfriends. It didn't register right away, but by the time I left the café I had my suspicions."

Fastwater nodded. "I only just learned that he'd dated Christine, the newswoman."

Simanich leaned forward. "There were more than a few things we didn't know about him. It never occurred to me that he got himself assigned to this case so he could monitor and steer the investigation away from him. You know, originally he tried to pin it on that homeless kid in Duluth."

"That poor young man," Arlene said. "Do you think Jepson killed him so he couldn't defend himself against the charges?"

Simanich simply stared at her, his non-answer an answer in itself.

Arlene frowned. "Well, his best bet was to pin it on Luc here. And again, if he'd killed him, Luc couldn't have defended himself. The circumstantial evidence may have been enough to close the case."

Fastwater shook his head. "You forget, Arlene, that Anna already had her suspicions."

"Yes. And look who was next on his list."

When everyone's eyes went to Anna, Fastwater shot a glare at his sister. Michael's arm went around his wife again, and Leonard used the uncomfortable quiet to say, "I was thinking about when we went out to the girls' campsite. Remember Detective Jepson got there before us? I always thought it was kind of strange. What do you suppose that was all about?"

Fastwater looked at Simanich who shrugged his shoulders and said, "I don't know. He said he thought we were meeting out there."

"Or maybe he was looking for something," the sheriff countered. "Something he didn't want us to see. Like that fur hat. I'm guessing he made all his attacks in costume, and maybe he lost the hat in the dark while struggling with that coed."

"That could be," Simanich agreed. "And I remember he was acting kind of defensive when we arrived."

"He couldn't have searched after the attack because the girl had that gun. But he knew the missing hat would give him away because he'd lost the tail at the scene of Niki's murder. I bet he found the hat before we got there and hid it inside his jacket."

"How do you know the tail was lost at the murder sight?" Simanich asked.

"Because I found it there. At the time I wasn't sure it was relevant; for all I knew, it could have been a real wolf tail."

"You never told me you'd found it," Simanich accused. "His DNA could have been all over that tail."

"The hat, Phil. Probably not so much the tail."

"And since then he replaced it with a new one," Leonard said.

"Yeah. A raccoon tail on a wolfskin hat," Anna added with a bemused shake of her head.

Marcy swooped in with a fresh pot of coffee and caught Fastwater squeezing his cup between two fat-fisted bandaged hands. "Are you managing that okay?" she asked.

Everyone looked away to hide their grins. The sheriff ignored her, but slid his cup across the table for a refill.

Matthew called to Abby and Ben. "Come on, kids. Time to hit the road for school."

Abby slid out of the booth and stacked their dishes to carry to the kitchen. Ben slowly got to his feet. "Aw, Dad, can't we stay home today?" He squatted next to Gitch and began petting him again. "I think Gitch needs extra attention today."

Smiles and chuckles appeared on faces, but even Ben seemed to know his argument wouldn't fly as he trudged toward the door. Gitch got up to follow, and Charles trailed along, not wanting to be left behind.

Anna said, "One child doesn't want to go to school, and the other can't wait." Raising her voice, she called, "Come back here, Charles. We're going home soon."

Charles acted as if he hadn't heard her while following Ben to the door. He stood close to the bigger boy, looking up at him with adoration. Abby returned from the kitchen, slipping her coat on as Gitch nudged Ben's hand for one last scratching.

Everyone watched the scene at the door as Charles pulled one of his carved wooden birds out of his pocket, handing it to Ben. Then he pulled out the second one and held it up. "Caw. Caw-caw!" he cackled.

Behind him, from the bench seat in the booth near the window where fat, fluffy snowflakes swirled, came the distinctive, melancholy whistle of a white-throated sparrow. Charles turned around and grinned. He ran toward them then, his arm held aloft holding the wooden bird in flight. "Caw. Caw-caw!"

The End